Beyond

THE

Rapture

Jennette Green

Diamond Press

BEYOND THE RAPTURE

A Diamond Press book / published in arrangement with the author

Copyright © 2014 by Jennette Green
Cover Design by Cora Graphics

ISBN: 978-1-62964-007-5

Library of Congress Control Number: 2014912119
Library of Congress Subject Headings:
Man-woman relationships—Fiction
Love stories
Rapture (Christian eschatology) — Fiction
The End Times — Fiction
Christian fiction
Fantasy
Inspirational fiction
Suspense fiction

Diamond Press
3400 Pegasus Drive
P.O. Box 80043
Bakersfield CA 93380-0043
www.diamondpresspublishing.com

Published in the United States of America.

*"And this gospel of the kingdom
will be preached in all the world
as a witness to all the nations,
and then the end will come."*

MATTHEW 24:14 NKJV

FUTURE

THE FAMILIAR ASH DARKENED the morning sun and choked the shadowed earth beneath. Crushed brown weeds, as dry as paper, lay in their shallow graves of cracked concrete. Oppressive heat radiated up from the broken asphalt of the city streets, permeating the very soul of the young woman who walked quickly over its surface.

She turned a corner, and strode rapidly down the middle of the empty lane. It was quiet now. Sunday morning; her favorite day of the week. Everyone still slept in their sweltering beds, savoring the luxury of sleeping in late on their one day off.

But not Isola. Swiftly, she strode toward her destination. She inhaled through gritted teeth, hating the burning taste of the smoky, bitter air which choked the city.

Isola was her middle name. It meant island, or isolated. Either one described how she felt now. Alone. Completely alone. And, if she was honest, bitter. Her new name symbolized the death of her old life. And her old self.

The desire to revisit the place had been building within her over the last month. It tugged at her empty soul. She wasn't sure why, but it felt like something waited for her there. Something valuable...

RmmmmRmmmR.

With a sharp inhale, she jerked her head left. Acrid air seared her lungs. She'd taken a chance, walking out here alone, while everyone slept. But she saw nothing...yet.

RmmmMRmMRM.

The mechanical rumble jarred the asphalt beneath her feet. It was about to turn the corner.

She had to hide.

Heart thumping, Isola paused to weigh her options. The pavement radiated heat up through the worn soles of her tennis shoes. She scanned the buckled concrete sidewalks and the dingy, crumbling buildings beyond. The broken windows looked like gaping black holes. But the stores weren't empty. Or safe.

Where could she hide?

The grinding, deafening roar made her want to run. Instead, she fought for the calm and logic that survival required. *Outwit and outsmart. Don't run like a rat into the nearest sewer.*

Her gaze focused on the stripped metal autos littering the sides of the street. She made a leaping, rolling plunge and dove into one of the vacant cars. The driver's side door was ripped off, the chassis bent double, seats gone. Its front end rested precariously on the tailgate of a rusted, dilapidated blue truck.

The hot metal seared her skin, and bolts ripped into her flesh. She yanked her knees to her chin and tumbled to the far, passenger side of the car. The back window revealed bits of her to the oncoming tank. And the leering, dangerous men inside.

The car swayed gently, cramming her neck uncomfortably into the crevice where floor and engine compartment met. She dared not breathe. Would the soldiers notice the car's movement? Would they stop to investigate?

She waited. The adrenaline and fear pumping through her blood made her feel sick. If the tank stopped, she would scramble out and run. She wasn't finished yet.

The familiar, cold lump of metal which dug into her waistband comforted her as the thundering rumble drew closer.

The olive green tank slowly heaved by, its nose dipping and falling as it rode the stationary waves of the demolished street. The American flag painted on its side said its soldiers were supposed to protect her. But she knew better. Oh, she knew better.

Knees touching her chin, she listened intently, waiting for the thundering rumble to fade. Soldiers liked to sport with their victims. They might stop a block away, and then creep back to take her... Nausea convulsed in her throat. She closed her eyes and drew a steadying breath.

She was sick of being afraid. Sick of the nightmare that had become her life.

When would it end?

Something wet rolled down her brown, dirty cheek. Was that a tear?

Stop it! Jerkily, she rubbed her work shirt sleeve over her aching eyes. She had to remain strong. Her life three and half years ago, versus her life now, was like comparing day and night. Life and death.

The rumble faded. Cautiously, she twisted her body into a kneeling position and peered over the dashboard. A hot breeze lifted a limp lock of brown hair from her forehead. Her gaze darted back and forth. Empty. The street was empty again. But not safe.

Carefully, Isola eased out of the car. She continued her journey, rapidly climbing and plunging over the broken pavement. Like a ghost slipping over her grave, she felt eyes following her, watching from the dark store windows. Squatters. They wouldn't bother her, as long as she stayed in the middle of the street.

Keeping her breaths even and shallow in order to restrict the bitter air flowing into her lungs, she strode on. The rising sun shone a dull red through the ashen haze. Maybe she had another half mile to go. This was taking longer than she'd thought.

"Hey. You! Stop!"

Isola froze, seeing no one. Then the *rat-a-tat-tat* of machine gunfire peppered the still morning air.

She dove to the pavement. Her right shoulder hit first, and she rolled beneath a derelict bus, which was crazily parked half on the pavement, and half on the sidewalk.

"Get out of here! Get!"

The jeering laugh of a soldier. Pounding feet ran toward her bus.

Tattered shoes and flapping pant legs sprinted by her hiding place. Looters. A few stores were still in business, and the military vigilantly guarded them.

She heard the gasping, laughing pant of the rebels. Then a shrill cry sounded above her, and the bus shook.

"Go man, go!" Vagrants in the bus cheered on the gang.

The machine gunfire halted. Pressing her cheek to the pebble strewn asphalt, she spotted four greasy-headed looters a block away, panting and grinning back at the soldiers. One held up a bag of potatoes and screamed an epithet.

Machine gunfire exploded. The thug made a quick, insolent hand gesture and darted off.

Isola's heart rate skidded to a gentle thud. Above, the vagrants muttered and thumped about to make their next hour of sleep a comfortable one. Finally, all was silent.

But fear dripped like poison through her heart. What was she doing out here? Why hadn't she stayed at home, where it was safe? She closed her eyes tight and drew quiet, even breaths.

It wasn't safe at home. It wasn't safe anywhere. If she wanted to survive, she must be courageous, and right now, that meant continuing on to her destination.

Isola slipped out from under the bus. A swift scan proved the coast was clear, and she backtracked a block, and then cut around and up a block so she would miss the trigger-happy soldiers.

Back on track at last, her stride lengthened. This was the home stretch. Regular people ventured out now, including a few old women with kerchiefs knotted up about their heads. They scuttled toward the food distribution center.

Her empty stomach growled, and pain cramped her mid-section. Unfortunately, she couldn't visit the distribution center yet. Her food token was only valid after twelve o'clock. She would have to wait.

Wait. Always waiting. But for what? For order to her life? For meaning and purpose and an explanation for the destruction around her? What could possibly explain the state the world had fallen into?

Her steps quickened. Kay had known the truth; her life had proven it. And that was why Isola had risked this journey today.

The Chairman boasted he knew the answers, too. He made a lot of sense. But an unease that bordered on revulsion twisted through her soul when she thought about him. She didn't like the man. He reminded her of a reptile—or better yet, a primordial fish; slippery, slimy, and scaly.

Isola trusted one person to tell her the truth; the absolute, painful, honest truth, and that was Kay. She would listen to Kay over the boastful proclamations of the Beast.

But Kay was gone. And had been for three and a half years. Why had she waited so long? Was it too late to find the answers? And even if she did find them, would it make any difference? She couldn't step back in time. She couldn't return to her old life. If only she could.

"Miss!" The harsh voice made her whirl.

A policeman stared at her. A lascivious smirk bared his teeth.

Straightening her shoulders, Isola hurried on, but fear squeezed her heart and stole a little more of the oxygen from her lungs. Casually, her hand slid across her abdomen and touched the cold metal weapon stuffed into the waistband of her dirty jeans.

The feel of it beneath her fingertips slowed her racing heartbeat. Her father's gun. The only good thing he had left her. Along with six bullets.

Ears straining, she listened, but heard no footsteps. Her palm sweated against the smooth metal handle, but she didn't let go. She swiftly walked another block before chancing a look over her shoulder.

The policeman was gone. She sucked in a relieved breath, and foul air burned her lungs. She coughed and gasped.

Slowly, the sharp edge of adrenaline dulled to a tight, constant tension. She'd never known State Street was so long. How much farther did she need to go?

Isola searched for a familiar landmark, but found none. She plodded on for more long minutes. Buildings on this side of Truesdale had all been thrown down by the great quake.

Her steps slowed. That earthquake had annihilated her old life; destroyed it as completely as it had demolished this house.

Isola had reached her destination. The skeletal tree in the yard looked just like Kay's old elm tree had in the winter time, except now the bark looked like ash, as though burned from the inside out. The poor, wasted tree mirrored how Isola felt inside, too; charred, dead, as if one puff might scatter her, body and soul, to the four winds. She swallowed back the sudden ache of tears in her throat.

Stop it. You can't go back. Face the future.

But to do that, she must finally face the past. Starting here. Right now.

Bizarrely, the rubble beckoned to her, urging her to step in and find something...anything.

What she was looking for?

Isola cast a quick glance over her shoulder. She saw no one. For this one moment in time, she was completely alone.

As she stepped carefully into the ruins, she questioned her sanity for the first time today. Why had she walked all the way out here? Nothing remained of the house, except for rubble and a crazily tilted, drunken half of the brick chimney. Surely looters had already picked Kay's house clean.

Concrete and mortar crunched beneath her shoes. A short beam that poked up through the rubble caught her toe, and she almost fell. Catching herself, Isola crept forward again, toward the back of the house. It was hard to believe this had once been a two-story house, and filled with people she'd cared about.

Memories seared her mind. How could life possibly have been so good just three and a half years ago? And now be so horrible?

She groped for a broken piece of chimney that rose from the ground. The warm, rough mortar rasped against her skin.

It didn't make sense. But then, in a confused way, wasn't that why she had come?

Isola brushed the sleeve of her faded, blue and gray shirt across her eyes. She didn't care how stupid this was. She'd keep looking until she found something. *Anything* to explain why she had felt compelled to come here.

Four steps brought her to the place where Kay's room would have been, had it been on the ground floor. Nothing distinguished the first floor from Kay's room. It was all a jumbled, twisted mess.

So what?

With determination, she bent and sifted through the gritty rubble.

The sun beat on her back and sweat trickled from her armpits. Isola kept digging, but found nothing but plaster and broken bits of wood. She swiped her hand across her brow and sat back on her heels. The red sun blazed down, burning her skin like fire from hell. How much longer should she look?

Despair, her all too familiar friend, told her to give up.

No. One last time, she would try. She hadn't talked to God in ages, but figured it couldn't hurt now.

"God," she whispered, "if I'm supposed to find something here, please help me find it."

No voice from heaven spoke, but she did hear muffled shouts down the street. She'd better hurry up, before soldiers caught her digging through the rubble. Looting was a crime, even if nothing was left to loot. She became aware that her fingers absently rubbed on a smooth piece of wood. It felt like the curved corner of a desk.

Kay's desk? Excitement quickened her spirits, and Isola dug beneath the jutting edge. She scooped out great handfuls of gray, gritty plaster and debris. Then she touched something flat and smooth. It felt man-made. Her fingers scrabbled, digging to free the slim plastic rectangle from the pile of plaster.

There!

An electronic notebook.

So now what?

Compelled by a force she did not understand, she dug deeper into the crumbling mound, beneath where the notebook had been buried. The dust felt coolly refreshing against her fingers.

And then she touched smooth leather.

A book? Her fingers dug deeper to get a better grip on it. She tugged it out and rubbed the slender, tan volume against her shirt. A Bible.

Puzzled, she surveyed this, and then the red electronic notebook. These were what she had come for. This certainty filled her soul.

But why would she want either one? And why was her heart hammering with excitement?

Isola stuffed the small Bible into the back waistband of her jeans, and stumbled to the remains of the fireplace, which offered a flat chunk of concrete to sit upon. Again remembering the danger, she scanned the dusty, deserted street. Still safe... but for how long?

She smoothed a hand over the scratched plastic and glass notebook. It whispered almost audibly to her, urging her to fold it open.

She did. A clear black screen greeted her. Wonder of wonders, it wasn't scratched or cracked. The "On" button mesmerized her, and she pushed it. Immediately, a lone icon popped up on the screen.

The battery still worked. Why wasn't she surprised? She rubbed the grime off of the tiny solar cell in the top corner, so it could recharge. It couldn't have much power left after all this time.

She double-tapped the icon, and black words rushed across the screen.

"Week One. Wednesday. Two guys tried to attack me today..."

It was Kay's diary.

She stopped. Guilt seared her conscience. How could she possibly read this?

But Kay wasn't on Earth any longer. Surely she wouldn't mind.

And when had Kay been attacked? Isola didn't remember that happening.

Knowing it was Kay's diary made her want to read it all the more. Events from three and a half years ago were recorded here. Perhaps memories of her old life, too, before her world had crumbled.

It would be so wonderful to escape, just for a little while, and remember the way things used to be, and to remember her old life and her old friends.

Surely Kay wouldn't mind. Isola wanted so much to remember.

She glanced about, feeling nervous and more than a little guilty. No one was near. No one cared.

A hot breeze touched her brow, and above, two vultures slowly circled, searching for their next victim. She'd read...just for a little while, she promised herself.

"SO, YOU'RE A CHRISTIAN?" My rescuer's question caught me off-guard.

"Yes."

Mitch did not look at me. "You'll want to be careful, then. Those two guys belong to a Christian/Jew hate club on campus."

"What?" I stopped in my tracks. "Are you serious?"

Unsmilingly, he met my gaze. This wasn't a joke. And why would he joke? People hated him, too.

"I can't believe this." I fell into step beside him again. "Why would anyone hate Christians that much? Or Jews? It seems so Naziish."

"I don't know." The slight inflection in his tone dismissed the topic as unimportant.

We reached the parking lot a few silent moments later, and stopped beside my old brown Mustang.

"Thanks again." I felt awkward now. He was an odd guy. Withdrawn, and obviously complex.

He smiled, surprising me. "Glad to be of help." He snapped the rolled up paper in farewell. "See you around."

But he must have snapped his wrist harder than he'd thought, for the paper cylinder flew from his hand and curled open, fluttering to rest on the hot asphalt, inches from my feet.

With a smile, I bent to retrieve it. A corner of the thin, curled open paper caught my attention as I straightened. It was a charcoal drawing.

"Are you an artist?"

"Yeah," his face flushed as he accepted the drawing back. "I draw what I see. Sometimes I don't understand what that is. Guess that doesn't make much sense."

"Sure, it does." Curiosity gripped me. "Could I look at it?"

He hesitated, and unrolled the roughly textured paper. "I understand this one a little."

But his comment faded as I stared at the spare, bold black strokes covering the page. Two eyes in heaven watched the earth. I couldn't look away from them.

Vaguely, I heard Mitch speak. "It's God watching the earth, and man, whom he created."

Feeling oddly befuddled, I tore my gaze from the page. "He looks angry." I don't know why I said that. The eyes didn't look angry. They looked loving, patient, and watchful. And yet anger lurked around the corner. In their depths.

Also by Jennette Green

Romance Novels

The Commander's Desire
Her Reluctant Bodyguard
Ice Baron
The Pirate's Desire

New Adult Romance

Beyond the Rapture
(Christian Apocalyptic)

Castaways
(a novellette)

Shorter Works

Toot of Fruit
(a children's story)

Murder by Nightmare
(a novelette)

Week One — Watch

KAY JAMESON'S JOURNAL

"Therefore keep watch,
because you do not know on what day your Lord will come."

MATTHEW 24:42

"What I say to you, I say to everyone:
'Watch!'"

MARK 13:37

WEDNESDAY

TWO GUYS TRIED TO ATTACK ME today in the journalism lab...

Wait. I guess I'd better write my standard paragraph first. Just in case someone else ever reads this—though I'm not sure why anyone ever would.

Anyway, my name is Kay Jameson. I'm a third year journalism student at Truesdale State University in California, and I live at home. I keep a journal like this because writing my life down in detailed story form helps sharpen my journalism skills. Besides that, it's fun to read over later. And maybe I shouldn't say "write." I talk, and my new notebook writes it down. It's pretty awesome.

Okay, enough of that.

Today was scorching and muggy. Even for late August, the heat this afternoon felt oppressive as I hurried over the deserted sidewalks for the journalism lab. The still air felt like a physical presence. It had a breathless quality to it; as if waiting for something sinister to happen.

Or maybe that was just my overactive imagination.

The computer lab was empty when I arrived. Since it was after four, and the first week of classes, that wasn't a surprise. In fact, I had counted on it.

My backpack slid to the floor, and the cool, air conditioned breeze bit through my teal, scooped-neck, Truesdale First Gospel T-shirt. It felt deliciously cool on my damp shoulder.

Truesdale State won't allow us to use our personal computers to gain access to the paid news subscriptions and services we need to research assignments. That means hundreds of students fight over the school computers each day. It's a prehistoric policy, as far as I'm concerned.

I flipped on the computer, tapped in my code, and set to work accessing information for my first journalism assignment. We were supposed to read the lead story for the Middle East from seven different papers, and then write our own article, pulling facts from each newspaper source.

I accessed the first newspaper, published in Britain, half a world away.

Two hours later, I relaxed back in my chair as the whirring printer spit out my two page report. I was glad to be done. I hate to have projects hanging over my head. Maybe that's a little obsessive compulsive, but I don't care.

"Hi, Kay."

The rich tenor voice startled me. As my head jerked left, a strand of sun-streaked hair slapped my face. I relaxed when I recognized the young man. And I quickly tucked the straight lock behind my ear.

Trenton C. Johns III. He was a new transfer into Truesdale State's journalism program, and we shared the same M, W, F Current Affairs journalism class. I'd never spoken to him before, and felt flattered he knew my name.

"Hi." With a smile, I retrieved my pages from the printer. "Are you here to work on Dr. William's assignment?" I felt pleased by the casual sound of my voice.

Trenton C. Johns III was very good looking. He was medium height, with a slim build, and he wore his light brown hair cropped short in back, and stylishly cut. Today he wore creased tan slacks, and a crisp, expensive looking white shirt. His features were classic, movie star handsome. But the first thing I'd noticed about him were his eyes. A brilliant, flashing royal blue.

"Yeah." Those incredible eyes drifted to the papers in my hand. "Hey, is that the assignment? Did you finish it already?"

"Yes." I reached for my backpack. "Decided to do it early."

He smiled and I blinked, mesmerized by his dancing blue eyes and even white teeth. "How long did it take you?"

A sharp movement near the door drew my attention back to earth. Two more guys from my current affairs class shuffled into the room. Tim and Randy. They were new, too. One was tall and thin, and the other broad and muscular. Both possessed a hungry, wolfish look.

I glanced back at Trent's handsome, smiling face. "Two hours. You could do it in less, though. I got sidetracked reading other articles."

"Could I buy it from you?"

Shocked, my whole body froze.

Trent's grin widened. He was only joking.

"I don't think so," I bantered back, and reached for the zip to my backpack.

Dark-haired Tim prowled up to me. "I want to see it."

I glanced at him, still smiling. But his flat gaze sent a flicker of unease through me. My smile faded. "Sorry, no. Dr. Williams wants us to do our own work."

Randy invaded my personal space next. His heavy forearms glinted gold in the fluorescent light. He wore a knotted black band around his bicep. Tim wore one, too. Some new, tough guy fashion statement?

"Maybe you ought to reconsider, girly."

Girly?

I glanced at Trent for moral support, but his tanned features had paled.

Randy and Tim's faces appeared oddly expressionless, but their eyes glittered. Sudden fear licked through me, because I realized they didn't want to see my paper at all. *They wanted to scare me.*

Tim stepped closer. His eyes looked like black marbles. I took a step back, and felt the computer table press into my leg. What was going on here? It was bizarre.

I glanced quickly around the room, looking for an avenue of escape, but saw none. What should I do? Who would help me? Obviously not Trent. More fear welled in my heart.

And then I remembered I wasn't alone. God was here too, even though I couldn't see him. I glanced up and silently prayed. *Help me, Lord, please!*

"What are you doing, praying?" Hatred snarled through Tim's voice.

"Looks like we've got a *Christian* here, Tim." Randy jabbed a finger into my midriff. "Says Truesdale First Gospel."

"Stop it!" I slapped at his hand.

"So that's why she won't give us the paper. It's the *Christian* thing to do."

Terror prickled. They hated me, just because I was a Christian? *Why? Help me, Lord, please!*

Suddenly, cool calm slipped into my heart. God had heard me. He was with me. He would help me.

I spoke before thinking, "Yes, it is the Christian thing to do. It's also the right thing to do. I won't do your work for you."

Randy's florid features convulsed. He pushed his face close to mine, and my confidence wavered under a curl of fear. Was God really with me? Why hadn't I shut my mouth, for once in my life?

Randy drew a mighty breath. I imagined hatred inflating his lungs like a balloon. He exploded, "Don't force your Christian way of thinking on us, girl! We've got rights. And one of those rights is to see that paper!"

"Hey." Trent spoke up at last.

Randy ignored him. His meaty fist painfully clamped around my wrist. I twisted my arm, futilely trying to free myself.

"Give me that paper," he hissed. His breath smelled like rotten eggs and day old fish patties. Panic threatened to overwhelm me. *Where are you, Lord? Please help!*

"Let her go." The new voice sounded quiet and authoritative. Deep, too.

All eyes in the room swiveled to stare at the intruder.

The guy was a stranger to me. He had short, wavy dark hair, and a knapsack over one shoulder. Of medium height and build, he wore a plain white T-shirt, blue jeans, and topsiders with no socks. The shirt clung to his well-defined muscles, which gave the impression he worked out.

His unusual face arrested my attention. He had piercing black eyes, a nose that was a little off kilter, and dark brows, the left of which tilted slightly higher than the right.

An odd, concentrated energy radiated from him. He advanced further into the lab, and gestured with the rolled up paper in his left hand. His muscles rippled. "Let her go, guys."

Randy's lip curled. "A Jew. Come to help a Christian. Now, isn't this a pretty sight?"

To my surprise, I found myself free. Randy had transferred his attention to the newcomer. Hands shaking, I snatched up my backpack. I had no clear idea what might happen next, but I was ready to run.

"Leave her alone." The stranger stood relaxed, with his feet slightly apart. A ready stance, should Randy or Tim try to rush him. But they didn't.

Why not?

Long moments ticked by. Then a surprising thought crossed my mind; Randy and Tim were afraid of him. They were brave enough to bully a woman, but not someone who'd offer them an even fight.

With a disgusted snort, Randy jerked his shoulders. "We're outta here. We know her paper's trash."

Tim's black eyes slitted, but he swung away from me, too. Both men shouldered past the stranger and vanished into the hallway.

I leaned against the table, feeling shaky with relief. God had answered my prayer. He had sent this stranger just in the nick of time.

"Hey," Trent's wobbly voice drew my attention. "I'm sorry. I never thought..." He looked shaken.

"It's okay." But I wondered why he hadn't spoken up sooner—but that wasn't fair. Who knew Randy and Tim would back down if confronted?

"It wasn't your fault," I told him.

Movement caught my eye as the stranger slipped from the room. Knees still feeling a bit wobbly, I moved toward the door. "See you in class Friday?"

"Yeah! See you then." Trent's voice sounded over-eager.

The stranger swiftly strode down the hall. I trotted after him, determined to thank him for stepping up for me. Seconds later, I walked quickly beside him.

Up close, he topped my five foot six by only a few inches, and he wasn't good looking. He had seemed bigger in that small room. Maybe it was the force of his vibrant, tightly leashed personality.

"Thank you. I don't know what I would have done if you hadn't..."

"Forget it." His mouth was straight and unsmiling. Striding rapidly ahead, he held the door open for me, and we both stepped outside. Humid, hot air enveloped us.

"I'm Kay Jameson." I said, unperturbed by his uncommunicative silence.

Did his mouth twist up slightly? It did. "Mitch Rubenstein." He glanced at me. "Where are you headed?"

"The parking lot."

"Good, I'm headed that way, too." His bass voice sounded casual.

But my back suddenly prickled. Did Mitch feel the danger, too? If so, the relaxed set of his stocky shoulders gave no indication. Randy and Tim were watching us. *Watching me.* I was glad Mitch was with me.

"So, you're a Christian?" His question caught me off-guard. "Yes."

He did not look at me. "You'll want to be careful, then. Those two belong to a Christian/Jew hate club on campus."

"What?" I stopped dead in my tracks. "Are you serious?"

Unsmilingly, Mitch met my gaze. This wasn't a joke. And why would he joke? People hated him, too.

"I can't believe this." I fell into step beside him again. "Why would anyone hate Christians that much? Or Jews? It seems so Naziish."

"I don't know." The slight inflection in his tone dismissed the topic as unimportant.

We reached the parking lot a few silent moments later, and stopped beside my old brown Mustang.

"Thanks again." I felt awkward now. He was an odd guy. Withdrawn, and obviously complex.

He smiled, surprising me. "Glad to be of help." He stepped away and snapped the rolled up paper in farewell. "See you around."

But he must have snapped his wrist harder than he'd thought, for the paper cylinder flew from his hand and curled open, fluttering to rest on the hot asphalt, inches from my feet.

With a smile, I bent to retrieve it. A corner of the thin, curled open paper caught my attention as I straightened. It was a charcoal drawing.

"Are you an artist?"

"Yeah," his face flushed as he accepted the drawing back. "I draw what I see. Sometimes I don't understand what that is. Guess that doesn't make much sense."

"Sure, it does." Incredible curiosity gripped me. "Could I look at it?"

He hesitated, but unrolled the roughly textured paper. "I understand this one a little."

His comment faded as I stared at the spare, bold black strokes covering the page. Two eyes in heaven watched the earth. I couldn't look away from them.

Vaguely, I heard Mitch speak. "It's God watching the earth, and man, whom he created."

Feeling oddly befuddled, I tore my gaze from the page. "He looks angry." I don't know why I said that. The eyes didn't look angry. They looked loving, patient, and watchful. And yet anger lurked around the corner. In their depths.

"I know," Mitch looked at the picture again. "I get that feeling too. Strange, isn't it?"

I nodded, and my gaze returned to the sketch. It *was* odd.

"A verse kept coming to mind when I drew it." Mitch slowly rolled up the sketch again. "Jeremiah seventeen, verse nine. 'The heart is deceitful above all things and beyond cure. Who can understand it?'" He glanced at me; maybe wondering how I felt about him quoting scripture.

I stared at him, fascinated and surprised.

He slowly went on. "And I also thought of a verse in Isaiah. 'We all, like sheep, have gone astray, each of us has turned to his own way...'"

"'And the Lord has laid on him the iniquity of us all,'" I finished.

What a strange conversation to have in the middle of a hot, muggy parking lot. I said, "That verse is a prophecy of Jesus Christ."

Mitch's piercing black eyes shuttered, and he hefted his knapsack more securely up on his shoulder. "Of course you'd think that. You're a Christian." His shoulders twisted away. Clearly, the conversation was over. The realization filled me with disappointment.

"Thanks again, Mitch."

When he glanced back, a smile twisted his lips. "See you around, Kay."

My car coughed long and hard, as usual, before starting, and then I pulled out of the parking lot. When I entered the smooth flow of traffic east on High Street, my thoughts returned to Mitch, his picture, and the scene in the journalism lab.

What a strange afternoon. Frightening. Very frightening. And yet the time with Mitch had eased my fear.

Why did Randy and Tim hate Christians? And what did Mitch's picture really mean?

I turned the corner onto West State Street. The street is home to one of Truesdale's upscale neighborhoods. Each house is built on a half acre of land. My own home is no different. It's two stories tall and painted white, with brick trim and pillars. Dark strips of wood frame the windows and the huge, mahogany front door. Brass lamps adorn each side of the garage.

I knew the garage was full, so I parked on the street. Grabbing my backpack, I stepped over the clean gutter and onto the sidewalk. With the rolling green lawn, and stately elm tree gracing the front yard, it looked like the picture of peace and tranquility.

On the outside.

I pushed open the door and stepped inside. I didn't realize I was holding my breath until my lungs protested. It was almost seven, but silence enveloped the house. My spirits lifted with hope.

I slipped by the gargantuan living room, decorated by my mother in soft earth tones, and followed the short hallway to the kitchen.

That's when I heard voices. The television murmured in the den, to my left. Dad was home, watching T.V. And Mom and my eighteen-year-old sister, Theresa, spoke quietly in the kitchen.

I turned right, into the kitchen.

The low-voiced conversation at the expensive teak table, near the French doors, stilled instantly. Two heads swiveled toward me. Mom's was a fashionable silver blond cap, and my sister's a dark, artistically curled wave to her shoulders. The expression on each of their perfectly made up faces was identical: frowning, and pinched with displeasure.

Mom rose gracefully to her feet and smoothed her sliver pantsuit with wrists encircled by slim, fashionable bracelets. She was thin. Thinner than me, and that wasn't good.

"Dinner is in the oven." Her voice sounded brittle, as usual. "We've already eaten."

I dropped my backpack on the counter and turned away from those frosty blue eyes. "Thanks, Mom. I'm hungry. Had to finish up a paper for journalism class."

I offered a smile over my shoulder, but it faltered when I saw her expression—tight, disappointed, sad. Because I had missed dinner? I glanced back at the oven. Had I missed it on purpose? I hadn't considered it until this minute. Maybe I had.

Silent moments ticked by while I fixed my plate, poured a glass of milk, and joined Theresa at the table. She eyed me. Her light blue eyes looked hostile, and slightly contemptuous.

"I can't believe you're working so hard. This is the first week of school. My professors haven't even given me home-work yet."

Familiar resentment surged. Luckily, I'd just popped a forkful of meatloaf in my mouth, so I couldn't spit back the irritated reply that flew to mind.

I hate it when she talks down to me.

Swallowing at last, I said evenly, "Things will be different when you're a junior." *You'll be taking harder classes than Dance 101 and English 1a, for one thing.* But I didn't say that.

The artificial highlights in Theresa's hair gleamed red as she turned. "Momma? Can I have twenty bucks for my date tonight? We might stop by the mall, and there's this to die for scarf I'd love to pick up."

"Ask your dad, honey." Mom's voice sharpened. "You know he controls the finances in this house."

"Okay." My sister's full face dimpled. Long ago, she'd learned how to wrap Dad around her little finger. He never refused her—or me, either, to be honest—anything. We were his weaknesses.

Long, silent moments dragged by. Theresa's red nails rapped, *rat a tat rat a tat,* on the table. Annoying in the extreme.

"So," I broke in. "Who are you going out with tonight?" I tried to sound interested, although I didn't quite feel it. Theresa dated a different guy every night. My parents said it was okay, as long as she kept her grades up.

"Tom." Theresa eyed me with disinterest. "I suppose you've got that church group tonight."

"Yes. We're going to watch a movie."

"That's nice." Theresa glanced at her watch and jumped up. "Gotta go. Tom will be here soon." She sneered this last bit over her shoulder. I couldn't help but glare at her as she swept from the room.

This was her constant taunt. She went out on tons of dates, and I barely dated at all. She thought it was completely abnormal. She also thought I was strange because I loved going to church activities with my best friends.

"Do you need anything else, dear?" Mom hovered near the door. Her eyes looked soft for the first time that evening. And there, just for a second, I saw the unhappiness glimmering in them.

"No. But thank you, Mom." I offered a quiet smile. I knew she loved me. It's just that we seemed to have so little in common these days. I dug again into my meatloaf.

"*Come to Burger B. . .*"

My fork faltered when the volume of the T.V. soared in the den.

"Would you turn that down, Winston?" My mother's shrill voice tried to drown out a honking fast food commercial. "I'm trying to talk to you!"

My father rumbled something unintelligible.

"I have a woman's auxiliary meeting tonight. Remember? Did you put gas in the car?"

A small silence ensued. I heard only the voice of the newscaster cutting in, announcing a dozen murders in the city today, compared to fifteen yesterday, and the sound of my teeth slicing through mushy green beans. I hated to listen to Mom harangue Dad. But I was stuck in the kitchen until I finished my supper.

"What about the brakes?" Mom charged. "When are you going to fix those? I've asked you a thousand times! You know they make that awful squealing noise. I tell you, I'm embarrassed to drive it anywhere."

Another rumble.

"What? I can't believe you, Winston. It's not like we're poor, for heaven's sake! Why can't we just buy a new car? I..."

"There's gas in the car, Helen!" Dad's angry voice cut her off.

The newscaster blared into the sudden silence, "And Senate challenger Woodward is coming in October..."

"*Fine.* I can see how important I am to you. Go ahead, listen to your stupid news."

Rapid footsteps crossed the carpet. Then Mom's heels clattered down the hall. The front door slammed. And with it, the volume of the T.V. dropped to a murmur.

Feeling sick to my stomach, I swallowed one last time, and then rose and scraped my plate into the sink. Not even the harsh, grinding noise of the garbage disposal could erase the sound of my parents' quarrel from my mind.

I hate it when they fight. It doesn't matter who starts it. This evening was Mom. Tomorrow would be Dad. It never seems to end.

Thankfully, tonight I could leave the house. I just wanted to escape and have fun with my friends. First, though, I would see how Dad was doing.

"Hi, Dad." The television flickered in the far corner of the dimly lit room. My father sat in his favorite recliner with his back to me, and the sports section of the newspaper open before him. All I could see was the top of his silver, neatly styled head. And his stocky arms, encased in a crisp white shirt.

Theresa has inherited her body type from him, and she hates it. Maybe that's another reason why she hates me so much. I take after Mom. Both of us are thin. But Theresa has inherited Mom's classic beauty. I look more like Dad.

"Hi, kid." Dad lowered the paper when I slipped toward the couch, to his right. His patrician features softened for a moment, and his hazel eyes glinted behind his reading glasses. "How was your day?"

"Okay." I didn't tell him what had happened in the journalism lab. He had enough to worry about.

"Good."

"Dad." Theresa popped in, her tone wheedling. Bright gold baubles hung from her ears and dripped from the necklace around her throat. She wore a ruffled designer dress. "Can I have twenty dollars? Mad money, you know. In case Tom decides to dump me." She let loose a small, self-deprecating giggle.

I mentally rolled my eyes. What had happened to that scarf she'd just told Mom about? She probably still meant to buy it. But she knew how to play Dad to get what she wanted.

Dad smiled at his youngest daughter. "That won't happen to you, honey. But here," he extracted a bill from his wallet and winked at her. "Go buy yourself something pretty."

Theresa flushed, and smiled. "Thanks, Daddy." She gave him a kiss just as the doorbell rang, and whirled from the room.

Dad sat very still and listened as Theresa shrilly welcomed "Tom." His faint mumble blended into a T.V. commercial attacking Senator Gilroy.

Dad's gold watch flashed when he raised the paper again. "Sounds like a nice guy." He'd given up checking out all of Theresa's boyfriends. It took too much effort.

"Bye, Dad." I brushed his scratchy cheek with my lips. "I'm going to church."

"Okay, honey. Guess the old man gets a little peace and quiet tonight."

Truth lay behind his joking tone. Dad treasured his quiet time. That was one reason why he took long, solitary walks every afternoon after work.

I ran upstairs, brushed my hair, brushed my teeth, dashed on a natural rose lipstick, and then scampered downstairs again. It was almost seven-thirty. I would be late.

"See you, Dad!" I called out, and slammed the front door behind me.

It was dusky outside, and I halted on the front doorstep, battling the familiar feeling of unease. Dark figures hurried west along the sidewalk, toward the college.

Evenings were dangerous, even in the nice neighborhoods. Especially in the nice neighborhoods. I knew gangs patrolled our street, because I had seen the graffiti. And last week an old lady down the block was assaulted and robbed.

I slipped quickly down the walk to my Mustang and locked myself inside. The car coughed again and again, but finally started. Engine roaring, I pulled away from the curb, zipped around the block, and headed east for the church, which was located two miles away and a few blocks south.

I parked in the lot behind the small, steeple-topped church and hurried to the front entrance. I had attended Truesdale First Gospel ever since I'd become a Christian, four years ago.

I sniffed deeply as I entered the sanctuary. I loved the smell of this church. Warm wood, furniture polish. And love. People here loved God, and loved other people.

"Kay!" A flash of bright red hair and a waving arm beckoned me. "Come on, you're late. Bobby's about to start worship."

Trotting after Joyce, I slid down a smooth wooden pew.

"Hi." David's lanky form scooted in after me. "Looks like we're both late."

"Shh!" Joyce touched a manicured finger to her lips. "Bobby's about to speak."

David grinned and leaned forward, well used to Joyce's focused, no-nonsense manner. "You guys want to get coffee afterward?"

Joyce sent him an annoyed look. "Fine, but would you please..."

"Sounds like a great idea," I said, sending a quick, quelling look to my two best friends. I was not in the mood for a petty squabble tonight.

Thankfully, Bobby spoke into the microphone.

"Good to see everybody tonight!" His enthusiastic tone sounded a bit artificial, which was strange, but his grin widened to encompass the college students who dotted the sanctuary. "We'll start off with worship, led by my lovely wife, Laura." A smile for her. "Then we'll see the movie. But first, let's have a word of prayer.

"Father God, we ask that you bless this evening, and use this worship and the movie tonight to minister to our hearts. In Jesus' name, Amen."

I poked David's T-shirted torso with my elbow. "You're not playing the guitar?"

He shook his dark head, his brown eyes gleaming. "Bobby wanted to keep it short and sweet."

While Laura played the piano, we all stood and sang a few of our favorite praise songs. Then the movie started.

The lights dimmed, and the title flashed across the screen which hung behind Pastor Warner's glass pulpit. Red block letters on a black background read, *"Are We Living in the Last Days?"*

When the movie ended, I felt as though I'd been hit by a truck. So much information! I couldn't grasp it all. But one fact rang clear. The Bible listed clear signs that would precede Jesus' second coming; that nation would rise against nation, and there would be earthquakes, famines, diseases... Those signs were happening right *now*. Jesus could return soon. We just might be living in the last days. And I hadn't known it. I hadn't even *thought* about it before.

Bobby ended the meeting with another prayer, and invited people to stay and discuss the film if they wanted to.

I turned to David, overcome with wonder. "That movie was great!"

He grinned at me. "Yeah. You know, Snickerdoodle, when you smile like that, you remind me of a little kid..."

"Thanks a lot!"

"No, I'm serious," his dark eyes laughed at me, enjoying a good joke at my expense. He flicked a lock of my hair with one lean finger. "Hair like warm sunshine, eyes like clear green marbles..."

I kicked him in the foot. "Get out of my way." What a pain he was. And I'd been trying to share something serious with him. I tried to frown at him, but a smile twitched my lips instead—quite against my will, might I add. He was incorrigible, and loved to tease me.

My shoulder-length hair is usually golden brown, but this summer the sun had streaked most of it blond. David appeared to be fascinated by this phenomenon.

Joyce shoved impatiently at my back. "I need to talk to Bobby, guys. Will you move your big hulk, David, so I can get out?"

"Aye, aye, captain, ma'am." He smartly snapped his fingers to the edge of his dark, carelessly styled hair.

The instant she escaped, Joyce caught up to Bobby, a few steps away, and spoke earnestly to him. Up close, his brown face looked strained and tired.

I turned to David. "Do you have to provoke her like that?"

A grin stretched his angular cheeks. "Calm down, squirt. It's just in fun. Joyce knows that."

Maybe she did. I glanced at Joyce's carefully tailored appearance. She was so businesslike these days. Her major in college was business management, but this attitude seemed to be flooding into every area of her life.

Joyce turned to us then, her blue eyes snapping and red hair swirling in a crisp, stylish manner about her shoulders. Grinning, she hooked an arm through each of ours, and strode between us, urging us to the door. "Are you finally ready? Let's get some coffee!"

This was the old Joyce we knew and loved.

The coffee shop was only a block away, so we walked. Safety in numbers. Actually, it was a diner, but they served coffee all night. And dessert, too. I scooted into the booth beside Joyce, across from David. The restaurant was cold. I hadn't realized how hot it still was outside until now.

"I need some chocolate mousse pie," I announced, ignoring the menu.

"You always order that," Joyce said. "How about apple pie? Or this heavenly chocolate brownie?" Saliva dripped from her words. We all knew Joyce would get the chocolate brownie, topped with ice cream. She always did.

We ordered coffee and dessert, and then David spoke up, his tone serious for once.

"So, what's up with Bobby? He seemed stressed out tonight."

Our attention turned to Joyce. She was Pastor Warner's daughter, so she always knew the inside scoop.

Her brows knit together, which sent a wrinkle toward her lightly freckled nose. "A rumor is going around that the church may have to let him go. Lack of funds."

"What?" I gasped. Bobby had been our youth pastor for the last four years. "What does your dad say?"

Joyce shook her head. "He doesn't deny it. Finances are tough right now. And the national headquarters for our church—First Gospel of America—might be cutting back our support money."

"Why?" David's voice sounded deeper and more serious than usual.

"I don't know. Dad said they're sending some bigwig here Sunday to check out the church. Then they'll decide what to do. Money offerings keep getting smaller. Maybe that's the main problem. Dad thinks so. But I can't help thinking that all the hate mail we're getting is why they're coming, too."

"Have we received more?"

"Yes. Fifth piece in three weeks. This one had a skull and cross-bones on it, and a nasty warning."

"Saying what?"

"Shut down the church, or we'll shut it down for you." Her lips pressed tightly together. "Dad's starting to feel pretty unpopular. Maybe the FGA thinks the same thing. Like maybe that's why giving is down in our church. I think they're coming to see if we're doing something wrong."

"We're not the only church getting hate mail," David pointed out.

"I know."

I leaned back as the waitress delivered our drinks and desserts. For a few minutes we silently sipped the scorching, bitter coffee. My pie was delicious. Melted in my mouth.

"You two will be on a caffeine high after this," David said, scooping up a big bite of apple pie.

"So?" Joyce raised a brow.

My mind slipped back to the college service. "Wasn't it great?"

"She's talking about the movie," David told Joyce.

I looked at my friends. "You know, I've never thought about the end times before. I didn't even know what they were, really. But now, I can't stop thinking about them. Jesus said things would get really bad before he returned. That there'd be famines, earthquakes, and diseases. Everything would get worse and worse, like it is now. I mean, those things are happening now. He could come back any minute!"

"Whoa." Joyce shook her head. "It *is* interesting, Kay, but face it, people have been saying the end is near for years. Focusing on that can be dangerous. People can get too heavenly minded to do any earthly good. We need to focus on the here and now. That's where all the needs are."

"But Jesus said to watch."

David's brown eyes looked serious. "She's right, Joyce. We are supposed to watch. And be prepared. Knowing Jesus could return soon should inspire us to use our time better."

"That's right." Encouraged by David's defense, I said, "Do you know what's really interesting to me? How these last days are laid out in the Bible. I mean, I never knew any of it before. I knew Jesus would come back again, but I didn't realize there was a sequence to the events. First the last days, then the Rapture, then the seven year Tribulation, and then Jesus' Second Coming."

Joyce remained silent, stirring her coffee, so I eagerly rattled on, "If we really are living in the last days, the Rapture is next. What did the movie say?"

"First Corinthians fifteen, verse fifty-one," David said. "'We will not all sleep, but we will all be changed—in a flash, in the twinkling of an eye, at the last trumpet.'"

"Can you imagine that?" I turned to Joyce. "Some of us will never die! Our bodies will be changed in an instant to immortal bodies. And we'll be caught up to meet Jesus in the air. Wouldn't that be fantastic? And to think it could happen in our lifetime!"

"I hate to dampen your enthusiasm, Kay," Joyce said. Her voice sounded tight. "But people disagree when the Rapture will happen. The movie said it will take place before the Great Tribulation. But some people believe it will happen after the Tribulation, or even sometime in the middle of it."

"I know." Discomfort twisted inside me. Why was she trying to kill my new interest?

A bit bullheadedly, I quoted the movie again. "But doesn't it make sense that Christians would be taken from the earth before the Tribulation? I mean, the Tribulation is when God pours out his wrath on mankind. It says in First Thessalonians that God didn't appoint Christians to suffer his wrath." (1 Thessalonians 5:9)

"And," I continued, "in the Old Testament, when God poured out his anger, he first rescued the people who were faithful to him; Noah in an ark, and Lot fled from Sodom and Gomorrah."

"Fine." Joyce raised her hand. "Believe what you want. But I'm focusing on what's going on right now. *This* is our life. And I think that's where our focus should be."

Feeling even more uncomfortable, I fell silent. No one spoke for a while.

I changed the subject. "I saw Mary Campinella today. Remember her from junior high?"

David looked blank, but then he hadn't moved to Truesdale until high school.

"Oh, yes." Joyce's smile looked too bright. "I remember her. How is she doing? How did she like Catholic high school?"

"I don't know. I didn't get a chance to talk to her much, but she looks happy. I plan to talk to her more before class on Friday."

We reminisced about old times, and then Joyce said she had to go.

Stepping outside was like stepping into a hot sauna. Cloying, close, and uncomfortable.

Joyce stopped at her car. "'Night, guys." She glanced at me a bit sheepishly. "I'm sorry, Kay, for raining on your parade back there. It's just that Dad talks about the last days all the time. I'm sick of it, that's all."

"It's okay."

"Hey, let's do something Friday night." David spoke up behind me. He'd been unusually quiet ever since I'd persisted in discussing the end times. Had I alienated both of my friends?

"Bowling?" Joyce slid into her car. "We can meet at my house."

"Sounds like a plan. What do you think, Kay? Seven-thirty?"

I nodded. "Okay. Great."

Joyce's car turned over smoothly, and with a wave, she eased out of the parking lot. Her house was only a few blocks away, but she'd rather drive than walk over the dangerous streets.

David walked me to my car, which was parked beneath the single lamppost in the middle of the parking lot. He leaned against the car as I unlocked the door.

"You okay?" His voice was quiet.

I quickly glanced up at him. His face and tall frame were cut into sharp relief by the bright light. Good old David. He wasn't mad at me. He was concerned about me.

"I'm okay," My lips smiled, but I suspected my eyes did not. I gave the door handle a strong pull, and the Mustang's door creaked open. "What about you? You seemed kind of quiet after that little discussion I started."

He unexpectedly grinned, and his features, which looked curiously sculpted in that light, relaxed. I intently stared at him for a second. I'd never noticed before, but he was actually handsome. The foreign thought disturbed me, so I shoved it into the back of my mind. He was David. My good friend. It felt strange to think about him like that, even for a second.

"I was fine," he said. "But I could tell Joyce was a little uptight, so I decided to play it cool."

"Unlike me." I ruefully sank onto the worn leather seat. "Always rushing in where angels fear to tread."

He chuckled. "Sometimes I think the world needs more people like you, Kay. People not afraid to speak their mind."

I turned the key in the ignition. "You're not afraid." I listened to the engine turn over. Again and again. A long, rasping cough. But it didn't catch. I tried eight times, then ten.

David poked his head in the window. "Doesn't sound healthy."

"It's been giving me trouble for weeks."

"Pop the hood." I did, and David spent a few minutes checking the battery, fuel, and hoses. Finally, he drove his old, beat up looking sports car to face mine, and attempted to jump-start the Mustang. That didn't work, either.

Wiping his hands, David disconnected the jumper cables. "Looks like you'll need it towed to a shop."

Frustrated, I frowned at the dashboard. Why had it chosen now to break down?

"I'll give you a ride home." David slammed the cords into his trunk.

I climbed out and looked at my car, soon to be alone in the small lot. "Do you think it's safe? What if someone steals it?"

"It'll be just as safe here as in front of your house," he pointed out. "Besides, it won't start. How would someone steal it?"

That did make sense. I'd call the tow truck tomorrow morning, since I didn't have class until noon. Plenty of time to take care of my capricious car.

I relaxed back in David's sports car, and listened as he turned the key to his ignition. One turn, and it started. Figured. He loved to work on his old car. And his father owned an electronics shop which specialized in rebuilding or locating hard-to-find parts for older cars. So if any special parts died, he or his dad could order or custom-make replacements.

Taking a deep breath, I closed my eyes as David bumped through a gutter, and onto the main street. His warm car smelled familiar and safe. An old pine air freshener hung from the rear view mirror. The scent mingled with the musty seats and the faint smell of gasoline. I smiled to myself. Funny how that combination could be so comforting.

"How was your day, anyway?" David's voice interrupted my pleasant thoughts. He rolled down the window, letting a gentle breeze slide into the car. "Anything exciting happen at school?"

The afternoon's disturbing events flooded back. I told him what had happened in the journalism lab, and about meeting Mitch. I ended with Mitch's statement about the hate club on campus.

"Can you *believe* that?" I said, turning to him. "A hate club toward Christians?"

David shrugged one shoulder, his gaze fixed on the road. "It's not that surprising, Kay. Look at all the hate mail our church is getting. And look at the news media. They've been doing a good job of demonizing Christians lately—especially ones who influence politics."

"I know." I watched a lot of news, but had never thought much about how the hostile news reports could influence the public. Prejudice them, really. But to hate?

David went on, sounding thoughtful. "It's like an unspoken war. Freedom of religion versus freedom from religion. I think pressure is building to make people confine their "religion" to their homes and churches. That way, Christians can't inflict their way of thinking on others. Or infringe on other people's rights to hear only what they want to hear."

What David said made sense. But my reporter's instinct told me there was more—much more—to the hate group story than that.

We pulled up in front of my house. I looked out across the peaceful lawn. The house was quiet, the porch light was on, and a faint glow backlit the living room curtains. Both of my parents were probably in bed by now. It was safe to go inside.

"Don't let Joyce discourage you, Kay. I think it's great you're interested in learning about the end times. I've been studying it for a long time now."

David had been a Christian since he was ten—twelve years ago. A lot longer than me.

I felt comforted by his encouragement. "I know I have a lot to learn. I might read Revelation. What do you think? I'm afraid I won't understand it."

"Maybe you won't." He shrugged. "But a lot of prophecies about the end times, including Revelation, are opening up now. People are understanding more now than they ever have before. You should read Daniel chapter twelve..." His voice faded when twin headlights flashed into our eyes.

A dark sedan twisted in front of us and bumped into our driveway. Theresa flounced out, slammed the door, and the car squealed backward, lunged onto the street, and roared off.

"Wham, bam, thank you ma'am," David muttered.

Theresa saw us and teetered her way over. To my surprise, she wobbled around the car and stuck her full head of hair in

David's window. I stifled a snort of laughter when his eyebrows shot up, and he tilted his torso away from my sister's panting lips. Puffs of stale alcohol drifted over to me, and I wrinkled my nose.

"What do you want, Theresa?" I said.

Theresa ignored me, and instead fixed her glazed blue eyes upon David. Her mouth curved into a pouting smile. "How..." David leaned even further back in his seat, "was your group tonight? Hope you had fun." Another dewy-eyed smile.

I felt embarrassed for my sister, and uncomfortable, too. Apparently, Theresa found David attractive. I glanced at him out of the corner of my eye. It must be because she was drunk. Although David was certainly good looking, he wasn't classic, movie star handsome—not on a level with the scores of men my sister dated, anyway.

"We had a lot of fun, thanks," David said gently. "How was your date?"

"Oh," Theresa jerked her head back, and bumped it against the car's roof. "Ow!" She frowned, clearly angry. Whether at the car or her fleeing date, I wasn't sure. "He was a joke...a jerk. You know how it is."

She gazed at David again, speculatively, and I decided it was time to break up this little tête-à-tête.

I sent him an apologetic look, and climbed out of the car. "I'd better let you go, David. I know you have a busy day tomorrow."

Thankfully, Theresa took the hint. She waved coyly to David, and staggered to join me on the sidewalk. He revved the engine once, and shot off. I smiled dryly. Theresa wasn't scoring well with men tonight.

Indoors, Theresa silently stumbled up the stairs, but at the top, she tossed her head. Her light blue eyes looked disdainful. "I see now why you're so faithful to your church group. That David...what a dish." Her cold eyes stared at me. Watchful. Waiting.

Anger flushed my cheeks. Even though I knew she'd provoked me on purpose, I snapped, "That is *not* why I go. And you know it. David is my friend. Period."

"*Whatever*." Condescension dripped from her tone.

Oh, I was mad. I stood there, quivering with fury, and finally escaped to my room before I said something hurtful.

Theresa makes me so angry, Lord! I know I'm supposed to be loving and forgiving and turn the other cheek and all that, but I just can't. Please help me.

After I'd calmed down, I found myself thinking about the movie again. And that reminded me of Mitch's picture. God watching the earth. What did it all really mean? With a cool sheet draped over my body, I stared at the ceiling for a long time.

Jesus had told us to watch for the signs of the end.

A still, small voice told me to pray for Mitch, and for my relationship with my annoying sister. I did, and I thanked God for delivering me from Randy and Tim today.

THURSDAY

TODAY WAS FAIRLY QUIET, but I'll write down a few things of interest.

I read a chapter in Luke while I ate breakfast. And I prayed, too.

I like to start my day off with God. It helps me have a better attitude all day—at least, usually.

Dad called and got my car towed to the mechanic. That meant I had to take the bus to school for my philosophy and mathematics classes this afternoon.

Nothing exciting happened at school. I didn't see Joyce, or David or Mitch. I knew I wouldn't see David. He only goes on Monday, Wednesday and Friday mornings. He's finishing up his last semester, and taking a few classes in business so he can become a partner in his father's electronics shop.

After class, I rode the bus to the mechanic's garage. Dad had already arranged for payment. I know—I'm lucky to have rich parents. In two more years, I'll be out in the real world, paying my own way, Dad says.

By the time I got home, Theresa had already flitted off on another date. Unfortunately, I was glad. I was having a real problem being nice to her. I wanted to act like Jesus, and I wanted God to be glorified by my life, but it was just so hard. *Lord, please fill me with your love, so I can love my sister like you do. And my mom, too.*

Mom and Dad barely spoke tonight. The tension was thick at dinner, and I fled upstairs as soon as I could, under the pretext of doing my homework. Well, I did do homework, so it was the truth. But I couldn't wait until tomorrow night. Bowling with Joyce and David would give me a chance to escape from this house.

I read Daniel 12, too, like David had suggested. Here are a few verses that caught my eye:

(Note: By now in the book of Daniel, God had revealed all kinds of things to Daniel about the end times.) Verse 4:

> *"But you, Daniel, close up and seal the words of the scroll until the time of the end. Many will go here and there to increase knowledge."*

Then more prophecies were revealed to Daniel, but he did not understand what they meant. He asked what the outcome of all of these things would be.

Verses 9-10:

> *He replied, "Go your way, Daniel, because the words are closed up and sealed until the time of the end. Many will be purified, made spotless and refined, but the wicked will continue to be wicked. None of the wicked will under-stand, but those who are wise will understand."*

So that was what David had meant. Prophecies about the end times would open up in the time of the end. People would understand them like they never could before.

I wondered if I would be one of those who understood.

I also read the first chapter of Revelation. One verse surprised me right away. Chapter one, verse 3:

Blessed is the one who reads the words of this prophecy, and blessed are those who hear it and take to heart what is written in it, because the time is near.

It sounds like a blessing is promised to everyone who reads the book of Revelation! God must really want us to read it.

FRIDAY

I SAW MARY CAMPINELLA in World Religions class this morning.

By the way, we learned on Monday that our teacher, Mr. Carlisle, is an atheist. Seems strange that an atheist would teach a world religions class, but he claims he brings a refreshing, objective view to the subject. We'll see.

Anyway, today I had a chance, for the first time since school started, to really talk to Mary. I learned something that shocked me.

"Hi." I slid into the seat across from her.

Mary looked up, startled. Her thin fingers fiddled with an earring hidden beneath her chin length, chestnut hair. She was classically pretty, with dark, arched brows. But her face had a pinched look to it this morning.

"Hi." Her chocolate brown eyes looked tired. She wore faded jeans and a worn, but stylishly cut print blouse. Her burgundy book bag on the floor looked dented and battered. She offered a faint smile. "Sorry if I seem like a poop, but I was up late last night, working at the supermarket."

"Oh." Interesting. Mary's parents were rich, like mine. At least, they had been seven years ago. I unfortunately spoke before thinking, "Why are you working? Do you need the extra money?"

"You could say that." Although Mary laughed, she watched me carefully. "I need it for the baby. My parents threw me out of the house four months ago, when they found out I'm pregnant."

My gaze shot to her waistline, which was covered by the loose, cotton blouse. "You don't look pregnant." What a brilliant thing to say.

"Thanks." Mary looked uncomfortable. "I'm only five months along. Wearing loose clothes helps cover it up."

I glanced quickly at her left hand. No ring.

"I can't believe they threw you out." Finally, a supportive comment left my lips. I was just so shocked. Mary, an upright Catholic girl, pregnant. It didn't fit the image I remembered of her. But then again, both of us had changed a lot in the last seven years.

"What is your life like now?" Mary apparently didn't want to talk about herself. "You've changed a lot." She looked wistful.

"Seven years can make a big difference."

Mary shook her head. "No. Something is different about you, but I can't put my finger on it."

"I became a Christian four years ago. That's the biggest change in my life."

"Oh." She eyed me uncertainly.

An idea flew to mind, and I smiled. "I know. How would you like to come to my house this afternoon? We could look at photo albums, and remember the good old days. It would be fun."

Mary smiled for the first time. "I'd like that. My last class is over at four. But I have to be at work at eight."

"I need to do research at the library until four. Would you like a ride to my house? Or is your car here on campus?"

"I don't have a car. I take the bus."

Mr. Carlisle strode to the front of the classroom. The dark soul patch growing on his chin complemented his worn jeans and rumpled plaid shirt. He wasn't old—probably under thirty—and every time he entered the room, a few girls giggled and fluffed their hair. While he wasn't bad looking, his self-confident swagger bordered on the arrogant, and scraped on my nerves.

"Let's meet at the library, at four." I whispered. "Outside. West entrance."

Mary nodded as Mr. Carlisle flipped on the overhead projector. The nearby computer projected a picture of the Buddha onto the screen at the front of the room.

He offered us a small, condescending grin. "Who wants to hear another fairy tale?"

Current Affairs journalism class was next.

Apprehension slowed my steps as I neared the doorway, and a warm, sweaty sock aroma assaulted my nostrils as I peeped inside. The last teacher must have taught with the door closed. With a wrinkled nose, I scanned the lightly populated room. Randy and Tim weren't there.

The knot in my stomach eased. Good. Maybe they'd drop the class.

I chose to sit at a desk in the middle of the room, and pulled out my report.

"Hi!"

The rich tenor voice made my head swivel.

Trent flashed a warm grin as he slid into the desk beside mine. I couldn't help but notice that his aqua polo shirt intensified the royal blue of his eyes.

"Hi." My response lacked a bit of his warmth. Quickly, I chided myself. What was my problem? Trent hadn't assaulted me. And it wasn't his fault those two thugs had decided to get ugly.

His grin faded, and his aristocratic mouth drooped. "I'm really sorry about what happened." His gaze darkened with sincerity. "I feel bad about the whole thing. Tim and Randy never would have demanded to see your paper if I hadn't...you know. Asked you to give it to me."

He was incredibly attractive, oozing that puppy dog charm! How could I be angry with him? None of it was his fault.

Although he could have at least said *something* to those two thugs, I sharply reminded my slipping senses. "It's okay. It wasn't your fault."

"Sure you're not mad?" His hopeful grin charmed me, and I found myself laughing.

"No, of course not. Don't be silly."

"Good." He leaned closer, which made my heart flutter. Trent was entirely too good looking for his own good. I ordered myself to focus on his perfect, movie star features, rather than sweep, misty-eyed over his square shoulders, defined by his clinging knit polo shirt, and up over the flat planes of his cheeks that dimpled now as he smiled at me.

He murmured, "Will you come to coffee with me after class?"

Chagrinned, I returned to earth. His grin said he knew I'd been admiring him, and he liked it.

"I can't." I glanced at the front of the room, where Dr. Williams wrote on the board. The class had filled up in the last few minutes. Out of the corner of my eye, I spotted Randy and Tim sidling to the far back corner. "I have a class."

Trent slumped back in his chair. "Maybe another time, then." His tone sounded hopeful.

My lips twitched into a smile. "Maybe so."

Mary waited on the library steps when I finally flew out, clutching a pile of library books. The hot, still air hit me like a blast from a furnace.

"Sorry I'm late. The check-out line was longer than I expected."

She glanced at her watch and smiled. "Only five minutes. Hardly a crime, Kay."

Laughing and talking, we walked quickly to my baking hot car. The leather seats were toasty warm, and the hot metal buckle bit painfully into my fingers. Thankfully, the car started on the first try. Amazing what a new fuel pump could do.

Turning onto High Street, I glanced at Mary.

"So, where do you live now?"

She gestured. "At the east end of High Street. On Driscoll. My boyfriend, Jack, is letting me stay with him."

I heard an odd inflection in her voice, and wondered about it. "How does he feel about the baby?" I assumed it was his.

"Oh," Mary twisted her hands and stared out the windshield. "He doesn't want it. But he's promised to take care of us. He's a good guy, and he loves me."

Aghast, I wondered how a good guy could not want his own child. *And* tell the woman he loved that. But I kept my comments to myself, and changed the subject. "What sort of work do you do at the supermarket?"

Mary relaxed. "I'm a checker. I zip the products over the scanners, and take money. It's pretty easy, and it pays well, which is great. I need it."

"Are you paying your way through college?"

"My parents are helping. When I was a baby, they put money in a college fund for my tuition." Her voice grew quieter. "But Dad says I'd better hurry up and declare a major, or he'll cut me off. So I'm saving money in case that happens. Plus, I pay half the rent and food, and I'm buying clothes for the baby."

I slid into the parking spot in front of my house. "Sounds like you keep busy."

Cool air sliced through my blouse when we stepped indoors. Mom sat on a tan couch in the living room, her nails flipping through a fashion magazine. The house smelled freshly polished, and fresh flowers graced the elegant blond coffee table. She looked up as we entered.

"Kay!" She smiled. Tonight she wore a pale peach silk dress, delicate diamond drop earrings, and her favorite silver bracelets. She always dressed up in the afternoons. For Dad? Considering the tension between them, that was hard to believe.

"Mom," I turned to my guest, "this is Mary Campinella. Remember? We were friends in junior high."

"Of course! Mary." Gracefully, Mom stepped over and clasped Mary's hands. "You look wonderful!. So tall, and thin." She eyed Mary's tasteful, yet obviously old clothes with a bit of horror, but tugged on her hands, leading her to the couch.

Mary glanced at me, smiling, and followed my mom.

"Tell me all about yourself. How is your mother?" Mom's frosty blue eyes melted a little around the edges. She and Mrs. Campinella had been strong acquaintances for years.

"I haven't seen my mother in a while." Mary said awkwardly, "I'm not living at home anymore."

Just then, the front door slipped open. Dad was home early. His stocky, business-suited form strode by, programmed to ignore my mother. Then he did a double-take and stepped back.

"Mary?" he boomed. "Is that you?" His face blossomed into wreaths of smiles. "How wonderful to see you again! Come here."

Mary grinned shyly, and hugged my dad. Both were the same height. Mom watched, her lips thinned, eyes jealous. Dad never greeted her like that anymore.

Dad held Mary at arm's length. "Gaining a little weight, are you?"

Mary flushed, and touched her stomach. When she did, I finally saw the obvious bulge. "I'm pregnant."

Mom's gaze zipped to Mary's bare ring finger.

"Isn't that lovely." The distaste in my mother's voice rang painfully clear to us all. "Are you living with the father?"

"Yes." Mary's face drained white, and she withdrew her hand from Dad's. "My parents threw me out."

"I'm sorry to hear that," Dad boomed, and smiled warmly at my friend. "But a child deserves a celebration. Can you stay for dinner tonight?"

"Oh." She glanced at me, uncertain.

"Yes!" I smiled, surprised by my father's warm charm. "What a great idea, Dad."

Mom rose stiffly to her feet. "Yes, what a perfectly lovely idea. Let me make sure I have enough potatoes roasting."

"You girls have a lot of catching up to do." Dad patted Mary on the back. "We'll see you downstairs for dinner. Six sharp."

Mary and I spent the next hour laughing over junior high yearbooks, and remembering old classmates and teachers. At six o'clock, we trotted downstairs, eagerly inhaling the warm, spicy smell of roasted chicken and fresh baked rolls.

"...of course I agree with you, dear. It's the Christian thing to do. That poor girl..." Mom's righteous, stilted words halted the instant we stepped into the kitchen.

I hoped Mary hadn't heard, but knew she had.

My mother's peach painted lips stretched into a thin smile. "Did you girls have fun?"

"Yes. Thanks, Mom," I said tightly. I felt upset and embarrassed for my friend. "Are we eating in the dining room?" I brushed by her.

The chandelier in the dining room sparkled down on the fine china, polished silver, and cloth napkins on the table. Mom had gone all out, doing the "Christian" thing for Mary.

You're judging her, a voice whispered in my spirit. That was just as bad as what she'd done to Mary.

"Hi, Mary. Good to see you again." Seated already, Theresa offered Mary a smile.

Mom served up baked potatoes, roasted chicken, a fresh salad and rolls. Despite the delicious food, the atmosphere at the table felt strained. Dad and I tried to make light, friendly conversation, but poor Mary looked desperately uncomfortable. She stared at her plate and poked at a lettuce leaf.

The doorbell came as a relief.

"I'll get it." Theresa jumped up. Her pink cheeks matched her sleeveless top and complemented her white jeans. "Richie said he might be early."

But the high, harmonizing trill coming from the living room moments later said it wasn't Richie who had arrived.

Laughing over her shoulder, Theresa returned. Joyce trotted behind her, red hair tied up in a pony tail, and she wore a huge T-shirt and slim-fitting workout shorts.

"Hi, Mrs. Jameson! Hi, Kay." Joyce's gaze traveled around the table, but stopped when she came to Mary. "Is that *you*, Mary?" She dashed over and flung her arms around her neck. "Kay told me you're in one of her classes. Look at you! You look great!"

Mary's pinched face blossomed. "So do you. Kay and I have been catching up."

Joyce sighed. "The good old days. Nothing to worry about but boys and what to do for summer vacation." She turned to Theresa and held out a pair of sunglasses. "I almost forgot. You left your sunglasses at the gym, so I thought I'd run them over on my way home."

"Thanks, Joy." Theresa accepted them, still smiling. I stared at my sister, certain I must be hallucinating. I hadn't seen my sister this relaxed and friendly in months. And I hadn't known she and Joyce knew each other so well, either.

Joyce turned next to my mother. "See you at the gym tomorrow, Helen? I have a few ideas that could help your workout."

Mom's eyes sparkled. "Yes, I'll be there. Thank you, Joyce."

Breezily, Joyce spun toward the door and waved. "Gotta run. Great to see you, Mary. See you later, Kay."

The door slammed behind her.

I felt stunned, and honestly a little jealous of Joyce right then. I could barely speak to my sister, had nothing in common with my mother, and yet Joyce was on perfect terms with both. It didn't seem fair. Not at all. Was it me? Was something wrong with me? Blinking quickly, I stared at my chicken.

A few minutes later, Mary glanced at the maple clock on the wall. Seven. "I'd better be going." Her smile still looked a bit stiff. "I need to change for work. Thank you for dinner. It was delicious."

"I'm so happy you came, Mary. Come again soon." My mother could be gracious now. She had fulfilled her Christian duty. I felt appalled by my horrible, sarcastic thought.

I dashed upstairs to grab my purse. After calling out that I'd be back later tonight, we hurried to my old brown Mustang. It was still hot and muggy outside.

The sun was setting in a blaze of glory, firing the west end of State Street a dazzling orange. I eased into traffic, and drove around the block to High Street.

"Your parents still look the same."

"I'm so sorry. I feel terrible about how my mom treated you."

"Don't apologize. I'm used to it. Remember? My own parents kicked me out of the house."

Minutes later we turned left, and then pulled up in front of Mary's apartment complex, located on Driscoll Street. It was in an older, run down section of the city. Groups of toughs strolled the streets. A few eyed my car.

"Want to come up and meet Jack?" Mary paused, her hand on the door, and tone hopeful. "Just for a minute?"

"Of course." I tried to ignore my unease. It was still light outside. And I was curious to meet Jack, whom Mary had bubbled on and on about while we'd flipped through old photo albums. He sounded like quite a guy.

After locking the car, I stepped across a strip of sweet smelling, freshly mowed grass to the sidewalk, and followed Mary inside the apartment building. It was old. Apartments branched off of a central, linoleum hallway. The walls were painted dark brown, and the smell of frying onions wafted from under one of the green doors.

We climbed upstairs, to apartment 201. Mary's key rattled in the gold doorknob, and she pushed it open.

"You home, Jack? I'd like you to meet someone."

"Hey, babe." Beer in hand, a slim, dark-haired man sauntered up and slung his free arm over Mary's shoulders.

He wore jeans and a tight white T-shirt, obviously designed to showcase his bulging muscles. His hair was black, short in back, and stylish, with a long, straight lock drooping over his forehead. Twin black brows slashed devilishly above two hard brown eyes. He was handsome. And he knew it.

I didn't like the way his gaze raked me. Speculatively. As if he was a bird of prey, circling for new game. He swigged back his beer, keeping his black eyes fixed on me. "So, who's this, Mare?"

Mary's happy smile faltered. "Kay. Kay Jameson. And Kay, this is my boyfriend, Jack Ignacio."

"Nice to meet you." I smiled politely, and glanced at Mary. "I guess I should go. My friends are expecting me. See you in class on Monday?"

She smiled. "See you then."

Since the area outside was clear of toughs for the moment, I made a beeline for my car and slammed the door behind me. With a faint shiver, I pulled away from the curb.

I did not like Jack. He gave me the creepy crawlies. Hopefully he treated Mary a whole lot better than that encounter seemed to suggest. She obviously loved him.

David's old sports car was parked outside Joyce's house when I arrived. The Warners owned their modest, two-story home, since the church did not provide housing for its pastor. As I parked behind David's car, my spirits lifted. I was looking forward to this evening. It was a welcome chance to forget about the tension in my life.

David answered the door with a grin. His dark hair looked rumpled, as usual. He wore a casual brown shirt and jean shorts. Shorts! I did a double-take, and grinned up at him.

"Hey, haven't seen your skinny stick legs all summer," I teased. "What's the occasion?"

He gave a fake leer and hissed, "They're my secret weapon. You girls will be so distracted by my sculpted legs that you won't be able to concentrate." His eyebrows wiggled. "And I'll win the bowling tournament."

"Right!" I rolled my eyes. "More like they'll blind us. They're as white as a sheet."

"Hey," David looked hurt as he closed the door, but only for a second. He glanced over my head and grinned. "Hi, Pastor Warner. Is Joyce ready yet?"

"Here I am!" Joyce emerged from the hall.

"Don't you girls look nice." The overhead light shone off of Pastor Warner's balding red head and beaming face. Reading glasses rested on the tip of his nose, and loose, comfortable clothes enveloped his stocky body.

I smiled, happy with his sincere compliment. Tonight I wore a soft rose blouse and nice, dark gray jeans. I suspected the bowling alley would be cold. Joyce wore pale blue jeans, and a stylish aqua blouse over a camisole. Her hair was still in a ponytail, but she managed to look elegant anyway. Like my mom and sister. Maybe that was the tie that bound the three together.

"Thanks, Daddy." Joyce kissed his cheek. "I'll be back by eleven."

David jangled keys behind my head. "I'll drive."

I squeezed into the back seat, because Joyce hated climbing into that tiny space. "Which alley are we going to?" I asked the back of David's head.

"Comden. Down on Driscoll."

"I just came from there!" I sat back, enjoying the feel of being chauffeured.

Joyce twisted her head. "Really? What were you doing there?"

"Dropping Mary off at her apartment." I gave them a sketch of my evening, but glossed over my mother's reaction to Mary's illegitimate pregnancy.

"That poor thing!" Joyce shook her head after learning about how Mary's parents had thrown her out of the house.

We approached the old Comden bowling alley. Cars filled the lot, and bands of smoking young people clustered next to the dingy building.

"Looks run down," I observed. We hadn't visited the alley in a couple of years.

"It'll be okay inside," David said optimistically.

"I hope so," Joyce muttered.

David was right. Although the faded red carpets looked shabby, it seemed safe enough inside. A few people sat at tables, drinking, but most clustered at the lanes, intent on bowling. Besides the crash of falling pins, it was quiet inside.

"See?" David raised a supercilious brow at me.

After paying for shoes and depositing one of our own with the slack-faced cashier for insurance, we limped down to our lane. Number sixteen.

"I hate these shoes," I said, lacing up the red and blue striped footwear. My narrow feet always ended up slipping around inside.

David returned with his ball; a hefty, blue sixteen pounder. I raised my eyebrows. "Be careful that ball doesn't roll *you* down the lane, David."

He ignored the comment. Disappointed, I slipped over to search for a ball for myself. A pretty, green and black swirled ball immediately caught my eye, and I pulled it into my arms.

Joyce chose black. When I returned, she already sat at the scoring computer, logging in our names. "There. We're ready to start."

My first game was awful. Unlike Joyce's. Each time she threw, she studied the lane for a full minute, frowning, and then precisely swept to the line and rolled the ball.

David played well, too. I watched with a narrowed eye as he easily lifted and bowled the sixteen pound ball. Was that the weight he'd always bowled? I couldn't remember.

David won the game by ten points. I lagged behind both, ringing in at 79.

"Good game," I congratulated him.

"Thanks, Guttersnipe." He grinned at me. His various, imaginative nicknames for me had become a longstanding joke between us. "I'll give you a few pointers, if you're interested."

I shrugged. "Okay." What did I have to lose?

We trotted out to the wooden bowling floor.

"This is what you're doing," he lectured. He grabbed a ball, dashed to the line, paused, whistled a short tune, and then hurled the ball. It arched, and then crashed halfway down the lane.

"No way!" I sputtered into laughter. I turned to Joyce for support. "That's not true, is it?"

Her smile looked maternal. "I'm afraid it is."

"See?" Triumphantly, David loped up and grabbed another ball. "Now I'll show you how it's *supposed* to be done."

Unable to suppress a small smile, I stood back to watch.

Bowling ball curled to his chest, David bent a little at the waist, and then stepped once, twice, thrice, and smoothly released the ball. Instead of flying halfway down the lane like mine, it touched down softly, only feet from where David released it, and rolled straight, right down the middle of the lane. A full strike.

David pumped his elbow to his knee. "Yes!" He grinned at me. "See how the master does it?"

"Okay, mister know-it-all. Move out of my way." Grabbing my ball, I slipped into place. I was ready. Video streaming through my mind, I copied his steps. Only his strides were longer than mine, so I had to add in an extra one. That really messed me up. Next thing I knew, my legs tangled, and the ball flew through the air.

SLAM! It crashed into the gutter, and almost flew into the next lane.

David and Joyce gasped, laughing, until tears streamed down their cheeks. Determinedly ignoring them, I tried again, and this time it went better. At least the ball went down the middle of the lane....until the end. Gutter ball.

I improved as the game progressed, but not by much. Joyce was last up. I had lost, with 86 points, but David led Joyce by a strike. Could she do it?

No...eight pins down. She walked back, smiling.

I suddenly felt David's hand on my shoulder, shoving me down hard to the floor.

"Wha..." I gasped, and struggled against him. But his surprisingly strong arm held me down.

"Get down!"

Joyce dove onto the floor beside us.

"What is it?" I stared at my two best friends. Their faces were inches from my own.

"Knife fight!" David cautiously poked his head up, and then ducked back down again. His arm still protectively rested across my back, holding me down. "They're headed this way."

I heard the shouts now, for the alley had suddenly fallen silent. No balls rolling. No pins crashing. Just deadly, hate filled screams. Right behind us.

"I'm going to kill you!"

My hands suddenly felt cold, and fear filled me. *Lord, please protect us.*

Compared to this, the journalism lab incident was nothing. These men had knives, and probably guns. A live-eye news report flashed before my eyes. "Three college students were gunned down tonight, victims of gang warfare..."

I cringed against the floor. We could die. Right now.

"It's okay," David's arm squeezed my shoulders. "Everything will be fine. Don't worry."

The shouts sounded hoarse now, and enraged. I heard scuffles and grunts, and the sounds of fists hitting flesh. One of the seats moved against my ankle, and someone screamed a curse.

"All right, that's enough! Break it up!" The authoritative voice strode our way. "The fight's over, boys."

After a filthy mumble of language and more threats, the fracas moved away. David urged us up, and we backed away from the group of angry young men. Blue-suited security guards herded the toughs toward a side door.

I didn't realize that tears slipped down my cheeks until David offered me a hanky. He looked grim, and white etched his high cheekbones. Although wide-eyed, Joyce appeared composed.

"Let's go," I said quietly. Stumbling to a chair, I pulled off my bowling shoes. The bowling alley was quiet now. The rowdies had moved outside. We could leave through a different entrance.

Legs trembling, I approached the desk.

"No charge, no charge." The man looked apologetic as he handed over our shoes. "Come back again soon?"

I could barely see him through the tears filling my eyes. I hated myself for being weak. Joyce wasn't crying. Why was I?

I crammed into the back seat of the car, and tried to stop shaking. I wanted to be somewhere safe. Logically, I was safe in David's car, but emotionally I didn't feel it yet.

David bumped onto the main road. The comforting scent of pine and musty seats, and the smooth purr of the car soothed me. Slowly, my breathing quieted, although a few tears still slid down my cheeks.

"I can't believe it," Joyce snapped. "We can't go anywhere anymore. Crime is all over the place. At the bowling alley, at the mall, at the movies! What is this city coming to?"

"I know," David said, and glanced at me in the rearview mirror. "Makes a person want to stay home."

Although it was warm in the car, my hands felt like ice, so I crossed my arms and pressed my curled fingers into my armpits. Unobtrusively, I dipped my head and wiped the last of the tears from my cheeks onto my shoulders.

We pulled up in front of Joyce's house a few minutes later.

"Do you want to come in?" She hesitated. "We could watch a movie or something."

"Thank you. But I think I've had enough for tonight." I just wanted to get home.

"Okay. Well, see you Sunday at church. Can you get out, Kay?" She flipped up the seat. "Are you okay?"

"Yes." I took a small breath and managed a smile as I climbed out. "I was in shock, I think. That's all."

She gave me a brief, concerned hug, waved to David, and disappeared up the walk.

"Kay."

"What?" I bent to peer into the car.

David motioned with his hand. "Come sit in here a minute."

Slowly, I complied. I looked out the windshield, feeling a bit foolish. "I feel like a crybaby." I glanced at him, but his brown gaze caught mine so I couldn't look away again.

"Don't be stupid, Kay. It was scary. Don't apologize for how you feel."

"I know." I pulled my gaze from his. "It's just that even Joyce..."

"Forget Joyce. She's not you. Joyce has a tougher skin. She was scared, though. So was I. We'd be stupid not to be."

"I know." With a sigh, I stared out the windshield again.

"Hey." The brief touch of his warm fingers on my cold ones brought my attention back to his shadowed face. "I'm glad you are who you are. If you can't be real with your best friends, who can you be real with?"

"Thanks, D." I gave him a small smile. "You're a great friend."

His familiar, endearing grin flashed. "You are, too. In fact, you know what?" He thought for a second. "Yep, it's true. I wouldn't trade you for a bunch of horny-backed toads."

"Thanks a lot!" With a laugh, I crawled out of his car. Suddenly, I felt a whole lot better about the whole disastrous evening.

"Although," he poked his head back into my line of vision. "I might trade you for a new computer chip."

"You are a pain," I told him, but couldn't help but smile.

He touched the gas, and the old sports car revved, gently. He stuck his head into view again, looking serious now. "You going to be okay getting home?"

"Yes, thanks. Goodnight, David."

He revved the engine in farewell.

At home, I trotted upstairs. I had a lot to thank God for tonight: rescuing us from danger, and for good friends.

At 1:20 a.m., the door slammed downstairs. Theresa, finally home from her date with Richie. Must have gone better than her date on Wednesday night.

I thought about saying "hi," but decided against it when I heard her stumble into a wall. She was drunk again.

SUNDAY

DAD SAT AT THE BREAKFAST BAR, eating cereal alone. He wore a T-shirt and walking shorts, and his silver hair looked wind-blown.

"Morning, Dad." I'd woken up in an inexplicably good mood. Today I wore a pale ochre dress for church.

"How was bowling on Friday night? Forgot to ask you yesterday." Dad had worked all day Saturday, which was unusual for him. His hazel eyes smiled at me as I splashed milk over my healthy breakfast flakes.

"It was okay. Until the knife fight." I popped a spoonful of cereal in my mouth.

"*Knife* fight?" A vein popped out on Dad's forehead. "Where did you go?"

"The Comden." When he reprovingly shook his head, I explained what had happened.

"That's a bad side of town, Kay. I don't want you going over there at night. It's too dangerous."

"I wasn't alone, Dad. But you're right. I don't want to go back there, either." I shoveled more cereal in my mouth. The service would start in ten minutes.

After gulping down orange juice, I asked, as I always did, "Do you want to come to church with me?"

"No. Thanks, honey."

I'd never stop asking. My parents know what Christianity is about, but I felt pretty sure they'd never committed their lives to Christ.

When I arrived at church, a crowd of people clustered near the western corner of the building. Curious, I adjusted my path to see what they were looking at. Only by standing on tiptoe could I see it.

A black, ugly skull and cross-bones had been spray-painted on the white wall. And scrawled beneath: *Death to all Christians.*

The hatred and evil of it made me draw a breath and step backward. *Why?* Why had someone done that?

I slipped inside the church. After a quick scan, I spotted Joyce and her mother in their usual position: front row, on the right. I slipped onto the pew before Laura struck the first chords on the piano.

"Hi," I whispered.

Joyce's chin jerked left to look at me. She scowled. "Did you *see* what they did?"

I nodded. "When did it happen?"

"Last night. I can't believe it!"

"Who would do such a thing? And why?"

"I don't know."

"Shh," Mrs. Warner shushed us. We rustled to our feet to sing the first hymn.

I found myself scanning the room as we sang. For whom? The person who had defaced our building? It wasn't likely he'd come to church.

I did see one unfamiliar face. David came in late, so he had to sit in the back—next to the pinched-faced man I'd never seen before.

The sermon was good. Pastor Warner talked about forgiveness and loving our neighbor. And that meant our own family, too. My heart burned with conviction. I loved my family, but I hadn't been showing it enough lately. Except maybe to Dad.

After the service, the stranger cornered Pastor Warner in the foyer.

"That's Mr. Crawford from the FGA." Joyce nodded toward the spectacled, dark-haired man.

"FGA?" David appeared by my side.

"First Gospel of America. Remember, I told you they were sending someone to inspect our church?"

"Oh, yeah." He glanced at the two conversing men and raised an eyebrow. "What exactly is he inspecting?"

"I'm not sure. Supposedly he's here to find out why our revenues are down. But Dad doesn't think that's the whole reason. Neither do I."

I remembered Joyce's theory about the hate mail. "That graffiti must make us look awful."

"It certainly won't help matters."

"We're not the only church with graffiti," David pointed out. "First Methodist was spray-painted last week."

Joyce shook her head. "I don't think that matters to these people."

"I wonder what he's saying." We stared at the grim, gray-suited man. But we weren't close enough to overhear their conversation.

We attended Sunday school, and then I drove home. Homework unfortunately beckoned, so I spent the rest of the afternoon catching up. I also read a few more chapters in Revelation.

And I prayed that God would help me be a witness this week. So I could speak his words to anyone who might need to hear them.

MONDAY

"WHAT A BEAUTIFUL DRESS," I exclaimed to Mary, dropping my forest green backpack beside my desk in World Religions class. "Is it new?"

Her casual dress was simply designed: wine red, sleeveless, with a delicate design at the neck. Something I'd choose if I could wear bold colors. And was pregnant.

"Thank you." Mary offered a small smile. "I bought it at a thrift store over the weekend."

"It's gorgeous. I'll bet Jack likes it, too."

Mary glanced away. "No. He doesn't." When she looked back, her smile wavered. "He thinks it's out of style."

"But that's ridiculous. It's a classic. It'll never go out of style."

"Jack has his own ideas about fashion."

We both watched Mr. Carlisle stride to the front of the classroom. I wondered which religion he'd make derogatory remarks about today.

A quick smile brightened Mary's face. "Did I tell you I'm going to the doctor tomorrow? I'm going to have an ultrasound. It'll use sound waves to look at the baby. I'll actually see a picture of it."

"Neat!"

"I'll get a photo made and bring it to class on Wednesday, if you're interested in seeing it."

"Yes, I'd love that."

Mr. Carlisle used a remote control to flip off the lights, and then a snapshot of thousands of devout, kneeling worshippers lit up the projection screen. He chuckled. "Looks painful. Being an atheist definitely has its perks."

Dr. Williams, my hard-eyed, blond-haired current affairs teacher, gave us a new assignment this morning. He told us to search the newspapers and choose a topic for a major, in-depth article. Like a term paper, I guess. Our thesis statement was due on Monday.

Mulling over ideas, I gathered up my books and headed for the door. Someone fell into step beside me.

I knew without looking that it was Trent. He'd come in late, and had to sit in the front of the classroom. I'd had a hard time keeping my eyes from straying to his light-haired, perfectly sculpted head during class.

"Hi." A smile warmed his rich tenor voice.

A reluctant grin tugged at my lips when I saw how soulful his expression looked.

"Hi." I still felt unsettled by the contrary emotions Trent evoked in me. Strong attraction, and yet a good amount of caution, too.

"Do you forgive me? For what happened in the lab last week?"

"There's nothing to forgive, Trent. It wasn't your fault."

"I'll only really, *truly* believe you if you'll come to coffee with me this afternoon," he wheedled.

Why was he so interested in spending time with me? Guys didn't exactly beat a path to my door. I was passably pretty at best, but that was it. And especially not guys like Trent, who were handsome, charming, sophisticated and fun.

I glanced at him out of the corner of my eye. He wore a snug, tan polo shirt today, and gray shorts. He had tanned, well-formed legs, too. I stopped myself when my gaze lingered. What was I doing? Looks weren't the most important things about a person. And the only way I'd discover more about Trent was to spend time with him.

Trent grinned, perhaps amused by how long it was taking me to respond.

"Okay," I said, hoping my smile looked composed, and not like a teenager with a silly crush. "Three o'clock, at the student union?"

The full power of his electric blue eyes beamed down on me. My heart fluttered. "Great! I'll see you then. I'm looking forward to it."

As he strode off, questions danced through my mind. What did he see in me? A slim, blond-haired girl wearing an old caramel blouse and jeans. I had no idea. But it would be fun to find out.

I pushed through the crowded student union, heading for the table where a light-haired young man sat alone.

Trent immediately leaped up and pulled out a chair. "Kay! Great to see you. Would you like some coffee?"

Letting my backpack slide to the floor, I sniffed the air. A delicate, mint aroma wafted from his mug. "I'll have what you're having."

He grinned. "One chocolate mint coming up."

I crossed my legs and rested my elbows on the table as I waited for him to return. I noticed that he'd placed Dr. William's assignment sheet on the table before him.

"Thank you." I accepted the steaming mug from him, and nodded at the paper. "Have you decided on a topic yet?"

"I have a few ideas." He flashed a white smile. "I've been thinking about it for a while, though."

"Really?" Puzzled, I sipped the coffee. "But we just got the assignment today."

"The assignment is in the syllabus he handed out last week." Trent's grin widened. "Don't tell me you haven't read his syllabus! It's Dr. William's bible for the semester."

"I haven't. But maybe I'd better. I'd like to get a heads up before more surprises come."

We sipped coffee for a few quiet moments. I searched desperately for something witty or interesting to say.

Trent's choice of topic surprised me. "I've been thinking about Tim and Randy's behavior in the journalism lab."

"Really? Why?"

"I can't understand why those guys hate you so much. It's because you're a Christian, right? Don't you go to Truesdale First Gospel?"

My mug halted halfway to my mouth. Hurriedly, I sipped. Where was he going with this? "Yes. That's right."

I couldn't quite decipher the gleam in his eyes. It looked satisfied. Pleased.

"I guess some people are religious fanatics," he mused.

"What?" Coffee sputtered from my lips.

He waved a hand. "I'm talking about the bigots who hate Christians, or Jews. They're fanatical. They have to be. I mean, what kind of decent person would behave like that?"

"Are you saying Randy and Tim are worse people than you?" My impulsive mouth spoke before my brain engaged.

"Well, of course they are." He looked surprised. "I don't attack people."

"Interesting." I stirred my coffee with the little red straw. "Sometimes I want to think the same thing. But I can't."

"Why not?"

"Because the Bible says something different."

Trent raised a brow. "The Bible is only one religious book."

"Do you believe in another one?"

"No. But at the same time, I'm not a Christian, either."

"So what are you?"

He grinned. "I like to describe myself as an open-minded agnostic."

"I see." After a moment, I said, "Mind if I ask you something?"

He shook his head.

"I was wondering how you decide what's wrong, and what's worse. For example, how can you say persecuting Christians is worse than lying to your mother?"

He laughed. His bright blue eyes looked oddly intrigued. "Ah, a philosophy question. Well, to me, it's simple. If you hurt someone—whether it's murder, rape, stealing, whatever—that's really bad, and should be punished. But smaller things, like telling white lies, aren't that important."

"How do you know?" I pressed. A bit of anxiety twisted in my stomach. This confrontational boldness wasn't the norm for me. "I mean, are your opinions the ultimate authority on what's right and wrong?"

He grinned. "I knew you'd be interesting to talk to, Kay." He remained silent for a few moments. "To answer your question... Yes, I think I'm right. I've thought about good and evil a lot, and I stand by what I said."

His blue gaze snared mine, pulling me into a teasing challenge that I could not resist.

Casually, I said, "Making up your own moral rules, huh? It almost sounds like you're trying to play God."

"Whoa!" He sat back with a laugh. "I wouldn't go that far. I mean, I do believe there's a God. That's where I get my ideas about right and wrong."

"But you don't think you're as bad as Randy or Tim."

"That's right." He leaned forward, and his sculpted features relaxed into a charming smile. "So. What do you say about that?"

Did he actually want to hear what I thought about God? The student union suddenly seemed chilly. I shivered. But I met his gaze boldly enough.

"Have you ever done something you *know* is wrong?"

"Yes." His eyes sparkled; almost as if flirting with me. "But nothing big. Nothing God won't overlook. God is loving, right?"

The hot mug warmed my icy fingers. I smiled at him. "You're right. God is loving, Trent. But he's also holy, righteous, and just. He looks at things a whole lot differently than we do. Since he's holy, he hates sin. That means every bad thing we do—no matter how big or small. And human beings are sinful creatures by nature. So we sin a *lot*."

Trent leaned back. "That's where I disagree. Christians' opinion of human nature is too pessimistic. We're not that bad. And I don't see how little white lies could ever compare with murder."

I sensed that his interest was fading, so I decided to finish up. "The Bible says two things. First, it says, '...all have sinned and fall short of the glory of God.' It also says, '...whoever keeps the whole law and yet stumbles at just one point is guilty of breaking all of it.' So, if we break just one law or commandment, we're guilty of breaking all of them, in God's eyes." (Romans 3:23 and James 2:10)

He did not like that. His aristocratic nose flared, and I felt him emotionally withdraw from me. But in the next instant, he surprised me.

His mouth curved up into a slow, devastating smile, and he leaned forward and captured one of my hands.

"You know," his rich tenor vibrated with intimate warmth, "this is what I admire about you. You stand up for what you believe in. Just like you stood up to Randy and Tim. It shows strength of character." His warm, tanned hands rubbed mine while his brilliant eyes held me mesmerized. "It's very attractive."

I felt like I was drowning. His potent, heady charm washed over me, making me feel giddy. I found myself smiling foolishly. From then on, we talked about other subjects; his family, extremely rich, and his plans for the future—to become a foreign news correspondent.

I hurried home after my coffee date with Trent. My mind felt drugged with infatuated excitement. I liked Trent. A lot. He was fascinating, and we had so much in common. Current affairs, journalism...

Mom stood alone in our spacious kitchen, which was decorated with Italian white Carrara marble floors, and pale blond wooden cabinets. The warm, herbed aroma of chicken and gravy permeated the room, and my mouth watered. Chicken pot pie. Dad's favorite. Mine, too.

Mom turned quickly, her silver-blond cap of hair whirling, at the sound of my footsteps. But the spark in her eyes died when she saw me. She looked suddenly sad and lonely.

I longed to rush over and give her a hug, like Theresa would. The emotion was so strong that I actually stepped forward and began to reach out to her. But before I'd gone a quarter of a step, she turned back to face the sink.

I stopped, feeling rejected. Of course, that was ridiculous. She hadn't known I'd wanted to give her a hug. I drew an unhappy breath. An inseparable gap was growing between me and my mother. It made me feel sick, but I didn't know how to fix it. I didn't even know what she felt about me these days. Worse, I felt like I couldn't measure up to Theresa, who was my mother's favorite.

"What's wrong, Mom?" I moved to stand beside her at the counter.

"Oh, nothing, honey." Her smile looked forced, and a visible, frosty shell slipped over her blue eyes. Vigorously, she scrubbed a chopping board. Her silver bracelets jiggled against the sleeves of her stylish denim dress. "It's just your father." Her voice cut, like the expensive knife lying in the sink. "He's usually home by now. I wish he'd call when he's going to be late. I just put supper in the oven!"

She slapped down the rag and squirted slimy yellow dish soap over the marbled board. Mouth pressed tight, she glanced at me. "You didn't happen to see him drive up, did you?"

I watched her vigorously scrub the board again. "No. But I'm sure he'll be home soon. It's only six."

"Yes, I know. But you know your father." Her voice rose a strident octave. "He always has to be home in time for his *walk*."

The front door slammed, and our heads swiveled.

"Anybody ho...ome?" Theresa yodeled. She burst into the kitchen, still dressed in her black and pink gym attire. Perspiration beaded on her brow. "It's *hot* outside!"

After plucking a water bottle from the refrigerator, she leaned against the counter near Mom and gulped noisily. "It feels hotter today than yesterday. Is it? What did the weatherman say, Mom?"

Our mother flicked water from her pearly fingertips and reached for the dish towel. She seemed distracted, as if lost in her own thoughts. "It reached a hundred and seven today. Sixth day in a row—apparently that's some kind of a record, since it's almost September."

"I know!" Theresa rubbed a wrist across her beaded forehead. "I wish it'd break. Thank goodness the gym is air conditioned. By the way, Joyce asked why you didn't work out yesterday, Mom."

"Oh. I was busy, honey. And it was so hot. How was your workout?"

"Great. Joyce lent me a new dance tape, and I love it. She's so together!" My sister's voice sounded admiring.

"She's a nice girl." Mom glanced at the silver watch on her wrist. Her tone sounded distracted again. "Do you have a date tonight, dear?"

"No." Theresa's haughty, disdainful gaze flicked to me. "Thought I'd take a break, since I had dates *all* weekend."

I ignored the slur, and adjusted the heavy weight of the backpack on my shoulder. "I'm going upstairs, Mom. Call if you need help setting the table."

She gave me a pleased, if somewhat surprised smile. "I will, honey, thank you."

Theresa's eyes narrowed, and I guessed she'd probably set the table herself.

I looked up from my English paper. The warmth of the setting sun blazed through my bedroom window. It was after seven. Mom's chicken pot pie must be burned by now. Why hadn't Dad come home yet?

The garage door opener whirred beneath my feet. There he was. My fingers curled tightly around the pen in my hand. I wouldn't go downstairs. Not yet.

My mother's strident, hurt voice echoed up the stairwell. "Why didn't you call, Winston? Thanks to you, dinner is ruined!"

"I was busy at work."

"So, the work I do isn't important?" Her voice rose. "You don't appreciate *anything* I do, Winston! I cook for you, clean for you, raise your children for you..."

"I'm always the ogre! Right, Helen?" Dad barked. "Maybe you should look in the mirror sometime. Really look, before you cake on all that makeup. You've turned into a shriveled up prune of a shrew, Helen. Take that and feed it to the kids!"

I gasped. Dad had stepped over the line. While Mom wasn't perfect, she did try to please him.

Understanding finally clicked. That's why she always dressed up in the evenings when he came home. That's why she always cooked his favorite meals. Dad just never noticed. Mom wanted his attention, but never received it. That's why she was so angry, and complained all the time. But her bitterness was driving Dad further away.

Didn't they love each other anymore? Would they get a divorce?

I pressed the heels of my hands against my suddenly hot eyes.

God, why is this happening? Please heal their relationship. Please.

Tears slid down my cheeks. I buried my head in my arms and poured out all my troubles to the Lord, my Father in heaven.

Warm sunshine touched my cheek, and I felt like God whispered to me to be quiet and still, and drink in his peace. Everything rested in his capable hands.

FUTURE

A LOUD, PIERCING blast made Isola jump, and Kay's notebook snapped shut on her finger. The noonday sun beat down on her dark head.

What in the world...?

Another piercing blast ripped the air, and she lurched to her feet, wide gaze fastened on the gray, ash filled sky.

Air raid! She glanced toward the street. With a gasp, she dropped down and crouched near the broken brick fireplace. Her heart hammered hard.

Soldiers! Six of them. They swept the streets now to make sure everyone was safely inside, and out of danger. But she wasn't. She was outside, and alone. Easy prey.

She had to get to an air raid shelter. Fast. But where was the closest one?

The soldiers were coming closer. Soon they'd see her.

She had to hide. She couldn't let them find her.

Chest tight with fear, Isola crawled behind the chimney. Jagged pieces of mortar and wood poked painfully into her kneecaps and palms as she peered around it. Had they seen her?

Two soldiers broke away from the central group. Dressed in olive green military fatigues, they cut across the street and headed directly toward her hiding place.

Week Two — Wars

*"Nation will rise against nation,
and kingdom against kingdom."*

MATTHEW 24:7A

FUTURE — CONTINUED

SHE HAD TO ESCAPE, NOW! Fear screamed at Isola, urging her to run like a scared rabbit. But that's what the soldiers expected her to do. She was smarter than that.

The air raid siren screamed again and again, like a cacophony from hell.

She glanced left and right, weighing her options. Fifteen seconds remained, tops, before they reached her. Already, their evil, self-indulgent laughter rang in her ears. The air raid wouldn't stop them from having their bit of fun. Their lives were empty and meaningless, too.

Isola twisted to look behind her. And then she saw it. Her route of escape. Broken pieces of wall, a tree, a bit of broken fence, and more jagged house remains cut in a diagonal line away from her. They led toward High Street, a block north.

Bent double, she darted for the next hideaway. The air raid signal blasted every few seconds now, drowning out any noise she made.

Ducking behind the piece of wall, she glanced back. The soldiers had almost reached the chimney. They hadn't seen her run.

No time to lose.

Bent double again, she sprinted for the tree, and then the bit of broken fence. There she paused, and glanced back again.

"Hey!" One of the crew cut heads stared at her. "Come back here!" Both soldiers broke into a run.

Isola bolted, her feet stumbling and twisting over broken plaster and timbers. Her heart pounded like thunder in her ears, drowning out the shriek of the air raid siren.

She sensed them drawing closer.

Reaching High Street, she glanced wildly right and left, and then suddenly, in a flash, remembered where the nearest air raid shelter was located.

She flew over the jagged, broken concrete. The foul air seared her lungs, and she gasped.

She heard them now. The heavy drum of boots followed her.

Hands shaking, she yanked the tiny gun from her jeans and flicked off the safety latch with her thumb. She'd kill them if they tried to harm her.

Although she'd never shot anyone before, this deadly resolve calmed her nerves.

Her straining eyes spotted the outline of the high school gym through the gray, dirty air. Three blocks to go. Hazy throngs of people flooded into the building.

Another block passed beneath her flying feet.

The air raid blasts were continuous now, and she couldn't hear her pursuers. One block remained. Panting, she whipped a glance over her shoulder.

The soldiers were three steps behind her, but the lead man's gaze was fixed on the gym. Isola read uncertainty in his eyes. Hope shot through her, and it added a spurt of energy to her pounding feet. Too many people were nearby. He was having second thoughts.

The soldier's split second hesitation was her salvation.

Moments later, she burst through the doors of the gym, choking and coughing on the awful, searing pain in her lungs.

She stumbled to a free foot of wall space and quickly shoved the gun deep into her waistband. Weapons were outlawed. She didn't want to give the soldiers an excuse to arrest her. Or worse, execute her.

Still gasping, and bent double to catch her breath, she watched the olive drab uniforms stride toward her. But she was safe now, and they all knew it. They elbowed by, their automatic guns snapping painfully against her shoulder. The lead, blond-haired man—a Captain, by the two bars on his uniform—

gave her a hard stare that seemed to say, *You may have won this battle, but we won't forget you.*

A fit of coughing prevented her from glaring back. Probably for the best.

Finally, as her gasps quieted to a gentle pant, Isola took note of her surroundings. The gym was hot and humid. And packed with people. Every person stared at the large television monitor suspended in the far left corner of the room. Fear rippled in tangible waves from those around her,

Images of war planes streaked across the television screen, but air sirens drowned out the sound. Isola hugged her arms across her chest, and tried to ignore her own surge of fear.

That's when she realized she still held Kay's notebook. How she had hung onto the diary while the soldiers chased her, she had no idea. She had no memory of carrying it.

Somehow, hugging that small plastic rectangle to her body gave her a feeling of comfort as she stared at the monitor's flickering screen. The cloying fear that permeated the room touched her, but did not penetrate her soul.

Had the United States been bombed? Was this the dreaded start of WWIII?

What if it was? Isola closed her eyes, as she realized the truth. Death by nuclear attack seemed antiseptic, compared to how she'd felt a few minutes ago, fleeing from her fellow human beings.

That was the true horror. Trusting no one. Fearing for her life every second of the day.

The bleat of the air raid siren faded from her mind. When had the world turned so terribly wrong?

Fewer than four years ago, talk of peace had circulated on the European continent, and throughout the world. At the time, the U.S. had been financially limited, and couldn't take care of every world problem. So world problems and responsibilities were parceled out and shared.

Then the Chairman—or "the Beast," as she liked to call him—came, promising lasting peace to troubled regions, and proving in miraculous ways that he could achieve and keep it. Treaties were signed, and peace did last for a while. But now huge wars waged, and more could come. Millions had already been killed.

A sudden silence made her look up. The siren had stopped, and the gymnasium, filled to overflowing with people, hushed. Everyone stared at the television monitor.

The newscaster's crisp voice said, "More bombs have fallen in the Middle East today. The United States is on red alert, and ready to protect herself, should that prove necessary. The Chairman held a news conference a few minutes ago..."

The image of soaring jets cut to a picture of the Chairman, who smiled grimly at the camera. He exuded a potent charm, but his eyes looked hard and empty, which was a direct contrast to the boastful words flowing from his mouth.

"...I have everything under complete control. Haven't I proven myself before? Hasn't my military proven itself? The countries threatening world peace will be brought to their knees. Every country of the world must agree together to be subject to me. Only then will true world peace prosper."

The picture cut away to show devastated swathes of land.

Beside her, an elderly man muttered, "I'd think that guy was crazy if I hadn't seen all the miracles he's done. Seen 'em with my own two eyes! Makes a person wonder if the Chairman really is God, like he claims."

"He does seem to have divine powers," whispered a woman with wide eyes and a sallow face.

Isola's attention returned to the newscaster.

"Rumors continue to circulate that the Chairman is having trouble keeping his coalition together. Insurrection continues to bubble up in a variety of trouble spots. This has been especially prevalent lately, ever since he set himself up in the Jewish temple in Jerusalem as God."

Another camera pan showed the Beast speaking at a news conference.

"The Chairman will hold another press conference this evening. Sources say he'll announce a change in his economic policy at that time."

Isola stared at a still picture of the Beast, and a crawling, repulsive feeling squeezed her gut. True, he had done some pretty miraculous things. But did that mean he was God?

No. There had to be another explanation. Was that why she'd felt compelled to go to Kay's house? Maybe Kay had known...

A shout drew her attention back to the television. Old news footage replayed the two Witnesses of God standing in front of the temple, crying out, "The Chairman is the abomination of desolation spoken of by Daniel the prophet!"

The Witnesses' deaths, over a week ago, had solidified the Beast's power. Afterward, the worldwide glee and gift giving over their killings had sickened Isola. And when the men had come back to life...the news channels were still replaying the Witnesses' ascent into heaven, and the tremendous earthquake which had followed. The news networks couldn't seem to satiate viewers' desire to relive it, over and over again.

Now, seeing it played out again on the television screen scared Isola. Something horrific was happening in this world. What would happen next? She had a feeling Kay would have known.

"Air raid's over!" The announcement trumpeted over the gymnasium's speaker system.

Isola blinked. It was over. The air raid was over. The United States was still safe. For now.

Turning as one, the crowd shoved for the doors. But Isola remained where she was, pressed up against the wall.

Someone watched her.

She twisted her head slightly left and glanced out the corner of her eye. It was the blond-haired Captain. He didn't move.

As casually as possible, Isola snaked her way through the crush of people. She headed for the far side of the gym, where a cluster of cots and elderly people congregated. She would be safe there.

After reaching the other side, she glanced back. The soldier still watched her.

With the cool wall against her back, she slid to the floor near a group of gossiping elderly people. She'd stay in the gym for a while. Sooner or later, the soldier's commanding officer would come looking for him. Then she would head home.

Kay's red diary lay in her lap. Its call was nearly irresistible. She would love to escape again.

Feeling less guilty than the first time, Isola began to read.

WEDNESDAY

WITH MY HAIR UP IN A PONY TAIL to try to combat the inhuman heat, I trudged up the sidewalk, bumping elbows with fellow students streaming into Wilson Hall. Perspiration dripped down my neck. It was only nine a.m., but was already hot and muggy. It was supposed to reach 108° today.

My white cotton top and khaki shorts clung to my skin, and I wiggled uncomfortably. When would the heat break? It was almost September.

Cold air embraced me when I stepped into Wilson Hall, and I relaxed. The hall reeked of pungent janitorial cleanser. Room 101 was empty.

I slipped into my seat and pulled out my freshly printed essay on Buddhism.

"Morning, Kay!" With a warm smile, Mary dropped her red book bag onto her chair. "Remember my ultrasound?"

"Yes! How did that go?"

"See for yourself." With a proud grin, she handed me a black and white photo. The print was mostly black, but a light-colored, pie slice shaped area filled the center. Curled inside this were a conglomeration of round knobs and swimming limbs. I refocused, and stared at the biggest bulge.

"Oh," I gasped. "There's the head."

Mary's eyes glowed. "Look. Those are his legs, and his arms."

"It's a boy?"

She smiled, clearly delighted. "Yes."

"Congratulations! Has Jack seen the picture?"

"Yes, but he couldn't tell what anything was. Men!" Still smiling, she tucked the photo into her bag.

I wondered what Jack thought about the baby, now that he'd seen it, but decided not to ask. Mary seemed so happy now. I didn't want to ruin that.

But I did want to learn more about Jack. I hoped my first impression was wrong.

"So, what's Jack really like, anyway? I didn't get a chance to talk to him much when we met. He's very handsome."

Mary flushed. "Yes. He is." She shrugged one thin, cotton clad shoulder. "He's really nice, once you get to know him. He might seem a little rough around the edges at first. But he means well."

"Oh." I smiled and hoped that was true.

"In fact, he bought me a new dress last night so we can go dancing this weekend." Her eyes seemed to shadow, however.

"Don't you want to go?"

"Well, I don't mind. I like to make him happy. And I don't want him to think I'm a fat, boring pregnant girl."

"You're not," I said indignantly. "You are very thin and graceful. And you have a definite glow about you. I hope I have that if I ever have a baby."

"Thank you. So, what are you doing tonight?"

"My church college group meets on Wednesday nights." An idea flashed. "Do you want to come? It's fun. We sing, learn about the Bible, and then talk and eat desserts afterwards. Sometimes we play games."

"I can't. Sorry." Mary looked apologetic. "I have to work tonight. One of the checkers is sick, and I have to cover for her."

"Maybe some other time, then."

She nodded, as if giving it serious thought.

Mr. Carlisle asked for our papers, and as I handed mine forward, I wondered which religion he'd make snide remarks about today.

My hands trembled, and I found myself glancing repeatedly at the door. When would he arrive?

And then Trent stepped into Dr. Williams classroom.

A thrill of excitement tingled. I hoped my small, casual smile masked the jumping butterflies in my stomach. Trent grinned, and made a beeline for me.

"Hey, Kay." He slipped into the seat beside me.

"Hi." We didn't have time for more than a few whispers, though, before our humorless professor cleared his throat. I glanced up, and for an unexpected second my gaze locked with Professor William's. His lips curled, as if in disgust. Taken aback, I blinked, but his face had already smoothed into an expressionless mask.

He turned to the board and wrote down today's topic. I felt disturbed. Surely he hadn't directed that look at me, personally.

Of course not. He'd probably had a rough morning.

At the end of class, Trent and I gathered up our books.

"May I walk you to your next class?" he said with a warm smile.

"Okay." My return smile was quick.

Sauna-like heat blasted us when we stepped outside. Not a breath of air stirred the limp leaves. Late blooming jasmine sprawled around the base of the journalism building, radiating up a heavy, sweet perfume.

We walked slowly. I savored my time with Trent, and hoped he felt the same way. Several moments passed before he spoke. "Uh, I was wondering, Kay."

"Yes?"

"I was wondering..." A dimple flashed in his tanned cheek. "Would you like to go out Friday night?"

"Oh!" Whatever I'd expected, it wasn't this. "Well. I..."

Why was I hesitating? He was handsome, charming, and we had tons in common.

But he wasn't a Christian. This fact surfaced for the first time. Jumbled emotions added to my confusion. What should I do?

As the seconds passed, a faint look of hurt crossed his features.

"Umm," I finally mumbled intelligently. "That sounds fun. But could I get back to you? Some friends of mine...I think might be..."

A relieved smile lit his face. "Sure. Let me know. Hey, I understand if you already have plans."

I smiled, but felt horribly confused inside. What was I going to do? Could I date a non-Christian? The Bible warned Christians not to be unequally yoked with unbelievers. Surely, there must be a good reason why.

But what did "yoke" mean? Did it mean date? Or did it only mean something serious, like marriage?

Still feeling conflicted about the subject of dating Trent, I immediately looked for Joyce when I arrived at church that evening. I needed to speak to her. She was practical and level-headed. She'd provide good advice. We hadn't had a good talk in weeks, anyway, thanks to summer jobs, and now because of school. It would be good to talk to her.

"Hey, Sunshine." David's lanky form appeared beside me. His guitar was slung across his chest. "We could use an extra singer. Sylvia's sick. Want to help out?"

As I gazed up at David, I couldn't help but compare him to Trent. Trent was shorter than David, and just as lean, but he wore crisp, fashionable clothes. Tonight David wore a neat black T-shirt and jeans, but there was something intrinsically rumpled about him. Especially right now, when he was worried about getting an extra singer. He was goofy, casual, and easy to be with. But not sophisticated. Not polished. Not vibrantly, breathtakingly attractive.

"Do I have a bug in my teeth?" His left brow winged toward the rafters. "And are you going to help out, or not?"

"Yes, I'll help." Exasperated, I crashed back to planet Earth. I still wanted to go out with Trent. Definitely. But was it okay with God?

On stage, I stood beside Laura, Bobby's wife. She touched my arm, her eyes radiant—she always looked joyful, and it was genuine, too. How did she do it? "How are you, Kay? I haven't had a chance to talk to you in ages."

David slashed his pick over the guitar strings, which cut my reply short.

"First song we'll sing is an old one, but a good one," he declared. "'Shine, Jesus, Shine.'"

Clapping and singing, I felt my worries melt away. Finally, I could focus on Jesus. And praise him. It felt good, to the depths of my soul. I suspected my eyes were shining, much like Laura's, when we finished.

As we slipped toward the front pew, Bobby, our stocky, curly-headed youth pastor, brushed by us. A faint frown puckered between his black eyebrows. His feet thunked up the stage steps, and he gripped a small duffel bag in his hand.

"Great to see you tonight." His voice echoed in the sanctuary, and his brow smoothed out. "We have a great evening planned. We'll break into teams and look at James chapter four. Afterward, we'll have a question and answer session. I know you guys are chomping at the bit to get started, but before we do..."

He unzipped the duffle and pulled out a bunch of giant, swirled lollipops. He twirled them enticingly. The glossy candy glittered, in all the colors of a rainbow. "Prizes! For the team who answers the most questions right. Okay?" His white teeth flashed in his dark face. "Only one problem. No study guides. No one knows my questions except for me."

"And Laura," David muttered, with a speculative glance at Bobby Page's blond wife.

Another team snatched up Laura.

We didn't win, although every time Bobby asked a question I thought I knew, I leaped up and waved my hand. Other people were quicker. Our team came in second. No lollipops.

That was okay with me, because I wasn't a big sugar fan. But David was. With a mournful droop to his mouth, he watched Laura's team trickle outside, licking their huge, yellow, green, blue and red swirled wheels.

"Guys!" Joyce motioned us away from the chattering college students. "I have something to tell you." She glanced at Bobby as he hurried by. A frown worried his brow again.

I remembered the rumor that his job might be cut from the church, and wondered if it might be true. Poor Bobby. He'd moved all the way from Hawaii four years ago, just to take the Youth Pastor position at Truesdale First Gospel. He couldn't lose his job now.

"Remember that Crawford man who came to church on Sunday?"

The dark-suited, spectacled guy who'd cornered Pastor Warner. "Yes."

"Well, Dad just told me the FGA didn't like the service." She paused for effect. "They've put our church on probation."

"*What?*"

"How can they do that?"

"They're in charge of our church. Just like they're in charge of *all* the First Gospels in the United States. The FGA is a huge organization, in case you didn't know. If we don't run our church exactly like they say, they can boot us out. Literally. Stop all funds. And kick us out of this building."

"Wow." David's voice deepened. "What do they want us to do?"

"They want Dad to go to a vision meeting next month. It's supposed to teach him FGA's vision for the future. Mr. Crawford says our church is unpopular because we're stuck in the past."

"What is *that* supposed to mean?"

David's black brows drew together. "It means they don't like how we run our church."

"Because we have low revenues? Because we're getting hate mail?" I said incredulously.

"Maybe. But it must be more than that." David snapped his fingers. "You know what this sounds like? A public relations ploy."

Joyce frowned. "What do you mean?"

"The elections are coming up. And one of the FGA's board members is running for the U.S. Senate. Oak Woodward."

The name sounded familiar. I'd heard scores of political commercials on T.V. lately.

David's voice turned thoughtful. "Maybe they're trying to sanitize First Gospel's image, so the public can't find fault with it. So they can't find fault with Oak Woodward."

"That's scary," I said. "How can they convince people to like our church? I mean, Christians are pretty unpopular right now. In fact, some people hate us. They'd only like our church if we taught whitewashed, publicly agreed upon values. And ignored God!"

"Anyway." Joyce looked disturbed. "From now on, Daddy has to clear all of our activities through the FGA first. At least, we do until Dad goes to their vision meeting."

"*Every* church activity?"

"Everything. But especially community events."

David raised a brow. "Sounds like that fact proves my hypothesis."

"We don't know that." Joyce frowned.

David departed to help break down the sound equipment. I turned to Joyce, who sat uncharacteristically silent. A frown knit her brows together.

"Are you all right?"

"Yes," she said curtly. But her gaze softened a bit when she saw that I was bursting to tell her something. "What?" she smiled. "What's going on?"

I grinned foolishly. "I've been dying to talk to you all night. I've met a *great* guy at school."

"You have?" Her eyes snapped with instant interest. "That's terrific!"

"The only problem is, Trent's not a Christian." It hurt to say that.

"Oh." Her smile faded, and she eyed me with concern, but before she could speak, David returned. Evidently, his help wasn't needed on stage.

"What's up?" He grinned. "Or am I interrupting a female pow wow?"

"It's nothing." I glanced at Joyce anxiously. I didn't want David to know about my love problems.

"What do you want?" Joyce tilted her chin to him.

"Sorrr...ee!" David looked hurt. "Guess I can tell when I'm not wanted. I came to ask if you want to get together Friday night. Movies, at my house. I'm inviting the whole college group."

"Sounds fun," Joyce agreed. "What time?"

"Eight." He looked at me. "What about you, Kay? Are you in?"

Staring up into his warm, expectant brown gaze, I remembered Trent. David's gaze sharpened over my brief hesitation.

"Sure. Sounds great."

He let the incident pass. "Well, I'll let you girls finish talking. I've got to go. Got a bunch of homework to do tonight."

After goodbyes, I turned back to Joyce. "Well?" Apprehension tinged my tone.

Joyce's advice, as usual, was pithy and to the point. "I don't think you should get romantically involved with him, Kay. I'm sure he's a nice guy. And of course it's great that you're friends with him. But that's not the issue, is it? The Bible tells us not to be unequally yoked with unbelievers."

"But he's only asked me out on a date. Is that yoking? I mean, to me it's like going out with a friend."

"With one big difference. What's the purpose of dating?" She answered her own question. "To find a husband."

"No. I just want to get to know him better, that's all."

"And that's why your whole face lit up a second ago." Her expression softened. "Look, Kay. I know you like him, but in the long run, you'll be happiest if you obey God. First Corinthians seven, thirty-nine puts it pretty plainly. '...she is free to marry anyone she wishes, but he must belong to the Lord.'"

"I'm not going to marry him, Joyce! And how can getting to know someone be wrong?"

She shook her head. "You want to be more than friends. That's obvious. Just remember, Trent doesn't share a huge dimension of your life. If you get seriously involved, it's eventually going to cause problems. Look at what happened to Sylvia and Jeremy..."

"I know." I didn't want to hear anymore.

"Just think about it. I don't want you to get hurt." But Joyce knew me well enough to know I'd do exactly what I wanted to do. She sighed. "You know I'll be here if you need to talk."

"Thank you." She was a good friend. I could always count on her to be there for me, no matter what I decided about Trent.

When I lay in bed that night, I reluctantly remembered Sylvia and Jeremy's stormy relationship. Sylvia had belonged to our college group, and was a Christian. Jeremy was not. They'd met, dated, fallen in love, and married two years ago. And divorced a year later.

While they dated, Sylvia had stopped going to church. I saw her four months after the wedding. She'd said she felt spiritually dry, and wanted God in her life again. So she returned to church.

But Jeremy didn't understand Sylvia's renewed interest in God, or why she'd returned to church. He became increasingly angry and jealous of the time she spent reading the Bible and going to services. He attacked her faith constantly.

Sylvia later said she'd felt suffocated from the inside out. Jeremy could not—and did not want to—understand the most important area of her life. And she'd finally realized a truth she never had before. Faith encompassed all aspects of her life. And in many areas of her life, her beliefs and Jeremy's values clashed. Horribly.

Eventually, he'd forbidden her to go to church. She stopped going to church, but she'd never stopped reading her Bible. God was all she had to cling to anymore. Her marriage disintegrated right before her eyes. Finally, Jeremy divorced her.

Sylvia was devastated.

Last year, she'd begun to pick up the pieces of her life again. But she still looked terribly unhappy.

I lay in bed, thinking about all of this. Logically, I understood what I should do. But emotionally, I did not. I liked Trent. A lot. And I had no intention of marrying him, or turning away from God, like Sylvia had done. I just wanted to be Trent's friend. Certainly, nothing was wrong with that.

As long as that was all I really wanted.

Was it?

I could not ignore Trent's charm and attractiveness. *And* he was interested in spiritual things. He wasn't closed-minded, like Jeremy. At least, Trent seemed to be open-minded. We'd had a good discussion about God on Monday. Maybe God was calling his heart. Maybe I should spend more time with him, and tell him about Jesus.

And Trent liked me. That was still a wonder to me. Here was a guy who could have any woman in the world, and he'd chosen to spend time with me. I still didn't fully understand it, but didn't plan to question it any longer, either.

Was it wrong to enjoy his company? To get to know him better?

Half-heartedly, I prayed. *Lord, please tell me what to do.*

THURSDAY

I'M NOT SURE WHEN I MADE THE DECISION, but when I saw Trent on campus at noon today, I made a beeline for him. The hot air whipped my hair as I jogged for him, and it cooled the perspiration dripping down my neck. The sky was a deep, brilliant blue, and sunshine reflected off of the empty, white concrete sidewalks, blinding my eyes. Most people were in class. I should be, too.

"Trent!" Steps behind him, I slowed to a ladylike walk.

He turned with a grin. "Kay. What are you doing here?"

I glanced guiltily over my shoulder. "I have a class. But I saw you and wanted to...to ask you something." Suddenly, I felt incredibly shy. A foreign emotion to me.

His eyes sparkled with invitation.

Nervously, I licked my lips. "A group of my friends plan to watch movies tomorrow night. Would you like to come? With me?"

"I'd love to." His grin widened with clear pleasure, and the nervous knot in my stomach dissolved. He did like me. He did want to spend time with me. Warm happiness bubbled up, until I felt like I was beaming from the inside out.

He pulled out his cell phone. When he glanced up, a funny smile quirked his mouth. "You know, Kay, when you smile like that, your eyes turn an incredible green. Like the color of a clear emerald sea."

"Thank you," I murmured. Joy radiated to my toes. It was a far cry from David's declaration that my eyes looked like green marbles!

"What's your address?"

I told him, and we parted ways after he said he'd pick me up at 7:45. Then we both laughed with embarrassment. We'd see each other in class tomorrow.

When I arrived home, I smelled stew bubbling on the stove. Both of my parents sat in the den, watching the news.

"Hi, dear." Mom patted the couch beside her. She carefully avoided eye contact with Dad, whose arm chair was at my elbow.

"Hi." Moving to the couch, I gave them both a smile. Dad only nodded, his eyes glued to the news announcer. Mick Murray reported current world events.

Pulling the heavy backpack between my feet, I listened, too.

"While the U.S. struggles to bring internal problems like crime, poverty, and the aftermath of natural disasters under control, world conflicts continue to escalate in the Middle East, Europe, and all over. In the midst of these crises, the financially limited U.S. is forced to choose its conflict involvements carefully. We're sharing more and more of the world's burden with the European Union and other alliances.

"Turmoil is wracking our planet. Is there hope for the future?" Pictures of war torn countries, body bags and flying planes marched across the screen.

Cut to a political commercial.

"Crime's worse, the economy's worse; everything's worse since Senator Gilroy took office. Maybe that's because he spends most of his time playing golf." A shot of a heavyset man swinging a golf club on a fairway flashed on the screen.

"Oak Woodward is for people. Neighbor helping neighbor. Working hard." The commercial transitioned to reveal to a tall, toothy man with an arm wrapped around a bristle-faced, grinning vagrant. "Vote for Oak Woodward. He's for you."

"Oak Woodward! Is that his real name?" Theresa snorted. She stood behind Dad's chair.

The newsman cut in again. "Senator Gilroy will speak at Truesdale State University tomorrow. Challenger Oak Woodward says he'll address the university in a few weeks.

"A final, interesting note. Although he's the head of the nationally recognized church organization, First Gospel of America, Oak Woodward is receiving endorsement from liberals, as well as moderates. Perhaps that's because he's vowed to keep religion off the table if he becomes elected. Instead, he's running on mainline people issues, such as improving the lot of the average citizen in the United States. And who can disagree with that?"

The credits rolled.

"First Gospel of America." Dad glanced at me. "Isn't that the head organization of your church?"

I nodded.

He snapped open his newspaper. "I like Woodward's philosophy. Religion has no place in politics. I believe in God, but it's not right for people to push their faith off on others."

"Why do you say that, Dad?"

His newspaper lowered. "Faith is personal. People can come to God in a multitude of ways, Kay. Who's to say one way is more right than another?"

"I agree." Mom spoke up. Then she looked quickly at Dad.

A verse I'd memorized for college group came to mind. John 14:6. "Jesus said, 'I am the way, and the truth, and the life. No one comes to the Father except through me.' Jesus said he's the only way to be reconciled back to God."

Dad shook his head. "That's too harsh. Why can't God just forgive us? He knows we're not perfect."

"That's true," I agreed. "But God is holy, too. He can't just ignore sin. Romans six, verse twenty-three says, 'For the wages of sin is death, but the gift of God is eternal life in Christ Jesus our Lord.'"

"What the heck does *that* mean?" Theresa gave a sneering, contemptuous little laugh.

"It means," I frowned, "that forgiveness costs something. For example, say I crash Dad's new car. I'd know I did something wrong. So I'd ask for his forgiveness. Let's say he completely forgives me, because he loves me."

Dad raised an eyebrow, but his mouth twitched. I grinned, and went on. "The car is still wrecked, though. Who pays the price to fix it? Dad does, because he knows I can't. That is true forgiveness.

"That's how God loves us. We sin, and God hates sin, so our relationship with God is broken. But God loves us, and wants to forgive us and restore that broken relationship. But for healing to take place, a price has to be paid for the sin. Jesus paid the price for the consequences of our sin. He did that for us when he died on the cross in our place. He's paid the price so our broken relationship can be repaired with God. He's the *only* way to God."

Dad shook his head. "That's too narrow-minded for me to believe." The newspaper snapped up again around his face.

Frustrated, I blurted, "It's a tremendous gift. And we're the ones who are too small-minded to realize it."

"Mom." Theresa cast me a disparaging look. "How do I look? Thad is picking me up in ten minutes. Should I change?"

Mom sprang to her feet to fuss over Theresa.

I said nothing more, but I have to admit I felt rejected and ridiculed right then. My family just didn't understand how much God loved them. And none of them seemed to care, either.

"Okay, I'll change my blouse," Theresa's flouncing exit drew my attention back to the present. Theresa would party another night away.

What about homework? I hadn't seen her study yet.

That night I felt the urgent need to pray for my family. For their eyes to be opened, for them to hunger for God, and to give their lives to him.

The Lord loves us so much. If only my family *knew* that. If only they *knew* he exists. If only they understood that he wants to have a living, vibrant relationship with them. That he wants to give them *life*!

My soul wept, for I could not make them see. Only God could. So I prayed for them, and for Trent, too.

I read another chapter in Revelation, and a chapter in one of the books I'd bought today at a Christian bookstore. Both books were about the end time prophecies, and one was just about Revelation. I hoped they would help me understand Revelation better. So far, I found it pretty confusing.

FRIDAY

"*JACK AND I ARE GOING DANCING* tonight." The dark circles under Mary's eyes almost disappeared when she smiled. "I'm glad my boss gave me tonight off." Mary had worked the graveyard shift at the supermarket four nights this past week, filling in for a sick co-worker.

"That sounds like fun." I eyed her. "Do you want to go? You didn't sound too sure about it on Wednesday."

"Oh," her brown eyes sparkled, "I think it'll be fun, after all. It'll be like a real date. Jack and I haven't been out—alone—in a long time."

"That should be great. Looks like we'll both have dates tonight, then."

"Really? Who are you going out with?"

"A guy named Trent Johns. He's in one of my journalism classes."

"Oh, I know him. He's in my poly sci class. He's nice. But he seems pretty fanatical about journalism."

What an odd remark. I explained, "That's normal. You have to be intense if you want to make the cut in today's news markets. That means living and breathing journalism, starting now."

I didn't have a chance to talk to Trent in class. But he flashed me a white smile, which said he looked forward to this evening.

At noon, I flowed outdoors into the heat, pushed by the throng of people exiting from trigonometry class. My stomach growled noisily, and a few people sent me amused glances. How embarrassing. With my thumb hooked through my backpack's green shoulder strap, I took the short cut to the student union, which was located across a football length stretch of lawn. My feet sank deep into the grass.

The campus was crowded today. In fact, a huge knot of people roiled around the open air stage in front of the student union.

Were those television cameras? Curious, I headed closer.

"College is for the rich!" The chant reached my ears. Placards sliced the air.

Discrimination!
Poor and rich get college. What do we get?
The middle class counts, too!

"We want *our* tuition subsidized!" a girl screamed.

The portly, silver-suited man on stage mopped his perspiring brow. He grabbed the microphone.

"Robert Gilroy is for you! I understand what you want. Everyone should be able to afford college. Not just the poor and the rich."

"Then do something about it," yelled a blond man with dreadlocks. "We don't need promises! We need an education!"

"Yeah!" Dozens of fists pummeled the air.

"Wewantcollege! Wewantcollege!" The hoarse chant swiftly escalated into a hysterical frenzy. A line of campus police marched toward the unruly crowd.

I stopped a safe distance away. So that was Senator Robert Gilroy. The evening news had said he'd be stumping on campus today.

"Bet he didn't expect this." David's voice startled me. He stood beside me, his blue backpack casually slung over his shoulder. His dark eyes scanned the scene before us.

"Probably not." My gaze returned to the milling crowd. "They seem mad. Like they're out for blood."

"Maybe they are."

"What?" I glanced back at him.

He shrugged, still not looking at me. "I understand why they're upset. I couldn't get financial aid, either. My dad makes too much money. But not enough to put me through college. So I had to work, since I didn't want loans."

"Oh." I felt ashamed, and suddenly ignorant.

David had never mentioned before how hard it was for him to get through college. Neither had Joyce—although she did receive financial aid. I'd never suffered like that.

"Hey." David's smile washed away my guilt. "Don't feel bad about being rich. You're lucky." His gaze returned to the angry crowd. "Something needs to be done, for sure. But starting a riot isn't the right way to do it."

I wondered what was the right way. Anymore, it seemed like something terrible had to happen; some sort of violence, or tragedy or accident before the media would focus on a problem. It was awful. They wanted sensationalism to sell the most basic stories. Real needs were ignored until something awful happened.

I wanted to make a difference in the world when I became a reporter.

"Have Randy or Tim bothered you again?" His dark eyes looked serious.

"No." Nothing except for a few sneers, and an elbow in the side from Randy the other day. But that could have been an accident. Maybe. We'd all been jostling for the door. I chose to believe it meant nothing.

"Good. Gotta go. See you tonight?" He suddenly grinned.

"Yes." I watched him leave, his long strides loose and relaxed. And wondered why I hadn't told him that Trent was coming.

The crowd boiled now. I skirted the far edges, and headed for the student union. I didn't want to get caught in a riot.

"Kay!" A deep voice caught my attention, and I glanced toward a trio of shady trees.

"Mitch!" Beaming, I hurried over. I hadn't seen him since the night he'd rescued me from Randy and Tim. "It's great to see you. How have you been?"

"Good, thanks." He grinned. Again I noticed how arresting his oddly put together face was, with his left brow tilted higher than the right, and his asymmetrical nose. His muscled shoulders hunched slightly over his sketch pad.

My eyes riveted upon the charcoal sketch resting in his lap. I'd never quite been able to shake his old drawing from my mind. God's eyes. Watching the earth.

"Are you an art major?"

His smile faded. "Not quite. My dad wouldn't go for that."

"Why not? Is he against art?"

"No. But he thinks business is the only way to go. He owns a string of grocery stores." His lips twisted. "He wants me to follow in his footsteps. A good Jewish boy, following in the family business, and going to synagogue every Saturday."

"Do you? Go to synagogue?" The impetuous question flipped off my lips.

"Yes." His black eyes turned serious again, and he rolled the charcoal between his fingertips. "I am pretty serious about that. Just like Dad."

"So that's why you know the Bible so well." He'd quoted Jeremiah and Isaiah to me in the parking lot.

His face darkened—perhaps a mixture of embarrassment and firm pride. "Guess so." His added a few more strokes on the sketch.

I leaned closer. "What are you drawing?"

The grin flashed back. "See for yourself." He turned the sketch toward me. "I don't have a clue what this one means. What do you think?"

It was a picture of the campus. And slicing through the center was a gigantic sword.

"Wow." I didn't know what to say for a second. "It looks like war. You know, I read something last night that reminds me of this." I whipped out the pocket Bible I kept in my backpack, and flipped through it. "Here it is. Revelation six, verse four."

I glanced at him, suddenly feeling doubtful. Here I was, bulldozing ahead, not even considering how Mitch felt. "Do you mind if I read it?"

Looking intrigued, he sketched a short wave. "By all means, go ahead."

"First, a little background," I felt excited to share my new interest with someone. "This is about the Great Tribulation. Chapter six is about a scroll with seven seals that's being opened. Verse two is about the first seal. It says, 'I looked, and there before me was a white horse! Its rider held a bow, and he was given a crown, and he rode out as a conqueror bent on conquest.'

"But verse four is the one your picture reminds me of. The second seal has been opened. It says, 'Then another horse came out, a fiery red one. Its rider was given power to take peace from the earth and to make men slay each other. To him was given a large sword.'

Mitch looked thoroughly confused now. "What's the Great Tribulation? And why is there a scroll with seals?"

Alarmed, I realized I'd dug myself a deep hole, and wasn't sure I could climb back out. My prophecy knowledge was slim. But I did understand a few things, thanks to the first chapters of my new prophecy books.

"The Tribulation is a seven year time period when God pours out his judgment on the world. All kinds of terrible things will happen then. The Old Testament talks about it in the book of Daniel, chapter nine, verses twenty-five through twenty-seven. Daniel's seventieth week is the Great Tribulation."

Mitch stared at me for a moment, his eyes piercing. Maybe he didn't believe what I said, but it fascinated him, all the same. His next question sounded like a test. "And when does the Messiah come?"

He understood more than I'd imagined. "Jesus will return at the end of the Great Tribulation. He'll be the conquering Messiah. He will rule the nations with an iron scepter."

His expression remained impassive as he picked up the piece of charcoal again. His next comment seemed unrelated. "I plan to move to Israel soon."

"Really? Why? Because it's the Jewish homeland?"

"Yes. Partly." He flipped the page and began to sketch. Beneath his flying, bold strokes a portrait of a person emerged. Me. He glanced up, and let the bit of charcoal rest on my collar. "I'm not sure why I want to go, to tell you the truth. It's like these pictures." He motioned to the one he'd flipped over. "I feel like I need to go. That that's where all the action's going to be."

"Israel is central in God's plan during the Tribulation."

Mitch seemed to think about this while he put the finishing touches on my portrait. Then he ripped it off and handed it to me with a faint smile.

The drawing was more complimentary than I'd expected. The main features were my eyes—which looked somewhat mysterious—and my wide smile. My first, instant impression was of someone who would be fun to know.

"You're an interesting person to talk to, Kay."

"Thank you for the picture." I awkwardly shifted the pack on my shoulder. The conversation was over. Mitch seemed withdrawn, even pensive now. "I guess I'll see you around."

He sketched a wave, and I trotted off, skirting the flying placards. Had I said too much? It was odd how the conversation had swung around to focus on God again. Just like in the parking lot. Only this time, we'd talked about the end times. Why? Was he really interested? Or was I just pressing my new interest off on anyone who cared to listen?

Then I remembered his pictures. They were unusual, and so was Mitch. He did seem interested in what I had to say.

What's the purpose in this, Lord?

For I felt sure there must be a purpose in it. I just could not see what it was.

Dinner was silent, except for Theresa's monologue about Adam, her unbelievably cute date. Tonight he was taking her to *the* party of the semester.

Theresa lifted a haughty brow at me. "And what are you doing tonight, Kay? More homework?"

"I have a date." I smiled sweetly.

She blinked.

Mom's strained voice said, "That's wonderful, dear!" Her blue eyes softened. "What's his name? Is he someone we know?"

"No. His name is Trent Johns the Third. He's in one of my journalism classes."

I watched Mom and Theresa both do a double take when I said "the Third." I'm not sure why I did. Maybe because at heart, I craved their approval. I glanced at my watch. "He should be here any minute."

"I'm so happy for you, dear!" Mom looked inordinately pleased. As if her wayward daughter had finally stepped into the normal order of living. Dates. Boys. Clothes. Those were things Mom approved of and understood. Not my preoccupation with God.

There I went, being judgmental again. I had no idea what Mom thought these days. But I did wonder if she understood that my deep, satisfying relationships with my friends meant everything to me—certainly more than dates with casual acquaintances. Trent being the exception, of course.

"That's great, Kay." Shoving away his plate, Dad gave me a gruff smile. "I'd like to meet him when he gets here." He rose to his feet.

"Promise you'll be nice." I didn't go on many dates, but Dad always gave them the evil eye.

His hazel eyes twinkled. "We'll see."

A frown flashed across my sister's face, and she stared down at her plate and poked her food with a fork. I guessed it hurt that Dad didn't greet her dates anymore. But there were so many. They were like ships in the night, passing one by one. It was exhausting. She never dated the same guy twice. If she did, Dad would probably show more interest.

Mom intercepted Dad in the hall. "What are you going to do now, Winston?" Her tone sounded accusing. "Watch T.V. all night?"

"Yes," Dad snapped. "What else can I do around here?"

"It'd be nice if we went out once in a while."

"Make the arrangements, then, if you want to go."

"You could show a little enthusiasm!" Mom's rising, brittle voice sounded hurt.

"Really? *Why?*" Dad snarled. "Why should I want to go out with you?"

Mom gasped. "Are you ashamed of me? Do you really think I look like an old prune?"

My shoulders scrunched as their voices rose. I stopped chewing, and pressed the rolling balls of peas against the roof of my mouth. I couldn't stand it.

"I hate it when they fight." Theresa stared at her plate.

"Me, too."

It was the first honest, heart-to-heart communication we'd shared in months.

The doorbell pealed, ending my parents' bitter quarrel.

Mom's heels snapped down the hall, and the front door swished open. Voices. Was Trent here? My stomach gave a funny, skipping lurch, and I slipped into the hall.

I'd forgotten how handsome he was. My heart somersaulted when I saw him. Trent wore casual khaki slacks, and a gray polo shirt. His deep blue eyes smiled at me over my mother's head, and I gulped, almost choking on the forgotten peas in my mouth.

"Hi, Trent." My voice came out a garbled, high squeak. I swallowed and stepped forward. "I'd like you to meet my parents." My hand flew toward Mom, whose stiff mask had relaxed into an approving smile. "This is my mom, Mrs. Jameson. And my dad, Mr. Jameson. Mom, Dad, this is Trent Johns."

Dad shook Trent's hand. His sharp eyes assessed Trent in an instant. I couldn't tell what he thought.

Trent's aristocratic mouth curved into a blazing white grin, and he vigorously returned Dad's handshake. "Good to meet you, sir. Ma'am." His gaze flickered by me.

Theresa brushed up. "I'm Theresa," she breathed throatily. "Kay's sister."

"Nice to meet you." Trent's smile seemed warm, but a bit amused.

Dimpling, Theresa floated to Mom's side, and then she glanced at me, both perfectly plucked brows raised in astonishment. And approval.

"Let me grab my purse, and I'll be ready to go."

My heart sang when Trent gave me a special smile and nod.

Aware his eyes were upon me, I smoothly traversed the length of the hall. But upstairs I burst into high speed. I had to brush my teeth, brush my hair. Put on lipstick!

Skidding, I barely remembered to snatch the small purse from my desk. Normally, I didn't carry a purse, for it was difficult to manage with my backpack at school. But the leather scrap matched my silk blouse, accented in cream and canyon colors. And white jeans went with anything.

Flushed, I jogged downstairs.

After a chorus of goodbyes, Trent ushered me into the hot, muggy twilight. I spotted a low slung, vintage silver Porsche parked behind my Mustang.

"Nice car!" I slid onto the smooth, cream leather seat, and Trent closed the door after me. Fastening my seat belt, I inhaled deeply. The car smelled new. Of warm leather and Trent's cologne.

"Like it?" Trent slipped in across from me, and a waft of his spicy, citrus cologne tantalized my nostrils. Light, and yet heady, just like Trent himself. He was easy to be with, and yet potently attractive, all at the same time.

"I love it. Are the seats new?" I was happy my voice sounded smooth, and maybe even sophisticated.

"No." Trent's arm cupped the back of my seat, and he glanced back, easing the car into reverse. The hairs stood up on my neck. "They're two years old. A high school graduation present from my dad." His arm returned to his side. A smooth change of gears, and we slid onto State.

"Where do we need to go?"

Mesmerized by Trent's presence and the purring car, it took a second for my mind to resume normal function. "David's house is south about five blocks, and a mile or two east."

Obligingly, Trent eased left at the next light.

"We can turn left again on Market. That next light," I directed, relaxing still more. The seat was so comfortable! It enveloped me in a hug.

As we purred closer to the light, a feeling of discomfort slid through my spirit.

I straightened up as the yellow light approached. The turn lane was only yards away.

"Don't turn!"

Trent shot me a strange look, but continued straight and pressed on the brake as the light turned red.

"We can take the next street," I said weakly. "It'll take us right to David's house." Why had I done that? I felt foolish.

When the car stopped, I glanced out Trent's side window, and gasped.

A gang, armed with blazing torches, advanced down the middle of the street. Black figures broke off and darted up residential lawns. Metal glinted, and a window shattered. One porch light winked out. Then another. The closest figures were only yards away.

"What the..." Trent stared, too. He jammed his foot on the gas, and the Porsche leaped forward like a nervous stallion. Gun shots barked, and I ducked, covering my head with my arms.

Trent drove like a race car driver. Engine roaring, we skidded onto David's street. Then he grabbed his cell phone. "Thugs are getting braver and braver!" he choked out. "It's barely dark."

He called the police. My heart hammered with fear as I stared out the window. A quiet residential neighborhood slid by.

It could have been this street. It could have been my street. I realized I was shaking.

He hung up. "Wow!" His rich tenor sounded unsteady. "Didn't expect our date to be so exciting."

We chattered nervously for the remaining mile. The block around David's house was parked up, so Trent settled for a space across the street.

I was still trembling when I climbed out. My cream colored sandals crushed the dried grass beneath my feet. That was how I felt, too. Dry, brittle. On edge. I'd experienced too much violence lately, and too much fear. First it was Tim and Randy's attack in the lab. Then the knife fight at the bowling alley. Now gangs torching Market Street. What was happening to this city?

But the violence wasn't really new, I realized. It had been there for years—growing worse all the time. Only I'd never experienced it for myself.

"You okay?" Trent solicitously cupped my elbow.

I managed a small smile. "I'm fine, thank you."

Joyce opened the door on the first chime. "There you are! We've been waiting for you." Her interested gaze rested upon Trent. She extended her hand. "Hi. I'm Joyce, a friend of Kay's."

"Trent." Trent's royal blue eyes smiled, unleashing his potent brand of charm. "Good to meet you."

Joyce blinked a little, and glanced at me. "What took you guys so long?"

Following her inside, I told her about our harrowing experience. We each grabbed a cup of punch and hovered near the cookie table. Cinnamon oatmeal raisin. *Mmm.* They smelled heavenly. Mrs. Matthews was a wonderful cook. In fact, David's mother had become famous for these cookies at the Sisters of Mercy charity, where she volunteered part-time.

"How awful!" Joyce said when I finished the tale. "What is this world coming to, anyway? Did I tell you, Kay? Last Monday my grandmother went grocery shopping, and when she got home her apartment had been vandalized! Right in the middle of day. Bold as brass. Can you believe it? Luckily she wasn't home at the time."

"We need more police," Trent commented.

"We need fewer criminals!" Joyce retorted.

An idea flashed. Crime. It might be a good topic for my article in Current Affairs class.

"Hey." David ambled up beside Joyce, his curious gaze fixed on Trent. He smiled and stuck out his hand. "Hi. I'm David."

"Trent." Trent returned the vigorous shake, and smiled.

"Kay's date," Joyce threw in. This made Trent's smile widen, but I frowned at her. Why had she said that? Trent and I were just friends. I still clung to this illusion.

"Oh," David's grin faded, and he glanced at me, slightly puzzled, suddenly withdrawn. "Well, I just wanted to say the movie's about to start." His opaque brown eyes glanced at Trent. "Hope you like old movies."

"Sure do," Trent's smile was relaxed. But when he watched David walk away, his gaze narrowed slightly.

Did Trent see David as a threat? A small smile tugged at my lips. Of course that was ridiculous. But Trent didn't know that.

"Come on," I touched his arm. "Let's find somewhere to sit."

I noticed that David and Joyce sat on the far side of the room, a good distance from me. They didn't want to intrude on my time with Trent.

I'd seen the first movie, but it was a great classic. *Forrest Gump*. At the end I felt sad, but inspired at the same time.

David leaped up and gestured grandly toward the refreshments. "We'll take a short intermission, and then watch the last movie."

"What is it?" a girl called.

"Uhh," David glanced at the case. "*Sleeping Beauty*."

Beside me, Trent groaned, along with a few others in the room. I knew Joyce had picked out that movie.

David only shrugged and grinned. "Classic Walt Disney, folks. Stick around." Stepping carefully over the people sitting on the floor, he made his way to the back, to the refreshment table.

"You don't want to watch it?" Standing to stretch my legs, I glanced at Trent.

He made a slight face. "Not really. Maybe we could do something else." One brow arched. "I know. We could get frozen yogurt. I know a great place."

I remembered the gang marching down Market Street, and apprehension gripped me.

"It's in a good neighborhood." Trent seemed to read my mind. "And the owner has a shotgun. The gangs don't give him any trouble."

I wasn't sure if that made me feel better, but decided to go anyway. "Okay."

"Great." Trent wound his way over to David and stuck out his hand. "Thanks for the hospitality, and for the movie. I really enjoyed it."

"Sure." David firmly returned the shake. "Where are you headed?" His dark, unreadable gaze touched my own, and then slid away.

"Yogurt." Trent smiled, and touched my shoulder. "You ready, Kay?"

I nodded, and grinned a farewell for David. I looked around for Joyce, but she had disappeared.

The night felt warm and sticky. The dark asphalt street dully reflected back the yellow streetlights. It was still. And quiet. No gangs here.

My fear eased. The Lord would watch over us. He'd kept us safe from Market Street, hadn't he? Praise bubbled up in my heart. Why hadn't I thanked him before?

Thank you, Lord, for protecting us. Peace stole into my heart, and when I prayed that he would keep us safe for the rest of the evening, I knew he would.

Trent was right. I couldn't imagine anyone messing with the proprietor of Kruger's Yogurt.

The place was empty when we walked in. The tables, walls, floor and ceiling were stark white. I blinked, dazzled. Antiseptic counters gleamed a shiny aluminum color. And the air conditioning was on full blast. A sharp contrast from outside.

Only one man inhabited the room. Kruger, I guessed. He was huge, and dressed in jeans and a white T-shirt. A green tattoo bulged on one bicep, while another was stamped across his thick neck. He was bald, with thick, black bushy brows suspended millimeters above beady black eyes. I could vividly imagine the shotgun nestled behind the clear, well-polished display case.

His voice was deceptively mild. Even a little high. "What can I do for you folks?"

We ordered, and sat to eat our frozen yogurt under the protection of his stony gaze. I did not feel comfortable, but didn't feel scared, either. Nervous was the word. I swallowed a spoonful of double chocolate fudge. Mmm. Good.

Trent dipped into his vanilla yogurt. "So, tell me about your friends. Do you all go to the same church?"

I nodded, and scooped up another ladylike bite. "Yes. Truesdale First Gospel."

His eyes narrowed. "I've heard of it. Is it affiliated with First Gospel of America?"

"Mmhm," I agreed.

He returned to the original topic. "So, you've all been friends since high school?"

"I met David in high school. I've known Joyce since the first grade." I glanced at him. "Where did you grow up?"

"In a little town two hundred miles north."

"I'll bet it was hard to move here, and start all over."

"Yes." Trent's eyes crinkled at the corners, and he reached over and clasped my hand. "But it's getting easier every day. I'm glad I met you."

My tongue stumbled. "I'm glad I met you, too." My cheeks warmed. Why did he have to be so attractive? Why was my heart pounding like a trip hammer? I felt like I could drown in his tender blue gaze.

Thankfully, another topic flew to my mind, and I latched onto it, glad to direct the conversation away from the two of us. I wasn't ready for that. Besides, I just wanted to be friends with him, right? Gently, I extricated my hand.

"I'm thinking about applying for an internship soon. How about you?"

"I plan to do the same," he agreed. "Even though it's not required until our senior year, more experience can't hurt." We talked a little more about the journalism program.

Half an hour later, Trent walked me to my front door. He didn't touch me. But my heart jumped as I fumbled in my purse for my house key. Awkwardly, I turned the lock.

Was I supposed to ask him in? But it was after eleven. My parents wouldn't approve.

He took my hand and turned me to face him. "Goodnight, Kay." A little breathlessly, I stared up into his warm gaze. "I had a great time tonight."

"We'll have to do it again. Soon," I said. My lips tingled. Was he going to kiss me?

"Yes." He smiled slowly, and lifted the back of my hand to his lips. "Goodnight."

I felt like I was going to faint. What was happening to me? Usually I wasn't the light-headed, swooning type. I suspected his good looks were addling my brain.

"Goodnight," I whispered.

It was hours before I fell asleep. My mind wouldn't stop spinning. All I could think about was Trent, and how much I liked him.

I didn't want to be just friends. Joyce was right. I was looking for more.

What was I going to do?

SATURDAY

"I CAN'T BELIEVE THIS!" Joyce's voice crackled in my ear. I sat at my desk, phone tucked between my chin and shoulder. My fingers hovered, motionless, above the computer keyboard.

"You said *what* happened?" I stared at the computer monitor, not seeing anything except for the picture Joyce had just painted with her words.

"Last night someone vandalized the church! All the windows are broken." Joyce's voice wavered. "And Dad's pulpit is smashed to pieces."

"Are the police there?"

Joyce's voice faded, and I imagined her turning to look at the scene inside the church. "Yes. They don't have any clues. Except they found a black cloth tied to the railing outside. Around another hate note."

"So they don't know who did this?"

"No."

"Do you need help cleaning up? I can come right over."

A short pause ensued. Joyce sounded distracted now. "Thanks, but don't bother, Kay. It's a crime scene now. And after that, it's just a lot of sweeping. We'll manage. I just had to talk to someone."

"Well, of course you did. Are you sure you don't need help? And how will you replace all the windows?"

"The church carries insurance." Joyce sounded grim now, and eager to get off the phone. "Thanks for the offer, but people are already helping out. No sense in you coming over, too. Those horrible hate mongers have wasted enough people's time today."

"If you're sure." My tone indicated doubt.

"Look, I've got to go. Talk to you tomorrow?"

"Okay."

"Bye." The line clicked dead in my ear.

I disconnected the line. The hate mail writers were getting braver. Why? What was their goal? When would they stop? Or would they?

An uneasy feeling lodged in my heart. Crime seemed to be getting worse lately. I thought back over everything that had happened in the last two weeks. Four unsettling events. Three of them outright crimes.

It was crazy, but for a second I saw it as a jigsaw puzzle. Some of the pieces fit together, and I had a weird feeling something Joyce said had sparked that idea. But what? I couldn't remember.

Whatever the case, I had a bad feeling this was only the beginning.

SUNDAY

WHEN I ARRIVED AT CHURCH on Sunday morning, the building seemed awfully dark inside. Like a morgue. The windows were covered with brown paper, and only a few people had shown up. Word must have got out about the vandalism. It seemed so solemn inside, as if someone lay sick, or dying.

At least, it did until Pastor Warner delivered his fiery sermon from behind his new pulpit—a music stand. The part I remember most is this:

"'What, then, shall we say in response to this? If God is for us, who can be against us?'" (Romans 8:31) He looked around the sanctuary, his eyes blazing, his voice challenging. "We will not cower in fear! We will not!" He closed his eyes, and lifted his hands in supplication.

"Lord, protect our church! Deliver us from evil. We pray that you would be glorified in this church, and in this congregation. Let us be a light, Lord, to the dark, dying world around us."

Then he flipped his black Bible open.

"'The righteous cry out, and the Lord hears them; he delivers them from all their troubles. The Lord is close to the broken-hearted and saves those who are crushed in spirit.

"'A righteous man may have many troubles, but the Lord delivers him from them all.'" (Psalm 34:17-19)

Pastor Warner's sermon lifted my heart. By the end of the service, it didn't seem quite so dark inside the church anymore. Our church hadn't been destroyed. God was still with us. He was protecting us, and we would go forward.

We didn't have Sunday school today. And I didn't have a chance to speak more than two words to Joyce, either. She rushed off the instant the sermon ended.

MONDAY

"HOW DID YOUR DATE GO ON FRIDAY NIGHT?"

Mr. Carlisle had let us out of class a few minutes early, so Mary and I sat outside on a hot bench, relaxing until our next class.

I'd woken in a good mood today, but tried to pretend it wasn't because I would see Trent in my next class. I'd thought about him all weekend. It was both a pleasure and an agony. I liked him, but felt pretty certain I shouldn't get romantically involved with him. But right now, I didn't care. I just wanted to see him.

"It was okay." Mary shrugged.

I eyed her with concern. "What happened?"

She attempted a smile, but it didn't erase the weary look of unhappiness in her eyes. "It wasn't just Jack and me, after all. All of his friends showed up." Her shoulders drooped. "I just don't fit in with them. Jack's always telling me I should try harder to be witty. Funny. Loosen up more." She looked ready to cry.

Appalled, I said, "That is ridiculous! How can you believe that? You are fun. And witty. You're a wonderful person."

She shook her head. "Jack never seems to think so."

I didn't know what to say. But I was upset for her. It was a glimpse into Mary's personal life, and I didn't like what I saw. My opinion of Jack plummeted, and with it, concern for my friend grew.

"The rest of the weekend was good," she said. "I went to Mass on Sunday."

"How was it?"

Mary shrugged. "Okay. Same old stuff."

"Do your parents go now?"

"No."

Mary's parents had sent her to Catholic Mass since the day she turned five. But they never went. I'd never visited her church before, either.

With curiosity, I said, "What's the Catholic church like, anyway? What kinds of things do you do there?"

She blinked. I'd never shown interest in her faith when we were kids. "Well, we sing and listen to a scripture reading. Then the priest says a few things and we take communion."

"Do you go to confession? What's that all about?"

"Sometimes I do. Only it's called Reconciliation now. After I confess, the priest usually gives me a penance to do. Sometimes it's a rosary—although most churches don't do actual rosaries anymore. The priest may ask people to recite some of the same prayers as for the rosary, depending on what they've done, but only a few churches still do the full rosaries."

"What is a penance? Is it a punishment for your sins?"

"No. It's complicated. God forgives us, but penance is a way for us to show how we want to make amends for the damage our sinful actions have caused in the world. The penance depends on the sin. It might be an offering, a prayer, works of mercy, or other things. In our church, I've only been asked to say certain prayers." Mary reached into her bag and pulled out a necklace laced with different sized beads. It was a rosary. She pointed to the small beads. "I say a Hail Mary prayer on these beads, and an Our Father prayer on the larger ones."

She pointed to a cross and another large bead above it. "I say a different prayer for each of these. After I've prayed all the way around, I've done one rosary." She slipped it back in her bag. "I do everything I'm supposed to. All the confession, penance, communion... Everything."

I detected a note of bitterness in her voice. "What's wrong?"

"None of it ever helps. I never feel like I can do enough."

"You mean to feel good about yourself?"

"Yes." Her eyes shone suspiciously bright. "Jack is always disappointed in me. My parents, too. Especially my dad. I never do enough to make him proud of me. I think God feels the same way. Sometimes..." a tear slipped down her cheek, and she quickly brushed it away, "sometimes I think I could do rosaries day and night, and God would never forgive me."

Tears stung my own eyes. Mary was hurting, deeply. How could I help her?

"Mary, none of us can ever *earn* God's forgiveness. Not with prayers, penance, or good works. We can't pay the price ourselves. You're right about that. But the good news is, we don't have to. It's a free gift. God became man in Jesus, and he paid that price himself. That's how much he loves you, Mary. Listen to this."

I fumbled in my backpack for my Bible. Matthew 11:28-30. "Jesus says, 'Come to me, all you who are weary and burdened, and I will give you rest. Take my yoke upon you and learn from me, for I am gentle and humble in heart, and you will find rest for your souls. For my yoke is easy, and my burden is light.'"

"And listen to what Ephesians two, verses eight and nine say: 'For it is by grace you have been saved, through faith—and this not from yourselves, it is the gift of God—not by works, so that no one can boast.'

"No good works or rituals can buy forgiveness for our sins, Mary. Forgiveness is a gift of God. All we need to do to be saved and receive God's complete forgiveness is to put our faith in Jesus, and what he did for us on the cross."

A small spark of interest shone in Mary's eyes as she stared at my Bible, and then it slowly died. "That's interesting, Kay. And I do believe in God, but I have to be honest." Her brown eyes looked sad. "I'm just not sure I believe in Jesus, or that he died for my sins. To me, that's a whole lot harder than doing all the rituals."

It was my turn to be shocked. For Catholics believed in Jesus, just like I did. But Mary did not.

At least she was honest. And she did seem to have some interest in the subject. So I flipped to Galatians 2:15-16.

"The Jewish people were used to following rituals and laws, too. But Paul said, 'We who are Jews by birth and not Gentile sinners know that a man is not justified by observing the law, but by faith in Jesus Christ. So we, too, have put our faith in Christ Jesus that we may be justified by faith in Christ and not by observing the law, because by observing the law, no one will be justified.'

"And another verse says, 'And without faith it is impossible to please God, because anyone who comes to him must believe that he exists and that he rewards those who earnestly seek him.'" (Hebrews 11:6)

Pain flared in Mary's eyes, and she stared at my Bible, reading the words for herself. "I've never heard that before."

Had I said too much? I was afraid I had. Sometimes I didn't know when to stop. Reaching for my backpack, I said, "If you want to learn more about Jesus, we have a college study group on Wednesday nights at my church. You're welcome to come, if you'd like."

Mary hesitated, but then shrugged a shoulder. "Maybe I will."

I paused in the doorway of Current Affairs class, and scanned the room for Trent. The excited thump of my heart slowed. He wasn't here. Yet.

A hard forearm hit my shoulder blade and made me stagger forward.

"*Hey.*" I turned.

Randy's murky eyes glared down at me. His heavy shoulders hulked forward in a threatening manner. "You're in my way, girl!"

"No need to be rude."

His lips curled back. "Get. Outta. My. Way!"

I glared at him, trying to hide my fear. But rather than exacerbate the situation, I decided to turn away. I felt his eyes burning into me as I marched to my seat. Why did he hate me so much? Because I was a Christian?

I didn't know. But whatever the reason, it scared me.

I glanced at him out of the corner of my eye. He sat at his own desk now, in the back corner of the classroom. He still stared at me, hatred evident by the vicious thrust of his jaw.

I gripped my pen, fingers trembling a little. Randy had enjoyed threatening me just now. So he'd probably do it again. Unless I managed to avoid him.

Trent walked in the door a few moments later. His friendly smile was a welcome relief.

To my great disappointment, I only had time to whisper "hi" before class started. And he left early, too, after we'd handed in the topic ideas for our articles.

But he did give me a rushed explanation. "I have an interview scheduled for an article. See you on Wednesday?" He smiled, his bright blue eyes warm.

Of course I agreed, smiling like a fool.

I sat beneath a magnolia tree, munching my sandwich and trying to read my history textbook.

"Hey, Kay." David swung his long body to the ground near me. "Good book?" His gaze lacked its usual gleam. It looked watchful. Maybe even a little guarded.

"As good as a textbook can be." I offered a playful grin, hoping to break him out of his somber mood.

It didn't work.

He peeled open a sandwich and began to munch.

Clearly, something was wrong, and I had a good guess what it might be. Fine. I would jump right into the frying pan.

"How did the party go, after Trent and I left?" Since we hadn't had Sunday school, I hadn't seen David since the movie on Friday night.

"Good." He raised a deliberate brow. "But I guess the real question is, how was your date?" He took another casual bite, but it felt like his dark eyes bored a hole right through me, pinning me to the magnolia trunk. My temper sparkled.

"Why don't you say what you mean, David? I'm sure Joyce told you Trent's not a Christian. So come right out and tell me what you think. I know you're dying to."

I crossed my arms and leaned back, trying not to feel defensive, but failing.

His gaze held mine. "Do you think it's a good idea, Kay? Going out with a guy who's not a Christian?"

My heart beat harder, but before I could speak, he went on. "I just want to make one point, okay? Hear me out.

"God told the Israelites not to marry foreigners. That meant people who didn't worship the Lord. First Kings eleven, verse two says, 'You must not intermarry with them, because they will surely turn your hearts after their gods.' And away from the Lord."

"I'm *not* marrying Trent!" This was unbelievable. First Joyce. Now David. With trembling hands, I scraped my belongings together. "We're just dating. So...so just stop it. I'm going to do exactly..." I threw an apple into my lunch sack with unnecessary force. *"Exactly* what I want to do. Get that?"

I stumbled to my knees, but his fingers on my arm halted me. I glared at them, and then at him.

"Stop *touching* me," I hissed.

His hand jerked back, as he'd touched a hot poker. Pain flickered in his eyes. "I don't want to fight about this."

I sat back on my heels and frowned. "Then talk about something else."

I knew I was being unreasonable, but both Joyce and David seemed so close-minded. Judgmental, even. I could accept that I probably shouldn't marry a non-Christian. But what about dating one? I just wasn't sure. But if I was going to fall, I'd have to do it. Maybe that was the only way I would learn.

We both sat silently for a long time.

"How's your Revelation reading going?" David's voice, when it came, was quiet.

"Fine." I glanced at him, suddenly ashamed of how I'd snapped at him. He'd been straight with me. He was only trying to be my friend. But I couldn't apologize. Could I? Wouldn't that be tantamount to admitting he was right? Or worse yet, open up the whole conversation again? I couldn't bear that.

I said, "It's hard to understand, but I'm reading a Bible prophecy book, too. It helps make things clearer."

"Have you read Matthew twenty-four?"

"Yes." I understood this, at least. "It says nation will rise up against nation, and there will be famines and earthquakes, and things will get worse, like birth pains, as the end gets closer. I see those things happening now."

"I know. Wars are springing up all over. So are floods and natural disasters." David took another bite of sandwich. He didn't look at me, as if lost in his own thoughts.

"And if crime was a war, it'd be one trying to take over this country," I said. "I'm going to do a paper on it. I'll compare the crime rates now with a decade ago."

"Sounds interesting." David crumpled his lunch bag. Silently, he stared across the campus. "The more I learn about Bible prophecy, and the more I see what's happening in this world, the more convinced I am that the Tribulation is just around the corner." His glance looked serious. "Maybe closer than we think."

A small sliver of affirmation slid through me. Could David be right? Was it really close? Was it at the doors?

He swung to his feet. "I have to go."

I eyed the apple in his hand. He hadn't even finished his lunch. I suddenly felt horrible. I hated things to be wrong between us.

"I'm sorry," I blurted, squinting up at him.

"It's okay, Cookie." He smiled, but his voice was rough. "See you later."

"Wednesday?"

He lifted an arm in farewell.

I felt oddly bereft, sitting there. And very alone.

Voices murmured in the kitchen when I entered the house that afternoon. Undoubtedly Mom and Theresa sat talking at the kitchen table. I still felt unhappy about my conversation with David, and decided I needed to try to be a whole lot nicer to the people who mean the most to me. Including my family. Perhaps especially my family.

"Hi!" I said cheerily, and dropped my backpack on the kitchen counter.

"Hi, honey," Mom smiled. Shadowed half-moons underscored her eyes. She looked fragile. I wondered if I'd interrupted a heart-to-heart chat, but decided to behave as if nothing was wrong. I'd stay for a few minutes, and then leave them to finish their chat.

I poured a glass of milk and plopped down at the table. "How was your day?"

Mom blinked, as if surprised I'd decided to join them. A small smile touched her lips. "Good, thank you, Kay. I went shopping. Bought these new earrings," she touched the silver discs hanging from her ears, "and this new outfit." It was a gold and silver threaded pantsuit, and very slim and fashionable. "And I bought some new tablecloths..."

I nodded with interest, but when she started talking about a new dress she'd put on layaway, I got worried. What would Dad think about all of Mom's new purchases? Money seemed to be a growing source of contention between them.

Mom looked at me hopefully. "I don't suppose you'd want to go shopping with Theresa and me tomorrow. I need to look at new drapes, and I'd like your opinion."

Theresa sneered. "Kay doesn't know the first thing about shopping, Mom. She's worn the same clothes for years."

"I have *not*." My determination to be nice, no matter the cost, cracked and resentment oozed out. I was heartily sick of how Theresa kept putting me down.

"Right. Looks like you shop at a thrift store." Theresa rolled her eyes.

I gasped, and my temper snapped, sending my last good intentions tumbling, like leaves caught in a hurricane. "At least

I'm not a clotheshorse," I shot back. "I mean, how shallow can you get?"

Theresa blanched, but worse, deep hurt flashed across Mom's face. Immediately, I felt horrible. I hadn't meant to include Mom in my snapped comment.

"I'm sorry," I fumbled, "I didn't mean..."

"It's okay, honey." She stood. "I understand that you're interested in other things."

I felt awful. I tried to apologize again, but Mom wasn't buying it, and Theresa continued to sneer at me. Clearly, I could say nothing to patch things up. My big mouth had created trouble again.

Why couldn't I love my family?

Please forgive me, Lord! I'm so sorry. Please help me love my family. Help me to be loving and kind and patient and good.

TUESDAY

MY ENGLISH PROFESSOR gave us a new project today, and I was thinking about it as I hurried for the school parking lot this afternoon, eager to head home. As usual, it was hot and sticky. I couldn't wait to get in my car. Oh, for blessedly cool air conditioning.

Mr. Carlisle left the parking lot just as I arrived, wiping his darkly smudged fingers on a tan car rag. Was something wrong with his car? I didn't ask, though, since he brushed by as if he hadn't seen me.

Thank goodness my car was in working order. I hate car trouble.

I'd parked on the far side of the lot, as the parking area had been full this morning. As I hurried over the sticky asphalt, a familiar, light-blond head caught my attention. And a low slung Porsche.

Trent! With a glad spring to my step, I adjusted my route.

His back was to me, and I heard him say into his cell phone, "Done. I'll get more dirt..." He unexpectedly pivoted on his heel and saw me. A startled, guilty look crossed his handsome features. "Talk to you later," he muttered, and shoved the phone into his pocket. "Kay! Good to see you."

I wondered who he'd been talking to. "How did your interview go yesterday?"

"Great! I got all the information I need for the article." A charming grin lifted his lips. "Maybe you'll read it later this week? I'd appreciate your opinion."

"Sure. I'd be happy to."

"Great." He flashed a glance at his broad, expensive looking silver watch. "I have to go, but let's get together soon. Sound good?"

"Sounds great." I headed for my car. A moment later, Trent's Porsche glided by, heading for the exit. He seemed to be in an awful hurry.

I wondered again who he'd been speaking to on the phone about "dirt." And what he'd meant by "dirt." Was he researching a dirty politician? Was it regarding an article in another class?

A faint, noxious odor assailed my nostrils as I threaded through the final row of cars. My car was parked on the last row, nosed into the far bushes that lined the lot.

I wished shady trees bordered the parking area, and was glad I'd put the sunshade up in the windshield, or else my car would feel like an oven when I climbed in.

I wrinkled up my nose and fished the key from my bag.

Eww. Smelled like doggy doo.

I unlocked my Mustang and slid into the baking interior. The smell seemed particularly strong in here, but I couldn't figure out why. I stashed my backpack on the seat next to me and pulled down the silver, reflective sun shade from the window. And gasped.

Brown goo was smeared all over my windshield.

Dog poop.

It streaked over every square inch of the clear glass. Large chunks dotted my windshield. And into the feces someone had scrawled an obscene phrase, my name and the word "Christian," written upside down and backwards.

My heart hammered.

Someone had vandalized *my* car. On purpose.

It was a deliberate attack against me. Clearly because I was a Christian.

Had it been Tim or Randy? Or their hate group?

Randy's shove in Current Affairs class returned to mind with sinister clarity. So did the scene in the journalism lab at the beginning of the semester. The two men hated me. But enough to go to all the trouble of gathering up pounds of dog doo and smearing it on my windshield?

Yes. I could easily imagine Randy doing it, and with glee. Tim, too.

But how had they transported it here? Surely the dung had left a trail somewhere—in their car, or on their clothes or hands.

I rocketed out of the car, suddenly shaking with rage. If there was a trail, I'd find it.

Unfortunately, I found nothing but an empty, smelly brown sack shoved into the bushes. Dog feces littered the ground around my car.

I glanced around the parking lot, wondering if Randy and Tim were watching me now. Were they sharing a good laugh at my expense? If so, I didn't want to give them a reason to salivate over my distress. I'd try to appear calm and collected. As much as humanly possible, that was.

I grabbed a roll of glass cleaner wipes out of the trunk and wiped enough of the windshield so I could see out. After depositing the soiled cloths in the trash and thoroughly wiping my hands with several clean wipes, I returned to the car and drove to the nearest car wash. I tried to ignore the stares of the car washing attendants, drove my car onto the moving car conveyor, and let the shooting soap and swishing blue bristles work their magic. And as water rained down on my car, I finally let myself cry.

I hated Randy and Tim. I hated them so much.

When I got home from the car wash, I still felt defiled, and the interior of my car stank, even though I'd left the windows open all the way home. Leaving them unrolled at home was out of the question, however. My car would be stolen in two seconds flat. So I sealed up the car, and with a sick, angry feeling resigned myself to the fact that my car would stink like dog doo for some time to come.

"What's wrong, Kay?" Mom said, the moment I entered the kitchen. She pulled fresh dough from the bread-maker and plopped it onto a flat, round pan. Pizza. At least that was one good thing to be thankful for, and to look forward to tonight.

Theresa sat at the table painting her fingernails. She wrinkled her nose when I placed my backpack on the chair beside her. "*Ew*. Gross! Did you roll on the ground at the dog park?"

I scowled. "No. Someone smeared dog poo on my windshield."

"*What?*" Mom gasped. "Why would someone do that?"

"I don't know. I think I've made some enemies." I briefly told them about the journalism lab incident.

Mom gasped again. "I can't believe this. I am going to call the school right now."

"No, Mom. I have no proof that Tim or Randy did it."

"But what if they do something worse? They've *attacked* you. Twice, now!"

"They're small-minded jerks. I plan to ignore them. If they don't get a reaction, they'll give up." I hoped.

"I still think you should report this to the dean." Mom returned her attention to the pizza dough.

"If something else happens, I will," I agreed, to pacify her. But if I had no proof, it wouldn't do any good. Otherwise, I'd definitely do it now. After all, I wanted Randy and Tim to pay for what they had done.

I hated that I felt more scared now than before. But I wouldn't let Tim or Randy win the psychological war. What was that verse?

For God has not given us a spirit of fear, but of power and of love and of a sound mind. (2 Timothy 1:7, NKJV)

God was on my side. I'd be extra careful from now on. And I'd pray for protection.

Although these thoughts comforted me a little, I still felt angry about the personal violation of my property. I didn't want to be a victim.

I dragged my backpack from the chair and, suddenly feeling tired, took the vacated seat.

Theresa gave a moue of disgust. "*Ew*. Get a shower. You stink."

I glared at her. "Really? You have to attack me right now?"

"Just sayin'..." With an eyebrow lift, she popped her gum.

"You are so *shallow*." I could not believe her insensitive words and disdainful look. "I was attacked, and all you care about is yourself. And your stupid nails!"

"Kay," Mom cut in.

I leaped to my feet. "Sure! Take her side. Like always!" I grabbed my bag and stomped upstairs. I was shaking, I was so angry. But my mother and sister weren't the real problem.

I flung myself on the bed and burst into tears.

WEEK THREE — EARTHQUAKE

*"…There will be famines and earthquakes in various places.
All these are the beginning of birth pains."*

MATTHEW 24:7B-8

Wednesday

This morning, I got up early so I could spend more time praying and reading the Bible. I needed it. I read a few Psalms and 1 John. They encouraged me that God still loves me, even when I fail.

I felt bad about lashing out at my sister and mother yesterday, and what was worse, it wasn't the first time. Yes, I'd been angry about the horrible dog poop, but I felt my attitude toward them both, and toward others in my life, had been less than desirable lately. I wanted it to change.

1 John 1:9a says, "If we confess our sins, he is faithful and just and will forgive us our sins and purify us from all unrighteousness."

What encouragement! *I want to be a better person. Lord, please help me. And please protect me from Randy and Tim.*

I slipped into my seat in Current Affairs class. Trent hadn't arrived yet.

I tried not to think about Randy or Tim. Hopefully, they would skip today. If they did come in, I wouldn't cower. In fact, I'd stiffen my spine and ignore them.

Students trickled through the door. Then my tall professor stalked in. My attention remained glued to the door, but a prickling sensation crept down my spine.

I turned my head, and was surprised to find Professor Williams staring at me. His eyes looked like pale green ice chips, and a faint, hostile smile lurked in their depths.

His stare creeped me out. Then his lips twisted, as if at some secret joke, and he turned to the board.

I remembered the odd, disgusted look he'd directed at me last week. Did he dislike me for some reason? If so, why?

"Hi!" Trent's voice gave me a start. He slipped into the desk next to mine.

"Hi." I was glad to see him. Finally, a friendly face.

"Want to meet for lunch?"

My dark, cloudy feelings dispersed, like the sun breaking through on a rainy day. I smiled. "I'd love to, thanks."

Although crowds of students filled the student union, I managed to find a free table, and set down my coffee cup. Since Trent was nowhere in sight yet, I reluctantly decided to make good use of the time. An English essay was due tomorrow, and I needed to outline it. A topic sentence was my first hurdle.

Unfortunately, my mind wandered, because I kept thinking about Trent. I wondered again why he'd acted so strangely in the parking lot yesterday. Not that his phone call was any of my business. We were barely more than acquaintances. However, I was looking forward to this lunch, and the opportunity to get to know him better. Maybe at some point he'd tell me what the phone call had been about.

About ten yards away, a husky blond man and a dark-haired one caught my attention.

Perhaps because they were staring at me.

My heart gave an apprehensive lurch, and I glanced away, pretending not to see Randy or Tim. With vicious, disgusting force, the dog dung on my car returned to mind, and so did Randy's shove in Current Affairs class. The two scared me, but I refused to let them see it.

Out of the corner of my eye, I watched them. Randy headed for the door, but Tim suddenly drove through the milling bodies and headed for the far side of the student union. "Pete!" he called out.

The crowd thinned enough for me to see Tim speaking to Mr. Carlisle, my World Religions teacher. Standing side by side, they looked remarkably similar. Both were tall, wiry and muscular, with dark hair, and strong, angular jaw lines. Were they brothers? Cousins?

The two headed for the exit.

"What's up?" Trent had arrived.

"Not much."

"I'd believe that if you weren't frowning."

"I just saw Tim and Mr. Carlisle talking together. They look alike. I was wondering if they're related."

"I heard they're cousins. Why? Does it matter?"

Cousins. Tim was a member of the hate group on campus. And I'd seen Mr. Carlisle wiping his hands on a rag in the parking lot after my car had been defaced. It wasn't a far reach to wonder if Mr. Carlisle was a member of the hate group, too. And if he had vandalized my car.

Was I grasping at straws? Mr. Carlisle certainly didn't care for religion in any form. But did that mean he was a bigot? Or that he would skate the criminal fringe?

"You look pretty serious," Trent said. "What is it?" He pulled a sheet of paper from his notebook.

My thoughts took another sinister twist. I couldn't help but remember again how Trent had looked startled and guilty when I'd approached him in the parking lot yesterday. And why had he said, "Done. I'll get more dirt..."?

But when I looked across the table into Trent's eyes, and his smile that so easily charmed me, I couldn't believe that I'd just—even for a second—linked him to the crime against my car. He'd never hurt me. Never.

I glanced down at the paper he'd just scooted before me. "I'm fine. What's this?"

"An interview for a class project. I'd really value your opinion. Would you read it?"

"What do you think?" Trent smiled at me across the table. The noisy bustle of the lunch crowd swirled around us, but by now my unease regarding Randy, Tim and Mr. Carlisle had finally melted away. They had long since disappeared, and I felt cocooned, insulated from the others in the student union. It was just Trent and me, alone, set apart, somehow.

I slid the paper back across the table. "It's good. Very concise. A good article."

"But?" Trent caught my slight hesitation, and glanced down at the interview he'd typed up.

"But..." Uncharacteristically, I hesitated again, but only for a moment. I had to tell him the truth, even if he got mad at me.

"It's pretty biased, don't you think?" I took the paper back and pointed to a sentence. "Here, for example. 'Bishop Carletti, and others like him, cling to their simplistic faith, brandishing it as a cure-all for the woes of modern society.'"

I glanced at him. "Simplistic faith? How can you say that?"

He leaned back in his chair. His eyebrows rose and eyes gleamed, as if he'd just accomplished a hidden agenda. "Christianity is based on events that happened two thousand years ago, Kay. Things are a lot more complicated today than they were then."

"You don't think Jesus is relevant today?"

"I mean we have to find our own truth. Jesus was a simple carpenter. We're a lot more sophisticated now. We ought to be able to come up with better answers. Just look at all our new technology and knowledge."

What can I say, Lord?

An idea came to mind. My palms felt suddenly moist, but I tried to relax in my chair. I desperately wanted Trent to like me, but I had to defend my faith, too.

"How will you know the truth when you see it, Trent?"

His eyes sparkled, and he rocked back on two legs of his chair. "The world is filled with different 'truths.'" He waggled his fingers for the quotes. "But I guess I'd recognize the real truth if it felt right. In my heart."

"That's pretty subjective."

He rocked a little more, but all the while watched me closely. "Maybe. But your truth is pretty subjective, too."

Nervously, I licked my lips, but met him eye for eye. "No, it's not. Jesus Christ claimed that he is God. If he is God, then the words he said have to be true. Agreed?"

Trent crashed forward. "Whoa! Wait a minute." He held up a hand, laughing. "Jesus was just a good teacher. He never claimed to be God!"

"Yes, he did. More than once, too. Listen to this." I whipped out my handy dandy Bible. I'd never used it on campus as much as I had during these last few weeks. "John eight, verse fifty-eight says, "'I tell you the truth,' Jesus answered, 'before Abraham was born, I am!'" I looked up. "The Jews were furious when he said that. They wanted to kill him."

"Why?" Trent still smiled, but his eyes looked disbelieving.

"Because Jesus just claimed he was God. 'I AM' is a name reserved only for God. In Exodus it says, 'God said to Moses, "I AM WHO I AM. This is what you are to say to the Israelites: 'I AM' has sent me to you."'" (Exodus 3:14)

"So in that little sentence Jesus claimed to be God?" One of Trent's aristocratic brows shot up.

"Yes. I can show you other…"

"No. That's okay." His blue gaze latched onto mine. Slowly, deliberately, he shrugged one shoulder. "So he claimed to be God. So what?"

He poured on the charm now. My insides melted like jelly, but I forced out my final words anyway. "This is my point. Either he is who he claimed to be, or he's not. If he is, we should follow him, and take his word as the truth. If he's not, then none of it matters."

His warm hands closed around mine. "Awfully black and white," he said softly.

My heart bumped, double-speed. How could he do this? Turn a conversation about God into an intimate, charged moment?

His mouth curved into a warm smile, but I glimpsed the mocking challenge lurking in his blue gaze. Blinking, I pulled back. Was he using charm to throw me off track?

"It's the only way that makes sense to me," I replied crisply.

Trent laughed then, and his eyes sparkled with merriment. He recaptured my hands. "That's why I like you, Kay. You're sharp. You're interesting to talk to. And you can read me like a book."

I couldn't help but melt again. I grinned back at him. He was a fascinating guy. I liked him. I never knew what to expect when I was with him.

He leaned forward. "Do you have plans for Friday night?"

"No."

"Would you like to go out? Maybe play miniature golf?"

"I'd love to." I hoped he couldn't feel my racing pulse.

"Good." He smiled deep into my eyes. "I'm looking forward to it."

My heart sang all through dinner, even though my parents bickered the entire time. Dad was mad at Mom for spending too much money. Theresa had vanished on a dinner date.

I escaped as soon as I could into the warm, dusky twilight, and bounced into my car's baking interior. Pressing the air conditioning on full blast, I drove toward Mary's apartment. She'd agreed to come to our college group tonight.

Mary stood waiting on the curb in front of her apartment building, and jumped in as soon as I geared down to a stop. I was glad I didn't have to go upstairs and meet Jack again.

"Hi!" She slammed the door behind her, and I rolled back into traffic. "Perfect timing. I just got downstairs."

"I'm glad you could come tonight." I smiled happily, buoyed by the joy still bubbling up in my soul.

She laughed at me. Teasingly, she said, "Has something happened, Kay? You're glowing."

I couldn't contain my grin. "Trent asked me out for Friday night."

Mary's smile sparkled approval. "That's wonderful. You really like him, don't you?"

"He's great," I sighed dreamily. I couldn't wait until Friday night. At seven o'clock Trent and I would meet up, and enjoy an entire evening together.

We were late. So we tiptoed in and quietly slid down a pew beside Joyce. As I glanced about the church, I did a double-take. All of the brown paper had been removed. Glass gleamed in the windows.

"Hi," Joyce whispered, waggling her fingers. Sunday's unhappy tension seemed to have vanished.

"How did your dad replace the windows so fast?" I hissed.

A smile brightened her face. "It's great, isn't it? Dad has a friend in the glass business. We became his number one priority. Of course, the stained glass will have to be replaced later."

"But still, that's terrific. It looks so much better now."

At Mary's questioning look, I explained what had happened over the weekend. She looked shocked.

That brought to mind the dog poop on my windshield, and in a whisper, I told them both about it. Their indignation made me feel better.

"Something has to be *done*," Joyce hissed. "Those criminals are taking over the town. Worse, the police aren't doing one thing to stop them."

"They're understaffed," Mary murmured. "Crime is really bad on Driscoll, where I live. Gangs break in and vandalize apartments all the time. And apparently just for the fun of it."

In a strange way, it helped to know I wasn't alone—that I wasn't the only victim in this town.

Bobby's tired voice drew our attention back to the stage. David stood behind him, with his guitar slung around his neck. Laura stood to the right, smiling radiantly at her husband.

"We have some great news." Bobby's smile didn't look wide or happy enough for great news. "Laura and I," he glanced at his wife, "are going to have a baby. Due in the spring."

Our college class erupted into whistles and pounding applause.

Bobby's smile dimmed a little. "That's the good news. Now the bad. Rumors are flying that my position might be cut." He paused. "It's true. I have one month left before I'm laid off."

A collective gasp rippled.

"Pastor Warner is negotiating to keep me on longer, but I'll be honest. It's unlikely he'll succeed. This situation scares us, especially now. We'd really appreciate your prayers. We desperately need this job."

"How awful," Mary whispered, touching her stomach. She, more than anyone else, could understand the joys and fears facing the Pages.

"I'd like to pray for Bobby and Laura." David stepped forward to take the microphone. Bobby melted into the background and wrapped an arm around his wife. Blond head and dark head bowed together, touching.

"Lord, you know all of Bobby and Laura's worries, and we know you love them. Please comfort them now. Please assure their hearts that you'll provide for them, no matter what comes. We pray for a secure position for Bobby. And that his job here could be saved, if that's your will. We trust you to take care of them, Lord. And if there's anything we can do to help them out, please tell us.

"Thank you for your great love, Lord. And I pray that all of us, Bobby and Laura included, may be able to comprehend more fully the width and length and depth and height—to know the love of Christ which passes all knowledge. In Jesus' name, Amen."

"Amen," I murmured.

Mary stared at the stage, watching Bobby hug Laura tightly and kiss her. She looked down into her lap, and her fingers clenched white.

"What's wrong?" I whispered.

"Nothing." Mary looked up with a clearly forced smile. "Nothing. I'm fine." Her face was an expressionless mask now, and she stared straight ahead.

Jack must be the reason for her unhappiness, I guessed. He didn't want their baby. How horrible. It must be doubly hard to see how much Bobby loved his wife, and the baby to come.

Bobby gave a short lesson, and then we broke up into groups and talked and prayed. Mary seemed to enjoy it. This evening, we learned more about one of my favorite stories in the Bible—Luke 10:38-43—when Jesus visited Mary and Martha.

In short, Martha was distracted by all the preparations that had to be made for Jesus' stay, but Mary sat at Jesus' feet, listening to what he had to say. This made Martha mad, for she was doing all of the work. She asked Jesus to tell her sister to help her out, but Jesus said, "Martha, you are worried and upset about many things, but only one thing is needed. Mary has chosen what is better, and it will not be taken away from her." This story always tells me how important it is to spend time with Jesus by reading the Bible and praying. I need to do that more.

After the groups broke up, Mary and I slipped toward the stage, where Joyce and David talked with Bobby. Bobby broke off the conversation and immediately stretched out his hands to Mary.

"Hello! It's wonderful to see a new face." He winked at me. "Get tired of seeing the same old mugs all the time."

I grinned. "Bobby, this is Mary."

Bobby briefly clasped Mary's hands. While he talked to her, I glanced at my friends. David's back was to me, and he pulled the guitar strap over his head. A thought struck me. He'd never met Mary before. Mary had left for Catholic high school the same year Joyce and I had first met him.

But when Bobby slipped away a moment later, Joyce spoke up before I could. "David, have you met Mary? Kay and I went to elementary school and junior high with her."

"No." His white teeth flashed in a slow, easy grin, and he stuck out his hand. "Good to meet you. I'm David."

"Hi." Mary smiled shyly.

"So, what do you think of our group? Exciting enough for you?" With a grin, he clicked shut his guitar case.

She laughed. "I don't know if exciting is the word. But it was interesting."

"You should come to our Friday night get-togethers. That's when we really cut loose. Movies, bowling, games..."

Mary looked regretful. "I'd like to, but I have to work on Friday nights."

"What about you, Kay?" His gaze seemed to shutter. "You coming Friday night? We're playing games at Bobby's."

I couldn't help but smile, for warm anticipation bubbled up inside me again. "No. I have other plans." I didn't say they were with Trent, but he knew. And so did Joyce. Her keen gaze sharpened, but she said nothing.

"Oh," David shrugged slightly, and turned to grab his guitar. "Guess I'll see you Sunday, then. Joyce, I'll pick you up. Mary, nice to meet you." The shadows of the soft stage lighting made his face look incredibly gaunt just then, with his high cheekbones, and slightly hollowed cheeks. I suddenly wondered if he was getting enough sleep. I knew he worked full-time at his father's electronics shop, and attended school full-time, too.

His gaze slid past me. "Got to go. See you guys later."

"Great playing tonight, D," I called as he strode down the aisle.

"Thanks." His voice was tight, and he did not look back.

"Is something wrong between you two?" Joyce frowned.

"We had a fight on Monday." But I'd thought we'd made up. Evidently, I was wrong.

"About Trent?"

"Yes. He made his opinion clear. But I made mine clear, too. I'll do what I think is best. So now he's mad. But I don't care what he thinks."

Joyce's brow rose. "I think you do."

She was right. I did. "He needs to accept that I'm dating Trent." I still didn't understand why I felt so upset. Well, it hurt that David was mad at me. But we'd work it out, wouldn't we? We always had before.

But it also hurt that he didn't approve of something so important to me. I turned to Joyce. "What do you think of Trent?"

"He seems nice. And he's very good looking," she added frankly.

I relaxed a little. "He is. Very nice," I agreed. "And we almost always end up talking about God. It's kind of strange."

"That's good." A movement from Laura caught Joyce's attention, and she waved. "Got to go," she apologized. "Nice to see you again, Mary. Come back soon."

Mary and I walked into the parking lot. The unholy heat lingering from the daytime still radiated up from the hot pavement, making my feet stick to the gel-like asphalt.

When we climbed into my Mustang, Mary broke the silence. "Why is David upset that you're going out with Trent? Is there something going on...between you two?"

"You mean between David and me?" I choked on a surprised laugh. "No. *No.* That is not the problem."

I explained what the Bible said about yoking with unbelievers. However, I confess my statements lacked conviction. Mary looked confused by the end of my cryptic statements, but I didn't try to clarify the subject further. I wanted to go out with Trent. And so I would.

I wasn't going to marry the guy, after all. Everyone was making a very big deal out of nothing.

I was still arguing with myself when I went to bed. Trent was interested in God. Maybe God wanted me to witness to Trent about him. Maybe that was the reason for my overwhelming attraction to him.

It sounded good enough to believe.

FRIDAY

TODAY WAS THE NINETEENTH DAY of our hot spell—108°. But today felt different. I couldn't explain why.

A thin layer of clouds drifted overhead all day, providing bits of relief from the blinding blue sky. But no breeze touched the earth. Again. Today's stillness felt eerie. Like the earth had caught its breath and was waiting. But for what?

I felt on edge all day, even though nothing happened. No one touched my car, and my professor didn't give me any strange looks.

Even odder, my parents sat silently at dinner. They didn't even speak to Theresa or me. I felt like an explosion had already detonated in the house, and we swam through the suffocating smoke left behind.

Theresa methodically chewed through her food, and rarely looked up from her plate. Maybe she was daydreaming about her time with Bill or Bob, or whoever her date might be tonight.

I retreated to the living room to wait for Trent.

"Are you going out tonight?" Theresa perched on the couch beside me, snapping a piece of gum. Her chilly eyes scanned me. "You look nice," she said indifferently.

I glanced at my pale green, scoop-necked dress, and matching, casual flats. Had my sister just complimented me?

"Thank you. You look nice, too." Theresa wore a new designer dress. It was white, with a ruffle around the hem. She must be going to an upscale party tonight.

"I had to get out of there," she said unexpectedly. "I love them, but I can't stand their fights anymore."

"Did they fight tonight?"

Her thin eyebrows arched. "Yes. A wing-dinger of a blow out." She swung her heel against the couch. "I'd never heard Dad scream before."

I was glad I'd missed it. But despair caught at my soul. "Was it about money?"

"That, and everything else under the sun." The doorbell pealed, and Theresa jumped up.

"Jeffrey!" Lifting her heel, she kissed him, and peered over his shoulder. "And Trent! Good to see you again." She dimpled.

I hurried over so she couldn't dig her claws into my date.

"See you later!" Theresa whirled gaily past Trent, with her hand caught by the tanned, blond-headed Jeffrey. A black limousine waited in the driveway.

"She's a social butterfly." With a smile for Trent, I closed the door behind us. The hot night enveloped us. It felt eerie. Still. Waiting.

"Mmm." Trent glanced after my sister. "She's not as happy as she looks."

The statement surprised me, and I glanced at him. He wore a classic tan polo shirt tonight, and white slacks. The picture of a smooth, sophisticated man. I followed his neatly attired form to his Porsche.

"Why do you say that?" I asked, sliding inside. The warm scent of leather and citrus-tinged cologne tantalized my nostrils.

He scooted into the driver's side. Unexpectedly, he stared straight ahead without speaking for a moment.

"I've seen her type before. I've even run with the same crowd." He smiled at me, and turned the key in the ignition. "But I like this a lot better. Getting to know one person is more fun than going to a bunch of parties."

But I wondered if he did miss the parties. Or if he went, but didn't ask me, because he knew I wouldn't enjoy them.

Quietly, the Porsche purred to the mini-golf course. The amusement park was well secured, I noticed, when we stepped inside. High walls, electronic sensors. The owners had to protect their customers, or they'd lose business. Most mini-golf courses had already closed—they were too open to the public and vulnerable to crime.

I grabbed a club and followed Trent down the dimly lit path to the first hole. The objective was to putt the ball through a clown's mouth. Biting my lip, I lined up the ball and swung.

Whack! It bounced off the shining red nose.

Laughing, Trent fetched the ball for me. "Try again."

After three tries, I finally shot the ball down the clown's gullet.

It was fun, playing with Trent. He was easygoing and fun to be with. We talked about inconsequential things, like how we'd both loved miniature golf when we were kids, and how we'd gone to the same popular amusement parks, and loved the same rides... The Matterhorn. Mr. Toad's Wild Ride.

Gradually, the subject turned to school.

Trent carefully aimed his putt. "So, what's the subject for your Current Affairs article?"

He sank the ball.

"Crime. How it's reached epidemic proportions. I'm comparing it with crime rates ten years ago."

Trent rescued the ball. "It was terrible then, too."

"I know. Maybe I'll compare the crime rates every five years over the last twenty years." I swung carelessly, but the little white ball zipped between two obstructions and then bounced and stopped, inches from the hole.

"Good job! You've got the hang of it."

"Just swing and pray?" I laughed, and putted the ball in. "What is your paper about?"

Trent carefully lined up his next shot, and sank the ball with one stroke. I looked on a bit enviously.

Slowly, we walked to the next hole. The moon shone down, looking orange and hazy behind the clouds. Tall, lush trees studded the deserted golf course. Soft lights and music whispered across my senses, masking the eerie stillness. It was an incredibly romantic night.

As if sensing my mood, Trent slowed, and so I did, too. He smiled at me. His eyes looked deep and fathomless, and he leaned forward and kissed me. Quickly. Gently. But my lips tingled when the light pressure left them.

Smiling a little, Trent took my hand and we walked companionably to the eighteenth hole. There he reluctantly, it seemed, released my hand.

"In answer to your question," he bent to place the ball on the starting mark, "I'm doing an article on the Senate race between Robert Gilroy and his challenger, Oak Woodward."

"Really?" I watched him swing. A little off, this time. My turn. "Are you comparing their campaigns?"

"Yes."

A minute later, the game ended, and Trent had won by a landslide. It was only nine-thirty.

"Want to go for a drive?" Trent held the car door open for me. "Maybe you could show me around town."

As we drove, the feeling of warmth and companionship grew between us. He laughed at all the things I laughed at. I discovered his family owned a newspaper in his home town. So, he was following in his family's footsteps.

"Been on the newspaper beat since I was eight," he confessed, turning onto Morning Drive, the ritziest street in Truesdale.

"Then you must know the best kept secrets to flushing out a story," I remarked, gazing at the mansions nestled behind huge security gates.

"I know a few." An odd catch roughened his laugh. He pointed to a house on the right. "Who owns that?"

I commented on what I could, and was sorry when we finally pulled up in front of my own home. Now it was after eleven. I couldn't believe the time had flown by so quickly.

Trent walked me to the door, but didn't wait for me to open it before he took me in his arms and kissed me. Hungrily.

My instincts screamed a warning, and I automatically pushed away, feeling confused, incoherent. It felt like too much, too fast.

"Sorry." Trent released me and offered a sheepish smile. But his gaze looked curiously haunted. "You're a special girl, Kay."

"Thank you." I desperately wanted a sophisticated comment to roll off my tongue and diffuse the sudden tension. But it didn't. "I had a great time."

"I did, too." Trent smiled at me, which melted my insides all over again. "I'd like to do it again. Soon."

"Me, too."

His lips touched mine again, gently, and then he was gone.

I'd planned to read one of my prophecy books tonight, but it was no use. All I could think about was Trent. And how much fun I'd had tonight.

I sighed. Good conversation, nice kisses...

But once or twice, I'd received the fleeting impression that Trent was holding something back from me. Was he deliberately hiding something? Or was he just a complex man?

It would be fun to learn more about him.

I turned over and fluffed my pillow. My digital clock read one o'clock. Theresa wasn't home yet. I thought of my baby sister out drinking and surrounded by fraternity guys, and worried about her. She should be more careful. One of these days she could really get hurt.

Lord, please watch over Theresa tonight.

SATURDAY

I AWOKE TO A LOUD RUMBLING. My bed shook.

The mirror on my wall shuddered, and the floor rippled. The noise grew louder, like a freight train roaring through my room, threatening to rip it to shreds.

Earthquake!

I'd experienced earthquakes before. But nothing this strong.

The bed unexpectedly bucked and tossed me into an untidy heap on the floor. I scrambled up and mindlessly lunged for the doorway. Old instructions from school teachers pounded in my brain. My only coherent thought—get to the doorway. I'd be safe there.

The door smacked me in the back of the head. I staggered, knuckles white, clenching the door jamb. I wouldn't fall. *I wouldn't.*

I clung to the door jamb, and watched everything in my room crash first one way, and then the next. My laptop computer leaped off the desk and bounced off the carpet. Books flew across the room, tangled in my sheets, and one flew out the open window.

I heard Mom scream, and Dad's hoarse shouts, asking if I was okay. I couldn't answer. My tongue felt stuck to the roof of my mouth with terror.

Would I die? Would we all die? I hung on desperately.

It seemed for an eternity.

Slowly, the noise faded, and the bucking stopped. I realized I was kneeling on the floor. I scrambled up, shaking, not trusting the ground beneath my feet.

"Kay?" Mom screamed, stumbling down the hall. Her silver-blond hair stuck out in all directions, and she wore only a thin nightgown. Dad staggered behind her, wearing red boxer shorts.

"Are you okay?" he shouted.

I didn't know why he was shouting. His arm clamped tightly around my shoulders, and he glanced wildly about. "Theresa?" he bellowed. "Where are you? Are you all right?"

Silence.

Mom ran into my sister's room. She whirled back out, hand to her mouth, her eyes wide in horror. "She's not home."

"She's still *out?*" He peered at his watch and roared, "It's six o'clock in the morning, Helen! Where is that girl?"

"I don't know!" Tears trickled down Mom's pale face. Suddenly, her knees buckled, and she fainted. I don't know how Dad caught her before she fell.

"Grab some blankets," he ordered me. "And meet me downstairs."

Dragging a pink furry blanket, I staggered down the staircase. A complete disaster met my eyes. Everything glass had broken. Except, miraculously, the exterior windows. Books, vases—everything lay scattered in the tan and white living room.

"Tend to your mother." Dad shoved a wet washcloth into my hand. "I'm going to turn off the gas."

Mom lay still on the couch. Her eyelids fluttered, but she did not wake up. I cast a nervous glance at the walls and ceiling. No cracks. Structurally, the house still seemed intact. I breathed a short prayer of thanks to God, and for earthquake building codes.

Dad took over for me. "She's okay," he said, noticing my worried expression. "Her body told her to relax for a few minutes."

I wished I could relax. I was nervous. And strangely hungry. Legs feeling rubbery, I stumbled to the kitchen. Pots and pans lay strewn across the floor. Cereal was scattered in the wooden pantry. I grabbed a couple of bowls and scooped up what I could, and then joined Dad in the living room.

We ate silently, and listened to fire trucks roar down the street.

"I can't stand this." Dad disappeared for a minute, and returned with a radio. The electricity was off, but luckily the radio's batteries worked.

The announcer sputtered in. "Preliminary estimates put the earthquake at an 8.0 magnitude. The epicenter was located twenty miles east of town. It's unknown how many are injured. East Truesdale, especially along Driscoll, has virtually collapsed. There are fires, sewer splits, demolished houses and apartments..."

Mary lived on Driscoll. Horror welled within me. And where was Theresa?

Mom stirred awake. "Lucky Parrot," she whispered.

"What?" Dad bellowed, mad she wasn't making sense. But I knew his anger covered a deeper concern. His gaze, which rested on my mother, looked more worried and tender than I'd seen it in months.

"Lucky Parrot," I repeated. Comprehension dawned. "It's an all-night dance club. Is that where Theresa went last night, Mom?"

When she weakly nodded, dread seeped into my heart. The Lucky Parrot was located on Driscoll.

"Call, Winston," Mom urged faintly. "See if she's okay."

"I doubt the phone lines are working, Helen." But he picked up the old fashioned phone lying on the floor. He pressed for the dial tone twice, and his eyebrows rose. "Phone's working."

He dialed for directory assistance. Then he dialed again. "Busy," he explained. He hit the redial button. "Hello? Operator? Give me the number for the Lucky Parrot." He dialed more numbers. Finally, he hung up and tried his cell. He shook his head. "All I can get is a crackling sound."

Had the Lucky Parrot collapsed?

I suddenly couldn't sit still any longer. I had to do something. I ran upstairs, threw on jeans and an old T-shirt, and splashed water on my face. A comb through my hair, and I felt a little better. I didn't feel quite as shaky anymore. I clutched the doorway as an aftershock shuddered through the house. When it stopped, my knees trembled again.

Mom's shrill, accusing voice assaulted my ears when I descended the stairs. "Why don't you go look for her, Winston? My baby could be lying somewhere, hurt!"

"I'm going to find her, Mom," I broke in before Dad could explode. I hovered on the steps leading into the sunken living room. "I'll try to call Joyce and David. Maybe they'll help."

My parents fell silent again. Mom wept quietly. Dad looked stiff, like an angry, frustrated bull.

Miracle of miracles, I was able to contact David with my cell phone. Only crackling came when I tried Joyce's number. David offered to pick up Joyce and be at my house within the hour.

In the meantime, I helped Dad pick up the mess in the living room. After a bit, Mom felt well enough to sit up and direct.

The radio newscaster continued to broadcast the latest news. "Thousands of homes and businesses are destroyed in Truesdale. But amazingly, few reports of injuries so far..."

Jesus' words about the last days flooded my mind. Earthquakes, wars, famines, diseases. Each part of Jesus' prophecy was happening now. Unprecedented natural disasters were taking place in the United States. Earthquakes, floods... Were they signs? Was God warning our country to repent? In the Old Testament, weren't natural disasters a sign of God's displeasure and judgment?

When the doorbell rang, I answered it gladly. Anything for a distraction from Mom's thin, reedy commands, and Dad's sniping. Couldn't they get along? Especially now, of all times.

"Hi, Kay. Are you okay?" Joyce gave me a quick hug. "I can't believe this, can you?" She slipped by to hug Mom, too. She murmured to my parents.

David dropped his keys in his pocket. "Hey, Munchkin." He grinned awkwardly. "Glad you're okay."

He was happy to see me. A great relief rushed into my heart. I hadn't realized until this moment how much I hated the tension between us.

Tears sprang to my eyes, and my smile wobbled. "Give me a hug," I said shakily. I reached him first, and he pulled me into a warm, secure hug. His heart thumped quietly beneath his dark green T-shirt, and a sense of security washed over me. Everything would be all right now. It just had to be.

He released me the instant I pulled back. I managed a smile for my parents, who now stood in the doorway. "I'll give you a call if we find her."

"Be careful, honey." Worry puckered Mom's brows.

"Stay away from gas leaks," Dad said gruffly.

"We will, Dad."

We piled into David's car. Slowly, the old sports car bumped over the cracked street, keeping well to the right side. Every few minutes, fire trucks or ambulances wailed by.

The breeze blowing through the window bit into my skin, and I shivered. "It's cold."

"The heat spell finally broke," Joyce said.

"We'll have to stop here." David geared down to a stop. "Fire trucks are blocking the road."

Driscoll Street was a mess. Emergency vehicles parked catty-corner across it. Firemen pointed streaming hoses at blazing apartment buildings and businesses. Water, covered with a shiny, oily film, rushed down the gutters and into the storm drains.

The air smelled awful; of gas, acrid smoke, and the foul, gagging odor of broken sewer lines.

"This way." After several blocks, I turned left. If the phone book was right, the Lucky Parrot should be a block north of

High Street. A few steps later, Joyce spotted a huge plastic parrot lodged in a tree overhead.

"This must be it." The remainder of the black building smoldered, and half the roof had collapsed. The fear I'd been trying to ignore threatened to choke me. Was Theresa buried inside?

All of our recent squabbles suddenly seemed petty and pathetic. We were sisters. And I loved her. Tears burned in my eyes.

A yellow slickered fireman swam before my eyes, and rough hands shoved me away from the building. "This is an emergency scene, folks! Back off."

Joyce plucked at my sleeve. "Come on."

"But I have to..." I whispered, fixated upon the smoldering ruin. "What if Theresa's in there? Can't we do something? Can't we help?"

"Come on, Kay," Joyce insisted.

David's hands closed around my shoulders. Gently, he urged me to follow Joyce.

"Look!" I said. "Those people look like they were rescued. Let's see if Theresa is one of them."

I scanned the line of ragged, soot-faced people. Their fine garments were in tatters, and their hair stood on end.

Then I saw her. Sitting alone on the end, her white dress grimy, hair a tangled mess, and her face tear streaked.

I flew over. "Theresa! Are you okay?"

She glanced up, looking dazed, and broke into sobs when I hugged her. "How... How did you guys find me?"

In that moment, as tears streamed down both of our faces, I felt closer to my sister than I had in the past year. Theresa wasn't looking down at me anymore. She was a person, just like me, needing the comfort of her big sister.

"Jeffrey left me," she choked out, rubbing her eyes. "The jerk!"

"What happened?" David knelt beside us.

Theresa managed a watery smile, and brushed her palms across her black streaked eyes. "I...I don't know, really. The whole place started to shake. Then people screamed, 'Earthquake!' and stampeded for the door. Jeffrey was the first one out, and people were pushing me..." More tears filled her eyes.

"It was horrible!" she whispered. "I was afraid they would trample me, and the whole world kept shaking. It was a nightmare."

"Are you okay? Any broken bones?" Joyce asked. "Maybe we should get you to a hospital."

"No." Theresa staggered to her feet. We rose with her. "I'm okay. Really. I just need a good bath."

I thought she might still be in a state of shock, and David must have wondered the same thing. He put a supportive arm around her shoulders. "My car is a few blocks away. We'll have you home in no time."

With a smile, Theresa rested her head against his shoulder. "Thank you," she whispered, and faintly fluttered her lashes.

I nearly rolled my eyes. She'd almost been killed, and she was already flirting with David! He didn't seem to notice, though, and I was too grateful she was alive to let it bother me for long.

"Mary lives down there." We had reached High Street again, and I pointed down the next block. "I'd like to see if she's okay."

"Let's find out," Joyce agreed immediately. "Are you up to it, Theresa? Or do you want David to take you to the car?"

Theresa put on a brave smile; perhaps for David's benefit. "I'll come."

Three apartment complexes remained intact on this block of Driscoll, and Mary's was one of them. I spotted Mary standing outside alone, arms hugged around herself. She looked pale, and in shock.

"Mary!" Joyce called. And suddenly the three of us were hugging and crying. Theresa joined in, too. In the end, our sobs turned to sputtered laughter. Maybe it was the relief of being alive, and together. I wasn't sure, but I couldn't seem to control myself. We sat down on the dry grass and laughed hysterically. Tears streamed down our faces. David looked on, looking a bit alarmed.

"Are you finished?" he said, when our gales of laughter quieted.

"This is how we cope, David," Joyce chortled. "Don't stare at us like we're freaks."

With a head shake, he wandered toward a growing commotion next door.

"My kitty!" a child wailed. "I hear her crying. Please save my kitty!"

That ended our laughter. We hurried over.

Most of the apartment had collapsed, but part of one wall remained, including a broken window and a slanted piece of roof. I noticed a small, dark space at ground level. Everyone else stared in the window.

"I see her." I ran forward, and scooted on my hands and knees toward the crack. I pressed my eye to the hole. Dust trickled out, making me sneeze. "Here kitty," I crooned. "Here kitty kitty. I'll save you."

A rough voice spoke behind me. "Better get away from that wall, miss. One more aftershock, and it'll fall right on your head."

I ignored this and continued my croon, waggling my fingers invitingly through the opening. "Here, kitty."

Suddenly, I felt a light, prickly paw bat my hand. "Kitty want to play?" I caroled. Another pat, and my fingers curled around the kitten. Triumphantly, I rolled out and smiled at the tearful little boy. "Here's your kitty, honey."

The child grabbed the cat. His blue eyes shone in his tear streaked face. "Thank you!" He ran off.

"You're quite the heroine." Grinning, David gave me a hand up. "Didn't know you had such a heart for stray kittens and children."

"Just goes to show there's a lot you don't know about me," I returned pertly, dusting off my jeans. Theresa, Joyce and Mary stepped up as the crowd dispersed.

"You know," Joyce said, "Kay has the right idea. We should stay and help out. A lot of people need it."

"I agree." David glanced at us. "I'm in. What about you guys?"

We all agreed, except for Theresa, who looked surprisingly regretful. "I'd like to stay. But all I have to wear is this." She looked at her soiled white dress.

"What size do you wear?" Mary said. "Maybe I have something you could borrow."

"Great!" Theresa followed Mary indoors.

The rest of us set to work. We helped people sift through the rubble for belongings, and swept up debris. Whatever help people needed, we gave it. Thankfully, at least in our area, no people were missing, and few were seriously injured.

Next door, a radio blared, giving us incremental updates on the earthquake's aftermath. Frequent bulletins warned us not to drink the water.

Luckily today was cool, but in a few hours my throat felt parched. We'd worked our way down one block, and had started in on another.

Dressed in jeans and an old red and white checked blouse, Theresa sat on a curb with the rest of us, taking a break. She'd stuck pretty close to David all morning. Her crush on him was becoming glaringly obvious to all.

Now she smiled at him and swiped a hand across her brow. "Whew! Have I got a hangover. Beer and earthquakes are not a good combo."

David offered an amused, almost paternal smile, but said nothing. Theresa took a fresh tack, and turned to include Joyce in the conversation. "This is so much fun, though. I've never met so many people in my life."

I spied a bottled water truck parked a few blocks down State Street—rumors were, water was being given away for free. "I'm going to get water. Do you guys want some?"

Everyone did.

As I hurried down the block, I suddenly remembered my parents. We'd been so busy for the last few hours that I'd forgotten them. They must be frantic by now. I pulled out my cell phone. Luckily, it rang through on the first try. "Hi, Dad. It's Kay. We found Theresa."

"Is she okay?" Mom's high voice shrilled in my ear.

"Yes, she's fine," I assured them both. "We're going to stay here and help out, okay? Right now, we're at State and Driscoll. Don't worry. We'll be back this evening."

My parents weren't enthusiastic about the idea, and urged us to return home soon.

Then I waited in the long line at the water truck. I glanced at my watch. Eleven-thirty. The others were probably wondering what was taking so long. I accepted two small water bottles from the man on the truck.

"Hi, Kay." The deep bass behind me was familiar. So was the oddly put together, arresting face, and the vibrant personality lurking behind the half smile.

"Mitch!" I grinned. "What are you doing here?"

"I used to live here." His lips twisted.

I noticed the water bottle in his hand and edged away from the crowded truck. "What happened?" His muscled form looked neat; a little dirty, but not like he'd just escaped from a collapsed building.

He fell into step beside me, heading back toward Driscoll. The foul odor of sewage filled my nostrils again, making my stomach heave.

"I was up in the hills watching the sun rise when it hit."

"What were you doing up there?"

The black eyes smiled a little. "Trying to draw."

"More of those strange pictures?"

"No. I haven't drawn another one since I saw you last. Just trying to figure out the ones I've drawn already." He fell silent for a moment. "I've been wondering about something, ever since our last talk."

"What?"

"What..." he seemed to choose his words carefully, "will be the sign that the Great Tribulation has begun?"

His intensity startled me. So did his fascination with this subject. Odd. A Jewish man consumed by the same topic that I was.

"Jesus said there would be wars and famines, earthquakes, and pestilences—diseases. All would get worse, like labor pains, as the day draws closer."

"You mean like now." His gaze swept the street.

"Yes. Some people think the Tribulation could start soon. But first, something else will happen. The Bible seems to say that all the Christians will be taken from the earth and transported to be with Jesus just before the Tribulation starts. That's called the Rapture."

His piercing gaze narrowed. "Interesting," he said finally.

"Kay! Where have you been?" Joyce demanded. Everyone crowded around me. David swiped a water bottle from my hand and took a lengthy swig.

"Hey," I cried out. "You big pig. Leave some for the rest of us."

Joyce stared at Mitch. "Hi," she said, as straightforward as usual. "I'm Joyce. We're Kay's friends."

I introduced Mitch. Theresa automatically dimpled, and David firmly shook his hand. I could tell the two instantly felt at ease with each other.

Recognition glimmered in Mary's smile. "Hi. We have a class together. Calculus. Two o'clock. Mr. Cassidy?"

Mitch's serious gaze melted when he smiled. "Right. I remember you."

Mitch was eager to jump in and help. He'd already dumped the few belongings he'd salvaged from his apartment at his parents' house, so he was free to help out. With him on our team, the clean up went a lot faster. He was a tireless worker.

He and David struck up an immediate friendship, and I was happy to see Mary talking with him, too. As we worked, his serious expression relaxed, and he joked easily with the others. I was glad Mitch fit in so well with my friends.

"I'm hungry!" With a limp wrist, Theresa tossed a stick onto the pile. One o'clock had come and gone, and now she stood between Mitch and David. She couldn't seem to help her compulsion to flirt with every available guy.

"A homeless shelter is down the street." Joyce wiped her brow with the hem of her stylish overshirt. "They're giving away free food."

"You could come to my apartment," Mary said. Her brown eyes shone. She looked happier and more self-confident than I'd seen her in a while. "I have plenty of food."

"Sounds great." David stretched his arms wide, and tossed me a grin. "I sure could use another bottle of water about now."

"Get it yourself," I retorted sassily, and sailed by him, with my own water bottle clutched firmly in hand. Again, I was really glad things had returned to normal between us.

A commotion behind me made me turn, though. Joyce smiled a welcome to a newcomer, and Theresa stood right beside her. The trim, light-haired young man was dressed in jeans and a faded cotton shirt. His blue eyes flashed at me, and my heart jumped with surprised pleasure.

"Trent!" I hurried over. "What are you doing here?"

His arm went around me and hugged me tight, in a shoulder to shoulder hug. "I was worried about you. I called your house, and your parents told me you were down here." He smiled. "So I decided to come."

"I'm so glad you did." I turned to my friends. "You know everyone, don't you? Joyce, Theresa, David..." my gaze slid by his unsmiling face to Mitch. Uncomfortably, the scene when Trent and Mitch last saw each other flashed through my mind. The computer lab, with Randy and Tim. "And Mitch."

Trent released me and stepped forward to greet Mitch. His smile looked friendly. "Good to see you again."

Mitch's black gaze measured Trent and sharpened. Why?

Unease slid through me, but I quickly dismissed it.

I turned back to Trent. "We're about to have lunch at Mary's apartment. Have you eaten?"

"Yes." He seemed to ignore the unfriendliness prickling from both David and Mitch. "But I'll keep you company." As we climbed the stairs, though, he threw Mitch a hostile glance and murmured to me, "I didn't know you were good friends with that guy."

I shrugged, but continued to smile. "We're acquaintances, really. I keep bumping into him."

"Kind of kooky looking, isn't he?"

I pulled away from Trent. "No. I don't think so. He's a very nice guy."

Trent squeezed my hand, instantly contrite. "Sorry. I guess I feel at a disadvantage. He rescued you at the lab, but I wish it had been me."

I understood how he felt. But still, his comment bothered me.

Lunch, consisting of cheese sandwiches and water, was half over when the front door slammed open and Jack strode in. He stopped in mid-stride, and his black, devilishly winged brows shot up as he took in his crowded apartment.

A long, uncomfortable silence ensued. Then a smile curved his thin lips. His jet eyes hardened to flint.

Mary quailed when he stared at her.

His false smile returned to us. "Hello. I guess you're friends of Mary's. I'm Jack."

"Hi, Jack," we chorused, and Mary introduced each of us. Jack's gaze rested on my sister, and a sordid smile twisted his lips.

"Nice to meet you," he said deeply. His meaning rang clear to all, especially to poor Mary.

"Hello." Theresa's gaze turned cold. It froze the sleazy smile off his lips.

Jaw tightening, Jack turned to his girlfriend. "Mary?" He stalked for the bedroom door. Clearly, she was to follow.

When the door closed behind them, we milled uncomfortably.

"What a jerk!" Joyce stated. Although the electricity was out, she jerked open the refrigerator door and stored the remainder of lunch inside. Then she slammed it shut. But the sound couldn't drown out the roar from the next room.

"*Ask* me the next time you plan to hand out *my* food to complete strangers, okay, Mary? Is that too much to ask?"

A despairing murmur.

Jack's strident voice overrode hers. "We're in an emergency, you know."

"Fine!" Mary's voice rose. "But next time don't make a pass at my friends, Jack. I don't come on to yours."

A sharp laugh snapped. "Right! Like they'd want *you*. Listen, missy. I'm doing you a big favor by taking care of you, and that brat you're carrying. I'll —— well do what I want!"

I jumped when the door crashed open. Jack stormed out the front door and slammed it behind him. The whole apartment shuddered. We stared at each other, stunned, not sure what to do. The guys looked outraged. Theresa and Joyce looked horrified.

I broke out of my stupor first. "Poor Mary!" I gasped, and hurried to comfort my friend.

Mary sat weeping on the double bed. Her thin hands covered her face. I hugged her. "Don't you dare listen to him!"

I glanced at Joyce, who hovered in the doorway, and silently pleaded for her help. I didn't know what to say. What *could* I say? Mary's boyfriend had just berated and belittled her in front of all her friends.

Finally, as a result of our encouraging, supportive comments, Mary's tears stopped. But I worried about her. Did Jack always treat her that way? Why did she love him? Why did she stay with him? No wonder her self-confidence seemed so shaky. Jack treated her like dirt.

That afternoon, back at work, we quietly cleared debris for the first hour or so. Gradually, though, we lightened up and began to tease each other again.

David and Mitch paid Mary a lot of attention, and I was glad. She needed positive male contact after that scene with Jack.

Trent and I worked together. We worked companionably, and didn't talk much, but I enjoyed his company. As the afternoon wore on, more space separated us as we picked up the scattered bits of wreckage.

We had one flash of excitement when the water streaming down the gutters suddenly caught fire and flames leaped up, scorching the toe of my shoe black. Before I could leap back, a strong hand gripped my arm and pulled me back against a tall, hard body. Instinctively, I knew who it was.

"You okay, Cricket?" David murmured.

I nodded, and he let me go before I was ready, relinquishing me to Trent, who'd run up. My heart pounded in shock. How could water catch on fire?

"See, Miguel, you had to have that cigarette, didn't you?" screamed a dark-headed girl.

Trembling a little, I watched the fire roar by. For a moment, I felt like a child again, in need of a secure, comforting hug. Shouting firemen rushed up and sprayed chemicals over the gas slicked water.

Trent whistled sharply. "Wish I had a camera right now!"

Swiftly, the blaze died before my eyes.

Aftershocks continued to rumble beneath our feet all day. Despite myself, I stiffened every time, even though I knew I was safe outside. I steered clear of anything that could fall on me.

When dusk fell, we finally stopped working. Trent's face was dusty, and his cotton shirt grimy. But his eyes sparkled, and charmed my tired spirit. He pulled out his wallet and flicked through the bills.

"Anyone for pizza? My treat!" he called down the pebble strewn sidewalk. It was growing dark fast, and the street lamps weren't working. Most emergency vehicles had already pulled out, leaving the street quiet and deserted.

"Sounds wonderful!" Theresa staggered up with a smile. I hadn't seen her this happy, messy and dirty in years.

David—reluctantly, it seemed—tossed down a board and trudged up to us. He looked tired. His dark hair was rumpled, and his dusty green T-shirt had a tear at the sleeve. "Sounds great," he agreed. "I have a couple bucks I can throw in."

"I have to go to work," Mary said regretfully. "But I car pool with a friend. She'll be here soon."

We said goodnight to Mary at her apartment, and walked to a pizza place a few blocks west, on State. Candles flickered in the windows, so we guessed, correctly, that it was open.

The menu was warm soda and pizza baked in a wood burning oven. The place smelled delicious, and my stomach rumbled as we slid down red vinyl benches. We faced each other across the candlelit, checkered table cloth. Girls sat on one side, and guys on the other.

We agreed on three large pizzas. Two pepperoni, and one vegetarian. It was good. Cheese stuck to my plate as I lifted a slice to my mouth. The strand caught on my chin, and when I pulled the slice back, another cheesy glob stretched away and snapped back on my lip. Laughing at myself, I wiped the mess off with my napkin and smiled across at Trent.

"Can't take you anywhere, Kay!" His lips curved intimately.

"Let's plan something for next Friday night," Joyce spoke beside me, interrupting my dewy-eyed smile.

"Bowling," David snapped out, and tossed a pepperoni slice into his mouth. He didn't look at me.

"That sounds fun," Theresa sighed.

"You should come," David told her seriously. Chewing.

"Really?" Her eyelids fluttered. "I'd *love* to. But I don't want to intrude..."

I seriously doubted that.

"No intrusion." He smiled, his teeth flashing white.

Trent glanced at his gold watch. "Yeah, sounds fun. How about it, Kay?"

"Sounds fine to me." My eyes narrowed a bit at David. "As long as we don't go to the Comden."

"Why not?" An edge bit through his words. "Add a little excitement to the evening."

"We'll go to the Sienna." Joyce put a quick end to the discussion.

"Great." Rising to his feet, Trent gave me an apologetic glance. "I hate to go, but I have to run an errand on the north side of town." Amid the chorus of goodbyes, he whispered, "See you on Monday."

Soon after, Mitch rose to his feet and tossed a bill onto the ever-growing pizza payment pile. He had to go, too. "Nice meeting all of you. Helped turn my day into a good one."

Everyone chorused warm goodbyes. "See you on campus," I called out. A final grin, and he was gone.

Joyce started stacking plates. "What a nice guy, Kay. Where did you meet him?"

"Oh..." I glanced at David. I'd never told Joyce the story. "He helped me out of a tight spot one day. And I've seen him once or twice since. He's an artist," I offered.

"What does he draw?" Theresa's light blue eyes looked considering.

I didn't know how to describe Mitch's drawings, and hesitated for a moment. "He draws landscapes, and portraits, too."

"Ready to go?" David had finished counting the money. He stood.

It was pitch dark outside, since the streetlights weren't working. And chilly, too. Only the thin sliver of the moon playing tag with wispy clouds gave light to our path.

Groups of people with flashlights brushed by us, heading toward Driscoll. Most were young men, but I saw a few women. Most wore dark clothes. A shiver slipped through me. Gangs? Or people returning home for the night? Whatever the case, they didn't bother us.

David's car sat alone near the curb, and Theresa and I piled into the back. More groups of people thronged the streets now, and headed toward the decimated, Driscoll section of downtown as we drove to Joyce's house. I wondered what was going on.

"See you guys in church tomorrow. And you at the gym, Theresa." When Joyce stepped onto the curb, Theresa sprang out and secured the front seat, next to David.

It bothered me; perhaps because I felt embarrassed for her. David obviously wasn't interested in her, and yet she kept throwing herself at him. Why?

I eyed him furtively. Yes, he was definitely handsome—it was a fact I couldn't seem to ignore anymore—but not movie star material, which was the sort of man my sister usually dated. And he wasn't sophisticated or charming—well, maybe he did have a boyish charm. He wasn't a partier, either, which appeared to be my sister's favorite activity.

We rolled up to my house. Bright street lamps beamed in my neighborhood, and warm light glowed behind the curtained living room window.

"Want to come in?" Theresa dimpled at David.

"Maybe for a minute. I'd like to see how your parents are doing."

I trailed them up the driveway, feeling strangely like an outsider. Theresa grabbed David's arm and walked close by his side. He didn't seem to mind, and that disturbed me, too. I didn't like any of these feelings. At all.

Theresa poked her head in the door. "Mom, Dad! We're home!"

"In here, dear," Mom called from the den.

I didn't realize how grubby we were until I saw my parents reclining in their easy chairs, watching the news. Mom wore a camel-colored pants suit, accented with silver bangles on her wrists, and her cap of silver-blond hair shone. Dad wore his usual creased slacks and polo shirt. We were muddy and dirty. I sniffed the air delicately. And we stank, too.

"Isn't that awful!" Mom tossed to Dad, her gaze glued to the set.

"Where's the police?" Dad rumbled.

They didn't realize they were communicating without shouting.

Mom noticed us. "Thank goodness you're home," she exclaimed. "I can't believe what's happening down there!" Her gaze fell to our clothes, and she visibly blanched with horror.

Then her gaze swiveled back to the white-haired anchorman on television.

Mick Murray spoke, and his sonorous notes rang like the tolls of doom. "With the fall of night, looting and rioting escalated on the east end of town. As you know, that's the area worst hit by the quake. Live-Eye Helicopter One is at the scene."

Black night, dotted with leaping orange flames, darkened the television monitor.

"Businesses are blazing out of control. Looters have set fire to a hundred buildings so far..."

The screen switched to a different aerial view. The helicopter's spotlight illuminated swarms of people breaking into businesses and streaming away with televisions, radios, blankets—whatever could be stolen.

"Two hours ago, at six p.m., the Governor declared Truesdale a disaster area. National Guard units are on their way. They'll help our police take control of the situation... This just in. Mayor Jenkins is ordering a curfew. I repeat, Mayor Jenkins is ordering a dusk to dawn curfew. Effective immediately."

Mick pretended to shuffle papers, buying time for the television prompter writers to update the latest news. "Officials warn all Truesdale residents to boil their drinking water. Lines have become infected by broken sewer mains..."

"Ugh!" Theresa snorted. "That is *sick.*"

"We have bottled water." Mom rose to her feet. "Speaking of that, does anyone want tea or coffee? I have a pot on the stove."

"I'd die for some tea, Mom," Theresa sighed.

"Anyone else? David?" At his shaken head, she disappeared.

Dad turned his chair so he could face us. He smiled at David. "Did your dad's business get much damage, son?"

"No." He glanced at the T.V. "I just hope the looters stay clear of the north side of town."

"Me, too." Dad's business was located in north Truesdale, also. His thick silver eyebrows rose. "I must say, I'm real impressed with you young people, helping out those folks who lost their homes. We caught a glimpse of you on T.V. a while ago."

"You did?" Theresa squealed. "We were on T.V.?"

Dad's leathery face creased. "And they had a close up of you, pumpkin, sweeping the sidewalks. Made me real proud."

"She was a real trouper." David gave her a warm smile. Theresa glowed.

Unaccountably, jealousy welled within me. I tried hard to ignore it. What was wrong with me? Theresa did deserve a pat on the back.

"I have to go," David edged toward the door. "I just wanted to see if you and Mrs. Jameson were okay."

"Thanks, David." Dad smiled. "Come back again soon. Don't see you around the house much these days."

"Oh, well..." He finally flicked a glance my way. It was opaque. "I've been pretty busy."

"I'll see you out." Theresa shepherded him toward the door. He didn't bother to say goodbye to me, and it stung. What was his problem tonight, anyway? First, he'd seemed distant at the pizza place, and now he was acting cool toward me. I'd thought we were getting along again.

I stuck my head into the hall. "'Bye, David!"

His reply was an uninterested mumble. Hurt, I jerked back into the den.

"He's a nice young man," Dad said approvingly, and swung around to reach for the remote.

"He's bullheaded," I returned crossly. Now I was pretty sure what his problem was. Trent. He was blowing my relationship with Trent way out of proportion. Again.

Enough was enough. I would confront him tomorrow in Sunday school. We'd have this thing out, once and for all. I was sick of his disapproving looks and condemning ways. Either he could see things my way, or he could take a hike.

Dad's laugh cut into my rash, hot-headed thoughts. "Don't want a man who's easily pushed around. You're pretty strong-minded yourself, missy."

I frowned. "At least I'm not hardheaded."

Theresa wailed to Mom in the kitchen, "How will I get this *stench* out of these clothes?"

I spent the next hour cleaning up the mess in my room. My laptop was first. It still lay on its side on the carpet. I inspected it carefully, certain it must be broken, but didn't find any cracks. So I turned it on. And it worked! A minor miracle. One that soothed my uncomfortably tangled, hurt feelings a bit.

As I lay in bed that night, feeling a little better after spending an hour reading Revelation and my prophecy books, I listened to the noises rumbling outside my window. Chopper blades beat the air. News helicopters relayed live pictures to the flickering T.V. downstairs.

I stiffened when the house shook again. My bed trembled beneath me, and a picture swayed on the wall. Another aftershock. I couldn't get used to them.

Outside, a fire truck wailed by, rushing to a new emergency. Driscoll had turned to bedlam. New fires were starting every minute, not to mention the looting. It looked like a war zone.

My mind returned to the united, neighborly effort we'd all taken part in today. Why had things turned sour tonight? And I remembered lunch, and Jack, and how horribly he had treated Mary. I felt awful for her. She needed to get out of that relationship.

Lord, I pray that Mary would turn to you, so you can heal her heart. Please give her wisdom about Jack. And thank you for keeping Theresa safe this morning. Thank you for answering our prayers.

Sunday

"We don't have to boil the water anymore," Theresa announced on Sunday morning. "Our side of town is clear." Smiling, she brushed by me, and headed upstairs. Yesterday's camaraderie lingered. I was glad about that.

Crunching cereal, I rested my elbows on the back of Dad's recliner and watched the morning news with my parents. It looked like they hadn't budged an inch since last night.

"Rioting continues in eastern Truesdale. Looters are robbing stores and homes. They're taking anything left behind by the quake. Victims of the earthquake are suffering. They have no running water, little food, and the shelters are overflowing. Officials fear disease outbreaks as a result of the impure water, and broken sewer lines. People have nowhere to go."

"This is just *awful!*" Mom murmured, taking a sip of tea.

"We're lucky our house was built to withstand a seven-point-five earthquake," Dad said. Last night, the estimated strength of the quake had been reduced down from a magnitude 8.0 to a 7.5. Dad had found cracks in the stucco outside, but that appeared to be the worst of it.

He glanced back at me. "You going to church today?"

"Yes." I moved to the couch to sit while I finished my breakfast. Today I wore pearl gray jeans and a pretty, silky print blouse. I didn't want to wear a dress because I didn't know what I'd come across outside. The city was a war zone.

"Be careful." Mom frowned.

"I will."

"Say a prayer for me—for the earthquake victims, I mean," Dad said.

I was surprised that he'd mentioned prayer. It wasn't one of his favorite subjects. "You can pray right here, Dad."

He grunted. "I don't feel I have God's ear here. He hears prayers best in church."

"No, Dad. That's not true. God is omnipotent and omnipresent. That means he's all seeing, all knowing, all powerful, and is everywhere at once. He can hear your prayer here, just as well as he can in church"

Mom spoke up. "Maybe we should go to church, Winston." But her expression faltered under Dad's incredulous look.

"Mom, why don't you come with me?" I wasn't surprised, however, when she cast a quick glance at Dad and said, "Thank you dear, but no."

Dad snapped open his newspaper. The discussion was over.

I touched his shoulder as I went by. Quietly, I said, "I'll say an extra prayer for you, Dad. See you guys later."

Few people were in church today. Again. Any damage done to the church last night, during the riots, had already been cleaned up.

I sat with Joyce and her mother, but did not see David. I hoped he would show up, for I still wanted to talk to him. Enough was definitely enough.

Pastor Warner spoke at length about the earthquake, people's needs, and God's provision. We prayed, and then he announced that the church was starting a food drive in conjunction with the homeless shelter down on Driscoll. The food would be delivered next Saturday.

"I like that food drive idea," I told Joyce as we wandered to our Sunday school class. "But I wish our college group could do something, too—something extra. Those people are still going to need help after Saturday."

David spoke up behind me, startling us both. "We could put on a dinner for the homeless."

Joyce spun around. "Great idea! I like it. We could give the dinner the weekend following the food drive. Then we could help the earthquake victims two weeks in a row."

"Food drive? Dinner for the homeless?" Smiling, Bobby ushered us into the Sunday school room. "What's this I hear?"

Chattering breathlessly, Joyce gave him a brief outline.

Bobby pursed his lips. "I like it. Let's talk about it more on Wednesday night."

I didn't have a chance to talk to David during class. He sat on the other side of Joyce. My stomach fluttered with sick apprehension, visualizing the confrontation to come. Did I really want to do it? Was *I* the one blowing everything out of proportion?

At the end of class, my fingers felt cold and clammy. I rubbed them together. I'd never felt afraid to talk to David before. What was my problem?

David picked up his Bible and glanced at Joyce. "I need to help my dad at the shop. See you guys on Wednesday night?"

Joyce did not look up from her purse, which she briskly rifled through. "Sure. See you then. Oh," she looked up. "If you get any more ideas, let me know."

"Sure." He swung away and headed for the door. He hadn't looked at me. In fact, he hadn't spoken directly to me all morning.

It hurt, terribly.

Legs trembling, I quickly followed him. He'd slipped out to the parking lot before I caught up. I darted and whirled in front of him, forcing him to stop. "What is your problem?"

He drew back, clearly startled. Then his dark eyes flashed, which startled me. David rarely got mad.

Jaw clenched, he brushed by me to his car. Then he turned. He knew exactly what I was talking about. "You want to know what I think? I'll tell you. I think you're making a big mistake with Trent."

"Why? Because he's not a Christian?"

A cool breeze ruffled a lock of hair across his black, frowning brow. "No." His voice sounded tight. "Yes... No." A muscle flexed in his jaw. "It's not about that. At all."

"Then *what*?"

"I'm trying to tell you to be careful!" He glared toward the street for a moment. When he looked back at me, the hard mask had fallen from his eyes. They were tender. Pleading. "I don't want to see you get hurt. The guy is slick, Kay."

"Oh, stop it!" Quick tears prickled in my eyes. "You're just saying that because..."

"I'm your *friend*. All right? I want you to be happy. But I'm afraid he's going to hurt you." I didn't have to hear the ring of sincerity in his deepening tone to know he was telling me the truth.

But I didn't care. I felt strangely torn apart inside, and my conscience burned, too. Unfortunately, that erupted into angry, defensive words. "You know, I *know* what the Bible says about being yoked with unbelievers, David. Okay? But I'm not going to marry Trent. We're just going out. We're only *friends*. Okay? What is the big deal?"

I felt him withdraw from me, but I could not stop. I hated myself, even before I said, "I'm going to do what I'm going to do, so stop being so...so judgmental. If you can't be supportive, then leave me alone!"

"Fine." The word was quiet. His car door slammed.

Knees trembling, I leaned against a nearby truck and watched him leave. My cheeks felt hot, and my fists clenched.

The rest of the day was not good, for I was in a bad mood. When I went to bed I finally admitted one thing to myself. I didn't want to hear what God had to say about my deepening relationship with Trent. I knew the basic friendship was not the problem. But based on what others had told me, and my own jumbled feelings, I had a strong idea what might be.

That night I prayed rebelliously for Trent and me. And I prayed that he would give his heart to Jesus.

And I prayed for my relationship with David, too. For that was what hurt more than anything else. I hated how I had spoken to him, and I hated that he was angry with me still.

Monday

I POUNDED ON THE BATHROOM DOOR. "Hurry up! I have a nine o'clock class."

I felt out of sorts this morning, and it manifested itself in a poor mood. Reading the Bible had not helped, and I had cut short my prayer time. I was upset; perhaps childishly, but I couldn't help it. Why had God put Trent in my life? Why did I have to like him so much?

"*Yeesh!* Take it, already." Theresa flung open the door. Her chilly blue eyes glanced disdainfully at my rumpled hair. "Looks like you need it."

I splashed cold water on my face, and then stared at my frowning face in the mirror. Real attractive, Kay. Real sweet and loving and kind. Suddenly, I felt horribly ashamed of myself. What was the matter with me?

Slowly, I dried off my face and acknowledged the bitter truth piercing my heart. I was rebelling against God, and it was making me feel sick. Worse, I was taking it out on David, Theresa, and everyone else, too. Could I be any more selfish, or shallow? I didn't like myself. At all.

Didn't God always want the very best for me? Why wouldn't I listen to what he had to say about Trent?

I'm sorry, Lord.

The soft terry cloth twisted in my fingers as I stared at the mirror. Shadowed green eyes stared back. It was time for me to face the truth. I needed to learn exactly what God said about the subject.

In my room, I looked up "yoked" in my Bible's concordance, and turned to 2 Corinthians 6:14-16. Heart feeling heavy with dread, I read:

> *Do not be yoked together with unbelievers. For what do righteousness and wickedness have in common? Or what fellowship can light have with darkness? What harmony is there between Christ and Belial? What does a believer have in common with an unbeliever? What agreement is there between the temple of God and idols? For we are the temple of the living God. As God has said: "I will live with them and walk among them, and I will be their God, and they will be my people."*

Slowly, I closed the book. It didn't specifically say anything about dating or marrying an unbeliever. But God's thoughts on the subject of being yoked, or joined together with an unbeliever were clear. And the quote Joyce had thrown at me two weeks ago made it clear a Christian shouldn't marry an unbeliever. But what about dating one? How did that fit in?

I felt convicted, but I still liked Trent. I still wanted to go out with him.

Resting my head in my hands, I prayed. *Lord, I'm sorry for my poor attitude. If you don't want me to go out with Trent, please tell me why, specifically, so I can understand it. And if you don't want me to go out with him, please change my heart, too, so I don't want to go out with him anymore. I want to do what is right, but I feel so confused. Please help me, Lord.*

I felt a lot better after that prayer. I wasn't running from God anymore. I was trying to face up to the truth. Half-heartedly, at least.

At school, all anyone could talk about was the earthquake.

"Did you have riots in your neighborhood?" I asked Mary.

"No. Thank goodness. I guess they figured we didn't have anything left worth stealing." Her expression shadowed. "It was scary, though, with no electricity. It was so dark. Gangs of people streamed by outside, and I felt even more scared when I smelled the smoke. But at least Jack was with me."

"I can't believe how he treated you on Saturday."

Mary looked away. "He apologized for that. On Sunday, he gave me a huge bouquet of flowers, and said he was sorry for being such a jerk."

I couldn't help but say what I thought. "Maybe it's not my place, but why do you put up with him? Why don't you leave him? It sounds like he puts you down all the time. You deserve much better."

"I love him." She stared down at her twisting fingers. "You don't understand, Kay. He's really not that bad."

I wished I could believe that.

Mary changed the subject. "We got our electricity back last night, but we still have to boil our water. What a pain!"

"I know."

Her face softened, and she touched her stomach. "The baby's been moving a lot since the earthquake. I guess he decided it was time to wake up."

The loud, rolling snap of the projection screen caught my attention.

Mr. Carlisle grinned. "Today we'll learn about cults. Who can tell me the difference between a religion and a cult? Or *is* there a difference?"

I frowned at the very question. How could he compare Christianity or Judaism to a cult? My hand flew up. When he nodded, I said, "Cults are destructive. They brainwash people."

"And how is religion any different?" he countered. "Both preach misinformation. Both twist their parishioners' minds so their sheep will blindly follow. Nonconformity means guilt. Acceptance means approval. Can you prove to me that Truesdale First Gospel is any different than your average cult, Miss Jameson?"

How did he know I went to Truesdale First Gospel? Had Tim told him? Or had he seen my T-shirt on that first day of class? My suspicion about his involvement in the hate group—and the dog poop on my car—again reared its ugly head.

"The gospel is about God's love for us, Mr. Carlisle. Salvation is free. It's given by God's grace. Not by our works. Cults preach the complete opposite. They demand compliance to their specific rules. They break down personal barriers between people. They attempt to control every area of their followers' lives. They subjugate their followers into compliance. Those are just a few differences."

My heart pounded. I wished I knew more about the subject, but I didn't like Mr. Carlisle's mocking suggestion that Christianity could possibly be equated to a cult.

"Other opinions?" Was his sarcastic smile accompanied by the barest eye roll? Or was I imagining things?

"I'll return your thesis statements on Wednesday." Professor William's hard gaze scanned the class, but lingered on me. "The earthquake interrupted my schedule. However, I did finish grading half of them last week. *Most* are acceptable." His pale eyes bored into me, and a smirk bared his teeth.

It seemed pretty obvious that he'd graded my paper, and found it lacking.

When he turned to the board, something flicked into the back of my head. It stuck. What...? My tentative fingers touched a wet, slimy object.

Ugh! A spitball.

I threw it on the floor, and with revulsion swiped my fingers against my jeans. A quick, angry glance over my shoulder revealed Randy and Tim staring at me. Tim's blank, flat eyes and Randy's vicious, curled lips sent a flash of fear through me.

They wanted to scare me. Gritting my teeth, I turned my back on them. I would ignore them. If they wanted more of a reaction, they wouldn't get it.

Trent slipped late into class. He sat one row ahead of me and one aisle to the right.

Throughout the hour, I glanced more than once at the back of his light, perfectly molded head. Having him nearby helped me to block out Randy and Tim and their infantile, malicious prank.

I felt oddly detached, observing Trent that way, and the feeling disturbed me.

I took in the side profile of his chiseled chin and nattily clad shoulders. He was very handsome. Classically so. And we had a number of things in common. Well, mostly journalism, it seemed.

Why did I like him? I mean really, why? What was the spark?

After class, I pulled my backpack up onto my shoulder.

"Kay." I looked up.

Trent's smile took me by surprise. My heart skipped a beat, and I found myself grinning back. His warm blue eyes banished my cold doubts like the sun melting frost on a warm winter day.

This was why I liked him. He was a terrific guy.

He slung a casual arm around my shoulders. "How was the rest of your weekend? Did you and your friends go back and help on Sunday?"

"No. It was too dangerous, with the rioting. And I had homework to do."

"How's your paper coming for Dr. Williams' class?" He steered us smartly around a clump of giggling girls.

"Okay. I'll do more research this afternoon." And I'd go over my thesis statement again and try to figure out why Professor Williams had disliked it so much. I wished he'd returned it in class today, so I'd know specifically what I needed to work on.

Trent deposited me at the door to my next class with a dazzling white smile and a promise to see me on Wednesday.

I did like him. I just couldn't help it.

And why shouldn't I? He was a nice guy.

I knew that liking him wasn't the problem, though. Neither was being friends with him.

God's rules seemed too strict.

Today, the journalism lab was overflowing with people. It wasn't a bit like last time, when Randy and Tim had tried to steal my paper. I scanned the room, hoping to find an available computer. There. In the very back. I slipped onto a blue plastic chair positioned behind a battered metal table.

I tried not to think about Tim or Randy, or their disgusting spitball. I'd managed to ignore them during the remainder of journalism class today, but couldn't help but notice them staring and smirking at me when I'd exited with Trent.

They were plotting something new. This certainty lodged in my heart. But what could it be?

Their malice scared me.

I tried not to dwell on it. I still hoped that if I ignored them enough, they'd lose interest and leave me alone. Maybe that wasn't completely realistic, but I didn't want to live in fear, either. I'd be careful, and make sure I was never alone with either of them.

I punched in my computer code and settled down to work. I could access all the information I needed by computer. Library materials, information sources around the world—all were available at my fingertips, through the library's multiple subscriptions to news sources and journals.

That afternoon, I learned that the violent crime rate a decade ago was about half what it was now. Five years ago, it was two-thirds what it was now. It was getting worse, steadily, just like I'd thought.

I jotted notes for my article, and saved it in my account on the school computer system, and on my flash drive, too. Done. Finally. It was five o'clock.

As I reached for my backpack, my blouse caught on the table corner. A slight tug, and a horrible *rippp* rent the air.

Feeling sick, I twisted the teal sleeve around. A three corner tear gaped at the elbow.

My favorite blouse was ruined.

Tears threatened as I marched from the room. Frustration overwhelmed me. Suddenly, all of the bad events of the last week lumped together to form a hard knot in my stomach.

Everything kept going wrong. Why?

Mom noticed my torn sleeve the instant I entered the kitchen.

"What happened, Kay?" She wiped her spotless hands on a cotton towel. A casserole sat on the stove, ready to be baked.

"Oh," I briefly closed my eyes, "I caught it on an old metal table."

"Isn't that your favorite blouse?" Mom's frosty expression softened.

"Yes."

"Let's buy you a new one. Would you like to go shopping?"

"Now?" Surprised, I glanced at the casserole.

"Never mind this." Mom whisked it into the refrigerator. "We'll leave Dad a note." She looked expectantly at me. "Do you want to go?"

"Yes!" I smiled, and my spirits lifted. Mom still had the power to make me feel better, just like when I was a child, and a kiss could heal the hurt.

We collected our purses and drove toward the mall. Anticipation ran high in both of us—until a traffic jam on Market Street slowed us to a complete halt.

After waiting patiently for a long while, Mom leaned forward. Her silver bracelets clicked against the wheel. "*What* is the hold up?"

I rolled down the window and craned my head outside. "I see a fire truck up ahead."

"I don't see smoke." Mom cast a quick glance at her watch. "How many blocks up is it? Maybe we can go around them."

"The truck is three blocks away." But when I saw more details, a cold feeling clamped like a fist around my heart. No. It couldn't be. *And yet it was in the exact location...*

"Mom. Can we park the car and get out? I'm afraid..."

With a frown, she inched over to a free parking spot and I leaped out. Her heels clicked behind me as I sprinted over the next few blocks.

My flying steps rocked to a halt. Fire engines flanked Truesdale First Gospel.

"Oh, my heavens!" Mom gasped, catching up. Her hand fluttered to her mouth. "Whatever could have happened?"

I hadn't told her about the attacks on the church.

"At least it's still standing," Mom's comment faded from my ears as I dashed across the street. She was right. The church was still intact—except for one blackened corner. Fire crews poked at this, making sure the fire hadn't spread inside the building.

A multitude of people milled about outside. Mom made a beeline to talk to Mrs. Warner, but my footsteps continued to carry me, unthinkingly, toward the six foot scorch mark.

"That's far enough, miss." A fireman with bristling white brows stopped me from coming any closer. His eyes looked kind. "We're making sure the fire is out."

"Of course." Disbelief made me feel oddly detached from the scene. I stopped beside a young tree about twenty feet from the building. It had lost all of its leaves during the recent frost. It was bare—except for a bit of black cloth hanging from one of the limbs.

"Kay?" Joyce appeared. "Can you believe this?" Her voice shook with rage.

"Was it the hate mail people again?"

"I don't know!" Her words snapped like fractured chalk. "But this has gone too far! The police had better do something. So far, they've been useless."

"Have they found any clues?" The question made me remember the odd piece of cloth hanging from the tree. I slipped over to it. "Look."

"What?" Joyce's glaring eyes rested on the bit of black cloth. It looked unremarkable at first. Until one looked closer. It didn't hang haphazardly. Instead, it was tied to the tree in a square knot. And tucked beneath it was a note.

Just for a second, the black cloth caused a memory to flutter, and then it was gone.

Joyce eyed it. "This is unbelievable. The police found a strip of black cloth when the church was vandalized, too."

"We'd better tell someone."

Within seconds, we'd rounded up the police and Pastor Warner, and we all clustered around the bit of black material. A policeman wearing gloves carefully untied the knot and unfolded the paper.

"'Stop preaching about Jesus, or you die.'" His mouth twisted into a dubious smirk. "Is this for real?"

Unfortunately, it was. And it had just become crystal clear that our church was the victim of a systematic series of hate crimes.

By the time Mom and I decided to head back to the car, Joyce had fallen ominously silent. She didn't want to talk about what had happened. We left her standing alone, her arms folded as she watched the firemen poke at the burn mark.

I understood how she felt. Helpless. And unspeakably angry to be made a victim of the hate mongers.

Who were they? And what did they hope to achieve?

Again, a memory niggled at the back of my mind. Closer now. A clue? But whatever it was, it just wouldn't jog into place.

The long ride to the mall was broken only by Mom's sharp comments that traffic was awful.

My enthusiasm for shopping finally revived when we entered the bright, clean building. What a stark contrast from the smoky scene at the church—almost like we'd entered another world.

Mom's steps quickened as we headed for her favorite department store. She was in her element.

The scent of new clothes and fresh perfume filled my nostrils as I followed Mom's swift, clicking footsteps to the back wall. Obviously, she expected to find the perfect blouse right away.

But we didn't. Isn't that always the way when you have a mission in mind and money to spend?

We shopped high and low. Finally, we found a dusky rose blouse that I liked, and Mom held up a soft copper one.

"This would look wonderful on you, Kay," she insisted.

A few minutes later, I stared at myself in the mirror and smoothed the copper top into the waistband of my jeans. It did look nice. I liked it, but I also knew Dad was worried about money. Would he be mad if Mom bought both blouses for me? Would it start another argument?

"Do you like it?" Mom looked hopeful. Eager.

I hesitated. My conscience warred with my desire for the blouse. "It seems like a waste to spend Dad's money on both. I just need one," I said weakly.

Mom's smile froze, and her eyes turned to glacial chips. "If that's the way you feel."

I'd hurt her.

"We'll buy the rose blouse." Lips thinned, she stalked from the dressing room.

The drive home was quiet and strained. I tried to explain. "I did like it, Mom. Thank you for offering to buy it for me. I just didn't..."

"It's all right, dear," Mom said clearly. She looked ice shell thin. And brittle. By bringing up Dad, I'd alienated my mother. Did she feel I gave more weight to his opinion than to hers? I didn't know, but I felt deeply unhappy. I'd hurt my mother, yet again. Couldn't I ever do anything right?

At home, Mom promptly disappeared into the kitchen.

Bag in hand, I slipped into the den, where Dad sat watching the evening news. His usual shot of rum rested at his fingertips, and the paper lay in his lap. A political commercial played on the screen: Woodward against Gilroy.

"Hi, Dad," I said softly, and patted his stocky shoulder. One step later, I collapsed into Mom's comfortable chair.

"Hi, honey." His hazel eyes smiled over his reading glasses. He noticed the bag. "Been shopping?"

"I ripped a blouse at school, so Mom bought me a new one." I showed it to him.

Dad smiled approvingly. "Nice color for you, pumpkin. How was the rest of your day?"

Relieved that he wasn't upset with the purchase, I relaxed. "Okay." I told him about the church, and we discussed it for a few minutes. He was upset about it, too.

Just for a moment, I wondered why it was always so easy to talk to Dad.

But then I knew why. I felt comfortable with him; unfortunately, more than I ever did with Mom. The realization made me feel guilty.

Why did I keep hurting Mom? It's not like I wanted to, but things kept turning out that way. It made me feel sick inside. Like a failure.

Mick Murray's face flashed onto the screen. "Officials announced that cholera broke out in east Truesdale today. Officials are afraid the abominable conditions will deteriorate even further. They voiced concern that typhoid and dysentery could be close behind. Medical teams have been dispatched to the worst hit areas.

"Hundreds of homes were declared condemned today, forcing out tearful residents, who insist they have nowhere else to go."

Earthquakes, diseases... As the scenes flipped across the T.V., a verse from Matthew 24 slipped through my mind. "All these are the beginning of birth pains."

Was the Truesdale earthquake one of the many birth pains Jesus had predicted? What about the cholera outbreak? What about the escalation in crime?

I stared at the television screen, not really seeing it, and pondered the information I'd learned today about crime rates here, and around the world. All worse. Much worse than a decade ago. And natural disasters seemed to strike constantly these days. Were things getting worse? *Is the end really near, Lord Jesus?*

Unshakable conviction gripped my heart.

It *was* near. Nearer than I imagined. The thought was overwhelming. Awe inspiring. And I remembered that David had recently said he felt convinced of the same thing.

And yet, what did that mean to me?

Clearly, again, a small voice spoke to my heart: I needed to tell my family about God, and my friends, too. I needed to be the kind of person God wanted me to be.

I felt like I was far from that person right now. I seemed unable to love the people closest to me. Why? What was wrong with me?

That night when I went to bed, my Bible fell open to Romans 7:21-25.

So I find this law at work: When I want to do good, evil is right there with me. For in my inner being I delight in God's law; but I see another law at work in the members of my body, waging war against the law of my mind and making me a prisoner of the law of sin at work within my members. What a wretched man I am! Who will rescue me from this body of death? Thanks be to God—through Jesus Christ our Lord!

That described me perfectly. I wanted to do what was right, but I kept saying the wrong things, or losing my temper. I kept hurting Mom's feelings, I'd shouted at David, and the list could go on and on. But the Apostle Paul had had the same kinds of problems. They were normal. And the hope was, Jesus could save me.

Please change my heart, Lord. Please help me be a faithful witness to my family and friends. Please love them through me. And please strengthen me so I can follow your will and do what is right.

I felt a little better then, and lay quietly, thanking the Lord. A gentle peace washed through my heart. Jesus still loved me, despite all of my failures.

After a while, I flipped to Revelation 6:12-14. I'd read something last night that had struck me, and I wanted to read it again.

I watched as he opened the sixth seal. There was a great earthquake. The sun turned black like sackcloth made of goat hair, the whole moon turned blood red, and the stars in the sky fell to earth, as late figs drop from a fig tree when shaken by a strong wind. The sky receded like a scroll, rolling up, and every mountain and island was removed from its place.

"...every mountain and island was removed from its place"? That would be an awful earthquake. Certainly a lot worse than the one that had just shaken Truesdale. A sudden urgency quickened my spirit.

Lord, please guide me in the coming days.
And please protect our church.

WEEK FOUR — PERSECUTION

"Then you will be handed over to be persecuted and put to death, and you will be hated by all nations because of me. At that time many will turn away from the faith and will betray and hate each other..."

MATTHEW 24:9-10

FUTURE

A PAINFUL GROWL in Isola's stomach pulled her attention from Kay's diary, and back to the present. Reluctantly, she glanced across the bare, scuffed gymnasium floor.

Cracked wooden bleachers had been folded back against the opposite wall, and empty white basketball backboards punctuated each end of the gymnasium. The hoops were gone. Probably ripped off long ago.

Three volunteers quietly shuffled at the far end of the gym, beneath the television monitor, and methodically set up cots so the elderly people could take their afternoon naps. But few had waited. The group nearest Isola already sagged in their chairs, mouths gaping. Snores rasped through the peaceful silence. Their thin, cotton clad chests rose and fell in shallow, rhythmic unison.

Her gaze swept the quiet hall. The soldiers were gone. Her stomach gurgled again loudly, insistently. The bright shade of gray outside the gymnasium door said it was afternoon. Her food token was valid now.

Isola crawled to her feet, stretched her aching back and straightened her cramped legs. It felt good to stand. It was a welcome relief from the hard wooden floor.

She glanced at the murmuring television monitor, which displayed a huge crowd of people. The camera zoomed in and focused on a few faces. Faintly, she heard, "One hundred and forty-four thousand Jewish men have come together to declare..."

Suddenly, her breath caught. Her eyes riveted to the screen. Had that been...? Was that...?

The camera panned back again, and she swallowed. Her throat felt suddenly dry and achy. It was Mitch. Over in Jerusalem. It wasn't clear if he was one of the 144,000, or if he was just one of the nearby bystanders who thronged the streets.

Tears flooded her eyes, and she took a step toward the monitor—as if by taking that step she could somehow bridge the distance between herself and her old friend; the only man on this planet whom she could trust.

Then the camera panned away, and he was gone. She could not help it. Hot tears spilled over her eyelids. Tightly, she squeezed them together and pressed a hand over her mouth, which twisted in a soundless cry.

Oh Mitch, how she missed him! Tears burned her cheeks, and she leaned back against the rough concrete wall, gasping softly.

Raw, half-forgotten memories flooded her mind. She'd last seen Mitch three years ago, when he'd entered the airport to board a plane for Israel. He'd been so full of mission and purpose.

He'd become a Christian shortly after Kay and the others disappeared. Nothing could have stopped him from flying to Israel.

Over the last few years, he'd sent Isola a few emails, but none in a while. She hadn't known if he was still alive, or dead. Christians were being singled out and killed in the Middle East, in Europe—all over. More tears filled her eyes. She feared—she ached for his safety. But what could she do? He wasn't a part of her life anymore.

Scrubbing her plaid work shirt over her eyes, Isola turned and stumbled for the door. She had to stay strong. Kay's diary had begun to peel away the tough layers that the last three and a half years had cocooned around her heart. But life wasn't the same anymore. She had to remember that.

After the dim light of the gym, the ashy gray sunlight seemed blinding. Automatically, she scanned the area. No soldiers.

People wandered on the street. Most wore torn, dirty clothes, and their eyes looked either vacant or hard. Her own eyes dry now, Isola gripped the notebook tightly and trotted for the food distribution center located near her home.

Again, she kept to the middle of the road, which meant accidentally bumping elbows with other passersby. The middle of the street meant safety; not only to her, but to other women and children. Although no one could be trusted, here she was safe from the worst of the lot, who either lurked in empty store fronts or old abandoned cars. And the soldiers wouldn't accost her in broad daylight—not with scores of other people thronging the broken streets.

It struck without warning.

The ground violently shifted beneath her feet, and threw her to her knees. A woman screamed.

Jerking and shuddering, the earth bucked, each shudder increasingly violent. Isola's body flew up, and crashed down on the cracked pavement. Again. And again, as though she was a rag doll. Arms clenched around her head, she closed her eyes and hung on, trying not to think. Trying to block out the terror soaring in her mind.

Her elbows and shins slammed repeatedly against the jagged asphalt, scraping against her tender skin. Tears gushed helplessly down her cheeks.

After long minutes, the motion slowed. She lay still, sobbing, until the hot pavement stopped moving.

People screamed and wailed in earnest then. Children cried. Machine gunfire spattered the early afternoon air.

Isola scrambled to her feet, scared of being trampled by a mob. But she had no reason to be afraid. People lay unmoving on the street, weeping, or moaning in pain. The legs of several were caught in new cracks in the pavement. Still in shock, she stood very still, and finally noticed that her arms were empty.

Hadn't she been carrying something? Fear, and the instinct of self-preservation, learned the hard way, spurted through her, drowning out concern for those around her.

The gun! A quick touch proved the gun was still wedged into her waistband, as was the Bible. Memory sparked in her fogged brain. The notebook! Where was it?

Wildly, she looked about, scanning the buckled pavement. Where was it?

Then she saw a flash of red, ten feet to her right. On wobbly legs, she stumbled over and snatched it up. For the first time, she noticed that her shirt was torn, and her arm scraped and bloody. But she did not feel it. Or care.

Behind her, a high sobbing caught her attention. A child lay face-down on the asphalt, with his arm caught in a deep crack in the pavement. Automatically, she slipped over to help.

"*Get!* Get away!" Someone seized her shoulder and shoved, hard. She staggered backward. A woman's black, hate filled eyes glared at her, framed by wild gray hair.

"He's my son, do you hear? Stay away from him!" Her breath smelled rancid.

Isola backed up, feeling sick to her stomach. She'd just wanted to help, but the woman didn't trust her. Just like Isola trusted no one.

She turned and stumbled away. Despair engulfed her. It was more than being unjustly accused and rejected by the child's mother. It was everything. She was sick of being afraid. Sick of constant disasters. Sick of how horribly wrong her world had turned.

The earth shuddered again beneath her feet, and violent, primitive anger surged.

The earthquake would not defeat her. Neither would this aftershock. Grimly, she staggered on. She would ride it out. She would conquer it.

The aftershock rolled to a stop.

Isola felt oddly victorious. She had triumphed. She would triumph over the next disaster, too.

This latest earthquake had caused little destruction. Tanks rumbled down the side streets, apparently unharmed. Most buildings already lay in rubble from the tremendous earthquake that had leveled most of Truesdale three years ago.

Today's earthquake had only left behind dust. And more rubble. A sardonic smile twisted her lips. She'd have plenty of work to do tomorrow. Sweeping was her job, assigned by the government. As payment, they provided her with a tiny apartment, a small bit of money in her bank account, and one meal a day. A fair deal, given the state of the economy.

Isola slipped into the downtown area. Recently, only one store window still boasted glass. Kruger's Yogurt. Fueled by curiosity, she cut around a throng of arguing men and stepped onto the sidewalk to pass by the storefront. Had the glass shattered this time? She sidestepped a gap-toothed old man who leaned against a withered tree.

No. The clear sheet shone dully, still intact in the hot, dusty air. Amazing. Kruger must have installed bulletproof windows.

Isola couldn't resist pausing to gaze at her reflection. She hadn't looked in a mirror in ages.

The face staring back at her was unfamiliar. It looked old. Like it had lived three lifetimes in the last three and a half years. She touched her straggly dark hair. Washed three days ago, it was now limp and dirty. Her face was filthy, and her eyes looked huge in her thin face.

The woman staring back at her looked soul weary and sad. A shapeless man's work shirt fell in sharp planes off of her thin shoulders. The washed blue and the large, gray criss-cross pattern weren't flattering colors for her complexion. Neither were her torn blue jeans, which had faded to gray. Her scuffed tennis shoes had seen better days. They'd worn down almost through the soles. She wore no socks. Holes riddled the only pair she owned.

A weight of depression settled on her, and Isola spun away. Did she really look like that? She looked awful. Old. She felt old.

She escaped into the street, fleeing the image she'd confronted in the window. Fleeing the reality that was her life.

As she neared the food distribution center, the smoky, acrid air turned foul. Gagging, she shoved her shirt sleeve under her nose. The sewer lines had ruptured again. Ugh, it smelled awful.

A giant rat scuttled across her path, probably disturbed from its lair by the recent earthquake. Shuddering, she scanned the street ahead. More rats headed for the vacant lot, which bordered the food distribution center.

Vomit rose in her throat. Disease was already rampant. Would it get worse now? Would the rats infest the distribution center's food supply? A large gray rodent scuttled across her foot, and she yelped and jumped back.

From the food distribution center, a long line straggled down the sidewalk which bordered the vacant lot, and stretched around the corner.

Her stomach gurgled. Everyone else appeared to be hungry, too. Heart sinking, she urged her suddenly sore feet to walk faster, and find her own place in line. The sooner she found a place, the sooner she would get her meal ration.

The end of the line was five blocks away.

Isola fell into place behind a black-eyed, muscled young man, and a woman with a toddler. Both ignored her. As if of one accord, everyone glared at the person ahead of them in line, as if wishing down fatal judgments on their heads. Resentment oozed like poison from each individual.

An old man and his wife crowded in behind Isola, muttering peevishly to each other. A block ahead, a tall, mean-looking blond man broke out of line and strode forward several places. He shoved an elbow into the small man standing there.

"Hey!" Their voices carried clearly in the still, putrid air. The smaller man's voice was high and indignant, and the blond-haired man's sounded rough and bullying.

Crack! The immediate, warning report of a gun.

An olive clad soldier, helmet in place, strode for the two struggling men. Another soldier jogged up and helped his comrade yank the two men apart. They marched the two across the street.

"Not a smart move," cackled the old man behind her. "Now neither of 'em will get supper tonight."

The military vigilantly patrolled the food lines.

The early afternoon sun beat down on Isola's head as she waited. Perspiration slid down her hot neck. Her tongue felt thick and dry. What she'd give for a little shade! But the trees in this section of town had dried to withered claws during the hot, dry winter. And thanks to the angle of the sun, the few standing buildings only cast a narrow strip of shade onto the crumbled sidewalk.

The line moved imperceptibly forward. At least an hour remained before she would reach the food window.

With a sigh, Isola glanced at Kay's diary. She could read more. Her initial guilt over reading it had disappeared. She was too involved in the story. Too fascinated to see her life, and the lives of those she'd been close to play out on the pages of Kay's electronic notebook.

Reading would help pass the time, and she wanted to learn more about Kay's research into the end times. Isola found it fascinating that the Bible events Kay had read about were happening now. The diary was answering a few of Isola's questions about why the world had changed so horribly in the last few years.

She folded the notebook open again. Her hunger for answers continued to grow.

WEDNESDAY

I COULDN'T SPEAK TO MARY TODAY, because she arrived late, and left class early. That didn't stop me from worrying about her, though. She looked desperately unhappy. Was Jack still abusing her? No wonder she seemed so unsure of herself all the time.

"Journalism is about facts, class," Dr. Williams impaled each of us with his pale, cold gaze. "Not warm fuzzies. Facts."

He spun to the board and the chalk snapped harshly. He wrote *Religion*. "This," he stabbed at the scribbled word, "has no place in journalism." His pale green gaze bored into me. "Can I see a show of hands? Any Christians in this class?"

Slowly, I raised my hand. A few others did, too.

A smirk twisted his lips. "I knew it." Pivoting, he snapped *preconceived ideas* on the blackboard.

"Kay is operating under this fallacy, class. Her preconceived idea is that the Messianic age is almost upon us. Thus," he stabbed at the board, "everything she writes uses this hypothesis as a conclusion."

I felt the stares of my classmates. How did Professor Williams know what I believed? The thesis statement I'd turned in last week hadn't mentioned Christianity at all.

Noting my discomfort, his lips hardened into a smile. "Listen to me, class. People who believe in fables have shut off their brains. And they won't make it in my class. I want facts. Sound hypotheses. Not half-baked religious ideas. No holier than thou attitudes. Is that clear?" He stared straight at me again, and tossed a red-marked page onto my desk. "I want your revised thesis on my desk by Friday."

My face felt hot. Now I knew the reason behind the strange looks he'd given me lately. He'd read my thesis early. Apparently, he'd been biding his time, relishing the idea of tearing me down in front of the entire class.

Out of the corner of my eye, Randy swam into my field of vision. He glared at me. Was it my imagination, or did glee burn in his murky eyes? Hostility seemed to bubble up all around me, oozing from each of my classmates. They hated me. They looked down on me.

I hunched in my chair. Of course, I was over-reacting. But the hatred felt so real, so palpable right then, that it was hard to ignore it.

Dr. Williams strode to the blackboard. "Today, class, we'll talk about facts."

I felt oppressed, as if a great weight of ridicule heaped upon my shoulders. *Why* did I feel this way? Clearly not everyone hated me—after all, I wasn't the only Christian in the class. But for some reason, my brain could not process that logical thought. I sank deeper into my seat.

I burned to tell Dr. Williams, Randy and Tim that they were wrong. That they were the ones who were blind. But I didn't, because I was afraid. I felt sick inside, and disgusted with myself for keeping silent.

When I exited from the classroom, I found myself boxed in behind Tim.

A burly elbow drove into my side.

Randy's low hiss electrified my ear, and shivered down my spine. "Guess that'll teach you, girly. Keep your religion to yourself. Hear? Or you'll pay the consequence."

"That's right," Tim sneered. "Keep your eyes open. You'll get a surprise sooner than you think."

I broke free and lunged right, toward the stairs, instead of toward the outdoor exit. Would they follow me?

No. The two gave me another vicious stare and disappeared outside.

Knees trembling, I leaned against the wall and hugged myself. What plans had they made for me? And why had the professor attacked me?

"There you are. Hey, are you okay?" Trent's voice drew me from my fearful thoughts. He stared at me, clearly clueless to what might be wrong.

"I'm fine." I pushed away from the wall and headed for the exit. Trent didn't know what was wrong. And obviously, *he* didn't hate me. Had I blown the incident totally out of proportion?

Trent caught up with me. "Are you mad old Williams cut you down?"

"Yes," I said tightly. And so much more, too.

"Why didn't you tell him off, then?"

I shook my head. Hadn't he felt the hatred filling the class? And it *had* been there. Tim, Randy and Dr. Williams hated me, and so did some of the others. And just because I was a Christian.

"I was afraid."

Trent hugged an arm around my shoulders and shook me a little. "Hey. Put it behind you. It's no big deal."

But it was a big deal to me. Trent just did not understand.

That disturbed feeling lingered all day. As a consequence, I wasn't in the best of moods when I got home, although I wanted to be. I wanted to break through the tension building between my mother, sister and me.

Why couldn't anything ever be easy?

"School's a breeze." Snapping gum, Theresa eyed me. Mom sat at the kitchen table, drinking a cup of tea. Quietly, I lay my backpack on the counter. "The high school profs built it up way too much."

"I'm glad you're not having a problem, dear," Mom said. "Hello, Kay. How was your day?"

"Fine." I poured a glass of apple juice. "But I have to rework my thesis statement for Current Affairs. The teacher didn't like it. Said the topic was too broad. He wants me to narrow it down."

Among other things. But I didn't elaborate. Earlier, during lunch break, I'd scribbled out a new thesis statement. Anger and resentment had pushed my pen. He wanted facts? I would give him facts. Facts he couldn't refute.

"Oh," Mom frowned. "I hope that won't be a problem."

"No. I've almost finished it." I relaxed against the counter. Both Mom and Theresa seemed friendly, and willing to include me in their conversation. A piece of paper lay on the table between them. "What's that?"

"Oh," Theresa's face lit up, and a dimple creased into her cheek. "We were deciding what clothes I should wear Friday night."

"Oh? Who are you going out with?" Helpfully, I peered at the page. Red dress, pink outfit, jeans...

"David, silly. Remember?"

Surprise caught in my throat. "What? David asked you out on a *date*?"

"We're going bowling. Remember? With your group."

Comprehension dawned. "Theresa, David didn't ask you out. You looked like you wanted to come, so he asked you to join us."

She arched a haughty brow. "I've been on hundreds of dates, Kay." Her tone sounded condescending. "I know a date when I see one. And this is definitely a date."

The disturbed feelings I'd been fighting all day abruptly twisted and intensified, although I couldn't say why. It threw me further off kilter. "It is *not* a date. How can you say that? He's not even picking you up."

A flicker of uncertainty crossed my sister's features, but she shrugged. "It's a casual date. I'll meet him there. He'll probably drive me home. You'll see." She cast me a slightly pitying look. "Do you have a date?"

The confused feelings continued to eat at me. David wasn't interested in Theresa, was he? It hadn't seemed that way on Saturday. Theresa was setting herself up to be hurt.

"I'm going with Trent."

"Good." Theresa smiled again. "Maybe we can double-date, and share a bowling lane. That would be fun, wouldn't it?"

"Yes." I managed. "That would be a lot of fun."

Throughout dinner, all Theresa could talk about was her "date" with David. It bothered me, but I said nothing more about it.

"Hi, Kay." Joyce greeted me in the foyer of the church. Her black mood from Monday seemed to have disappeared, although the scar on the church remained. "Want to help sing on stage tonight? Laura isn't feeling well."

"Sure."

"What's wrong? You're frowning."

"I am?"

"Yes. What is it?"

An exasperated puff of air escaped. "Nothing. Really, it's silly. Theresa said something and it's bothering me. I don't know why."

"Have you talked to her about it?"

"It's impossible to talk to her. All she talks about is clothes and men. Like at dinner tonight. All she could talk about was her so-called 'date' with David on Friday night." I drew an exasperated breath. "But he didn't even ask her out!"

Joyce gave me an odd look.

"I feel like I can't have a real conversation with her. Like she can't—or won't—see below the surface. It's frustrating."

"She's not as bad as you think." Joyce eyed me kindly. "I talk to her a lot at the gym. Your mom, too. They're both relaxed there. More so than at your house. We talk about all kinds of things—not just clothes and men."

"I never see that side of them." Again, a feeling of failure nagged at me. "Maybe they feel more comfortable with you than with me." Pain glimmered. What was so wrong with me? Why did my mother and sister get along better with my best friend than with me?

Joyce's sympathetic face did not take the sting from her next words. "Sometimes you can come off as pretty intense, Kay. As if you've got all the answers. Maybe it intimidates them."

"*What?* I don't feel that way. In fact, that's how *they* seem to me."

"I don't know." Her mouth twisted sympathetically. One of the sound technicians beckoned to her, so she took a step backward. "Are you and David still fighting? Maybe that's the real reason why you're upset with Theresa."

"No." At least, I didn't think so.

"I don't know, then. Look, I've got to go, okay? See you later."

But now I felt worse than I had before.

I wandered to the stage and glanced up at David. He stood fiddling with the guitar strings, making sure it was in tune. His dark brown eyes met mine, but before I could smile, his unreadable gaze fell away. He was wholly intent on listening to his guitar.

Heart feeling heavy, I climbed onto the stage. Our fight in the parking lot still loomed between us, and I hated it. More than anything, I wanted things to be right between us. I knew I needed to apologize, but found I just couldn't yet. Wouldn't that be saying he was right about Trent?

Maybe he was right. And maybe I was being childish by burying my head in sand and not facing up to the truth. But I couldn't accept it. Not yet.

I felt alone and depressed.

We clapped and sang songs to the Lord, and by the end I felt a little better. It helped to get my mind off myself and onto Jesus, and how marvelous he is.

When we'd settled down in our pews, Bobby jogged up the stage steps. His smile looked brighter than I'd seen it in weeks.

"Evening, everyone. Glad to have you here!" His grin stretched to include everyone filling the sparsely dotted pews. "Got some good news and some...*mmm*," he pursed his lips, "not so good news. Here's the good news. Pastor approved our idea of putting on a dinner for the homeless. It'll be a week from Saturday.

"I'm sure all of you have heard about the fire at the church. Well, the damage was minimal. We can praise the Lord for that."

"That's great!" I glanced at Joyce with relief.

But her face looked stony. "They still haven't caught the criminals."

A motion from Bobby drew my attention back to the stage.

His square dark hands rested on the podium, "The bad news is about the FGA—First Gospel of America. I think most of you know our church is on probation. That means we have to clear *all* of our public relations events through them. Today Martha got a nasty call from their national headquarters in Sacramento."

Martha was the church secretary.

"Turns out the FGA got wind of our food drive plans. They're angry because we didn't run it by them first."

"Will they let us do it?" Sophie Li spoke up.

"Yes. They will. Luckily, they like the idea of helping the earthquake victims. But they gave Martha a threat. Said the next time we don't consult them, they'll withdraw all funding from our church."

A murmur broke out, and Bobby fell silent for a few moments to allow us to digest the news.

"How did the FGA find out?" I wondered. "And *why* in the world are they so mad at us?"

Joyce jerked a shoulder. "I don't know."

It made no sense at all. Then David's theory about Oak Woodward and the FGA's political aspirations returned to mind. Was the FGA trying to put on a good face for the public?

I mused, "Maybe the hate crimes make them look bad."

"And those things are our fault?" Joyce shot back.

"No, of course not. But maybe they think so. I mean, think about it. We're the only church which has been attacked multiple times by hate crimes. They must wonder why. Maybe that's why they're trying to control us."

"Sounds pretty far-fetched."

I ignored her pooh, pooh attitude. "But we *are* the only church which has been vandalized, Joyce. *And* had a fire. And graffiti..."

"Stop it!"

I stared at her.

Her lips pressed tightly together. "Look. I don't want to talk about the fire. Or the vandalism..." her voice rose. "*Anymore*. Okay?"

Bobby cleared his throat, loudly.

"What's wrong?" I whispered. "Are you okay?"

"Yes!" Arms folded, she directed her attention back to the stage.

I couldn't help but feel concerned. It seemed as if Joyce might be taking the attacks too hard; as if they'd been personally directed at her. That was understandable, but unhealthy.

Bobby's voice broke into my thoughts. "We need to have the right attitude about this, folks. What does the Bible say about submitting to authority?"

The group fell silent. A few studious types flipped through their Bibles, but most, like me, stared at Bobby, waiting for him to tell us.

Bobby's lips quirked into a smile. "Titus three, verses one and two. 'Remind the people to be subject to rulers and authorities, to be obedient, to be ready to do whatever is good, to slander no one, to be peaceable and considerate, and to show true humility toward all men.'"

His smile softened in sympathy. "Sometimes that's hard, isn't it? But we know God's way is always the best way. Right?"

At the end of the meeting, Joyce gave an announcement. Now she appeared calm and collected. All traces of anger were gone—or tightly suppressed.

"Anyone interested in helping out with the homeless dinner, come meet me at the back of the church. And food drive volunteers need to show up at the church on Saturday morning at seven o'clock."

After chatting with a few acquaintances, I headed for the last pew, where a little group had clustered around Joyce. David hovered on the outskirts, balanced casually on the edge of a nearby pew. He paid no attention to me as I slid up. His gaze was fixed upon Joyce, who spoke impassionedly.

"...we have to do *something*! The city is doing nothing. And the state government is moving too slow."

"We need to raise money," Anne Triglori said.

Joyce snapped her fingers. "Of course! We could expand the homeless dinner. We'll make it a fundraiser, too. Then the poor people could come and eat. Donors could come, too, if they pledge a certain amount of money."

"We'd need to advertise it." Sophie pulled on her jacket.

"Flyers," David spoke up.

"A speech!" Joyce's gaze riveted upon me. "Kay, you could give a speech on campus."

I could?

"You have access to all the mikes and sound equipment through the journalism department," Joyce explained. "I'll okay it first with the school administrators. Then you can ask your department for the equipment. Free advertising!" Her eyes sparkled. She was on a roll. "And I'll get tickets printed up that we can sell for the fundraiser."

Everyone liked those ideas. But I didn't. Visions of throngs of hostile people swam across my fertile imagination. Randy and Tim led the pack.

I stood on a little platform, and they screamed at me, mocking me. Throwing tomatoes...

"You okay?" David's voice sounded rough. "You're as white as a sheet."

My hands felt clammy. "I don't think I should give the speech."

His mouth twisted into a shadow of its old, carefree grin. "Never thought I'd see you scared of speaking in public, Kay."

Was he mocking me? "Well, maybe you don't know me as well as you think you do."

And maybe I didn't know myself, either. What was wrong with me? Why was I so paralyzed by fear?

His smile faded, but his dark eyes pierced me. He did know me well. He knew something was bothering me. But he didn't ask what. And that hurt. Of course, whose fault was that? Mine. I was the one throwing up walls and being as prickly as a porcupine.

I felt lonely, and twisted up inside with unhappiness. I missed the long, easy talks we used to have. But I didn't know what to do to change things back, short of swallowing my pride and apologizing. Unfortunately, I didn't feel ready to do that just yet.

Thursday

While I ate breakfast and read two chapters in Luke this morning, the phone rang. It was Joyce, and she bubbled with too much enthusiasm for that hour of the morning.

"I talked to Administration on campus. They said the speech is okay with them. So it's scheduled for Friday at noon, on the plaza. Okay? Will you go to your department and okay it with them?"

My stomach gave a queasy lurch. "All right."

"If there's a problem, call me back. I'll let people know what's going on." Joyce clicked off.

"Who was that, dear?" Lowering her magazine to the table, Mom peered at me over the top of her reading glasses.

"Joyce. Apparently, I'm giving a speech on Friday." Slowly, I put down my cell phone. "It'll advertise a food drive and fundraiser our church is putting on for the homeless."

"What a wonderful idea! You'll do great, honey."

"Thanks, Mom." I said weakly. It *was* a good idea. So why didn't I feel more enthusiastic about it?

On campus, I said a half-hearted prayer, and stopped by the journalism department office to explain my request to the secretary. To my extreme surprise, permission was immediately granted.

"Two people from the journalism department must take responsibility for the equipment." Lois' pen rested on the form. "Who will help you?"

"Umm, Trent. Trent Johns," I improvised. I didn't know if he would help, but he'd probably be fine with the idea.

"Fine. Fill out this form, and return it to me before you check out the materials."

"Thank you." Still a bit amazed by how easy it had been—red tape was legendary at our college—I wandered into the hall with the form in hand. And nearly ran into Dr. Williams.

He moved smartly out of my way. "Hello, Kay." His light green eyes gleamed with barely concealed malice. "Hope you've reworked your thesis."

"I have."

"Good. I'll expect it tomorrow." He gave me a condescending smile and strolled away.

I frowned after him, itching to say something snarky. Thankfully, for once in my life, my mouth remained wisely shut.

Feeling at a loose end, I wandered outside. I didn't have class for another twenty minutes, since I'd arrived at school early to ask permission for the equipment.

I scanned the wide, grassy plaza. People dotted the lawn, eating lunch and enjoying the cool, crisp September day. Glossy green leaves fluttered in the breeze, and the sky overhead was a deep, brilliant blue.

It was a beautiful day. But I had no one to share it with. No one to talk to. Loneliness made me feel empty inside. Trent wasn't on campus, Joyce was too busy, and David was mad at me, which I understood completely.

I was about to toss my backpack beside a tree when a white sketch board, half hidden behind a burly oak tree a few yards away, caught my eye. Curious, and feeling hopeful, I walked closer.

I smiled. "Hi, Mitch."

He looked up, his left brow still quirked high in concentration. His intense expression relaxed into a grin. "Hi, Kay."

"What are you drawing?" I moved closer, hoping I wasn't being too nosy. But he didn't seem to mind, and even tilted the sketchbook so I could see better.

"What do you think?"

It was another of Mitch's odd pictures. Once again, I found my attention riveted to the page. Black, bold marks sketched out a burning person tied to a stake. Daggers inscribed with the words "hate," "evil" and "lies" stoked the fire, and smoke ascended to heaven, forming angry thunderclouds.

"Wow." A deep shiver slipped through my spirit.

"I know."

"It looks like a person being persecuted."

"I agree."

"I feel like that person," I blurted. "I'm afraid to talk about my faith." Then I wished I'd said nothing; I wasn't being burned at the stake, after all. My problems were miniscule by comparison.

Mitch's left brow rocketed. *"That's* hard to believe." His lips twisted in amusement. "You're sure not afraid to tell me what you think."

"But you're different. You're interested in what I say. At least, I think you are."

"I am interested." His intense black gaze rested on me. "Why are you afraid to talk about your faith?"

"I don't know." But after taking a deep breath, I decided to let it all tumble out. "Yesterday, my professor ridiculed me because I'm a Christian. He did it in front of the whole class." The torment washed over me again, sharpened by meeting Dr. Williams in the hall a few minutes ago. "I felt like everyone in the room hated me. Then two guys—the same ones from the journalism lab—threatened me. I was afraid to stick up for myself, and that's not like me."

Mitch fingered the charcoal stick. "You were scared. That's understandable." He hesitated for a moment. "I've been persecuted too, Kay. It is scary. But fear has a way of blowing the incident out of proportion."

"I felt overwhelmed. I didn't know what to do." It felt good to talk to someone who understood. Trent certainly hadn't. He hadn't even tried.

"Don't feel bad about it. Just remember something. You're never as alone as you think. Most people are not bigots. They're on your side."

And God was with me, too. I'd forgotten that yesterday. I hadn't even prayed.

I managed a smile. "Thanks, Mitch." I felt better. Mitch understood how I felt. And he'd given me some practical advice.

His serious gaze returned to the sketch. He tapped it. "What do you think of this? You've been telling me about the Great Tribulation. Does this fit in, too?"

I quickly reviewed the various Bible prophecies I'd read recently.

"The Bible does say persecution will be horrible during the Tribulation. Revelation has verses about it. Do you want to hear them?"

Although his shoulders appeared relaxed, Mitch's gaze looked tense, and watchful. "Why not."

"Okay." I opened my Bible to Revelation. "I remember three different quotes. The first one is chapter six, verses nine through eleven.

"'When he opened the fifth seal, I saw under the altar the souls of those who had been slain because of the word of God and the testimony they had maintained. They called out in a loud voice, "How long, Sovereign Lord, holy and true, until you judge the inhabitants of the earth and avenge our blood?" Then each of them was given a white robe, and they were told to wait a little longer, until the number of their fellow servants and brothers who were to be killed as they had been was completed.'"

"Who killed them? And who are they?" Mitch interrupted.

"They're Christians."

He frowned. "I thought you said all the Christians would be taken away—raptured?—before the Tribulation. So why are Christians living through the Tribulation?"

"Other people will become Christians after the Rapture. During the Tribulation," I explained. "Wouldn't you, if you saw things happening that were prophesied thousands of years ago? But those Christians have to go through the Tribulation, because they missed the Rapture."

"Oh." He stared at his drawing, and absently shaded in an area with his black charcoal stick. "What do the other verses say?"

"Umm... Revelation seven, verses nine, thirteen and fourteen. This takes place after the fifth seal I just read about. But I'm not sure when, exactly.

"'After this I looked and there before me was a great multitude that no one could count, from every nation, tribe, people and language, standing before the throne and in front of the Lamb. They were wearing white robes and were holding palm branches in their hands....

"'Then one of the elders asked me, "These in white robes—who are they, and where did they come from?"

"'I answered, "Sir, you know."

"'And he said, "These are they who have come out of the great tribulation; they have washed their robes and made them white in the blood of the Lamb."'"

I looked up. "This verse is hard to understand. It says that these people came out of the great tribulation. I'm not sure if that means they'll all die during the Great Tribulation, and that's how they'll come out it, or if it means something else—like maybe some die, and maybe others persevere through it. It also doesn't say if, or how many of these people might have been persecuted and killed. But I wonder how many might have been. So, I guess that's a question mark. I just realized I have more questions than answers about that verse.

"And the last verse," I finished up, "is Revelation thirteen, verse seven. It's talking about the beast—the Antichrist to come.

"'He was given power to make war against the saints and to conquer them. And he was given authority over every tribe, people, language and nation.'"

I closed my tan Bible. "I guess that's why I was thinking the Christians in the previous verses were persecuted and killed."

"So this Antichrist is the one who kills the Christians," Mitch commented.

"I think he's responsible for a great deal of it, if not most of it," I agreed.

"Interesting." Mitch wrapped the charcoal in a square of cloth and set it in a flat, worn cardboard box. "Here's a question for you, then. Why are you so afraid? No one's trying to kill you for your faith."

"I know." Mitch was right. No one would kill me for talking about my faith. Where was my courage? All I'd received were a few threats and hostile looks. "I'm glad I ran into you, Mitch. You've helped me see things a lot more clearly."

"Glad I could help."

I motioned to the grassy area behind me. "I'm going to give a speech tomorrow. Our church plans to hold a food drive for the earthquake victims."

"I'll be there." He smiled, seeming to understand that this change in topic directly related to my fears. "What time?"

"Twelve." I felt inordinately grateful I'd have at least one supportive person in the audience. "But I'll probably set up at eleven-thirty."

"I can help," he offered instantly.

My heart felt lighter than it had in days. "Thanks, Mitch." How lucky I was to have found a friend like him.

The talk with Mitch inspired an idea about how I could refocus my article for Current Affairs.

In the journalism lab, my fingers flew over the keyboard. Professor Williams wanted focus? I would give him focus. My article would still center upon crime and how it was getting worse, but I'd concentrate on hate crimes. Specifically, persecution against Christians. I'd certainly experienced enough of it first-hand, and so had my church.

I whipped out a new thesis statement, and then spent the next several hours researching new avenues of information for my article.

I drove home at five, pleased with the information I had found. Dr. William's nasty criticism had proved quite helpful. My article would be good. A real eye-opener for my professor, I promised myself.

"Curfew and martial law were lifted today in east Truesdale," newscaster Mick Murray droned. "But police and National Guard units remain on alert in case more rioting occurs.

"While problems tone down at home, trouble spots continue to sizzle throughout the world. In Azerbaijan today..."

Dad sank down in his easy chair. He'd just returned from his daily walk. His hazel eyes smiled at Theresa and me. We sat on the couch. "How was your day, girls?" He lifted a shot of rum to his lips.

"Good." Theresa shifted uncomfortably. Ever since I'd joined her in the den, she'd appeared to be on edge.

"Date all set for tonight?" Dad closed his eyes and rested his neat silver head against the leather seat.

"I'm not going out." Theresa tilted her chin, as if to fend off any wondering comments. She'd only been out once this week—a record for her. "I'm resting up for my date tomorrow night." Her uncertain blue gaze flickered my way.

Again, Theresa's claim of a date with David disturbed me. She was going to get hurt. But if she refused to face the facts, I couldn't prevent it.

"Actually," Theresa sounded hesitant, "I was wondering, Kay, if I could get a ride with you to the bowling alley tomorrow night."

Surprised, I said, "Sure."

"Thanks." She looked away.

I struggled to find something else to say to continue the conversation, but Theresa jumped up. "I'm going to help Mom in the kitchen."

Disturbed, I wondered if Joyce was right. Was I hard to talk to? Did I come off as a know-it-all, like Joyce had suggested?

Lord, please heal my relationship with my sister, and with my mother. Honestly, I feel like I'm the one who doesn't fit in. That they're looking down at me. Please break down the walls of pride and anger in my heart, Lord, and fill me with your love and compassion.

My heart felt heavy as I stared at the yellow sliver of the moon hanging outside my bedroom window later that night. Even though I didn't feel very good about myself, I knew the Lord still loved me. He would work out everything for the good.

I just woke up from the strangest dream!

It seemed so real. Colors were so brilliant, and sharp and clear. I'd never felt so alive; so...*there.* Here's what I dreamed:

It was Sunday. Mid-morning. Suddenly, I heard a great, panicked commotion, like a rushing, thundering herd. My back yard filled to overflowing with cats and dogs. They leaped over the fence and crowded toward the house.

I suddenly stood outside. They flowed by me, in a steady stream into my yard. I knew they were fleeing—coming to me in their distress.

Perplexed, I asked God, "Lord, why are all of these animals crowding into my yard?"

He answered me, "Take them in."

"But I don't have enough room."

He said, "Take them in."

So I took them in. Hundreds of them, into the house to protect them.

Protect them from what? And how? I awoke before I could ask God.

What a neat dream!

Was the dream from God? If so, I'd have to trust that he'd reveal what the dream meant, when it was time. He wouldn't leave me confused.

I felt perplexed, but above all, excited. Had God just spoken to me?

How much he loves me, even though I'm not perfect!

One thing was clear in my heart when my eyes finally closed again. I had to remain obedient to God to the end. His ways were far above my own, and I had to trust him always.

FRIDAY

"OF COURSE I'LL COME HELP OUT!" Mary seemed happier today than she had all week. Hopefully, it was a sign things were improving between her and Jack. "What time will you set up for the speech?"

"Eleven-thirty. The speech is at twelve." My palms felt cold and clammy with nerves. In only three hours, I'd speak in front of the entire school. This morning I'd sketched out a rough draft of what I wanted to say. Just the facts, that was all, I promised myself. Then it would be over.

"Don't worry." She laughed at my wrinkled brow. "You'll do just fine."

"You'll do great!" Trent's royal blue eyes sparkled at me. "I can help, but I'll get there late. I have a test at eleven, and I'm sure it'll last until the last minute of class."

"I put your name on the permission form," I confessed. "Is that okay? Lois said two people from the journalism department must take responsibility for the equipment."

Slowly, his white teeth flashed. "I trust you. Go get'em, tiger."

As I lugged my backpack out to the plaza, along with a microphone I'd retrieved from the equipment room, I was surprised to spot a small group hovering near the wooden stage. A large camera rested at one man's feet. Channel 23 News.

Oh, no.

My steps lagged. Did they plan to film my speech?

How had they learned about it?

Joyce whirled my way, excitement snapping from her eyes. She looked elegant and sophisticated in her tailored outfit, impractical heels, and with her hair done up in a chignon. "Isn't this great, Kay? Channel Twenty-Three agreed to cover your speech. Now we'll get more donations for the fundraiser! Isn't that marvelous?"

I did not feel marvelous. Thank goodness I'd decided to wear my new, dusky rose blouse today. But my jeans and sneakers...

"Why didn't you tell me the media would be here?" I hissed.

"Oh. Sorry, Kay. Guess I got busy. I forgot what I told different people." She looked at me anxiously. "Will you be all right?"

I nodded, and took deep breaths to calm my jumping nerves.

David met us as we entered the journalism building. He leaped ahead and held the door open for us.

A single bare bulb lit the equipment room. It was dusty inside, and a faint, chemical smell lingered.

David knelt beside me and pulled a few boxes from the shelves. "We'll need speakers."

I grabbed a microphone stand, and held the door open as Joyce and David lugged several speakers outside. While we set up the equipment on stage, Mitch showed up, followed by Mary. In quick order more speakers, sound equipment, and extension cords were lugged out to the plaza.

Laughing, Mitch and Mary appeared with the last pieces of equipment. The weight of a heavy black box was shifted well back into Mitch's muscled arms.

"Just tell me where to go."

"Let me help you!" Mary insisted.

"No," he said flatly. "You're in no condition for that. Might hurt you. Or your baby."

Mary looked surprised, and oddly touched. I wondered if Jack ever showed such concern for her, or their baby.

"You okay?" David spoke behind me, and I turned away from the microphone. His dark eyes looked quizzical, and his mouth had finally relaxed into a smile.

Plainly, he wanted to forget our last argument. A choking emotion constricted my throat. So did I. More than anything.

"David, I'm sorry!"

His smile faded.

"I was out of line on Sunday. I'm *really* sorry. And I'm sorry it's taken me this long to apologize."

His grin softened. "Apology accepted, Cupcake."

I grinned back. Sweet relief sang through me. Why hadn't I done this sooner? Why was I so pigheaded?

A noise made me glance at the grassy lawn. A crowd had gathered. My stomach clenched with nerves.

"You okay?"

"I think so. I hope so."

"You'll do great." His gaze suddenly narrowed.

"Kay. How are you?" A possessive arm squeezed around my shoulders.

"Glad you could help out, Trent," David said.

A heavy piece of equipment thudded gently onto the stage, making it shudder, and my gaze flew to Mitch. His black eyes rested on Trent, and his left brow winged upward with barely veiled dislike.

"Where do you want this piece, Kay?"

The remaining minutes flew by, and before I knew it, it was twelve o'clock. Drawn by the camera crew, a large crowd milled about my little platform now. My throat felt dry, and my fingers cold.

My gaze latched onto Trent, who stood at stage right. He smiled whitely, and gave me two thumbs up.

Taking a deep breath, I reached for the microphone.

"Hello." My loud voice startled me. It resounded across the grassy knoll.

I cautiously cleared my throat and started again. "Hi. I'm Kay Jameson, and I'd like to talk about our recent earthquake." I glanced at the notes fluttering in my hand.

"Thousands of people are without homes, food, or the basic necessities of life, and Truesdale First Gospel wants to help. So, tomorrow we're going to hold a food drive.

"For the food drive to be a success, we need your help. If you have any spare food, blankets, or clothes, please drop them off at the church tomorrow. We'll make sure they reach the people who need them most."

A strange mutter rumbled in the crowd, but I pressed on, determined to blurt out the rest of my speech.

"Our church is also hosting a dinner for the homeless the following Saturday night. The dinner is a fundraiser, too, and we hope to collect more food and donations for the homeless at that time. If anyone would like to contribute to either of these projects, please contact me," I glanced up as a hiss caught my attention, "or Truesdale First Gospel for more details."

"Get off the stage, do-gooder!" Randy shouted.

People booed loudly.

"Don't need Christians telling us what to do! We'll take care of our own. Right?" Tim's dark head bobbed above the crowd, his face red and pulsing with hatred. His fist slashed the air, and just for a second, I saw the black band tied around his skinny bicep.

Black band? I froze as a memory tried to jog to the surface.

A piercing whistle made me jump.

The multitude swayed before me now, seemingly in unison in their furious chant. "Do-gooder, do-gooder go home!"

Fear gripped me. What was wrong with these people? Why did they hate me?

Then the truth hit me. They didn't hate *me*. They hated what I stood for. The church, and the Lord.

My temper sparked. I could stand up for God, even if I couldn't stand up for myself.

"Then do something!" I shouted. "You say you care? Then love your neighbor as you love yourselves!"

"Shut up! We don't have to listen to *you*," a long-haired girl screamed. She picked up an apple and threw it at the stage. It fell short.

My heart pounded. *Lord, please help me.*

"Do your religious —— somewhere else!" Randy roared. A flurry of fruit and pens and pencils pelted the stage.

A voice shouted from the crowd, "Leave her alone!" I couldn't see who said it, but the mob roared its disapproval. An object whizzed by me, and I heard a soft squish.

The screaming hysteria pitched to a higher decibel. But I didn't move. A great calm had washed through me. I wasn't afraid anymore.

Someone grabbed my arm and jerked me toward the back of the stage. He threw his body in front of me as a shield.

"Get down!" David growled, shoving me down. We both dropped behind the stage.

A siren shrieked, once, twice, and three times. "Campus police," a voice blared. "Break it up! Move away from the stage."

I crouched with David and Joyce behind the stage until the crowd broke, and then I moved to the side of the stage. Perhaps foolishly, I still felt oddly invincible. And defiant, too. I would not cower in fear to the haters anymore.

"Miss Jameson!" The Channel 23 reporter rushed up to me. "Would you like to comment on what just happened?"

"Yes." I stared straight into the opaque, black camera eye. "I'd like to say two things. First, I can't believe the crowd attacked me. Truesdale First Gospel wants to help the homeless. Something they..." I pointed to the crowd, "say they want to do. Why haven't they? Why are the government and Red Cross the only ones helping the earthquake victims? Why is Truesdale First Gospel the first private organization to help the victims in our city?"

My jaw relaxed a little. "Second, I'd like to ask the people who are listening to help us. Help Truesdale First Gospel provide food and clothing for the homeless. We're taking donations this Saturday, starting at seven a.m. Your help is desperately needed. With your help, we can make a real difference in the lives of those who lost everything in the earthquake."

"Thank you." The reporter slipped away, just as the city police cruisers pulled up on the lawn.

Clearly salivating for the cameras, the remaining rabble rousers tried to press past the campus police, but gave up when they spotted the blue-uniformed, city police reinforcements. I didn't see Tim or Randy among them. Where had they gone? I remembered they had been the first ones to stir up the crowd.

The black band around Tim's arm reentered my mind.

The image was important. But why? What did black have to do with hatred?

Finally it hit me, and I remembered the blackened corner of Truesdale First Gospel—the smoke, the dirt, and the black cloth tied to a young tree. Joyce had said they'd found black pieces of cloth when the church was vandalized, too.

Black cloth. Black arm bands. Could the attacks on me and the ones on the church be related? The idea wasn't farfetched. After all, Mitch had said that Tim and Randy belonged to a hate group.

Organized hatred toward Christians. Not just on a small level, against me. But against the entire church.

Another question flashed to mind. If Tim and Randy's hate group had orchestrated the recent attacks on our church, then who was in charge of the group? Tim and Randy struck me as the grunt soldier types. Not leaders. Not organizers of something so complicated. I thought again about how Tim and my teacher, Mr. Carlisle, were cousins. And the dog poop on my car. Was Mr. Carlisle involved in the hate group?

A shiver coursed through me.

More trouble was coming. I felt it, deep in my gut. Worse, I didn't know how to stop it. Finding evidence would be a step in the right direction, but the police had found nothing yet. Could I do any better? If so, how? *Please help us, Lord.*

"Let's get this equipment packed up while the police are still here." David's voice interrupted my troubled thoughts. He stood on the stage, already disconnecting extension cords.

For a moment, though, I glanced at the crowd again. Blue-suited officers hustled unruly people toward the patrol cars. Too bad Randy and Tim had already made their escape. And I'd never seen Mr. Carlisle in the crowd at all.

With everyone helping, we managed to cart the expensive equipment away in two quick trips. Luckily, the flying fruit hadn't damaged anything. A damp cloth removed a few wet stains from the microphone stand and speakers.

The quiet journalism building felt like a sanctuary after the turmoil on the plaza. For a few moments my dark, disturbed thoughts eased.

"Great speech, Kay," Mary leaned against a cool wall. "You had a lot of guts, standing up to those people like that."

"You sure did!" Trent hugged me. His eyes blazed, and his body felt tense with excitement. "It'll make a great article for my interpretive journalism class."

Mitch clicked shut the supply room door for the last time, and swiped his dusty hands against his jeans. "Need volunteers on Saturday? I can help."

"Me too," Mary spoke up.

"Yes!" Joyce interjected. "We'll need all the help we can get." She smiled at Trent. "What about you? Can you come?"

"I'll sure try!" The exuberance in his voice sounded a bit forced. His arm hugged me tight again, and then let go. With an apologetic smile, he said, "Sorry, but I've got to run. Are we still on for bowling tonight?"

"Yes. The Sienna at seven-thirty," Joyce said.

I turned to Trent. In a low voice, I said, "Theresa needs a ride. Do you mind?"

"Not a problem." He hefted his thin stack of school books to his other arm. "Pick you both up at seven, okay?"

A wave for everyone, and he swung out the glass doors and headed for the plaza.

"It seems wrong to go bowling when so many people are suffering," Joyce commented.

"Should we stay at home with long faces?" David lifted a brow. "That won't help anyone."

He had a point.

Mitch pushed his muscled body away from the wall. "I have to go. See you tomorrow morning, bright and early."

Evidently, he didn't plan to bowl. I turned to Mary. "Will you come tonight?"

"I wish I could, but I have to work. I have tomorrow off, though."

We separated to drift off to our classes. The plaza had pretty much emptied by then. It was hard to believe only twenty minutes ago a crowd had roiled there, seething with hatred and anger toward me. Well, me and the church. A shiver slipped down my spine. But the Lord had protected me—through David—I suddenly remembered.

Right now, he strode off across the grass. I hurried to catch up with him. "Hey, David."

He glanced down, and a quick, surprised grin lit his brown eyes.

I grinned back. "I never did thank you for saving me back there. Thank you."

"No problem, Jellybean." He offered me a crooked smile and slowed his pace to match my own. "Somebody had to rescue you. Looked like you were rooted to the spot."

"I wasn't." I laughed. "It *was* kind of weird, though..."

"Turning into a popsicle?"

"No! Stop it." But my spirit took wing. It felt good to joke with David again. I'd missed it terribly. "What I was trying to say, if you'd let me *finish,* please, is that I didn't feel scared. Like I knew everything would be okay."

His tone deepened. "It did turn out okay."

I frowned up at him. "Then why do you sound like that?"

"I was afraid they'd start throwing something harder or..."

"Or what?"

He shrugged, and his pace quickened again. "Or start shooting."

"Shooting?" Suddenly, I felt sick. I hadn't thought of that. But nowadays, the thought wasn't far-fetched.

His grin flashed back. "Don't worry, Chickadee. I was just overreacting."

Dinner that night was silent. Mom and Dad didn't speak one word to each other. Earlier, when I'd arrived home, Mom had asked if I was okay. She'd seen the campus riot on the news.

Obviously, my parents had had a huge fight before I got home. About what, I had no idea, but wearily wondered if it mattered. Probably about money, or something trivial. Again. And Theresa seemed lost in her own thoughts—no doubt dreaming about her "date" with David.

My sister had decided to wear designer jeans, a pink blouse and accents of baubly gold jewelry. Not to be outdone, I wore my nicest black jeans and a casual silk blouse. I didn't know why I'd dressed to the teeth to bowl. Maybe to compete with

Theresa? I wanted Trent's attention to be fixed on me, not my fashionable sister, I finally decided.

Dad cleared his throat and picked up a dinner roll. He smiled at me. "Saw you on the news tonight, Kay!" His voice sounded too jovial. "I'm real proud of you. You're turning into a real community action woman. Just like your mother." The last sentence twisted, like a fist clenching.

Mom's breath hissed in, and she clattered to her feet. Blue eyes freezing, she stomped into the hall.

Dad's brows lifted. "Wonder what her problem is."

I glanced at my plate, feeling sick.

Theresa jerked back her chair and leaped up. "Dad! Why can't you just love her for who she is?" She ran from the room.

Dad's fork halted halfway to his mouth. After a slight hesitation, he popped the bite of meatloaf in. "Guess it's just you and me, Kay." His chuckle sounded hollow.

Tears blurred my eyes, and I stabbed blindly at my green beans. Finally, I said, "Why do you do it, Dad?" A tear slid down my cheek. I brushed it away, but another soon followed. "Why do you keep tearing each other down? Won't you please stop? I can't stand it any more!" I swiped away the slick tears with the back of my hands.

"I'm sorry, honey," Dad said gruffly. "It's just... Things are complicated between your mother and me."

I wondered how complicated it could be to treat each other with respect. But I didn't say anything further. I shoved green beans in my mouth and blinked back more hot tears.

"I hear your church is going all out for the homeless!" Dad spoke loudly, as if trying to sound light-hearted and happy—as if everything was okay. But it wasn't. "I mean, two events. That's a lot."

I swallowed past the tightness in my throat. "We want to show people we care. And that God loves them, too."

We didn't speak after that. Although Dad's face was expressionless, I knew angry thoughts swirled beneath the placid surface.

I felt desperately unhappy. What was wrong with my family? Why couldn't we get along?

Trent rang the doorbell at ten after seven. Mom had retired upstairs with a headache, and Dad sat in the den, watching sports. Both looked angry and sullen.

Dad did not come out to see us off.

"See you, Dad!" I called. I hesitated before closing the front door, and heard a faint "Mmmph" come from the den.

"Nice car!" Theresa gasped, approaching Trent's sleek, low-slung silver Porsche. She sent him an admiring glance. "Is it yours?"

"Sure is." He opened the door and guided her into the back, and I slid into the front. He closed the door firmly behind me.

"This is nice!" Theresa breathed, scooting sideways in the tiny space allotted to the back seat.

Trent grinned and hopped in. "'14 Porsche 911. Mint condition."

The Sienna was located on the north side of town. As we pulled into the brightly lit lot, my subconscious fears vanished. The Sienna was not the Comden. It was a new building with well-kept cars parked in the spacious lot. I didn't see one letter of graffiti painted anywhere, and no riffraff slouched against the rough walls smoking pot—or worse.

Inside, the bright bowling alley clashed with sound. Bowling pins clattered, and people shouted and laughed. Video machines beeped in the arcade.

"Look! There's David." Theresa hurried to the counter and adopted her prettiest smile. She touched his arm. "Did you just get here?"

His smiled. "Yep." He glanced up as Trent and I joined my sister. His smiling dark gaze froze for an instant, and then relaxed. "Hi, Trent, good to see you again. Kay." He raised his brow at me. "Got your technique polished up?"

I impertinently tilted my chin. "I'm ready to take *you* on again."

"Right." He grinned at Trent. "She has a deadly throw. Duck if you see it coming."

I lightly punched him in the arm and glanced around with a happy, glowing smile. Things felt almost normal with David, even with Trent there, and I was glad.

"Here she comes," Trent said.

Joyce breezed up with a smile for everyone. "Shall we all use the same lane?" she asked, exchanging money for a pair of red bowling shoes.

We agreed we would, since there were only five of us. Other people from our college group trickled in later, and they grabbed up the remaining lanes.

Joyce spent most of the evening flitting from one group to another, talking about the food drive and fundraiser. She had a one-track mind, and was clearly excited about both events.

When she slowed down for a minute, I asked, "Does the FGA know that the homeless dinner's been expanded to a fundraiser?" I remembered the last time we'd neglected to tell Truesdale Gospel's parent organization our plans, they had been incensed. And threatened to cut off our funding.

"Dad told them." Joyce grabbed her black bowling ball and stepped up to take her turn. "They said it's okay. Provided they approve how we spend the money."

"How are we spending the money?" David asked. Theresa sat close beside him. So far, she'd managed to monopolize his attention for most of the game.

Joyce shrugged. Concentrating intensely, she stepped forward. The ball rolled fluidly from her fingers. I watched with envy. My bowling ball still refused to cooperate.

Joyce held her polished nails over the air flow vent. "Dad's thinking about donating the extra money—after the expenses for the dinner are taken out—to the homeless shelter down on Driscoll. They really need the funds. And food, and everything else, too. In fact, Dad wants a group of us to work there tomorrow and cart over food and supplies donated to the church. Do you guys want to come?"

"Sounds good to me," David agreed.

Trent had been listening, but his mind had latched onto the FGA, instead of the fundraiser. "Tell me something. Why does your church have to report everything to the FGA? Is this new?"

While Joyce rolled a spare, I explained what I knew.

"We still don't know why they're so mad at us," I finished. "Not for sure, anyway. But our church is on probation until Joyce's dad goes to their vision meeting."

"Interesting. And what about Woodward, the guy who's running for Senate. Isn't he connected to the FGA?"

"Yes." Joyce plopped into the scorekeeper's chair. "In fact, Dad said Woodward plans to stump at Truesdale State in a couple of weeks."

The issue of politics fell by the wayside then, for Trent, Joyce and David were in a dead heat. Sadly, Theresa and I lagged behind with just eighty points apiece.

"Teach me how to bowl, David," Theresa's big blue eyes pleaded. She clutched her pink bowling ball to her bosom. "I don't know *what* I'm doing wrong."

I couldn't help it. My eyes rolled to the ceiling.

David showed her the same moves he'd shown me a few weeks ago. Minus the sarcastic replay of her faults. Theresa blatantly admired his rippling arm muscles, and I did a double-take. I hadn't known David *had* any rippling muscles.

Out of the corner of my eye, I watched as he scooped up the sixteen pound ball again. His black T-shirt was loose, but I could tell he had gained some bulk. From carrying boxes of inventory in his dad's shop? Probably.

This little drama inspired Trent. He leaned close to me, his eyes sparkling intimately. "Want me to show you a few moves?"

A sickening, silly smile crept across my face. "It couldn't hurt," I giggled.

David glanced sharply at me, and then turned to Theresa, who spoke in his ear.

Trent demonstrated the correct way to bowl. He didn't have many rippling muscles, but he was nicely trim. After all, journalism wasn't known for physical activity, and that was his life.

I did try to follow his instructions, but every ball immediately flew right into the gutter. At least my old technique got them down the middle of the lane. Most of the way.

Disgusted, Joyce rolled her eyes at me when I finally sat down. But I just smiled. I knew Theresa and I were acting like simpering fools. I never knew being silly could be so much fun.

The last frame came up. David and Trent were still in a dead heat, and Joyce could win, too, but she needed two strikes. Her next throw demolished all hopes for her win.

"Darn!" she sat back down, and glumly rested her elbows on the machine console.

David threw a strike, and then a spare of nine.

Rubbing his hands on his jeans, he nodded to Trent. "All yours. Go for it."

With his handsome features tense with concentration, Trent stepped up to take his turn. He eyed the pins and stepped, carefully, fluidly forward. One, two, three, four, swish. His right leg swung back, across his left. Breathlessly, we watched the ball spin down the middle of the lane, as fast and smooth as butter. The pins toppled. First five, and then all of them.

"All right!" I shouted. I shot David a grin.

The ball spun back. Concentrating intensely again, Trent stepped quickly, lightly, and released the ball. Only five went down. In the second attempt he knocked down three more. So David won, by a pin.

"Congratulations." Sportsmanlike, the guys shook hands. David warded off a squealing Theresa.

The next game was dull. David won easily. It was as if Trent had given up. We headed to the counter to pick up our shoes and pay for our games.

After daintily pulling on her shoes, Theresa lured David away from the group. Puzzled, I turned to the counter, but sensed David's eyes upon me. Then I heard him say, "Sure. No problem."

Theresa breezed up as I slipped on my flats. "David's driving me home." Her smile looked triumphant, like a cat lapping up cream.

A few moments later, David and Theresa headed for the door, but David paused by Trent, who had jammed on his shoes. "Glad you could come. Have a good night."

"Thanks." Surprised, Trent watched them go.

David threw me a brief, casual wave. Strangely, it made me feel dismissed. Despite our casual banter tonight, I still sensed a small distance between us. I didn't understand it. Obviously, he'd decided to welcome Trent into our group.

Joyce opted to stay at the bowling alley and chat with friends.

"Want to go for yogurt?" Trent opened his car door for me.

"Sure." I smiled.

He laughed suddenly as he pulled out of the lot. "You know what? I forgot to tell you my exciting news. I've been waiting all afternoon to tell you."

"What exciting news?"

"Remember when I left the pizza place early last Saturday?" He glanced expectantly at me as he eased the steering wheel right to turn a corner. I nodded. "Well, I went for an interview. At the *Truesdale Register*."

"Really?" He'd gone to an interview last week? A prick of disquiet slid through me. Maybe I was making too much of it, but it seemed like a big piece of information to forget to tell a journalism friend. Especially since I'd recently told him that I planned to apply for an internship soon, too. I tried not to dwell on the obvious question—had he wanted to get his internship wrapped up before I could compete with him for the position?

"Anyway," he grinned. "I applied for the internship, and got it! I just found out today. Isn't that great?"

"That is great!" I smiled. Finding an internship in Truesdale was next to impossible. "I'll bet your family is proud of you." I shook away my silly, unsettled feelings. He'd probably been afraid he wouldn't get the spot, so he might not have told anyone. And I hadn't even tried to get the internship, so what was my problem, anyway?

"Dad's ready to print a bulletin in the paper. Not that it's *that* exciting. But I'll learn a lot. I'm looking forward to it."

We talked more about his internship. It started tomorrow morning at ten, so he couldn't work long at the food drive. That detail didn't appear to trouble him. And why would it? It wasn't his church. The only reason he was coming at all was because I'd be there.

I enjoyed talking with Trent over yogurt. A lot. But I noticed we only skimmed the surface—journalism, our classes, and our childhoods. We didn't talk about any deep feelings or issues.

Was he still interested in God? I didn't know anymore.

As the evening progressed, I felt increasingly unsettled, but couldn't pinpoint why.

After eleven, he walked me to my front door. And there, finally for a moment, I managed to forget my unsettled doubts.

His blue eyes seemed able to cast a spell all their own. They held me mesmerized. My lashes fluttered closed as his lips touched mine. His kiss became deeper, and a little more demanding. . .

I jerked back when a car door slammed. I stared up at him, feeling jumbled inside. I'd wanted the kiss to stop before he'd ended it. Why?

Trent gave me a slow smile. "See you tomorrow."

"Okay." A disconcerted curve twitched my lips. He passed by Theresa, who positively floated up the walk. Out of the corner of my eye, David's sports car pulled away from the curb. Obviously, both of them had seen Trent and me kiss.

Maybe that's why I had pulled back. I'd felt self-conscious about people watching us kiss.

"Where were you?" I fumbled with the door lock.

"Out," Theresa breathed coyly, her eyes fluttering ecstatically to the heavens.

"What do you mean, *out*?" Unreasonably annoyed, I pushed the door open and Theresa sailed inside.

She arched a brow at me. "On a date. Remember? I told you it was a date, Kay. Looks like *you* had quite a date, too."

I pushed the door shut. It closed a little louder than necessary. "I had a very nice time, thank you very much. I gather you had a wonderful time?"

"Oh, yes." Theresa danced lightly up the stairs.

I decided to ignore her theatrics. I couldn't care less about her "date" with David.

But I did wonder where she and David had been for the last two hours. Alone. Was she right? Was he really interested in her? For the first time, I wondered.

SATURDAY

I READ A CHAPTER IN LUKE THIS MORNING, and Psalm 139, too. I love that psalm. It's my very favorite one. Verses 1-2, 7, and 9-10 say it all for me:

> *O LORD, you have searched me and you know me. You know when I sit and when I rise; you perceive my thoughts from afar... Where can I go from your Spirit? Where can I flee from your presence? ...If I rise on the wings of the dawn, if I settle on the far side of the sea, even there your hand will guide me, your right hand will hold me fast.*

Theresa bounced into my car bright and early that morning, dressed in jeans and a T-shirt, like me. At least she'd dressed sensibly, and not to impress David. Of course, maybe she'd already impressed him last night. The thought bothered me, although I could find no logical reason for it. I turned my Mustang into the crowded church parking lot. Bins lined the sidewalk, labeled "Canned Goods," "Clothing," and "Perishables."

After locking the car, Theresa and I wandered around to the front of the church. Joyce busily stacked canisters of infant formula in a box.

"Isn't this great?" she called out. "Thanks to the newscast, we already have enough food to make a run down to the shelter. We'll go as soon as David gets here."

An old blue pickup chugged up to the curb. After backfiring once, the engine died and Mitch leaped out. He looked fresh and relaxed, and wore light-colored jeans and a white cotton T-shirt, which fit loosely over his muscled shoulders.

"Hi." He grinned. "Thought the truck might come in handy."

"You are heaven sent!" Joyce declared, straightening, her face flushed from her exertions. "If you don't mind, we'll start loading it now."

Mitch and the three of us pitched in. By the time David showed up, Mary and Trent had arrived too, and the truck was full.

"I can put a few things in my back seat," Trent offered, hovering near his Porsche.

"Great." Joyce pointed. "We have boxes of Bibles over there."

Trent raised his eyebrows, as though taken aback by the idea of transporting Bibles. Under his breath, he whispered to me, "What are those for? They can't feed the homeless."

"They can feed their souls." Although last night I'd acted like a simpering fool, today I needed to be real with him. Fantasies were all well and good, but I wanted to know that Trent liked the real me. Not a starry-eyed girl's blind infatuation, which had to be fabulous for his ego.

After we'd loaded up, David slid into the truck with Mitch. Disappointment and uncertainty flickered across Theresa's face as Mitch and David drive off, laughing and joking together in the cab.

"Theresa. Mary! You guys can come with me," Joyce called, waving from her ancient red Toyota.

I drove with Trent. Only two people could fit in his loaded sports car.

A line already stretched outside the homeless shelter on Driscoll when we arrived.

"Looks like the word is out." Trent hopped out of his car, and the two of us lugged the boxes of New Testament Bibles to one of the tables set up outside the rundown building.

The co-director rushed up to us, her face shining. "We're so happy you're here!" she cried. "We need your help desperately, as you can see. Now, just put the boxes over there."

I soon learned a bit of information I'd never known before—Truesdale First Gospel, in conjunction with a few other churches in town, regularly supported Driscoll Shelter.

David and Mitch left to fetch another load.

Time flew by. Trent and I stationed ourselves at the clothing table and handed out children's clothes to young mothers with squalling babies planted on their hips. Trent seemed unusually quiet as he handed out free items. Maybe he was thinking about starting his new internship in a few hours.

Theresa and Joyce distributed food, and Mary the Bibles. As each person left the first two stations, Mary timidly held out a Bible. Most took one.

Before I knew it, it was a quarter to ten o'clock. Word had caught like wildfire about the free food at the shelter, and the line had lengthened to five blocks. People were remarkably courteous, though—I didn't see any pushing or shoving at all.

Mitch's pickup chugged up to the curb and David leaped out. This was their last load of the morning.

People cheered as the two guys carted boxes to the tables. Mitch looked surprised and embarrassed, but David hammed it up. With a bow, he graciously handed out goodies to the wide-eyed, grinning children.

Trent nudged my shoulder. "Sorry, but this is where I take off. Don't want to be late for my first day."

"Oh! The time went so fast." We'd had no time to talk.

"I know." His blue eyes crinkled at the corners. "I'll be thinking about you all day."

I doubted it, but smiled in appreciation of the thought. "Have fun."

"I will." As he turned away, though, an empty feeling caught at my spirit.

He called to my friends, "See you later. I have to go."

"Thanks again, Trent!" Joyce called.

The good-natured crowd whistled and clapped, and Trent gave a final backward wave before disappearing into his car.

I turned back to the table, wondering why I felt unsettled. Trent had been unusually quiet and distracted all morning. New job jitters, no doubt. That must be it. I hadn't felt a real connection with him today because he'd been preoccupied, and we hadn't had time to talk.

I handed a toddler-sized pair of overalls to a young, dark-haired mother. Things would return to normal on Monday. We could talk then.

David and Mitch finished unloading the truck, and then came over to help us. I moved down to help Mary with the Bibles, and the guys took over the clothes table.

"How do you do this?" David glanced at me. His smile seemed a bit off, and I wondered why. We had been so busy all morning that we literally hadn't spoken one word to each other today. He lifted up a frilly dress. "Who am I supposed to give this to?"

"Let the mothers look," I advised. "You're just the referee. Make sure no one gets more than their fair share."

"Okay." He relaxed a little.

The children and mothers jabbered to him. "Can I have this? How many can we have?"

He was good with people, I noticed, handing out another Bible. The women and children automatically warmed up to him. Charm. He did have a definite charm.

"Want to trade, Kay?" Theresa flounced up, her gaze fastened on David, who stood beside me.

"I'll trade," Mary spoke up. "I'm ready to do something different."

"Oh. Okay. Thanks, Mary."

Theresa moved into Mary's spot, but a moment later, I felt a sharp elbow jab into my side. "Let's switch," she hissed, with a significant look over my shoulder.

I stood between her and her true love. Inexplicably annoyed, I could think of no reason why I shouldn't do as she asked.

After switching, I silently handed out Bibles while Theresa chattered to David. *At* David would have been a better description.

He responded sparingly to her questions, and instead appeared to concentrate on the task before him. After a few minutes, Theresa's comments trailed off. She looked hurt.

Although I had predicted this would happen, I felt bad for her. I leaned over and whispered, "Men can be single-minded sometimes, can't they?"

She flashed me a surprised smile. And she looked a little happier after that. Knowing how resourceful my sister could be with men, though, I was sure it wouldn't be long before she cooked up another plan to monopolize his attention.

Jackhammer blasts rattled the air as the morning wore on. Driscoll's sewer and water mains still weren't working properly. And only a few neighborhoods had regained power. The shelter ran off of its own generator.

"Hello." An arrogant voice spoke to my left.

I immediately recognized the man. Black, devilishly raked brows, hard pebbled eyes. Jack Ignacio. Mary's loving boy-friend.

Jack's lips curled up. "Looks like a great turn out. Can I get some free food, too?"

"Get in line." My tone was sharp. I couldn't help it.

The black eyes slitted. "Think I'll pass. Where's Mary?"

"Down there." I wished he'd go home. Something inside me sensed that Jack Ignacio meant trouble.

But I had no idea how much.

A few seconds later, heads swiveled to stare down the group of tables. A deathly silence fell, and disapproval stamped across the older matron's faces.

Then I heard it.

"Come home. *Now!*" It was Jack's low, chilling voice.

Heart accelerating with apprehension, I stepped back so I could see better.

Jack jerked Mary up to him, her forearms clenched in his cruel hands. "Come with me now, do you hear?" He shook her, hard.

"Stop it!" I darted behind the tables to stand beside my friend. Jack was a lot bigger than me, but I was too upset to feel afraid. "What do you think you're doing? Let her go!"

"Butt out," Jack snarled. He yanked hard on Mary's arms and she wept, clearly terrified.

"Hey." David stood beside me. In a deep, soothing voice he said, "Calm down, Jack. What's going on?"

Jack's face blotched a livid, angry red. He released one of Mary's arms and stabbed a finger into David's chest. "You stay out of this, man. This is between me and my woman. Okay? Back off!"

"You're hurting her. Okay? Let her go. No one wants to cause a scene here."

Mary staggered when Jack flung her backward. He shoved his face into David's. Although David was a good four inches taller, his lean frame couldn't match Jack's buffed out, well-defined muscles. I felt a chill of fear for my friend.

"You!" Jack stabbed David's chest. "Mind your own business. See? This is my woman, and it's my concern. Got it?"

"Then treat her right." David stared Jack straight in the eyes.

Jack stepped back, hands balled into fists. "I'll take you out, man," he swore, jaw tilted cockily. "Come on, just say the word!"

"No!" Mary lunged forward. She grabbed one of Jack's bulging biceps. "No!" she wept. "I'll go. Please..."

Jack yanked Mary roughly to him. Dressed in her neat, thrift bought clothes, and shoulders crumpled by Jack's vice-like arm, she looked like a frail waif.

"That's right," he hissed at her. "You'll come. Because I take care of you, woman." He glared at the gawking crowd. "Get lost! Show's over!"

Viciously elbowing by people, he towed the weeping Mary through the crowd. Both quickly disappeared.

I was stunned. "What a jerk!" I cried out. I spun to David. "Can't we do something?"

He shook his head. His warm palm squeezed my shoulder. "Mary doesn't want us to get involved."

I couldn't believe it. We had to watch our friend be dragged off by that monster? What if he hit her? What if he hurt the baby? Tears of horrified frustration burned in my eyes. I wanted to do something. Anything!

Usually unruffled, Joyce looked pale and stunned. "That guy is bad news. Mary needs to leave him."

I blinked back tears. "But she won't. She loves him."

Even so, I couldn't understand. What did Mary see in Jack? Why would she stay with him? Didn't she think she deserved better?

"Then we can't do anything." Joyce's words sounded cold-hearted. She handed a can of beans to an elderly woman.

Upset, I stepped toward my table. But a touch on the shoulder stopped me.

"Hey," David's voice was quiet. "How about a break? Want to share a soda with me?"

It couldn't hurt. We retreated to the side of the building where it was quiet, and he pulled an orange drink from the cooler. He offered it to me first, but I shook my head. "Do you think she'll be okay?"

David swigged back deep gulps of the pop. He rested the can on his knee. "I think she'll be all right. Has he ever hit her before?"

"I don't think so." Mary had never come to school in dark glasses, or in any pain that I could remember.

"Then he probably calmed down after he left. In his eyes, we were the threat."

"I hope you're right." I held my hand out for the can and swallowed several times. The sticky, sweet liquid burned down my throat. Grimacing, I handed it back. "You can finish it."

"You okay, Punkin?" His dark eyes looked concerned.

"Yes." A faint smile wanted to touch my lips, but I didn't let it. It didn't seem right to feel any sort of peace when Mary was so sad. But this time with David felt good. Comforting. Like it had in the old days, before Trent.

"Good." With one noisy slurp, he finished the orange drink and flashed me a small smile. "Then you'd better get back to work. No more slacking off."

Smiling, I kicked him in the shoe as I walked by.

Theresa eyed me when I returned to the table. "What were you and David talking about?"

"Mary and Jack."

Her lips instantly curled. "Jack is a jerk!" She smiled and handed a Bible to an elderly gentleman who shuffled by.

At lunchtime we ate in shifts. Of course, Theresa managed to finagle her lunch break with David's. I glanced at them out of the corner of my eye. I wondered what they were talking about.

But when David finished eating, he wandered over to talk to Mitch. Theresa's lips puffed into a dissatisfied pout.

I felt sorry for her. But not for long.

My sister swept up to Joyce.

"Would you give me a ride home later? Like at three?" Her ringing tones carried clearly to all and sundry on the block. "I have a *date...*" she flung this subtly in David's direction, "tonight, and need to get home early."

"Of course."

Theresa and I worked together at the food table after lunch. Three o'clock came rapidly.

Joyce appeared at Theresa's elbow, purse slung over her shoulder. "Ready?"

"Yes." Reluctantly, it seemed, Theresa set down a can of tomatoes. She flashed me a quick glance. "'Bye. It was fun, today."

"Thanks for coming, Theresa."

I was surprisingly sorry to see her go. A little closeness had grown between my sister and me today, and I didn't want it to end.

By five o'clock, the line had tapered off to two or three casual passersby. Thank goodness, for I was exhausted. My shoulders ached from lifting and reaching, and my feet hurt from standing all day.

I rested for a moment on the only available chair. Warm, contented peace slid through me. People had been so nice today. Friendly, too. It was refreshing to see the good side of humanity again, instead of all the crime stories on the news, or the inexplicable persecution at school.

Mitch squatted beside me. His black eyes gleamed with satisfaction. "I'm glad I came."

I remembered he used to live here on Driscoll, before his apartment collapsed. "Have you found a new apartment yet?"

He rested his stocky shoulders against the wall. "I have a lead on a good one. In a secured building, believe it or not."

"Because of all the crime?"

He shrugged. "Partly. I like the neighborhood. It's in north Truesdale."

Nosy, as usual, I blurted, "What do you do? I mean, besides go to school?" I was wondering how he could pay for his own apartment.

"I freelance. I create graphics for websites. I'm a bit of a computer geek." He grinned at my surprise.

"You're a graphic artist? Well, I guess that makes sense, since you draw such wonderful sketches."

"Sketching is my first love. I pick up digital design gigs on the side, so I can live. My sketches don't bring in much money." His smile looked rueful.

"That's neat." Amazed, I digested this interesting tidbit of information. Mitch was definitely an interesting guy. "Is your major in graphic design?"

"No. It's business."

"Hey, you two!" Joyce appeared around the side of the building. "We've been invited to a barbecue. Do you want to come?"

Of course we did! Mitch and I leaped up. A few steps later, the smoky, sharp smell of burning wood filled my nostrils, and my mouth watered as I imagined roasted chicken and baked potatoes.

A group of refugees had set up camp in a rubble-strewn lot. Encircled by tents, bonfires lay scattered throughout the center of the camp. Joyce led us to the closest fire. The dirt encircling it had been swept clear of grass and briers.

I slipped down to my heels and sat softly, bottom crunching on a few pebbles. Assorted lawn chairs and people sitting on blankets fanned out around the fire.

A brace of jury-rigged iron pipes arched over the biggest blaze, supporting two black cauldrons. A handful of women poured cans of baked beans into one pot, and someone intermittently stirred the other with a long wooden spoon.

I felt content to sit alone for awhile, inhaling the rich, smoky flavor of the beans, and the other, tantalizingly familiar aroma from the mysterious cauldron. What was in there? Whatever it was, it smelled delicious.

The sky faded pink, and with it, cool air bit through my cotton top. I shivered, and leaned toward the warm fire. It would be cold tonight. I was glad I could go home and sleep in my warm bed. But the refuges would have to sleep out here, in the cold, on the rocky, uncomfortable ground.

"Get a plate, Firefly. Time to eat." David's voice pulled me from my relaxed, trance-like stupor. It had felt good just to sit and let my tired muscles rest from the day's hard work.

Grabbing a flimsy paper plate and plastic fork, I eagerly followed my friends to the bubbling cauldrons. My nose quivered as I inhaled deeply. *Mmm.* Pure ambrosia. Baked beans. And hot dogs! Slightly stale buns and an industrial sized mustard bottle completed the meal. All were items we'd handed out today at the shelter. It looked heavenly.

I scooted back to my place beside the fire and began to eat. It tasted heavenly, too. I had no idea I was so hungry.

The others dropped down around me and ate silently, too. Mitch leaped up after a minute to collect drinks from the cooler.

Slowly, the black, velvety night edged in. The orange fires were the only sources of light, except for a few car headlights that flashed across our tranquil little scene, as they turned onto Driscoll from State. It was peaceful. Crickets creaked around us, pulsing their rhythmic melody up through the trodden grass.

"What a great day." To my left, Joyce's eyes gleamed with satisfaction. "And what a great turn out, too, even with such short notice. The fundraiser next week should do even better."

"You mean the homeless dinner." Beside me, David scooped up the last of his beans.

Joyce shrugged. "It's the same thing."

"Let me know if I can help out," Mitch's bass rumbled.

"Don't worry. We will." Joyce smiled at him. "We really appreciate everything you've done already."

Mitch looked a bit embarrassed.

I staggered to my feet, still hungry. There were no more fresh plates. But plenty of baked beans still bubbled in the pot, so I scooped up another heaping spoonful. It didn't matter that the bottom of my thin, saturated plate dripped strained bean sauce. Like the refugees, I had to make do with what I had. It was like camping out.

I glanced up at the brilliant, twinkling stars. It was so quiet here. Just the soft, velvety night, the crackling fire, and good friends. Peace stole through my soul.

I slipped back to my place, between David and Joyce.

"More beans?" David raised an alarmed brow. "I'm not sure I want to sit next to you."

"Just live with it." I grinned back. "Look who's talking, anyway. You've eaten twice as much as I have."

"But I'm twice as big as you," he complained. He shot a glance at Joyce. "Guess you won't need any fuel to get home, Joy. Kay can power the car on her own."

I shoved him, hard, so he swayed into Mitch. After more good-natured ribbing, we finally wound down.

Joyce drove me to the church so I could pick up my car. The parking lot was deserted. Sliding into my Mustang, I slammed the door, and ignored the thrill of fear that being alone in the dark night usually evoked in me. I wanted to savor the feeling of peace from the campfire.

As I snuggled into my soft, warm bed later, I reflected sleepily over the day's events. It had been a great day... Except for Jack. My eyes opened again. Mary needed to get out of that relationship.

It was too late to call to see if she was okay. And a phone call would probably only incense Jack more, anyway. I'd talk to her on Monday.

Lord, please protect Mary from Jack's temper, and I pray she would accept that you died for her sins. Please give her a new, better life.

Just before I drifted into an exhausted sleep, I wondered where my sister was, and what time she'd get home tonight.

Sunday

CRISP MORNING SUN streamed through my window. I flung open my closet door so I could inspect my outfit in the full length mirror attached to the inside. The door thumped against the corner wall.

"Stop *banging*!" Theresa shouted, and smacked the wall adjoining our rooms.

"Sorry!" I shouted back.

I heard a disgruntled mumble. Theresa had a hangover this morning, surprise of surprises. I'd never heard her come in last night. Her party must have gone late.

My slim fitting dress in a soft blue-gray, along with silver sandals and clutch purse, looked fine for church, I decided. I didn't usually carry a purse, but liked how it complemented my outfit this morning. I wasn't sure why I was so concerned about my appearance today, but felt satisfied I looked nice.

I got to church early, and was surprised to see people dotted all over the lawn. Some were kneeling. Some were squatting. Some stood on tiptoes, scrabbling in the trees. What were they doing? David and Joyce picked through bushes on either side of the front steps.

"What are you doing?"

Joyce whirled. "Can you *believe* this?" Mouth pressed into a thin, furious line, her arm snapped out, gesturing to the church grounds.

Then I saw the small black pieces of cloth. Everywhere. Stuck in the bushes, the trees, and scattered across the far lawn. As if someone had flown over and rained down black soot from hell.

Black. Hatred. Black bands. Foreboding slid through me. I felt more certain than ever that the hate crimes toward my church and Tim and Randy's hate group must be related.

"They put up skull and crossbones flags, too," David's eyes flashed black; the only clue to his deep rage. "They were planted all over the lawn. We picked those up first."

"I can't *believe* this!" Joyce's hand shook as she smashed a bristling handful of black into a trash bag. "I mean, who do they think they are?" In a quiet frenzy, she snatched piece after piece of black out of the bush. "How are we going to get this cleaned up before church starts?"

"I'll help." I set down my purse.

"You can take over this bush, Shortcake." David stepped back, rubbing the heel of his dirty palm against his jaw. "I'll rake up the lawn."

"Thanks, D." Joyce barely turned. Her furious, agitated movements didn't slow for an instant.

I took over David's bush. A few moments later, he emerged from the church utility shed with a long-handled rake. People moved out of the way as he scraped up the worst of the mess remaining on the far side of the lawn. Black piles heaped up at strategic points across the grass.

It struck me as funny, seeing everyone in their Sunday best, scrabbling around outside doing a bizarre form of yard work. David's charcoal gray shirt didn't show the dirt, but my dress would. So would Joyce's elegant cream blouse and skirt. But she didn't seem to care.

Out of the blue, she spat, "I don't know why the police can't find who's doing this. There must be fingerprints everywhere!" She snatched the rustling bag open, and smashed it closed again. Her eyes blazed. "I don't think they *care* who did it."

"They do have a lot of crime to deal..."

"And religious persecution isn't high on their list?"

After a moment, I said, "I've been the target of persecution, too. Remember the dog poop at school? Two guys seem to have it in for me. So far it's just been the dog poop and some shoving, but it's scary."

Joyce's brows flew together, and for a second, worry about her own problems seemed to vanish. "I'm so sorry, Kay. That's awful."

"Both of them wear black arm bands. It makes me wonder if their hate group is the one that's attacking the church."

"Maybe. I'll mention it to my dad. But again, without fingerprints or witnesses, the police can't do anything. I wish *we* could do something."

I dropped a few filthy scraps into the bag. "Actually, I'm doing a paper on the persecution of Christians across the country."

"You think it's happening more often than ever before?"

"Yes. I'm not sure exactly why, but I do have a theory. I think it's a sign that we're getting close to the end."

"Of time?" Joyce stared at me, her eyes wide in disbelief. "You know, you should talk to Dad."

"Why?"

"Because he thinks the exact same thing!" She sounded disgusted. She smashed another fistful of black into the bag.

"Don't you? I mean, look at all the things that are happening. Persecution, earthquakes, famines, pestilences..."

"Stop it! Just stop it, okay?" She glared at me. "I don't want to hear it."

I gaped at her, surprised by the venom in her tone. "Why? Don't you think it's great that Jesus could come back any minute?"

Her lips pressed more tightly together. "I'll tell you what I think. I think you and Dad are living in an apocalyptic fantasy world. You see what you want to see, and you push it off on everyone else."

Her scornful words cut me to the quick. "So you don't think it's important to watch for Jesus? You don't think he's coming soon?"

"I think that's beside the point. Maybe he is. Maybe he isn't. We need to live life here and now. Then, if it does happen, fine. But I don't want to think about it."

"Why not?" I didn't understand her hostility.

"Because it's ridiculous!" She glared at me. Her hands shook as she smashed the bag closed and twisted it into a knot.

"I don't know *why* you and Dad keep talking about this! Think what you want. But leave me out of it."

"Why are you yelling at me? I'm not the one attacking the church."

"I know." After a short pause, she said, "Look." Her voice sounded tightly controlled. "I'm sorry, Kay. Really. But I don't want to talk about this anymore. Okay? I just don't. Honestly, I'm sick of it." Her voice wavered between anger and tears. "I have too much on my mind right now. I don't have time..." For an instant, her chin trembled. "Sometimes, I wish things could go back to the way they were."

She blinked, snatched up the trash bag and marched into the church.

Why was Joyce so upset? This was the second time she'd flown off the handle when I'd brought up the subject of the end times. Why? And with whom was she really angry? Me? Her father? Or the hate group?

I understood why she felt angry about the persecution. And scared? I was, too. So many bad things kept happening, and Joyce didn't know how to deal with it. She didn't seem to *want* to deal with it.

But why didn't she want to talk about Jesus' return?

Thanks to the efforts of the early volunteers, most of the black cloth was gone by the time the on-time attenders straggled in.

Joyce apologized to me again in church. Of course, I forgave her. But I still sensed distance between us. From her? From me? From both of us? Whatever the case, Joyce acted as if nothing was wrong, and I felt reluctant to bring up the subject. I didn't want to start another argument.

Pastor Warner didn't mention the black cloth strewn over the church grounds. I'm sure he didn't want to upset people even more, considering the other attacks our church had suffered lately. Instead, he praised contributors for the food donated yesterday, and he advertised the homeless dinner and fundraiser planned for next Saturday.

"Yesterday was just a drop in the bucket!" he announced with a smile. "We can do so much more. Dinner tickets to the fundraiser are on sale for fifty dollars a plate. I realize the price is steep, but we need to restrict seating. We want most of those who come to the dinner to be homeless. If you can't afford a ticket, please drop a donation into the offering basket this morning. Please realize, *any* contribution is very much needed and appreciated. The money will go to Driscoll Shelter's food relief program. Please, do what you can to help out. You can buy tickets from Martha, our church secretary, any day this week."

Each person in our Sunday school class received four tickets to sell. Afterward, Joyce, David and I pushed together some chairs for an impromptu meeting about the upcoming dinner.

"We need to put up flyers advertising the fundraiser," Joyce said, pen poised over her notepad.

"It should list the date, time and location of the dinner," I said.

"And the price for the tickets." Joyce wrote rapidly.

"And what we'll use the money for," David said.

Joyce stared at her notebook for a moment. "Words aren't enough," she said finally. "The flyers need a spark. Something to catch people's attention."

"Art?" I suggested.

"Yes! But who could draw it?"

"Mitch offered to help. I could ask him."

"Great!" Joyce boldly checked off that item. "Now, let's see. What else do we need to do for the fundraiser? We have the tickets already..."

"You know," David interrupted, "I have a little problem with this whole fundraiser thing."

Surprised, we turned to him.

"Isn't this a dinner for the homeless? So why are we focusing on selling tickets to the rich?"

"Because the *rich* people's money will pay for the food," Joyce sounded irritated. "They pay, so the homeless can get in for free. I'm learning all about this in my 'Church as Business' class. We need to play it smart to maximize income."

"The church is not a *business*."

Joyce ignored David's comment. "Personally, I think we could give people more food if we didn't do the homeless dinner at all. We could add up the money donated and buy canned beans or whatever, and then distribute them like we did yesterday."

"No!"

David's harsh tone made me jump. "People are homeless, Joyce. They're cold, lonely and depressed. A warm, home cooked meal would do a lot more good than a cold can of beans."

"We can't feed them all," Joyce said sharply.

"I know. But we *can* feed some. It will make a big difference to a few, at least for one night."

"Fine. But here's a problem. How will those earthquake people get to the church? Some people sold their cars to replace what they lost in the quake. Others don't have money to buy gas."

"They could walk," I suggested, careful to keep my tone neutral. "Or ride the bus. It's only a mile." An idea flashed to mind. "In fact, maybe we could put up flyers on the east side of town, advertising the free dinner. We could say first come, first served. After the seats are filled, we could give away canned and boxed food at the door, to the extra people who show up."

"I like that idea," David relaxed back in his chair.

Joyce frowned, clearly not liking the direction her meeting had taken. But her first words were conciliatory.

"I agree a warm dinner would be nice. But here's another problem: how do you think the big donors will feel to have their dinner overrun by a bunch of shabby homeless people? I mean, when they donate fifty dollars for a ticket, they'll expect..."

"Everyone to look like them?" David exploded. "I can't believe you just said that, Joyce! This benefit is for the homeless. Not the rich. What's your plan? To throw them out, and give the whole dinner to the rich? Is that what your *business* class would recommend?"

"Well," Joyce looked down at her notepad, as if trying to find answers there. When she glanced back up, she looked sheepish. "I'm sorry. I guess I was focusing a little too much on the contributors."

"And forgetting the victims."

Joyce tapped her pen on the pad. "I do have one concern, though, for the homeless. Won't they feel funny if the rich people are there—like they're charity cases, or something?"

"Exclude all the rich people," David said promptly, but Joyce ignored him and looked at me.

I didn't like being put in the middle. "Say casual dress only," I suggested. "Jeans, T-shirts and tennis shoes."

"I agree." This was from David.

Joyce frowned. "Okay. What will we serve?"

"Spaghetti is easy," I said. "And bread. Maybe green beans, too. And we could have cake for dessert."

Joyce's lips wrinkled. "That seems so plain. For contributing fifty dollars a plate, wouldn't you expect more? I mean, maybe we could serve chicken, at least, and pasta."

"To whom?" David pounced on this. "The rich people?"

"Well..."

"Everyone should get the same food," he stated unequivocally, his mouth set in a straight, hard line. "And how do you plan to single out the rich people at the dinner, anyway? Didn't we just decide everyone should wear jeans, and blend together?"

"Okay, fine!" Joyce glared at him. "Do it your own way. Ignore the fact I'm earning a degree in business. Obviously, you won't listen to anything I have to say."

"I'll listen if you'll stop focusing on the almighty dollar," David shot back. "How can you think it's fair to serve gourmet food to the donors and..."

"Stop it!" I glared at them both. "This is for the *homeless*. Not the rich. And not for our own personal egos. Stop acting like children. We have a lot of work to do, and we won't get it done if you two keep sniping at each other."

They continued to frown at each other, so I took it upon myself to fill the heavy silence.

"Here's another idea. We could take an offering at the dinner. At *all* the tables, I mean, so the homeless won't feel like charity cases."

"All right." Joyce scribbled darkly on her notepad. "Who will cook the food and serve it?"

"Our college group will do that," Joyce stared at her list for a second. "Our group can tack up the two sets of flyers, too. One for the fundraiser, and one for the dinner. Maybe on Wednesday night."

"Good idea," David said tightly.

Joyce glanced at him through narrowed eyes. "Kay, if you could get the drawings from Mitch and print up the flyers by Wednesday, that would be great. David and I will work on selling tickets to businesses..."

"No," he said emphatically. "I don't want to do that. I'd rather take care of planning the actual dinner. Buying the food, serving it, and things like that."

"Fine! Then I'll sell the tickets all by myself." Joyce's voice rose.

"You have the expertise," he said unkindly.

"Stop it!" I leaped to my feet. "You're both being ridiculous. We'll each take charge of one area. I'll do the flyers. David will plan the meal, and Joyce, you'll head up the fundraising. Okay?" I impaled each with a glare.

At the last minute, we decided that David would need extra help planning the dinner. I volunteered to help him, since Joyce would be too busy selling tickets. She also agreed to run all of our ideas by Bobby for approval, too.

The meeting ended soon after, to my great relief. I didn't know what had gotten into my two best friends. Then I remembered that Joyce and I had fought earlier, too.

Two arguments in one morning. What was happening to us?

"You're back late today," Mom hovered at the stove, ladling out my reheated soup. Dad read the sports section of the paper at the table.

"We were planning a big fundraiser and homeless dinner. Thank you, Mom." The steam from the hot, chicken noodle broth filled my nose. Mmm! My favorite, especially with oyster crackers, which Mom had also thoughtfully provided.

Dad looked up. Reading glasses partially obscured his hazel eyes. "You're putting on a fundraiser and a homeless dinner? Both at the same time?"

"Yes." I savored the soup. "We're selling dinners for fifty dollars a plate, and the homeless get to eat free. The church will give the extra money to a shelter down on Driscoll."

"What a wonderful idea." Mom hovered at Dad's elbow. "Maybe we should buy tickets, Winston." Her voice sounded a bit louder than usual, as if she wasn't sure how Dad would respond to the idea. "We have the money. It would be the Christian thing to do."

He lowered his newspaper. After a glance at me, he nodded. "All right. It's the least we can do to help out."

"That's great! Thank you. Will you come to the dinner, too?" My parents had never set foot inside my church.

"I think that would be fun." Mom cast a quick glance at Dad. "An evening out."

He shrugged, and flipped over the newspaper. "Sounds good to me. When, and what time?"

"Saturday. At six o'clock." What a miracle! The day had taken an unexpected turn for the better.

MONDAY

"SO, WHAT HAPPENED WITH JACK?" I asked Mary, the instant I saw her in class that morning.

Thankfully, she appeared to be unharmed. I slid down in my plastic chair, and my forest green backpack thumped to the floor at my feet.

"Oh," her gaze slid away. "Jack doesn't like it when I hang out with other people too much. He wants me to be there for him, and our relationship, full-time." She hunched down. "Not running around, being a little do-gooder."

Jack's jeering comment reminded me of the hate-filled crowd at my speech on Friday. It made me feel angry. "He's trying to control you."

"I know." With a distressed frown, Mary tucked a lock of hair behind her ear. "But I love him. I want to make him happy, but I want to have my own friends, too."

"Of course you do. It's not healthy to have just one person in your life." I couldn't keep my concerns bottled up anymore. "Mary, I'm worried about you. Jack treats you like dirt. And he won't let you spend time with friends. Why don't you leave him?"

"I love him," she repeated. "Please. I don't want to talk about it anymore, okay?"

"But I hate to see you treated so horribly. You deserve so much better! Don't you think so?"

She stared at her desk for a moment, and then lifted her chin. A thread of steel straightened her posture, and her mouth set into a stubborn line. "I'd like to talk about something else."

Frustrated, I fell silent. I couldn't live Mary's life for her. She had to make her own decisions. But she did need to break away from Jack. At least for a little while. How could I help her?

An idea flew to mind, and of course, it popped right out of my mouth. "Would you like to do something fun this afternoon? Like go to Kruger's Yogurt? We could forget all of our troubles for a while."

A faint, forgiving smile flickered, and then vanished. "Thanks, Kay. But I can't."

It wasn't because she had to work. Jack would be furious if he found out.

I felt worried about her. But what could I do? David was right. Mary didn't want to be helped. She didn't want my help.

Mary changed the subject. "Is your church still doing the fundraiser dinner on Saturday?"

"Yes." I bent to rummage through my bag. "I have two more tickets to sell. Can you believe my parents bought two? They're fifty dollars apiece."

Mary eyed the tickets thoughtfully, and extended her hand. "Maybe I could sell them to my parents. They have the money. And they're always interested in charity cases." Irony laced her tone. She obviously referred to herself.

"I thought you didn't see your parents anymore."

"I don't." Mary tucked the tickets into her purse. "But I need to go over soon and pick up a few things. I'll go during the day, when Dad's not home."

We watched Mr. Carlisle stride to the front of the room. A smile twisted his lips. I wondered which religion he'd tear apart today.

Mary leaned toward me. "I was wondering—how are things going with Trent? Is David okay with it yet?"

It was hard to figure David out these days. "I think so. He's accepted Trent into our group. And he and I are getting along better, so I'm glad about that."

"What about Trent?"

"Things are fine." I hoped so, anyway, remembering my unsettled feelings on Friday night and Saturday morning. "He's a nice guy."

"Then I hope everything works out for you."

Mr. Carlisle interrupted our conversation. "Listen up, class. To date, we've done a brief overview of six religions. Today we're going to have some fun. One representative for each religion will come to the front of the class. Debate time. I need six volunteers. Kay Jameson? I'm sure you'll want to volunteer for Christianity." Did his smile look a touch malicious?

I tried to hide my reluctance as I headed for the front of the classroom. *Lord, please don't let me make a fool of myself. Or you.*

I survived World Religions class by answering questions as quickly as I could, and then diverting attention from me by peppering new questions at the other "volunteers" in the hot seats. Mr. Carlisle gave me a grudging smile of admiration at the end of class. "Next time, it won't be so easy, Jameson."

I offered him a faint, sly smile of my own. "Next time, I'll be better prepared."

I was glad to escape to Current Affairs class. Unfortunately, Trent did not show up. I wondered where he was.

Later, I found Mitch in the student union, waiting in line at the soda machine.

"Hi," I grinned.

With a smile, he stepped forward to feed a dollar bill into the machine. "What's up?"

"Remember the fundraiser?" I pulled a paper from my pack. "We were wondering if you'd draw up a couple of flyers for us. All the information is here. We need two flyers. One advertising the fundraiser, and one advertising the free dinner."

"Let me see." Stepping away from the machine, he took the paper and scanned it. "When do you need them?"

"As soon as possible. I know this is short notice..."

"No problem." He tucked it into a folder. "I'll drop them off tonight."

"So soon?" I said, surprised, but pleased. "That would be wonderful."

"Sure." His serious face lightened into a grin. "I already have a few ideas. What's your address?"

"Fifty-seven-o-one State."

"Okay. I'll drop them off around eight."

"Thank you, Mitch." Again, I marveled at my fortune in gaining this remarkable young man as a friend. And all because of that scary situation in the journalism lab. Romans 8:28 sprang to mind.

And we know that all things work together for good to those who love God, to those who are the called according to His purpose. (NKJV)

When I got home, Mom told me that David had called. He wanted to come over tonight and talk over plans for the dinner. I called back and asked him to come over after six-thirty.

At seven, the doorbell rang, and Dad answered the door. "David! Great to see you again. Kay tells me you're working together on a homeless dinner."

They talked for a few moments, and David joined me in the kitchen where I sat at the table with paper and pencils scattered at my elbow.

His brown eyes gleamed down at me. "Glad to see you're prepared, Doodlebug."

"I'm prepared to have a constructive evening," I returned, remembering the bickering in Sunday school.

He slung his jacket over the chair and sat across from me. "Are you still mad about the argument Joyce and I had?"

"A little," I admitted. "I mean, aren't we supposed to be working together?"

"Joyce and I have different visions for the dinner. Raising money is important, but I felt the emphasis was getting off track. It sounded like she cared more about business principles than the people who need help. I didn't like it." He eyed me seriously. "Of course, that's no reason to start squabbling. I know I acted like a jerk."

"Well, as long as you can admit it now." I reached for my favorite blue pencil. "Are you ready to start?"

"Almost. How's Mary doing?" His frown indicated he'd been worried about her, too.

"She could be better." I related our last conversation. It felt good to share my worries with him. "She won't consider leaving Jack. In fact, she won't even talk about it. I don't know what to do." I eyed him. "What do you think?"

"I don't know." His expression looked grim. "Be supportive. Be her friend. It sounds like she needs one."

"I will." I glanced at the blank pad of paper before me, and then back up again. An unexpected smile pulled at my lips. "Are you ready?" Suddenly, I was tired of being so serious. I just wanted to relax and have fun for a while.

His grin matched mine. "You bet."

"What should we serve?"

We had decided on spaghetti, rolls and sheet cake by the time Mitch arrived with the drawings.

"Hey, Mitch!" We welcomed him with warm, delighted grins. "Pull up a chair."

I eagerly accepted one of the drawings. The sketch was professionally crafted, with the information neatly lettered in a bold hand. Clean, spare strokes caught the essence of the upcoming dinner and fundraiser.

The homeless dinner flyer portrayed an adult and two children sitting at a table with heaping, steaming plates before them.

The fundraiser flyer depicted a dollar bill dropping down out of the sky, where it transformed into a steaming plate of food before the same little group sketched in the first drawing.

"These are great!"

"What's going on?" Stifling a yawn, Theresa shuffled into the kitchen. She'd been out late last night, but had woken up early for class this morning.

"Mitch sketched flyers for the fundraiser." I shot a glance at David. "I mean, the homeless dinner."

A smile twitched his lips.

Theresa peered at them. "Those are good!" Her tired, red-rimmed eyes glanced quickly at Mitch.

With Mitch's help, and a few comments from Theresa—who flitted in and out, apparently revived by a new burst of energy—we planned the meal down to the last detail in fairly short order.

"Bobby and Laura Page offered to shop for the food." David sat back and flexed his shoulders.

My back ached, too. I glanced at my watch. After ten! I couldn't believe it.

David shuffled the papers together. "Thanks for your help, guys. I'll drop this list off at the church tomorrow."

Theresa batted her eyes. "Will you need help with the dinner on Saturday?"

"We sure will." His smile appeared carefully impersonal. It was painfully obvious my sister still had a crush on him. He glanced at Mitch. "It would be great if you both could come."

Mitch's mouth twisted with obvious regret, forming an odd angle with his off kilter nose. "Sorry. I have a job lined up that day. But I could drop off some rolls from my dad's supermarket."

"That would be great," I said. "You've already done a lot. Thank you so much for making up these flyers. They're terrific."

"Thanks." He flushed, looking a bit embarrassed.

We walked with him to the front door.

"Guess I'll see you on Wednesday," David nodded to me, and then he and Mitch slapped hands in some sort of male bonding ritual. "See you later, bud."

I watched them disappear down the shadowy walk. It was late, and dark. Dangerous. I wondered if either was ever afraid.

FUTURE

HER DRY, PARCHED throat was impossible to ignore now. Isola snapped shut Kay's diary. It had been hours since she'd last drunk any water. Thank goodness she was next in the food line.

Overhead, the dull, ashy sky was beginning to darken into twilight. Hard to believe it was spring, and that the days should be getting longer. Not shorter.

Swallowing with difficulty, Isola dug into her pocket and pulled out her small black food token. Ahead, the woman with the toddler moved out of her way.

"Token, please." Bored, the be-spectacled matron stared at her through the bulletproof glass.

Isola slipped the token into the retrieval box. The box slid out of sight.

"Water?" The owl-eyed lady nodded to a transparent bottle clenched in her fist. The liquid was a murky brown. "Decontaminated," she promised.

Isola's tongue felt thick and dry in her mouth, but she shook her head. Maybe the water was purified. Then again, maybe it wasn't. The risk was too great to trust the distribution clerk. She'd rather boil her own water and know it was safe to drink.

The box slid out. In it was a lunch-sized brown bag—her meal for the next 24 hours. Isola grabbed it, and greedily inhaled the warm, meaty smell. A hamburger. Her stomach rumbled angrily.

Feet flying, she set out for home.

When she turned the last corner, just a few blocks from her apartment, she saw it. The one thing that terrified her more than anything else these days: a man being beaten by two men in the middle of the street. One held the victim immobile, and forced him to kneel on the broken pavement.

Heart pounding, she darted behind a building. She was so close that she could hear the mocking cries of the attackers.

"Christian!" A bully sneered. "Curse your faith, and we'll let you go!"

"No!" the man gasped. Blood ran in rivulets from his nose, down to his chin, and dripped onto his chest. One arm was wrenched up painfully behind his back, but strangely, his face looked serene. "No. I will not renounce Jesus. He is Lord!"

Another sound of fist hitting flesh.

Isola cringed. How could the man stand it? How could he stay loyal to Jesus? Horror-struck, and yet feeling oddly jealous, she listened to him again defend his faith.

Oh, to have that kind of faith! To believe so strongly in God. She wished she had that. Kay had had it. But Isola felt empty inside. And she knew that her emptiness was much worse than the torment the Christian man experienced now. His pain would end. But hers would go on and on.

She blinked, and focused again on the struggle in the street. People wandering down the road skirted the little drama, ignoring it. It was a common enough occurrence. People hated the new Christians. Violently. But Isola did not understand why.

One of the attackers thrust his hand high in the air. A knife flashed in his fist.

Horror closed like a vise around her throat. They intended to kill that Christian man! She couldn't watch it. She couldn't allow it! But what could she do?

A distraction. Desperately, she looked around. Nothing. What she needed was...a gun.

With fumbling fingers, she jerked the gun from her waist-band and unsteadily cocked it. She'd shoot it over their heads. It would give the man a chance to get away.

As she watched, the knife plunged down.

Crack! The little gun recoiled in her hand, making her stagger. Eyes wide, she stared at it, and then at the scene in the middle of the street. The casual passersby scattered, but the two attackers gaped at her, comic disbelief written across their faces.

Forgotten for the moment, the Christian seized his chance. Twisting violently, he darted off between two buildings.

"Hey!" The men's heads whipped, first after the Christian, and then back at Isola.

One started for her. "Hey, girl!" he snarled. "I'll teach you…"

She didn't wait to hear more. Spinning on her heels, she fled, feet flying over the broken concrete, and darted into the maze of buildings that hid her apartment complex.

Week Five — Wickedness

*"Because of the increase of wickedness,
the love of most will grow cold..."*

MATTHEW 24:12

*"But mark this: There will be terrible times in the last days.
People will be lovers of themselves, lovers of money,
boastful, proud, abusive, disobedient to their parents,
ungrateful, unholy, without love,
unforgiving, slanderous, without self-control,
brutal, not lovers of the good,
treacherous, rash, conceited,
lovers of pleasure rather than lovers of God—
having a form of godliness but denying its power.
Have nothing to do with them."*

2 TIMOTHY 3:1-5

Future — continued

TWISTING AND TURNING, Isola sprinted. Each searing gasp rasped harshly in her ears. Surely he could hear her.

The whitish gray buildings stood close together, forming blocks and blocks of scattered alleyways; it was a maze that covered three square blocks. Her shoulder accidentally slammed into a crumbling, stuccoed wall, jarring the breath from her lungs. Gasping, she plunged on, her feet flying over loose rocks and plaster. She darted around a rusted air conditioner, and glanced over her shoulder. Nothing. But she heard him.

Twisting, she cut behind a building and sprinted down the narrow lane behind it. It was wider, meant for cars, and dangerous, for she was out in the open. Spotting familiar territory, she cut down another alleyway, and then slipped through a gate, and into an apartment complex.

Teeth clenched against the searing pain in her lungs, she flew past the empty swimming pool pit, past the dried stalks that had been geraniums, and through another gate, into another alley. Heart pounding, she stopped and looked right and left. She held her breath.

Nothing. She heard nothing.

But that didn't mean the man wasn't standing as still as she was, listening for any sign of movement.

Allowing carefully muted breaths to slip through her teeth again, Isola twisted the hot metal knob of the door that led into another crumbling apartment complex. Quietly, she slipped inside. It was dark in here, and musty. But familiar.

She opened another door, and peered out. The hallway was dim, but empty. Quietly, she crept out and walked swiftly down the hall, toward the rickety staircase at the end. Each puff of air burned her lungs.

She'd lost the man. She was pretty sure of that now. Still trying to slow her heaving, gasping breaths, she tiptoed up the creaking flights of stairs, and slipped down the dimly lit upstairs hall. At number 4E she stopped and fished a series of keys from her pocket. One, two, three, four, five locks all grated open. The creaking rasps sounded loud in the silent, decaying building.

After pushing open the door, she halted and listened. Nothing, except for the quick scurry of rodent feet overhead, and her own heaving breaths. Shuddering, Isola slipped into the filthy, dimly lit room and clicked all the locks closed behind her.

Trembling now, she closed her eyes and rested her back against the gouged wooden door. She was safe. Nausea rose in her throat, but she gulped it back. She'd escaped death three times today. Was she crazy? Walking all the way to State Street and back had been foolish. Chased by soldiers, murderous men with knives...

Shivering, she stumbled across the tiny room. Her dry throat burned. She was parched. A cup sat next to her little electric hot plate and radio, both of which were plugged into the one, double outlet in the bare room. She owned no furniture. The apartment contained nothing else, except for a musty old army blanket lying beneath the broken window.

Slipping out the Bible and her gun, which were digging into her flesh, she lay them and the notebook down on the dirty blanket. Greedily, she then took the extra step and grabbed the cup of murky water and gulped it down.

It tasted bitter. Awful. Contaminated by sewage lines and other, more horrible things. But boiled, as this was, it was safe to drink.

Grimacing, she set down the cup. Her throat still burned, but at least her mouth wasn't dry any longer. And her labored breathing had stilled. Isola glanced back at the locked door and listened. Silence. She'd tricked the man. She was safe.

Hefting a large kettle from the floor, she trudged to the bathroom. The door to this room was missing, and the grimy appliances were covered with the brown residue left behind by the filthy water. It was useless to clean anymore.

Plopping the kettle into the tub, she turned on the faucet. Brown water gushed out. The steady thrum rapidly filled the kettle. Quickly, she screwed the knob off before the pot could overflow. She didn't want filthy water to splash onto her hands. She planned to eat next, and did not want to contaminate her food.

After returning to the tiny living area, she set the kettle on the hot plate and flipped the switch on. The electricity wouldn't come on until six o'clock, but this way the hot plate would automatically turn on and begin to boil the water.

She had no watch. The only indicator of time she possessed was the time electricity came on, or the color of the sunlight outside her window. And right now, judging by the dark gray cast to the air, it was closing in on four o'clock. At five it would be pitch dark, thanks to the ash filled sky—in the old days, it would have stayed light until seven, since it was springtime.

The warm smell of hamburger meat tantalized her nose. She plopped down cross-legged onto the blanket beneath the broken window. She was so hungry!

Stomach growling, she eagerly pulled each item from the bag. A hamburger. That she knew. Two scrawny, shriveled apples. A small package of breakfast mix, fortified with vitamins and minerals, a sheaf of raw green beans, and four rectangular crackers. This was supposed to fuel her for the next 24 hours.

Bitterness touched her soul, but it vanished when she took a bite of hamburger. She exhaled softly. Pure ambrosia. She hadn't eaten a hamburger in ages.

While chewing, she carefully packed away the remainder of her meal. Food rations were getting smaller and smaller. Not only here, but around the world. No wonder she was so hungry all the time. Yesterday she had been unable to stop eating until the whole bag was empty.

She remembered the Chairman on T.V. He didn't look undernourished. But then again, neither did the other world leaders, or even rich people here in Truesdale. She'd seen them, occasionally.

She stuffed the hamburger in her mouth again, and tried to block out the empty, angry bitterness poisoning her soul. It wasn't fair. But the horrible thing was, she didn't expect life to be fair anymore.

Finally, she understood life, and accepted reality. She couldn't change the awful world she lived in. It was outside of her control. But maybe she could change on the inside. Maybe a healthier perspective would help her to better deal with the world around her.

But how? How could she change? What could possibly swallow up all of the bitterness and anger that had festered inside her for the last three and a half years?

Her gaze fell on Kay's diary. It pulled irresistibly to her. A small voice whispered that Kay's notebook held the answers she sought. It contained the solution—the hope, so she could triumph over her circumstances now. Isola wanted to hope again.

Her greasy fingers again reached for the notebook.

WEDNESDAY

Cold wind and rain buffeted me into World Religions class this morning. Gasping, and cheeks feeling cold, I dripped over to my desk. "Hi!" I chirped to Mary. "Great day, isn't it?"

"If you like rain." Mary glanced up with a smile. I peeled off my shiny blue slicker and hung it over the back of my plastic chair. "I like sunshine a lot better."

"But this is the first storm of the season!" My eyes felt cool against my eyelids. "I love it. I love the change of seasons."

Dipping into her purse, Mary handed me both fundraiser tickets and a hundred dollar bill. "My mom wanted to donate one hundred dollars, but neither of my parents will go to the dinner. So I'll give both tickets back to you."

"Oh. Thank you. I really appreciate it. How did that go, anyway? Seeing your mom?"

"Good," Her eyes sparkled. "We actually had a good talk about...things. She apologized for kicking me out."

"That was nice of her."

Mary smiled patiently. "It meant a lot to me. She even said she wishes I could come home, but Dad won't stand for it." She glanced down at her white knuckles. "But that's just the way he is."

"Will you see her again soon?"

"Yes." Her smile returned. "On Sunday we'll go to church together. To her church, I mean. I found out she's been going to Mass recently. I know. Surprise of surprises."

Neither of Mary's parents had ever attended church before, as far as I could remember.

"That's great news." God was calling the hearts of the Campinellas. First Mary, and now her mother. I could only pray that all of them, her father included, would give their hearts to Jesus, and accept him as their personal Savior. It rested in the Lord's hands. *Please turn their hearts and lives to you, Lord. And if you can use me in any way to speak to them, please show me how.*

"Can you help us with the dinner on Saturday?" I asked.

Her happy light died, and Mary looked away. "I don't think so."

I hadn't meant to upset her. Obviously, she wouldn't come because Jack wouldn't allow it. I changed the subject. "How is your baby doing? Have you seen the doctor lately?"

Mary smiled again. "Everything is going just fine."

"Hi, Kay!" The familiar, rich tenor halted me in my wet, squelching tracks. I was heading for Kale Hall, still endless yards away.

"Trent!" I welcomed him with a smile. It was good to see him. He was dry beneath his designer umbrella. His face looked thinner than the last time I'd seen him, and he appeared tired.

"Come under here." He motioned my dripping form under the wide umbrella. I readily complied. Although my hood was up, freezing rain dripped down my face, making me shiver.

"Where were you on Monday?" I struggled to match his hurrying strides.

"Umm... Internship had me out on assignment. Couldn't get out of it. Did I miss anything?"

"Not much. Dr. Williams lectured on protecting confidential sources."

"Oh." Trent didn't sound like he regretted missing the class.

"Kay? Is that you?" Joyce swam toward us, sheltered by a burgundy umbrella. "I thought so. Can't mistake that electric blue raincoat. Hi, Trent."

"Hi," he mumbled.

Joyce turned to me. "Have I got something to tell you! Remind me to call you later."

"What's it about?"

"The FGA—but I can't talk now. Got to run. Ta!" Joyce sprinted across the sidewalk, heading for the business hall.

A few minutes later, Trent snapped his umbrella shut and we dripped into Kale Hall.

"Some storm, isn't it?" I said with a small laugh.

His somber expression lightened, and he smiled for the first time. "Sure is. Sorry I haven't been all here. Hey, I wanted to ask you something. Do you want to go out Friday night?"

An unexpected catch of reluctance made me hesitate. It also confused me.

I chose to ignore it. "Of course. I'd love to. What did you have in mind?"

"A charity ball. It's formal. Sound like something you'd like to do?"

"Yes." I smiled. A ball. What fun!

But what would I wear? Then I remembered I still had a few old high school prom dresses hanging in my closet. Maybe one of them would work.

"Great. I'll pick you up at seven-thirty."

Dr. Williams shoved a paper at me when I stepped into the classroom. It was my reworked thesis statement, which I'd handed in on Friday.

He'd put a tiny check on it, meaning it was acceptable. But right below, in big red letters, he'd written, "Now you have a persecution complex. Stick to the facts. *If* you can find any."

I swallowed back a surge of anger. He obviously didn't think my topic was worthwhile.

After I found a seat, Professor Williams' sneering smile and cool, contemptuous eyes didn't reassure me. It was a warning. He'd let me pursue the topic, but he'd fail me if I couldn't prove that persecution was a real problem these days. And he'd take great pleasure in doing so.

Well, I'd prove it to him. I'd prove it, if it was the last thing I did.

Trent and I sat near each other and chatted about inconsequential things until class started. Trent's pensive mood had lifted. I wondered what had bothered him earlier, but oddly, felt reluctant to ask.

"Kay?" Mom knocked on my door. "Do you have your group tonight? If so, you'll need to eat before we do. Dad will be home late."

I opened my door. I suspected I looked frazzled. "Thanks, Mom." I'd pulled every gown out of my closet and they now dripped like sparkling gems around my room. I couldn't decide which one to wear to the dance with Trent.

Impulsively, I grabbed her hand and urged her inside. "Will you help me? Trent asked me to a charity ball on Friday night, but I don't know which dress to wear."

An instant, pleased smile softened the tense line of Mom's mouth. Her heels scratched softly across the carpet. "Of course. I'd love to. It's for a ball, you say?"

"It's formal." I hovered beside her as she fingered the five dresses draped over my bed, and over my chair back.

"This is lovely." Mom held up a silver, strapless gown. I'd worn it to a formal Christmas party given by Dad's employer. She stared at me for moment, lips pursed, and then shook her head. "No. That won't do. Too evening gownish."

She held up another, and another, until we came to the last dress. It was a cool, ethereal green with spaghetti straps. She smiled as she looked first at it, then at me. "This is it, Kay. It makes you look elegant. Sophisticated. And it brings out the beautiful green of your eyes."

We both turned so I could look at myself in the closet mirror. For a second, her smiling face tilted next to mine. "You'll take his breath away, honey."

My eyes glowed from her praise. The dress did look fantastic. I'd only worn it once before, to my senior prom. I hugged her. "Thanks, Mom."

"You're welcome, honey." She hugged me tight for a moment, and then let go. Her eyes looked suddenly misty. "I'll help you put these back. Dinner is almost ready."

I felt happy. At last, I'd done something right with Mom. I hoped the bond between us would only grow stronger.

"Did you bring the flyers?" Joyce stood at my elbow in the church foyer. College group would begin in a minute.

"Yes. In here." I patted my backpack. "So, will you tell me about the FGA? It was pretty cruel of you to toss that at me this morning. I've been wondering about it all day."

"Wondering about what?" David jostled my arm when he stepped out of the path of an incoming gaggle of girls. Rivulets of water ran down his dark blue slicker and through his rumpled dark hair. In typical male fashion, he hadn't thought to put up his hood.

"The FGA," I supplied.

We both looked at Joyce.

She sighed impatiently, and glanced toward the sanctuary. The group was about to begin, and she clearly wanted to be where all the action was. "Dad got a call from the FGA this morning."

"And?"

"They liked the food drive. But they didn't like that we gave out Bibles."

"Why not?"

"Apparently, the FGA didn't authorize buying Bibles." Joyce rolled her eyes. "They warned Dad that we'd better use church funds for approved uses."

"So now we have to get their approval for everything," David said grimly.

"Just about. And they delivered one more warning about Saturday's fundraiser."

"What?" Our church was caught in the middle of some bizarre game of chicken. Warnings from the FGA. Warnings from the hate group...

"They like the idea. But we can only spend the money we raise on food, and for setting up the event. They said they'd *review* our plan to give the extra money to Driscoll Shelter."

"That is ridiculous!" David's tone deepened with disgust.

"Why are they suddenly watching every move we make?"

Joyce shook her head. "Maybe all the hate group stuff is bothering them, like you said, Kay. I don't know. Anyway, Dad has to attend some vision meeting tomorrow. Maybe he can explain more afterward."

"I hope so."

Laura sailed by as our little group edged for the door to the sanctuary. Doing a double-take, she halted and gave us a radiant smile. "Hi, guys! How are you doing? I haven't been able to talk to you for a while."

"How are *you* doing?" I said with concern. "Have you learned anything yet about Bobby's job?"

"No." But Laura's eyes looked clear and serene. "We're just praying and trusting the Lord to take care of us. He will." Her smile gentled. "He always does, doesn't he?"

I admired, even envied Laura's deep, unwavering faith. I wanted to grow to know the Lord that well. A vivid picture flashed before my eyes.

I was on a journey, with ever widening pastures ahead of me. Waving, colorful oceans of joy, love, peace, wisdom, and righteousness that I couldn't comprehend yet, that God wanted me to have, beckoned me on...

I stumbled a little when David pushed on my back.

"Come on. Let's find seats."

I wondered where that vivid imagery had come from. From Jesus? Was he trying to tell me how rich and deep knowing him truly was? The thought took my breath away.

Or was the vision only a product of my overactive imagination?

Bobby's clipped voice filtered through my thoughts. "Tonight we won't have a regular meeting. I know it's raining, but we need to tack up flyers all over town. So any of you bold enough to brave the cold, stick around. We need your help."

His chin jerked down to view his notes. "Looks like one group will canvass the north and west sides of town, and another the east and south. We'll break those groups down into even smaller teams so we can cover more ground." His small smile looked a bit forced. "Who's in? Let's see a show of hands."

Thanks to the grit of our college class, everyone volunteered.

"Great. The north and west team will meet in the foyer, and the other group will meet up here."

"What are you guys going to do?" I asked.

"I'm going to lead up the north and west group." Joyce said. "Could you give me the fundraiser flyers, Kay? We'll put those up. The other group will do the dinner flyers."

"Oh. Okay." I dug the inch high piles from my backpack and gave the blue ones to Joyce.

"You keep some." She handed them back. "Would you put them up around campus tomorrow? I'll drop some off at the T.V. and radio stations, too."

"Good idea." We edged toward the aisle.

David said, "I'll head up the other group." His voice sounded a bit tight.

Palpable tension suddenly throbbed. Was David upset because Joyce kept babbling on and on about the fundraiser?

"Great!" Joyce trotted down the aisle and left us quickly behind.

"How about it, Buttercup? Want to come with me?" David's tone sounded too light.

"Sure." Why not? Joyce didn't seem to need or want either of us around. Already, she was jabbering with a little group of people clustered around her. She was in her element. Planning, directing. In control, as always. I had no doubt that her business career path was exactly on track, too.

Eight other people joined our east/south group. Since we had ten people, we elected to break up into five teams so we could cover more territory. That's when I realized we'd be covering all the bad sections of town, and Joyce, all the good sections.

Had she planned it this way? Was David right? Was she only interested in dealing with the rich and upper middle class?

It was a critical, judging thought, and Jesus' words, memorized a few months ago for Sunday school, flew to mind. Matthew 7:3-5:

Why do you look at the speck of sawdust in your brother's eye and pay no attention to the plank in your own eye? How can you say to your brother, 'Let me take the speck out of your eye,' when all the time there is a plank in your own eye? You hypocrite, first take the plank out of your own eye, and then you will see clearly to remove the speck from your brother's eye."

Ashamed, I quickly stuffed the thought to the back of my head. I didn't know what Joyce's motivations were. Only God did.

Bobby's voice rose above the chattering din. "That's it, folks. Laura and I will stick around here in case anyone needs to talk. Those of you who will be tacking up flyers, please meet back here at nine o'clock. I'd like you to drop off any extra flyers here, and also get a head count to make sure you've all returned safely. Call if you encounter any problems tonight. Other than that, see you later!" He scampered down the steps and disappeared toward the foyer.

"Guess we're on our own." David said with a grin. "Everyone got their assignments?"

Rowdily, we shouted back, "Yes, sir!"

"All right! Gooooo...team!" He pumped a fist toward the ceiling, and we erupted, giggling and jostling for the doors. Joyce's team still clustered in an orderly group, talking intensely together.

David and I decided to patrol the east side of town together, along Driscoll and High Streets.

Outdoors, the cold, pelting rain on my face felt like a shock after the warm church. I flipped up my hood and sprinted for David's sports car. My tennis shoes splashed through the shallow puddles dotting the parking lot.

Dancing a cold little jig, I waited while David unlocked my side, and then lunged in, teeth chattering, and unlocked his door.

"Whew!" Shaking his wet head like a mangy mutt, David slammed the door closed behind him. He grinned at me, his dark eyes sparkling, and shoved the key in the ignition. "This is going to be some night!"

I rubbed my cold hands together, and hastily buckled up when we bumped onto the main road. "Where do you want to go first?"

"Let's go straight north to High, then work our way east, toward Driscoll." Visibly charged with energy, he sped to our first stopping place.

"Let's each do one side of the street. We'll cover more ground that way." David eased over to the curb. Traffic on High Street was sparse tonight because of the driving rain. One blessing, at least.

"Two blocks," he said over his shoulder, and darted across the wet, slippery street.

Hunching my shoulders, I sprinted for the nearest telephone pole. A flyer and a tack secured the first flyer. They'd be tattered and rain soaked by morning, but what could we do?

I got an idea when I spotted a recessed business door. Quickly folding a flyer, I stuffed it in the doorway. Businesses could tell their customers about the free dinner, and if they wanted, the business could contribute money or food. A good way to kill two birds with one stone. Feeling proud of myself, I dashed to the next doorway, and then the next.

By the time I'd sprinted back to the car, the lights were on and David was creeping toward me. I lurched in, shuddering and shaking. My lips felt numb, and my jeans were soaked. It literally poured outside now.

"What are we doing out here?" I gasped. "We must be crazy!"

"Cold?" David cranked up the heat.

We edged forward two blocks, and then parked again. If anything, the rain pelted down even harder now, and pummeled the car roof with spattering, staccato blasts.

"Let's wait," I suggested, rubbing my frozen hands together. "Maybe it'll slow down in a minute."

"All right." David switched off the headlights, but kept the engine running and the heat blowing. Warmth crept back into my icy fingers, and I relaxed back in my seat.

It felt peaceful, sitting there. It had been a while since I'd been in David's car, I realized. I'd spent most of my time with Trent lately.

The sound of the rain beating on the metal roof, combined with the familiar musty, pine air freshener smell comforted me. As did David's presence. He was easy to be with.

"Trent left awfully fast on Saturday." Although David spoke casually, I stiffened. I thought we'd put the issue of Trent behind us.

And I simply did not want to talk about Trent. Not with David. I was dealing with enough confused feelings regarding Trent already.

"He had to work," I said carefully. "He has an internship with the *Truesdale Register*."

"Very impressive," Arms bent, he stretched forward. "So, you're still seeing him?"

Sudden, unreasonable anger gripped me. I could not explain why, but I felt shoved in a corner. For awhile now, something had been bothering me about my relationship with Trent, but I couldn't figure out what it might be. However, those uncomfortable, unsettled feelings inspired a fresh spark of anger toward David, who appeared ready to pepper me with hostile questions again.

"Yes, I am," I tried to speak evenly, but the words ended in a small snap. "You know that. Nothing's changed. Why do you keep bringing him up?"

He wanted to start a fight. Or maybe I did.

He shrugged. "Actually, I haven't..."

"Just stop it!" I glared at him. He clearly still disapproved of Trent. His implied criticism hurt me, deep inside. I couldn't even say how, exactly, but the desire to lash out and hurt him, too, overwhelmed me. Self-protective words, designed to make him back off and leave me alone, flew from my mouth. "You know, David, if I didn't know better, I'd think you were jealous!"

The words instantly delivered the desired effect. Perhaps more strongly than I had expected.

He jerked back, as if struck. "Don't be ridiculous!"

His fingers curled tightly around the steering wheel, and his knuckles briefly showed white. "You know, Kay, I'm trying really hard to stay out of this. And I think I've done a good job. But I won't lie to you. I don't like the guy. Period. Christian or not." His eyes flashed with temper. "I won't bring him up again. Okay?"

"Good!" I flopped back against my seat, arms crossed. The rain beat down on the metal roof. It was an empty sound. A lonely sound. We sat in silence.

A huge, uncomfortable barrier yawned between us. I hated it. Our relationship had finally gotten back on track again, but I'd just derailed it again.

Why had I gone off the deep end? He hadn't meant to turn the joking camaraderie between us into this stiff, angry silence. I had. Why?

Painful truth crept into my heart. Something *was* bothering me about Trent. But what?

I'd felt disconnected from Trent recently. Was that it?

A gentle probing could not explain what was wrong. David's comments had only served to rip it out. And make me angry.

"I'm sorry, David," I said softly. "I shouldn't have yelled at you like that. It was totally out of line, and I'm sorry. Honestly, I know you care about me, and that's the only reason why you say anything about Trent." I glanced at him, and then out at the rain pattering against the windshield. I knew that was true, and yet I still felt lost and troubled.

"I'm sorry, too. I didn't mean to upset you."

"Let's talk about something else, okay? Let's forget that ever happened."

"Okay." He eyed me carefully. "What do you want to talk about?"

"Did you know Mitch is interested in the end times?"

When David's brow lifted, I said, "He's drawn pictures that look like the Tribulation..."

The conversation went more smoothly after that. I made sure of it, and suspected he did, too. I wouldn't let Trent come between us again. My friendship with David was too important. David and I talked about Mitch's latest drawing; the Persecution one, I called it. Jesus had predicted persecution in the last days.

"You've had to deal with a lot of persecution at school lately," David settled back in his seat, looking serious.

"So has our church."

"True." But he turned back to his original topic. "Have Randy or Tim bothered you since that lab incident?"

I'd never told him about the doggy doo incident. I briefly told him about it, and his hands fisted white on his knees.

"Kay..."

"I'm fine," I assured him. "That was a few weeks ago. The worst was the speech. I know they're the ones who started the riot." I remembered class today. Randy and Tim weren't the only ones causing trouble for me because I was a Christian.

He picked up on my small hesitation. "What?"

"It's my professor." First, I told him how Dr. Williams had ridiculed me in class and rejected my thesis statement. Then I repeated the sneering warning he'd scribbled on my paper.

"That's not right." David's voice deepened.

"I can't do much about it. Mr. Carlisle doesn't seem to like me much, either. He put me in the hot seat on Monday because I'm a Christian. Of course, he doesn't seem to like *any* religion." I also mentioned his connection to Tim.

He frowned, and fiddled with the keys in the ignition. "Tell me if anything else happens. Okay? That harassment needs to stop."

I felt better after telling him everything. But honestly, I wasn't sure how either of us could stop my Current Affairs professor's subtle, mocking persecution. Anyway, it was minor; petty, really, when compared to the attacks on our church.

I turned to him. "You know what I think?"

"What?"

"I think Tim and Randy's hate group might be the one attacking our church." I'd told Joyce my theory, but she hadn't seemed too interested in it.

"Really." His brows drew together again. "Why do you think that?"

I explained about the black arm bands, and the black cloth at the church. "It's too much of a coincidence, don't you think? I mean, I don't have proof, but I would bet on it."

"It makes sense," he agreed. "And it's the first lead we have. If only we could prove they're behind it."

"You mean catch them in the act?"

He shot me a crooked grin. "I wasn't thinking anything so dramatic. But that would do the trick."

Unfortunately, neither of us could figure out how to keep a 24 hour watch on the church in order to catch the bad guys— short of hiring a security guard, and we knew the church couldn't afford that.

After a while we talked about Revelation again. David offered to lend me one of his prophecy books. He could give it to me on video night on Friday, if I decided to go.

"But it would be late," he remembered. "I have to take care of a family obligation that night."

"It doesn't matter. I can't go," I said quickly. I had a date with Trent. Although I didn't say that, just for a second I felt— or imagined—the uncomfortable feeling flood back between us.

But then David glanced outside and flashed me a grin. The rain had let up. "Bet I can cover the next block faster than you."

Laughing, we both dashed out into the dripping rain. The rest of the evening flew by.

But deep inside, something nagged at me.

Trent. What was bothering me about our relationship?

Lord, please help me to see Trent with clear eyes. I care about him, but I feel really confused about what that means right now. Please give me wisdom, Lord. I want to follow in your path, because I know your way is always the best way. Please help me.

And please forgive me for being so horrible to David, over and over again. Just because I trust him completely and can be real with him doesn't mean I can say whatever I want, and snap at him. I'm confused and frustrated, but that's no reason to take things out on him. I'm so sorry. Thank you for David's friendship. He means so much to me. In Jesus' name, amen.

THURSDAY

I FELT RANDY AND TIM'S EYES ON ME as I tacked up a poster on a public bulletin board on campus late this afternoon. I tucked the leftovers in my backpack and casually strolled down the corridor, hoping they wouldn't follow me into Kale Hall.

Flipping up my electric blue hood, I plunged through the swinging glass doors and out into the pouring rain. The heavy drops spattered off the pavement, swallowing up the sound of my shoes as I hop-skipped through the standing puddles. It was almost dark outside. Thick black storm clouds clustered overhead.

After a quick glance over my shoulder, I slipped into Kale Hall. They hadn't followed me. Thank goodness. The oppressive feeling of fear lifted.

I settled down to work at one of the free computers. Yards of research remained if I wanted to finish my outline, which was due on Monday. At five o'clock I stopped, stretched my aching back, and gathered up my notes and flash drive. A quick, furtive movement in the doorway caught my eye.

A shock of dark hair. A skinny arm.

Perhaps foolishly, I leaped up to get a better look. Tim darted down the hallway. I spun back to collect my backpack. Had he been spying on me?

Surely not. And what if he had? He couldn't steal my work. It was locked into the computer. Only I had the password.

Feeling a bit uneasy, I slipped down the hall. I longed to be home. Hunger gnawed at my stomach, and I was tired.

When I reached for the glass door, ready to push out into the pouring rain, I glanced at the bulletin board where I'd tacked a poster earlier.

What? I did a double take, and almost tripped because of my forward momentum.

The flyer had vanished!

A sick feeling washed over me. I whirled and dashed down the hall to check another bulletin board. Gone. And the last one. Gone!

Tim—and probably Randy—had torn down all of my posters. Shaking, I stood there, biting back angry words. All that work! They'd ripped down all of my work. They'd beaten me.

No. No, they hadn't.

I snatched the leftover posters from my backpack. I'd tack them up again.

My anger had petered out by the time I'd tacked up the last flyer. As I passed through another hall, I checked to make sure the posters remained up. Yes. Thank goodness. Randy and Tim must have gone home. They hadn't expected me to put the flyers back up again.

With a tired smile of satisfaction, I plunged into the rain. It was almost six o'clock, and dark. I longed for home.

Driving rain spattered off the dark, shadowed parking lot, and splashed onto my already soaked shoes. It was strange that the lot seemed so dark, for all the lampposts glowed. But the heavy rain seemed to bend their bright rays, forcing the light to pool at the lamps' feet.

I hurried through the shadows to my shiny wet car. It was parked alone, beneath a street lamp. No other cars were within fifty yards. However, just for a second, I had the intense, odd feeling that someone watched me.

Ridiculous. Surely Tim had left campus by now—otherwise he would have ripped down the posters again. And who else would lurk in the pouring rain, waiting for a victim? He'd catch pneumonia.

Unless he hid in a nearby car.

With quick, nervous glance at my empty back seat, I unlocked my car and slid in. I was safe. Everything was fine.

I slammed the door and shoved the key in the ignition. And froze.

My windshield was white. A cracked, smashed mess. Still intact, but barely. It looked like someone had beaten it with a baseball bat.

My shoulder hit the door, and I stumbled out again, still feeling the eyes watching me. The sensation felt more oppressive now. But I saw nothing except for the dark, shapeless forms of cars hunkered down in their parking spaces.

Fear curled like poisonous tentacles around my heart. I bit back a tiny sob and whirled back to my car.

Then I saw the tires. Both, on this side of the car, had been slashed.

Suddenly trembling so hard my knees felt like jello, I returned to the car and yanked out my backpack. I slammed the door, locked it, and blindly headed for the nearest building.

Don't cry! Don't cry. Don't let them see they've hurt me. Or scared me.

The words circled over and over again through my head. I clung to the bracing refrain.

I passed by the tires on the passenger side, and a glance proved they had been slashed, too.

Feeling numb, I walked steadily, keeping near the line of street lamps.

A car engine roared to life, and wet tires spun. Headlights glared, coming at me head on.

I gasped, and ran for nearest light post. Thick concrete wrapped around its base, and I flung my body against it, in some thought of self-preservation. Surely they wouldn't ram into a concrete pillar.

The car roared louder, and louder. It raced toward me, and then swerved crazily and skidded, so it faced the opposite direction. High, raucous laughter filled my ears. The driver gunned the engine again.

This time, he sped right for my light post. I stifled my instinct to flee like a frightened rabbit. The car passed so close that the concrete pillar almost took a layer of paint off the gray sedan. The man at the wheel wore a mask. Halfway across the parking lot now, he slammed on the brakes, skidded, and shot off toward the street.

Choking back a sob, I ran. He'd be back.

Chest heaving and lungs burning, I sprinted as fast as I could. Tears mixed with the rain streaming down my face. Tires squealed again. I'd made it to the sidewalk, and the administration hall lay right ahead.

Vision blurry, I burst through the doors. I glanced back. The sedan sped by, and then swerved crazily again, and jounced high off a speed bump.

Hand pressed to my mouth, I fled down the hall, desperate to find someone. Anyone still at work. But the offices were dark, and closed for the night. I needed to call for help, but I was afraid to stop. Afraid he'd find me.

I plunged down the hall, overcome by mindless fear. Finally, at the end, in a dark corner I huddled against the wall and pulled out my cell phone.

Trembling, and teeth chattering, I dialed home. Like a runaway freight train, sobs racked my body. One after another after another...

"Hello?"

"Dad!" The word ended in a high, keening wail. "Dad! Please come get me. Someone... Someone..." I could not speak. Unrestrained, convulsive sobs seized me.

"Are you all right?" Dad barked in my ear.

"Yes."

"Where are you?"

I gasped, "Admin. building. Dad, get a..." but the line clicked dead in my ear. He had already hung up.

Pressing cold hands against my eyes, I slid down to the floor, unable to stop the violent shudders wracking my body. I cried until no tears remained.

I managed to pull myself together enough to call for a tow truck.

Soon after, loud steps clumped down the hall. "Kay?" Dad bellowed. "Are you here? Are you all right?"

"Yes!" With a gasp, I dashed down the hall and flung myself into his protective arms. New tears burned my cheeks. "Dad, I can't believe this."

"Shh. Shh," he said, trying to calm me. "Tell me in a minute."

Finally, I gulped out the entire story.

His face turned a livid red. "Did you call the police?"

"No, I didn't."

Dad called the police. They arrived about the same time the tow truck did. I reported what Tim and Randy had done to me over the last several weeks. I felt sure they were behind this attack. I also described the car I'd seen, and the masked man.

"But I didn't get the license plate number." The policeman scribbled down my statement.

"It doesn't matter," Dad said grimly, his arm about my shoulders. "You'll get to the bottom of this, won't you, sergeant?"

"We'll try, sir."

Dad drove me home, and Mom fussed over me. Even Theresa hovered nearby with a worried frown as I related what had happened. I was thankful to be home, with my family circled protectively around me. They were on my side, no matter what happened.

The good feeling gradually trickled away when I retreated upstairs to my room. I couldn't stop thinking about everything Tim and Randy had done to me. It made me furious. They'd threatened another attack. Was this it?

My fingers curled into useless fists.

To make matters worse, my parents' vehement, cutting voices rose up from the living room. Worse, the argument was about me.

"It's too dangerous for her to be out there alone!"

"She's twenty years old, Helen. What do you want me to do? Give her a curfew? Five o'clock weekdays? Maybe five-thirty for the weekends?"

"If you ever cared about anyone but yourself, you'd *do* something!" Mom screamed.

It was too much. I leaped up and slammed the door. Then I fell on my bed and wept. Tears scalded my cheeks and soaked into my comforter. I felt completely alone. Why were they fighting? Didn't they know it made me feel even worse?

But Randy and Tim were the ones with whom I should be angry. They had victimized me. They hated me, and obviously believed they could do anything they wanted without getting caught.

They probably *wouldn't* be caught. The police were over-worked. Even worse, I had provided them with few clues, except for describing the generic gray sedan. I hadn't even seen the license plate number. The driver could have been Randy, Tim, Mr. Carlisle, Professor Williams...anyone. But I suspected Tim. And most likely Randy had been involved, too.

It wasn't fair.

God, why did you let this happen to me?

I grabbed up my Bible and thumped back against my pillow. God hated Tim and Randy's actions. They'd pay for their crimes. Maybe not now, but someday. God would make them pay. And the penalty for sin was death.

I flipped open to Revelation 8 and 9, which described God's trumpet judgments on mankind during the Tribulation. I read the chapters with relish, imagining the plagues heaped upon Randy and Tim's heads.

By the time I'd finished reading about those frightening events, however, I felt somber instead of vindictive. What tremendous, terrible judgments. Not just for Randy and Tim, but for all of mankind. And chapter 9:20-21 said,

> *The rest of mankind that were not killed by these plagues still did not repent of the work of their hands; they did not stop worshiping demons, and idols of gold, silver, bronze, stone and wood—idols that cannot see or hear or walk. Nor did they repent of their murders, their magic arts, their sexual immorality or their thefts.*

Mankind still would not repent, even though God had punished them for their wickedness. I couldn't understand how anyone could have such a bitterly hard heart.

Bitterness. The word pierced my own heart. I had to forgive Tim and Randy. Otherwise, my anger would grow into bitterness and poison my soul.

I didn't want to forgive them, even though I knew forgiving them didn't mean I was saying that what they'd done was all right. It absolutely was not. And it certainly didn't mean I should ever foolishly or blindly trust them, either. They were dangerous, and I needed to stay away from them. But I also needed to let go of my need for vengeance, and my desire to hang onto hatred. I had to give the whole miserable mess to God. For my own sake, I had to give God all of my bitterness and anger, and trust him to take care of those who had wronged me.

If only the police would throw Tim and Randy in jail, too. That would be the icing on the cake.

Bowing my head, I prayed.

Lord, I'm angry at Randy and Tim, and at what they've done to me. I don't know how I can forgive them, but I know that's what you want me to do. You said I should love my enemies. But I can't. I'm so angry! Please help me to live by your light, rather than stumble along in angry, bitter darkness. Please help me to forgive them. I give you my anger and my hatred. Lead me on your right path. In Jesus' name. Amen.

I felt a little better after that prayer. But I still didn't want to forgive them.

FRIDAY

"*I'D LIKE TO HOLD A QUICK MEETING TONIGHT* so we can tie up any loose ends." Joyce perched on a chair across the table from me in the student union. Our table abutted a streaming, rain blurred window. This was our third day of constant, nonstop rain.

"Good idea," I agreed, gingerly sipping hot chocolate through the whipped cream topping in my cup. "But can we meet at my house? I have a date with Trent at seven-thirty. I don't want to be late."

"Sure. How about seven? It shouldn't take long." Joyce reached for her bag. She'd only plopped down a minute before, but appeared ready to run off again. Casting me an apologetic glance, she stood. "I have an appointment at Channel Twenty-Three News in half an hour. They're interviewing me about the fundraiser."

"How wonderful!" I marveled that Joyce always seemed to have everything together. She was a planner, and always in charge and in control. And she always seemed so sophisticated, too, and easily hobnobbed with the business elite in town. Envy twinged, and then vanished. I could never be Joyce. And I didn't want to be, either.

"Well... Ta." Joyce flitted off.

I opened my history book, and took a big sip of hot chocolate. The hot, sweet drink burned my tongue and slid a fiery trail down my throat. Wiggling my scalded tongue, I pushed the cup away.

"Hi."

My burned tongue was quickly forgotten. "Hi." I smiled up at Mitch, delighted to see him.

"Are you busy?" He glanced at my open book.

I slammed it shut. "I should be, but honestly, I'm glad to take a break."

"Okay, then." With a crooked grin, he took the seat Joyce had just vacated. "I finished another strange sketch. Would you like to see it?"

"Of course." Eagerly, I pushed the book aside.

"This one looks like a shot from the daily news." He placed a white, roughly textured scroll into my palm. "But I know you'll have your own, unique interpretation."

Carefully, I unrolled it. The familiar, bold strokes instantly arrested my attention, and pulled me into the picture, as usual.

It was a street scene. People brandished guns, and shot at each other, and carried loot. Blood ran in rivulets down the streets. Men and women tottered on wobbly legs, their ill-gotten gain piled high on their heads: televisions, cars, refrigerators... Each faltering step crushed them nearer to the ground. Some people already lay in the street, crushed under the weight of their own greed. In the background, flames licked up buildings. Lightening bolts shot from roiling, angry black clouds.

"I know. It looks like the Tribulation." Mitch smiled.

"It does," I admitted. It reminded me of God's trumpet judgments on mankind that I'd read about last night.

"The Bible says love will grow cold, and wickedness of every sort will abound in the last days. God will judge the world during the Tribulation." Sadness pulled at my heart as I stared at the picture. "They won't repent," I said quietly.

Mitch twisted the picture back so he could look at it. His next question surprised me. "What part does Israel play in the Tribulation?"

"A big one," I said slowly, trying to remember what I'd read. "Things happening in Israel are key factors in Revelation. In fact, Israel's probably going to grab the attention of the whole world. Even more so than now, if that's possible."

"Wow."

"I wish I could tell you specific details. If you're interested in finding out more, you could read Ezekiel and Daniel, and the minor prophets. Of course, it would help if you read Revelation."

A faint smile tugged at his lips. "I think I'll pass on that."

"Do you still want to go to Israel?" At his nod, I said, "Why? Do you have family there?"

"No." The paper scratched as he rolled it up again. His serious eyes looked a little puzzled. "I don't know why I want to go, really. Besides the fact it's the Jewish homeland."

He hesitated. "It's kind of like these pictures," Mitch said finally. "I feel drawn, even compelled to sketch them. Like there's a reason, or a purpose for each one. I guess that doesn't make much sense."

"I think it does. Maybe you're supposed to go to Israel for a reason."

"Maybe," he said slowly.

"When do you want to go?"

"I don't know." His intense black eyes narrowed, and he glanced out the rain streaked window. "Maybe soon."

I tapped in my computer password twice in the journalism lab. But again the "file empty" error message flashed across the screen. A panicky feeling gripped me. Where were my files? What had happened to all of my work?

I jerked up my backpack and rummaged through it. The little red flash drive felt solid and comforting in my hand. My information was safe. Thank goodness. Good thing I'd kept everything backed up, just in case of a computer glitch like this...

No. Cold, unwelcome intuition told me this wasn't a computer glitch. Tim *had* spied on me last night. He must have seen me type in my password, and then returned and erased my files.

A slow burn of anger rose, drowning a more prudent flutter of fear. I was sick of Tim and Randy's stupid, raunchy tricks. One thing was for sure: they wouldn't get the best of me again.

After checking to make sure no one was watching, I changed my password. But I wasn't too worried. Neither Tim nor Randy had shown up in class today. Had the police finally caught up with them? I could only hope.

After transferring my back-up information into the school computer, I researched a few more sources for my topic. My working title was: "The Growing Persecution of Christians in America."

Then I organized the outline. I wanted to write a personal anecdote to back up each statistic. That way, each point of the paper would pack more of a punch.

Professor Williams wanted facts? He'd get plenty of them.

I splashed down from the bus in front of the auto repair shop, with my hood pulled protectively over my head against the drizzling rain. My Mustang, parked out front, sported a brand new windshield and tires. Thank goodness for Dad's mechanic.

And thank goodness for insurance. Carrying the receipt and my keys, I scooted into my cold car. The repair bill had run well over a thousand dollars.

Turning right, so I could drive around the block, my mind flashed back to Dr. William's class. Trent had been absent today, too. Where had he been? Hopefully, he wouldn't forget our date tonight. I looked forward to it. And I also looked forward to settling, once and for all, the questions in my heart regarding Trent.

White and orange road barriers suddenly appeared in the road ahead, and I slammed on the brakes. Dark, filthy water roiled a few yards beyond them, lapping up against the edge of the dip in Market Street. The black water swirled all the way to Driscoll and beyond, flooding the tiny valley that cupped the east side of town. I followed orange detour signs and turned right, onto Pine.

The earthquake, and now this! Mary hadn't been in class today, either. Had her apartment building flooded? I certainly hoped not. But I couldn't get any closer to find out.

The kitchen was quiet when I arrived home. Uncomfortably so. In silence, Theresa and I helped Mom carry dish after piping hot dish to the table.

"Are you okay, Mom?" I ventured.

"*Yes.*" Her eyes momentarily softened. "I'm sorry. Thank you, honey."

She set the last porcelain bowl, heaped with corn, on the table. "There." Her smile looked brittle. "Help yourselves, girls." Her heels made a hollow, clicking sound as she stepped out into the hall. It was the fifth time in the last ten minutes.

"Dad hasn't called to explain why he's late," Theresa whispered.

A bad sign. Dad always called Mom when he would be late, no matter how strained their relationship had become. But this was the second time this month he hadn't. Had something happened on the road home? Or was my parents' relationship deteriorating still further?

Both my sister and I drew a breath of relief when we heard the unmistakable "*rrrwhrr*" of the garage door opener. Dad was home.

Instantly, Mom returned to the kitchen, her heel clicks staccato with anger. Her eyes looked like frosty ice chips.

My fingers tightened around my fork. Another fight. I couldn't bear it.

But when Dad slipped into his chair, neither of my parents said a word. Not 'hello,' 'how was your day.' Nothing. Just freezing silence. It was worse than an argument.

I rapidly shoveled corn in my mouth, and stared at my plate. I longed to say something, but was afraid if I did, the whole situation might explode right before my eyes.

After dinner, I sought refuge upstairs from the glacial cold permeating our house. Only the doorbell called me down from the safe, warm cubbyhole of my room. It was probably one of my friends, arriving for Joyce's impromptu meeting.

David's easy grin and smiling brown eyes felt like a balm to my wounded soul. "Hey, Beautiful."

"Hi, David!" I offered an overly ambitious smile.

His eyes narrowed as he followed me inside. "What's up?"

I glanced toward the den, where Dad had retreated. I wasn't sure where Mom was. In a low voice, I said, "My parents are mad at each other."

"Oh." He looked surprised. He didn't know about the constant friction in my home. I hadn't told him. I hadn't told anyone; it hurt too deeply. Maybe I thought if I ignored it, it would go away.

He headed into the brightly lit kitchen. With David there, a little of the warmth returned to the cold room.

"Did you get new tires for your car? Noticed they looked different."

A chill of anger returned. "Yes!" I told him what had happened last night, and threw in the tale of my erased files this afternoon for good measure.

His eyes turned black. He was angry and concerned for me, both of which felt good. "Be careful, Kay. They obviously have it in for you."

"I won't let fear rule my life."

"Just be careful." Unknown emotions flickered in his gaze. "If you're late at school one night, and don't have someone to walk you to your car, call me."

"Thank you, David." His offer touched my heart, and uncurled a blossom of warm happiness in me. "That's wonderful of you, but I just couldn't. It's clear out of your way. You'd have to drive all the way to school—just so I could walk out to the parking lot!" Although he meant well, his idea was impractical.

"I don't mind. In fact, I want to do it." His deepening tone indicated he was serious. "I'm worried about what those guys might do to you next."

"I'll be okay, really, D..."

"*Promise me.*" He could be bullheaded, too. He raised his right hand in a swearing position. "Promise me, Kay. Please. At least until things cool off. Just for the next week or two. Really. I don't mind."

"Well..." The desire not to be a burden to David, or to waste his time, warred with the fear I'd felt last night. The danger was real. Randy and Tim had made that painfully clear.

"Well, all right." More warm joy flooded my heart. David cared enough for me that he'd come all the way to the school, just to walk me to my car. "Thank you, David. I really appreciate it." A soft smile tugged at my lips.

"You're welcome." His frown lifted, and his lips twitched into a return smile. "Anything for a certain bullheaded, blond-headed girl. You know, I should come up with a new nickname for you, Trouble. Maybe Moose, or..."

I gave him a mock eye roll as the doorbell rang.

Joyce and David greeted each other amicably enough. I hoped their arguments about the fundraiser would remain in the past.

As Joyce dropped her purse on the table, I said, "Didn't your dad go to that FGA vision thing yesterday? How did that go?"

"Bad." Joyce plopped into a chair.

"What happened?" This was from David.

Joyce took a deep breath. "You're *not* going to believe this. You want to know the real reason why the FGA is upset with our church? It's because Dad preaches the Bible as the literal Word of God."

"Isn't that what he's supposed to do?"

"Yes!" She looked disgusted. "But it gets worse. Not only is the FGA discouraging using the literal interpretation of the Bible in church services, but they want to dictate the kind of messages Dad preaches."

"What?" David frowned.

"Believe it. They want Dad to preach about neighbors helping neighbors, and other social issues. The FGA says those subjects speak *most* to people's needs today."

"So Pastor Warner can't talk about God at all?"

"He can, but only if he talks about God's love. He can't mention man's sin, or judgment or redemption, or the cross, or anything like that."

"So he basically can't tell people about Jesus."

"That's right. Dad is furious. He says those kinds of services are worse than useless. People might leave inspired to be better people, but good resolutions won't last. They won't be confronted with their sin and realize they need to repent and ask Jesus to be their savior. They won't learn how to have a real relationship with God. Only God can change our hearts to be the people he meant us to be. Our sin glitches everything up. If we don't deal with that, all the inspiration in the world won't help anyone. Good resolutions fail every day. We need Jesus!"

"Preach it, sistah!" I grinned. Joyce sounded just like her father.

"You're right," David said grimly. "We need Jesus. He is the way, the truth, and the life. No one comes to the Father, except through him. There is no life apart from him. And no way to heaven, apart from him, either."

"I know. Dad refused to sign their silly vision statement, and now the FGA is furious with him. They told him to *consider* it. But if he doesn't sign the statement, the FGA will withdraw all funds from our church. Basically, they'll throw us out."

"Can they do that?"

"Yes. And they gave Dad another warning. They said he can't preach the gospel at the fundraiser."

"Why not?"

"Because it's a community outreach project. Religion has no place there, they said. It would alienate the community."

"But that's ridiculous!" I gasped.

"Well," Joyce pulled a notebook from her purse, "that's the way it stands. Not much we can do about it. But Dad says he's glad the FGA only owns the church—and not our house, too." She glanced at her watch. "I know we're all busy tonight. Let's get started."

I fetched a pencil and paper of my own.

"Let's see," Joyce muttered. "Oh, yes. I know we decided to serve everyone the same food. But I still feel we need to do something extra for the donors, so they'll feel especially thanked for giving money to the homeless."

David frowned. "Like what?" His tone sounded guarded.

"Like special flowers at the table. Or their names engraved on cards. Maybe we could give..."

"I don't believe this!" David jerked back in his chair. "The money raised is for the *homeless,* Joyce. And it should be used for the homeless. Not wasted on giving the donors a self-congratulatory pat on the back!"

Joyce's eyes flashed. "You know what your problem is? You can't see past the moment. Those *donors* will help out again in the future, if we treat them right."

"They'll help if their heart is right! If they're giving for the right reasons. Joyce, what is your focus? Doing the smart business thing? Or following God?"

Joyce stared at David. Her lips curled. "Of course, *you* are following God."

David's face flushed. "I'm sorry. That's not what I meant." He turned to me. "We should all ask ourselves that question—have any of us prayed for this fundraiser? Have we asked God how he'd like it run?"

A silent moment elapsed. Obviously, none of us had.

"It's too late now," Joyce said impatiently. "I have it all planned out..."

"And we *can't* let anything upset your plans." An edge bit through David's words. "Just like your life, right? You've got it all planned out."

"What is *that* supposed to mean?"

"I mean, let's pray about it..."

"I don't have time for this!" Joyce slapped her pen into her purse. "If you can't see..."

"Stop it," I exclaimed. "We're friends, for goodness sake! Satan knows his time is short, so he's attacking us on all sides."

"You stop it, Kay!" Joyce spat. I stared at her, shocked. Her hands trembled as she gathered her things together. "Stop it with the end times lecture. You may think these are the end times, but that has *nothing to do with this*. All right? We're fighting because David is ignorant about running a fundraiser."

"Excuse me!" Eyes blazing black, David jerked to his feet. "I've had it. Where do you get off..." He cut the words short. After a brief pause, his white-knuckled hands shoved the chair under the table. I'd never seen him so angry before.

His jaw clenched. "It's obvious we won't get any work done tonight." He shot a glance at his watch. "And right now, I have somewhere to be. See you later. When you're calmer."

In two strides, he disappeared into the hall. The front door slammed.

Joyce stared at me. "I can't believe he left like that."

"He wants to cool off." I felt a little shaky inside, which was probably a reaction to Joyce's cutting words. At church last weekend she'd been hostile about the end times, too. But why? Quietly, I said, "He's afraid he'll say something he'll regret."

Several long, awkward moments passed. "I'm sorry, Kay."

"It's okay." I managed to smile. But I didn't feel all right. Why was Joyce so touchy these days? This was the second time this week she'd jumped down my throat. And it was her second fight with David, too.

"So," Joyce abruptly changed the subject, "how are things going between you and David? I know he was giving you grief about Trent."

"They're okay." It felt a little strange to talk to Joyce about David. Maybe because it had been a long time since Joyce and I had talked about anything important; meaning, anything beyond the surface level of church, or the fundraiser. Sadness slipped through me, along with a disturbing truth. In some ways Joyce and I acted more like acquaintances these days than good friends.

I saw my sadness reflected in Joyce's eyes, but then she glanced away, at her watch. With a short laugh, she crammed her notebook into her purse. "I really should go. I still have a ton of work to do for the fundraiser...dinner. My 'Church as Business' professor has given me a few great ideas to implement."

"Oh. That's great."

"Yes. The fundraiser is doubling as a project for the class, so it's beneficial all around."

Was that why Joyce seemed so focused on the business end of the fundraiser—because she wanted to get a good grade?

The doorbell pealed as we headed for the door.

Trent hadn't forgotten our date. He looked very handsome in a fashionable tan suit jacket, crisp white shirt, and tan slacks.

"You look nice." I smiled, relieved to see a happy, friendly face. I was sick of the tension between my friends, and sick of the strain in this house. I just wanted to escape for a while.

His deep blue gaze smiled back at me, and then glanced over my shoulder. "Hi, Joyce." Doing a double-take, though, his gaze slid down my outfit. "Are you ready, Kay?"

I wore jeans and a T-shirt.

"Oh, *no*." Seven-thirty had crept up on me.

Amused, Joyce said, "Go on up and change, Kay. I'll entertain Trent."

"Thanks, Joyce." I shot Trent a look of apology. "Sorry. I didn't realize it was so late."

"Take your time. I'm in no hurry."

But I hurried. I never ran late, and felt mortified that I'd forgotten tonight's date. At least, I had for this last hour.

I flung my closet door open and whipped out my gown. A few flurried moments later, I wriggled into it and twisted my arm around behind my back, and then awkwardly over my shoulder to zip it up. There! I stared at myself in the mirror. Not bad. But the girl looking back at me looked wild-eyed. I needed to calm down. Put on makeup.

Forcing myself to slow down, I slipped into the bathroom and carefully applied my makeup.

There. I pursed my rose colored lips. Good. Now earrings. I rummaged until I found the pair Dad and Mom had given me for my high school graduation. Delicate diamond drops. Flashes of white fire sparkled from my ears.

Now my hair.

I'd already been up here for ten minutes. Trent must be getting impatient. Making a quick decision, I decided not to put up my hair. It would take too long. Instead, I brushed the golden strands till they gleamed. Done!

I slipped on matching high heels, and then inspected myself in the mirror. I smiled, surprised and pleased by what I saw. I suspected Trent would be pleased, too.

My hair flowed in a golden shower to my shoulders, and the dress fit perfectly. Mom was right; the cool, ethereal green did complement my eyes. The gown's soft, shimmering lines fell to mid-calf on my left leg, and angled down to my ankle on the right. It looked elegant.

Flashing myself a self-conscious, impish smile, I grabbed my purse and a jacket and stepped carefully downstairs in the unfamiliar heels. I interrupted Joyce's high laugh. She smiled up at Trent. Was she flirting with him?

The thought didn't bother me, which seemed a little strange, but perhaps that was because Joyce looked happier and more carefree right now than I'd seen her in weeks.

Trent looked over her head. "Wow!" His whistle made me smile. "Nice dress."

Joyce's sparkling smile indicated her approval, too. "You look great, Kay."

Trent helped me slip on the jacket, and we all stepped outside. I pulled my hood up against the drizzling rain.

"See you later, guys." With a hurried wave, Joyce dashed down the path ahead of us, holding her purse over her head. "Have fun tonight!"

A moment later, Trent ushered me into his Porsche. He grinned at me. "Ready to dance?"

"I sure am." I relaxed back in the smooth leather seat. It took a few minutes to get to the El Dorado Hall, so we had plenty of time to talk.

"So, what's new?" He shot me a smile.

"I should ask you the same question," I replied with a laugh. "Haven't seen much of you in class."

"I've been working on a hot story for my internship. It'll double for Dr. William's class, too. And don't worry. I don't plan to miss any more classes."

"Probably a good idea."

"What about you? Anything exciting?" He glanced at me, hand resting lightly on the wheel.

"No. Except..." I hesitated, strangely reluctant to share Tim and Randy's attacks on me.

"Except what?" His gaze sharpened.

"Well, I kind of...was attacked yesterday."

"*What?*" His instant concern loosened my tongue, and I explained what had happened.

"That's bad." He frowned, and fell silent for a long time. "You okay?" His question sounded like an afterthought.

"Yes." I sat back, and wondered what he was thinking about.

A long silence stretched. Finally, I said, "I think Tim and Randy's hate group is the one that keeps attacking my church."

"Attacking your church?" Interest sharpened his tone, and when he glanced at me I saw that he had been thinking hard. Mulling over what I had said before? "Why do you say that?"

So I explained. Trent seemed fascinated by the black arm band theory. "You know," he said finally, as we pulled into the parking lot, "you should write an article about that."

"I am."

"I mean, for the paper. I'm sure they'd be interested. I'd write it, but I think you'd have a better angle. It's personal. You have something at stake."

"You think so?" The thought had never occurred to me. I'd never considered the idea that my personal problems might be of interest to anyone besides myself, and my circle of friends.

"Definitely." He jumped out of the car, and stepped around to help me out. His hand felt light on my elbow. "In fact, with the right facts, it could make front page."

"Wow." I'd never considered that idea. Pretty silly, since I was a journalism major. I guess I'd been thinking I'd publish big articles after I graduated.

Puddles dotted the black asphalt of the parking lot, and Trent kept his palm light under my elbow as we stepped carefully toward the hall. I lifted the right edge of my dress so it wouldn't dip into the puddles.

At last we climbed the steps and slipped under the banner emblazoned by the words, "Sisters of Mercy Ball." With flourish, Trent opened one of the double, white painted doors, and a rush of warmth and music tumbled out. The festive air swirled around us and carried us inside.

It was bright and cheery indoors. Chandeliers dripped with crystal beads and sparkled from their lofty appointments far above. Old paintings splashed with warm oil paints livened the white walls. The hardwood floor had a rich, warm glow to it; ready for a festive night of dance and romance.

"You can leave your jacket here." Trent guided me to the right. A long line stretched toward the hat-check area. It would obviously be a few minutes before we were helped.

He peered across the room as I peeled off my jacket. "I'll get us some drinks, okay? Be back in a minute." With a brief smile, he slipped away.

The line didn't move for several long minutes. An elderly lady at the front of the line lectured the poor hat-check girl on how to properly hang up her fur coat.

I scanned the room, looking for Trent. He should have returned by now. Maybe he'd seen someone he knew.

I stepped forward a pace when the stout matron at last shuffled toward the dance floor. The ballroom was crowded. The left and right sides were lined with conversing strangers. My gaze lingered for an explicable second on a tall, dark-haired man whose back was mostly to me.

I continued to scan the room, straining to see into the crowd of whirling, dancing bodies. They pulsated in the center of the dance hall to some new jazzy modern number. The punch bowl was located on the opposite side of the room, but I couldn't see through the crowd. I couldn't see Trent.

A quick observation hit me. Everyone here looked like high society people; the beautiful people. Most of the men were classically handsome...my eyes returned to the dark-haired man, who spoke to an older gentleman. He was probably the prime example of the clichéd tall, dark stranger. His black jacket emphasized the broad width of his shoulders, and the black slacks and jacket perfectly set off his trim, lean form.

I mentally shook myself. Why was I staring at a total stranger like that? I was looking for Trent. He was my date tonight.

I glanced across the room again, and stepped further to the right as a wave of people surged through the door behind me.

Still, I didn't see him. I was next in line.

I handed my purse and jacket to the hat-check girl, and then slipped forward a few paces, out of the way of incoming people.

The music faded. The gyrating bodies limped to a halt, and I found my gaze slipping to the dark-haired man again, as if drawn by a magnet. It didn't hurt to look, I justified myself. Besides, I found I couldn't tear my eyes away. Something about him intrigued me. The set of his shoulders. The way he stood...

His dark hair was cut short and combed neatly in place. I watched as he suddenly threw his head back and laughed at something the older man said. From this awkward angle I could see the firm, decisive cut of his jaw. A strong jaw line. A strong character, too?

Soft threads of a new song whispered into my ears, and the people on the dance floor swayed gently to the old, slow tune, "I Only Have Eyes for You."

The stranger's face turned ever so slightly, so I could see the slash of his dark brow. He had high cheekbones, I noted. Slavic descent, maybe. He was good looking. What did the rest of his face look like?

As if suddenly aware he was being watched, the man's head turned. Flashing dark eyes met mine... And all of a sudden he smiled. As if I was the only one in the room.

My breath caught, and my heart jerked out of rhythm when David turned and walked toward me.

My jumping heart felt like a trip hammer gone awry. David.

My eyes never left his as he stepped closer. I felt caught in a spell, unable to move.

"Kay." For one breathless moment, his dark eyes smiled down at me. "Want to dance?"

I nodded, unable to speak. My palms were perspiring, I realized. I put my left hand on the fine cloth of his black jacket and discreetly swiped my other hand against my dress before placing my palm against his. His fingers closed around mine. Then he stepped toward me, and we slipped into motion with the soft music.

I found myself staring at his shoulder. I felt strange. Shy. Did he feel it, too? This odd...spell between us? Or was it all in my imagination?

I couldn't look at his face. Strangely, it felt like I was dancing with a stranger.

Maybe I was. Because in that instant I saw him walking toward me across the room, the old mental picture I'd carried of David ever since high school—that tall, gangly, awkward boy—had been erased, replaced by this David.

He *was* handsome. And attractive. *Very* attractive. The realization took my breath away. For the first time, I saw what Theresa had seen in him. And I didn't know how to deal with it.

He was still David, my best friend. Right?

But I couldn't ignore the strong tension lacing like an elastic band between us. Did he feel it, too?

Why had he asked me to dance? He'd never asked me before. At least not to a slow dance, like this.

We moved fluidly, in perfect precision to the music. His low voice, when he spoke, was quiet. Not loud enough to jar me from the peculiar trance I'd fallen into.

"I didn't expect to see you here."

"Trent brought me."

I felt his shoulder muscles tense for a moment, and then relax. "Oh." His tone sounded light. He pulled me in close and whirled us both into an unnecessary half turn.

My cheek brushed against his shoulder. He was wearing cologne. The warm, spicy scent tickled my nostrils, and my lashes swept shut for an instant as I inhaled it.

"I should have guessed that," he murmured.

My pulse raced. I was very aware of how large and close he was, next to me. What was wrong with me?

This had to stop. Now.

"What are you doing here?" I tipped my head back and offered a small smile. I wouldn't let him see how confused I felt. I was being ridiculous. He was David. My friend. Nothing more.

But as his familiar brown eyes held mine, I couldn't look away. An unfamiliar expression lurked in them. I couldn't read it. Smiling? Yes. And something more.

"My mom is a chairperson for this charity. I had to make a duty appearance."

"Oh. That's right." I'd known that, but had forgotten.

I found myself staring at his shoulder again. My heart beat too fast. I felt if something didn't break this tension between us soon, I would...shatter. I didn't know what to do. Did he feel it, too?

What did it mean? Was it just the music? Was it the fact that I'd seen him across the room, thinking he was a stranger? Had we both been caught up in some odd sort of spell?

Someone bumped me from behind, and David pulled me closer to him. The dance floor was getting crowded. His chin brushed my hair, and the music crooned softly over my senses. My eyes closed, and with a sigh, I finally relaxed. I was enjoying this dance with him. Very much.

Perhaps too much. I lost track of our foot movements, and the next thing I knew, someone bumped me and my feet tangled together. I staggered and tripped sideways. David's strong hands easily checked my fall, but still I managed to stamp down hard on his toe.

"Sorry!" I gasped, jerking my chin up to look at him.

His eyes danced at me, and his teeth flashed. "Didn't know you were such a menace on the dance floor, Twinkle Toes."

His teasing comment broke the tension between us, like glass shattering under a hammer. But the sudden release left me feeling startled. Confused.

"If you didn't have such big feet, it wouldn't be a problem," I sallied back.

"You mean you can't keep up with the dance master."

I struggled to stifle a smile. "I *mean* you're a pain in the neck, David Matthews!"

He chuckled out loud, and his laughing gaze scanned my face. "Remind me to wear boots next time. At least that will protect my poor, innocent toes."

"If we ever dance together again."

"Hey." A new voice spoke up. Trent. "Can I cut in?"

"Oh." I glanced back up at David, strangely reluctant to end our dance.

But David released me at once. He gave us both a slight, mocking bow. "Be my guest. Just watch out for your toes. She looks as light as a feather, but her feet are lethal weapons."

I sent him a mock glare as Trent slipped over to take his place. The music faded.

David shot me one last impudent grin, and as the music whispered into silence, his black jacket disappeared into the throng of people. I felt jumbled inside, and aware of a feeling of letdown.

"Sorry to keep you waiting so long."

"David kept me entertained."

"I can see that." Trent pulled me close for the next song, which was another slow number. His possessive move inexplicably annoyed me. I didn't want to be so close to him; at least, not without being gently wooed first. But politely, I said nothing as we danced.

Trent's palms felt sweaty through my dress, and he seemed strangely shorter and slighter than he ever had before.

Why was I viewing him so critically? Was I upset that he'd left me waiting so long? Or that he'd cut in on David and me when we were laughing and joking and having so much fun? But that dance had pretty much been over when he'd cut in.

I didn't know. All I knew was I felt unsettled. And oddly dissatisfied.

Trent and I danced a dozen more dances. Most were fast. But after a while, I sensed he wasn't having much fun, either. Finally, he pulled me off the floor.

"How about we quit this joint? I guess I'm not in the mood to dance tonight."

"Me either," I agreed.

"Maybe we could go to Kruger's and talk."

"I like that idea. I'll get my coat." As we slipped outside, I noticed that David had disappeared, too. Had he gone to the movie night at Bobby's? For a second, I thought about suggesting it to Trent, but then discarded the idea.

The bald, burly proprietor of Kruger's Yogurt was busy tonight. I guess news of the great yogurt and safe dining was getting around.

For the first time, I noticed the small metal detectors positioned on either side of the doorway. The windows were probably bulletproof, too.

"So, now that we can hear ourselves think—what else is new in your life?" Trent licked his yogurt cone. His smiling eyes looked intense. Perhaps trying to make up for the odd distance that had lurked between us all evening?

"Not much, I guess." In a small part of my brain I noticed the beautiful royal blue of his eyes, but they weren't mesmerizing me like they usually did. "What about you? How is your internship going?"

"Great. They've given me free reign with the big article I want to write. That's a relief, because it's pretty much all I can think about these days." He fiddled with his spoon. "They may give me a part-time position next semester. With pay."

"That's great." I was glad for him. First, he'd landed the internship at the paper, and now he might get a paid job. Both were avenues I needed to pursue soon. I didn't feel jealous of his accomplishments, but something *was* bothering me right now.

I couldn't put my finger on what it might be.

Trent's next question captured my full attention. "So, how are things going for the fundraiser?"

"Good. Except the FGA keeps hassling us."

Trent frowned. "How so?"

I explained how the FGA wanted to regulate all of our church activities. I also told him what Pastor Warner had learned in his vision meeting.

"That doesn't seem right. Do they have the authority to enforce all those conditions?"

"I guess so, since Pastor Warner's taking everything so seriously." It felt good to talk out my frustration with Trent, and for a little while, I felt closer to him again.

But that feeling had seeped away by the time he deposited me on my front doorstep. He'd seemed distracted on the drive home, as if preoccupied by thoughts of his own. Just like earlier in the evening, when we'd driven to the dance. And during the dance?

"Goodnight." He smiled down at me, and kissed me softly. Tenderly?

Why did it feel like he was acting the part? And why did I feel like I was doing the same? My lashes fluttered closed, but I felt almost nothing from his kiss. Where had the magic gone?

Disturbed, I stepped away. "Thank you for the yogurt. I had a wonderful time tonight."

"Good." His smile seemed a little practiced. And his eyes? Strangely distant, as if still focused on inward thoughts. "See you in class on Monday."

"Have a good weekend," I called after him, a bit desperately. I felt alone. Lost. What was happening here?

The smile he flashed back seemed genuine. "You too, Kay."

My spirits rebounded for a second. Slowly, I turned to the door. *Every relationship has its ups and downs,* I counseled myself. Every date couldn't be perfect.

Then why did I wish I'd watched videos tonight after the dance, instead of going to yogurt with Trent? Would I rather be with my friends than with him? The thought seemed disloyal to Trent.

I slid beneath the covers. What did I really feel for him? The thrill appeared to be gone, and I didn't understand why. The knowledge only served only to emphasize the confused feelings that had plagued me all week.

I'd sensed a distance between us all night. We'd both been preoccupied by different things. He was obviously consumed by his big article—and his new internship—and I had my parents' fight and Joyce and David's fights nibbling away at the back of my mind. Not to mention that strange dance with David. Like we were dancing through a dream...

I tried to push those new, even more bewildering feelings into another room in my heart, and lock the door. I didn't know what to make of that dance, and found myself wanting to avoid thinking about it at all.

So, Trent and I had both been preoccupied. Logically, it made perfect sense that distance had separated us tonight.

My heart, however, could not be satisfied by logic.

What is going on, Lord? Please help me to understand. I'm tired of feeling confused. I want to figure out my feelings for Trent, once and for all.

SATURDAY

THE CHURCH WAS A SCENE OF PANDEMONIUM when Theresa and I arrived at three o'clock this afternoon to help with the homeless dinner. Large groups of people milled about in the cold, clear air outside. Some carried food, and others, clearly earthquake victims, tried to find the end of the line. Thankfully, the rain had ended at last.

Tables had been set up out front. Women's ministry would hand out food until eight o'clock tonight. I admired their fortitude. They'd been working since seven o'clock this morning.

"Hi, Kay! Theresa!" A bass voice rumbled from our left.

Mitch's oddly off-centered face smiled above the stacks of precooked rolls he carried. "Where can I put these? They're for the dinner."

"Where did you get them, did you say? From your dad?" Theresa arched a delicate brow.

I quickly led the way around the back of the building to the kitchen entrance.

With a nod, Mitch slid his load onto the island counter in the warm, quiet kitchen. "Yeah. My dad owns one of the local supermarkets. He sold the rolls to me at cost."

David swung through the doorway, wearing a dark gray sweatshirt and jeans. For an instant, another image flashed across my mind: David in his black tuxedo. And how we'd danced so closely together.

I gave myself a quick, mental shake. No. I couldn't—I *wouldn't*—think about him like that. He was my friend. Period.

My confused feelings evaporated when I noticed the white chef's hat perched on his head. What a goof ball.

"All right!" he crowed. "Thanks, Mitch. That will help a lot."

"What are you wearing?" I demanded. A giggle escaped. "You look like Chef Boyardee!"

David grinned and spun gracelessly. "Like it? Thought I'd really throw myself into the role."

"I like it," Mitch said.

"All right!" The two guys slapped high fives.

I rolled my eyes, but was unable to suppress a smile. "You are both ridiculous."

"Hate to leave so quick," Mitch edged toward the door. "But you know how it is. Work calls."

"Thanks again, Mitch!" we chorused.

When he'd left, I glanced around the kitchen. It looked ominously bare, and I looked at David. "Where is all the food?"

With a proud grin, he swung open the refrigerator door. A shelf was filled with fat, sausage-like logs. "There's the hamburger. Picked it up myself a few hours ago. Laura and Bobby are buying the spaghetti sauce and everything else right now."

"Okay." I looked around. "Where's Joyce?"

David's features stiffened for a second, but he shrugged. "I don't know. I think she's selling the last tickets. She'll be here by six to help serve dinner."

Theresa stared with distaste into the open refrigerator. "That's an awful lot of hamburger."

"Forty pounds," David grinned. "Enough for two hundred people."

Theresa and I both blinked. "I think we'll have leftovers," I murmured.

"That's okay. If we do, we'll give the extra food to people on the streets." David appeared totally unconcerned.

"What should we do first?" Theresa faintly fluttered her lashes at David, as though suddenly remembering why she had come in the first place.

David ignored this. "We've still got three hours until the dinner. We can probably relax for a while…"

"I don't think so," I interrupted. "That hamburger will take two hours to cook! How many frying pans do we have?"

"I don't know."

David opened cupboards, and Theresa and I joined him. We found two medium-sized frying pans.

I stared at them in dismay. "This will take forever."

David looked sheepish. Obviously, his great plans had not extended to the practicalities of cooking food for two hundred people.

I searched for a knife and spatula in one of the drawers, and then grabbed one of the hamburger logs and mashed one fourth of the contents into each pan. I turned the heat on "high," and waited for the meat to sizzle.

Bobby and Laura soon showed up, bearing grocery bags of canned spaghetti sauce, pasta, green beans, sheet cake, coffee, margarine, a container of iced tea flavoring, and disposable paper plates, cups, and other utensils.

I stood at the huge, industrial-sized stove, stirring sizzling hamburger, and watched Theresa and the others cart everything in. Spatters of grease and heat radiated up from the open pans, filling my nostrils with the warm, full smell of cooking meat.

"That's it," David said, dropping the last bag onto the crowded floor. Bags and jars covered every available square inch of the kitchen counters.

Laura peeled off her coat in the doorway. She pinched her nostrils closed. Her face looked green. The smell of frying meat, combined with her pregnancy, apparently was making her feel sick. Her usually radiant eyes looked clouded as she glanced about the crowded room. "How will we cook all of this food?"

It was a question I had been wondering, as well. We had almost three dozen cans of spaghetti sauce, 36 pounds of pasta, and untold cans of green beans. And the rolls to reheat. Not to mention the endless pounds of hamburger I cooked now. David and I had been in charge of planning the meal, but neither of us had imagined, nor prepared for cooking this overwhelming pile of food.

To my surprise, Theresa took the initiative. "We have six burners, right?" Glancing at David, she delicately pulled three huge stock pots from the cupboards. "We have these."

"We'll need more than that." Still pinching her nose, Laura hurried forward and bent to peer into cupboards with Theresa. "We'll need two pots of pasta going at the same time," she planned. "That way we can serve people in shifts. And we'll need another three stock pots just for the sauce and meat. And another one for the beans. We'll have to heat up the rolls in shifts, too."

I drained hamburger fat into an empty can, shoveled the cooked meat into one of the large pots, and then into the heated oven to keep warm. Laura and Theresa found three more pots. I'd only browned five pounds of hamburger. Thirty-five more to go.

By five forty-five the kitchen was hot, steamy, and spattered with grease. But I'd finished. Thank goodness. The browned meat was distributed between three stock pots. Helpfully, David poured sauce into the last of these while I rested my aching body on a hard, ladder-backed chair.

Out in the church gym, the twenty odd tables had been covered in dark blue, plastic table cloths. An odd assortment of the church's seasonal displays spruced up the centerpieces. Some tables boasted Christmas decorations made of red fabric flowers and pine cones, while reddish gold fall leaves and golden flowers decorated others. Despite the eclectic mix, it looked oddly tasteful. Glass vases, each filled with a thick red candle and tied with sparkle flecked gold ribbon, adorned each table, which helped to visually tie the groupings together.

Bobby, Laura and Theresa moved from table to table now, laying down place settings of clear plastic utensils and white paper napkins. Theresa seemed to have given up trying to catch David's attention. He was kind to her, but that was it. She seemed to have caught the hint at last.

"Hi." Joyce's voice startled us both.

The hollow, tapping sound of David's wooden spoon scraping the spaghetti cans halted, and he glanced over his shoulder. "Hi," he grunted.

I smiled, in an attempt to gloss over the sudden tension in the room. "Did you sell all the tickets?"

She smiled in return, and slung her purse onto the table. "Most of them." She looked around. "Looks like you guys have been busy. Everything under control?"

"I think so." I peered around David's shoulder. The pots were full. Very. A few were starting to simmer, although the last pot would take a while to heat through. "But we won't be ready by six."

"That's fine. Nobody expects to eat right away, anyway. Anyone from the college group shown up yet?"

"No."

"Well, they should be here soon." Joyce edged closer to peer into the pots, too. "Looks good," she remarked, barely glancing at David.

Suddenly, I'd had enough. "Stop," I said. "Both of you. Please. When will you make up?"

David slowly turned. He wiped his hands on a rag. "I guess this isn't the best way to start off an evening dedicated to God," he agreed quietly.

Joyce frowned. Her eyes looked hard. "I *still* say the donors should be thanked."

David slowly replaced the rag on the counter. "You're right."

"What?"

"They do deserve to be thanked. But I still think all of the money should go to the homeless."

"Well." Joyce looked flustered. "Thanks for trying to see things my way. But it's too late now, don't you think?"

"Maybe not. I talked over an idea with your dad. He liked it. Maybe it'll do the trick."

Of course, he didn't say what the idea was.

Joyce looked dubious, but seemed to relax for the first time. She sighed. "I'm sorry, David. I know I've been a real pig about this. And I know you're right, too. All the money should go to the homeless. I guess my focus slipped a bit."

David hugged an arm around her shoulders. "So we were both jerks. I'm sorry, too."

My friends had apologized. But for the briefest second, I wondered if the root of Joyce's anger had been dealt with at all. What was bothering her, really?

"Thank goodness," I said. "I couldn't stand it another minute. I hate it when you guys fight."

"Come here," David pulled me in with his other arm. We stood shoulder to shoulder. Behind us, the tomato sauce and green beans simmered. "Let's pray for the evening, okay?"

Nodding, we all bowed our heads.

"Lord, thank you for good friends, and thank you for providing all of this food. I pray it will warm and nourish the people here physically tonight, and that Pastor Warner's message will quicken their hearts and renew them spiritually, too.

"And I pray for the people who are coming that don't know you, Lord. I ask that they would really listen to your words, maybe for the first time in their lives. Please, I ask that many people will give their hearts to you, Lord Jesus, tonight, and be saved. We ask all these things in Jesus' name, and thank you. Amen."

"Amen," Joyce and I murmured. For the first time today, a warm glow of certainty filled my heart. This would be a wonderful evening. I could feel it down to my very bones.

By six-thirty, all of the food bubbled merrily, members of our college group had arrived, and the dining room nearly overflowed with people. Joyce, Theresa, Sophie and Anne dished out the food, and the rest of us served it. Laura and Bobby delivered pitchers of water and iced tea to the tables.

Mom and Dad sat at a table near Pastor Warner's podium, but someone else served them before I could. As I rushed in and out, bearing steaming, aromatic paper plates, Pastor Warner's words flowed around me.

"Glad all of you could come tonight. Right from the start, I'd like to say a special thank you to everyone whose generous donations made this dinner possible. Because of your help, all of these hungry people," a quick hand motion indicated the entire room, "can have a warm meal. Truesdale First Gospel church thanks you wholeheartedly for every can of food you brought, and every dollar you donated. Thank you."

I set down two plates, and backed away as the tired-eyed, but decently clad people at the table slowly rose, one after another, and clapped, loud and long. All around the gym, people stood. Everyone did. All of the earthquake victims, and apparently all of the donors, too; everyone congratulated the others who had contributed.

Was this what David had arranged with the Pastor? It did seem to accomplish what Joyce had desired. For a brief moment, I felt sure the donors felt set apart and appreciated.

As I hurried into the kitchen, Pastor Warner's words followed me. "Tonight, I'd like to say a few words about the One who has done infinitely more for us than provide us with a good hot meal..."

I hurried out again with more plates of food, following close on Theresa's heels.

"...many of you have lost everything. The future looks bleak. You feel like the weight of the world rests on your shoulders. You wonder if you'll ever get up again.

"I'm here to tell you, friend, that you don't have to carry your heavy burden any longer. Jesus wants to carry it for you. He said, 'Come to me, all you who are weary and burdened, and I will give you rest. Take my yoke upon you and learn from me, for I am gentle and humble in heart, and you will find rest for your souls. For my yoke is easy and my burden is light.'

"Do you feel empty and hopeless tonight? Has life thrown too many heavy burdens on your shoulders? Do you feel alone? Jesus doesn't want us to live like that! He wants to take our burdens. He wants to ease our cares. He wants to take away our loneliness. He came that we may have life, and have it to the full.

"Do you have that life, friend? Do you have that peace? Do you know Jesus as your own personal savior? If not, pray with me right now.

"Jesus, I know I'm a sinner. My life is a mess. No matter how hard I try, I just can't make things right on my own. But I know you can. I know you died on the cross to purchase forgiveness for my sins. I repent, Lord. I turn to you. Thank you for dying for my sins. Please come into my heart and be Lord of my life. Be my Savior. Be my Lord.

"Friend, if you just accepted Jesus as your Lord and Savior, please talk to me tonight, or talk to one of the young people serving you. They can answer questions, and help point you in the right direction, to begin your walk of faith. Remember, our Sunday service is at ten o'clock. We'd love for you to come."

I slowly turned into the kitchen. I'd hovered for a moment near the door, watching my parents and Theresa. *Please Lord, turn their hearts to you!* was the only thing I could think to pray. I'd seen them bow their heads during the prayer, like everyone else had in the room, but what did that mean? Would they ever realize how much God *really* loved them and wanted to call them into a relationship with him? Would they ever see that? All I could do was trust him.

We served the extra food to the groups of people lingering outside, and then retreated to the kitchen and devoured the few leftovers as we laughed and talked. The evening was a success. We could already tell.

While we served dessert, the women's ministry team carried the remaining canned food into the warm kitchen. They'd decided to shut down the outdoor table at 8:00 p.m. Martha, the church secretary, sat at the table and counted up the cash donations.

Joyce poked her head into the room. "Bobby? Call for you on line one."

Frowning, he disappeared just as Pastor Warner wandered in. The senior pastor immediately gravitated over to the counting table.

"Looking good?" he boomed.

Martha smiled, and her curly white head bobbed. "Better than we thought. Especially combined with the money we earned selling tickets."

"You mean you already have the total?"

"Sure do. Minus dinner expenses, the grand total comes to ten thousand, six hundred and seventy-one dollars!"

A piercing whistle split the room, and we all erupted into loud applause. David took his fingers from his mouth and pumped his fist in the air. "All right!"

Pastor Warner grinned. "Well, what do you think, kids? Shall we give the shelter the check tonight?"

"Yes!" Was the rousing response.

Earlier, Pastor Warner had made it clear that the FGA's demand to approve the distribution of the money would not change Truesdale First Gospel's pledge to give the funds to Driscoll Shelter. And we were behind him one hundred percent. Perhaps uncharitably, I suspected the FGA wanted to use the money for their own purposes; likely to funnel funds into Oak Woodward's political campaign.

The plan had been to pass a ceremonial envelope to the shelter director tonight, and then forward the actual check later. No one had thought we'd count up the money so fast.

"All right. I'll get the church checkbook." Pastor disappeared for a moment, and then returned. "Now what was that amount, Martha? Ten thousand..." He wrote laboriously, careful to be completely accurate.

"All right." He fluttered the thin piece of paper with a grin. "Here goes. Hope your numbers are right, Martha."

The older lady *pshawed* him out the door.

Cake plate and fork in hand, I slipped out with the others to watch. Pastor Warner leaned over and spoke to a silver-haired man seated near the front. He stood with a smile, and both men shuffled to the microphone.

"Folks..." the microphone squealed for a second. "Folks, I'd like to introduce Marv Driscoll, the man who runs Driscoll Shelter. Marv, I have a great surprise for you. Martha worked overtime adding up all the figures, and we've got a real check for you tonight! The grand total is..." He paused dramatically. "Ten thousand, six hundred and seventy-one dollars!"

Applause cascaded throughout the gymnasium.

When it died down, Pastor Warner gave Marv the check, accompanied by a stage whisper. "Don't cash it until Tuesday! We still need to deposit the money."

Sputtered laughter rolled around the room.

I grinned, too. Bobby stood at my elbow, watching Pastor Warner with a sad, troubled look in his eyes. I remembered that his job was still in jeopardy.

Impulsively, I touched his sleeve. "I wish we could have raised money to keep you on, too, Bobby."

He glanced at me, and an inexplicable look of guilt flashed across his face. "Thanks, Kay, for the thought. But these people need help a lot more than I do."

What a brave thing to say. His job could be cut any day, and the Pages had nothing to fall back on.

Gradually, the tables vacated, and everyone headed for home. Theresa left with our parents, the college kids left soon after, and then Bobby and Laura left the building. Finally, only Joyce, David and I were left—and Pastor Warner was in his office. He wanted to put a few finishing touches on his sermon for tomorrow. And keep an eye on the money in the safe for a little while longer.

Slowly, I hung up the dish towel. My back ached, and my arms ached.

Joyce clattered the last pot into the cupboard. "I hurt all over." She arched back her shoulders.

"And I've got dish pan hands," David complained.

"Let's go." Joyce grabbed her purse. "I already told Dad we were leaving."

The cold night air bit through my pale cotton blouse, and I shivered. I hadn't brought a jacket, for I'd thought it might get lost in the turmoil today. I regretted it now.

Joyce fumbled in her purse for the key and locked the kitchen door behind us. "Okay," she said, "I guess I'll see you guys..."

Black slashed through my vision. Instinctively, I screamed out a warning.

Like a flood, evil surrounded us. A gang, all dressed in black, surrounded us. Knives and pistols flashed in the moonlight.

"Give us your money!"

"We know you've got it!"

"We want it now!"

"All ten thousand!" The demands shot at us like machine gunfire.

Fear stabbed me, shocking my heart into a blood bursting gallop. *Help us, Lord Jesus!* My gaze winged heavenward. Psalm 121 filled my head. *...where does my help come from? My help comes from the Lord, the Maker of heaven and earth...*

"Give it *now!*" a young man screamed, slashing his knife through the air. The masked group of five tightened like a knot, squeezing closer around us.

Sudden, bracing strength surged through me, from the top of my head down to my toes.

"Get back! In the name of Jesus!" I cried out.

The gang halted. The leader gave a high-pitched, ridiculing sneer, and stepped forward again. A black arm band encircled his bicep, and those of his friends, too.

"It's Kay!" he jeered.

Shocked, I stood very still. A horrible feeling squeezed the air from my lungs. It sounded like...

"In the name of Jesus, Lord of heaven and earth, get back!" Joyce took up the cry, her voice clear, strong and unafraid.

"Go!" David's deep voice cracked like an authoritative whip over the menacing group of toughs.

The group faltered again. Then they snarled, "Fanatics! Jesus freaks!"

As if stepping against a great weight, they slowly pushed another foot forward.

The click of a cocked rifle cracked clearly through the still night air.

"Get lost, boys," Pastor Warner drawled. "Your kind of evil has no place here."

The group backed away, their eyes suddenly wide and wild.

"Bunch of crazies!" the leader panted. Saliva hissed from the side of his mouth. He spat an obscenity, and jerked a thumb to his minions. "Let's get out of here."

They ran. Their feet pelted across the asphalt parking lot, and out of sight.

David let out a long breath. "Glad to see you, Pastor."

Pastor Warner edged out of the shadows. A grim smile curved his lips. "You can thank the Lord. A minute ago, he sent me a strong message to get outside *now* with my trusty old rifle. Glad I've kept it here. I never feel too safe these days."

I knew the identity of our attackers. A tremble slid through me. Tim. Randy. And their hate group. Clearly, the attacks on me and the church were connected. They'd orchestrated this attack to steal the fundraiser money. But who had planned it? Not Randy or Tim. I still felt convinced of that.

"They could have killed us," I whispered, crossing my arms tightly, battling the cold shivers quivering through my body. "Why didn't they? Why didn't they take the money?"

Pastor squeezed my shoulder. "We can thank the Lord. He planted confusion in their hearts. They didn't know which way was up. They just knew they had to get out of here quick, or else."

"God did that a lot in the Old Testament, against Israel's enemies." A smile wavered on Joyce's lips. She blinked rapidly.

And that's when I realized that God truly had delivered us. He had been right here with us. He had protected us. Not only from Tim and Randy, but from the unknown person or persons who had formed a malicious vendetta against our church.

I shuddered now with cold and reaction. I felt amazed, unworthy and overwhelmed that Jesus had really protected us. Times like this drove it home to me that my faith was not a figment of my imagination. Jesus *was* real. God *was* really real.

God is exactly who he says he is. And he loves us. He loves *me*.

Pastor Warner gently touched my shoulder. "Are you okay?"

I nodded. "Just very, very thankful."

"Amen to that."

"Dad, will you come home now?" Fear quavered in Joyce's voice.

"No, honey. I still need to finish my sermon. Don't worry. I'll be home soon."

"I'll walk you to your cars," David spoke up.

With a nod of approval, Pastor Warner shouldered his rifle and disappeared back inside the church.

We had all parked on the street, in order to leave the lot open for the dinner guests. We approached Joyce's red Toyota first.

"Tonight's been something, hasn't it?" She slipped into her car. "See you two tomorrow."

I'd parked a block away, under a drooping dark tree, and far from the street lamp. I was glad David walked beside me. He was tall and substantial.

The night lay silent and still around us. Not even a leaf whispered. My key scraped in the lock, and then the door swung open. It was empty inside, and safe. I slid behind the wheel.

"Night, Peanut." David leaned against the open door frame.

"Night, D." I suddenly wanted to say more, but the words stuck in my throat.

"You okay?"

I swallowed, and decided to be honest. "I'm grateful God delivered us, but I'm scared, too. I recognized Tim's voice. He was the leader."

"Are you sure?"

"Yes." I gripped the steering wheel more tightly, and swallowed again. "When will it end? It keeps getting worse and worse. And tonight they didn't get what they wanted. I know they'll be back."

He squatted beside the car, so he was on eye level with me. His steady gaze held mine. "It is scary, Kay. But we have to remember one thing. God protected us tonight. He'll do it again. What is that Psalm?" He ducked his head for a moment to think.

He looked up. "Psalm ninety-one, verses fourteen and fifteen: "'Because he loves me," says the Lord, "I will rescue him; I will protect him, for he acknowledges my name. He will call upon me, and I will answer him; I will be with him in trouble, I will deliver him and honor him.'" He will take care of us, Kay."

I nodded.

His deep voice reassured me. "God is the Rock eternal, Kay. We can always trust him."

"I know you're right." I tucked a wayward lock of hair behind my ear, and his gaze flickered, following the movement. "Guess I'll see you tomorrow in Sunday school."

"You know it." His shadowed face smiled. "Have a good night, Kay."

"You too," I smiled as he stood and pushed my door shut. David was a wonderful friend. The absolute best.

I waited until he was safely in his car before pulling away from the curb. It was dangerous out tonight. For everyone.

"Hello, Kay!" Mom's happy, light voice hailed me from the couch in the warm, earth-toned living room. Dad relaxed beside her, and Theresa perched on a chair near the fireplace. My mother's elbow rested on the back of the couch, and her palm cupped her smiling face.

"Hi." Amazement and caution warred within me as I stepped down into the large, sunken room. A warm family moment?

I plopped into a soft chair near Dad. "So, did you enjoy yourselves tonight? Did you like the spaghetti?"

"Loved the spaghetti!" proclaimed Mom.

Dad smiled. "Me too. Meaty. Just the way I like it."

"We're so proud of both of you."

Dad nodded. "You two helped our community tonight. I'm real proud."

"Well, we coul..."

BOOM!!!

We jumped, and the windowpanes shuddered.

"What the..." Dad leaped up and dashed to the door. I impulsively shoved past him and stepped onto the porch. I froze.

A gang marched down the middle of the street, brandishing guns and blazing torches. Did they wear black arm bands, too?

They stomped closer, and closer.

Dark clad figures rushed up the steps of nearby houses and flung flaming torches at the buildings. Fire licked up the walls. It reminded me of the night I'd ridden with Trent past Market Street.

Fear mixed with an incandescent surge of anger. Too many innocent people had been victimized lately. It was enough. I stepped forward, clenching my fists. How dare they violate my neighborhood? How *dare* they?

"Get inside!" Roughly, Dad shoved me back. After an unwilling hesitation, I complied. He followed me in.

"Oh, my God!" Mom had seen. Her pale, waxy face melted dully into her silver-blond hair. Her blue eyes looked wide and terrified.

Dad rushed by us again, shotgun in hand. "Can't count on the police," he muttered.

"The police!" Hands fluttering weakly, Mom stumbled for the kitchen, and the phone.

Outside, Dad fired a round into the air. And another. And another. Other gunshots reported down the street. A bizarre thought flitted to mind. Had we returned to the Wild West? Shoot-outs in the streets... People trying to protect their homes from bandits...

Dad ducked back inside, his shells obviously spent. He smelled like burnt gunpowder.

He knelt by the window and peered out.

A series of explosive BOOM!s rattled the windows, and made me tremble with more anger and fear. I hated this. I burned to do something—*anything*—to scare off those punks. But I couldn't. It was out of my hands.

More gun reports.

"Neighbors are shooting," Dad flung over his shoulder.

Had I seen black arm bands?

Or was I becoming paranoid? Surely this wasn't another hate group attack. This gang meant to terrorize everyone. Not just Christians.

Mom returned from the kitchen, and Theresa clung to her. Their perfectly made up faces were blanched white with fear. Both dripped horrified tears.

"That's got'em! They're retreating." Dad leaped up and flung open the door.

"Winston!" Mom screamed.

But it was too late. Dad stood outside, minus the gun.

After several long moments, he returned indoors. "They've scattered," he said grimly. "But Wilson's house is on fire, and so is the Burns'. When is the fire department coming?" He strode for the phone.

We were safe? Relief didn't last long.

For they'd be back. I knew it.

Legs feeling a bit wobbly, I slipped over to the window and peered out. Our street looked like a scene from Dante. A burning inferno. Two houses blazed down the street.

Whirrr whirrr, whirrrrr. The cavalry approached.

Fire trucks and police cars parked haphazardly in the middle of the street.

"We're safe. We're *safe*," Mom wept. Dad held her in his arms.

Theresa collapsed like a deflated doll onto the couch.

Trembling, I rested my temple against the glass window. I couldn't seem to stop shaking. My anger had burned out, and now I just tasted bitter fear.

I didn't feel safe anymore. Not at home. Not at church. Not at school. I wondered if I would ever feel safe again.

SUNDAY

SUNDAY MORNING dawned cold, crisp and clear. A fresh new day. But nothing could blot out the black, scarred faces of the houses on our street. Mom didn't want me to go to church, especially after I told her what had happened in the church parking lot last night.

But I had to go. I wouldn't let the darkness win.

The bustle of the crowded church, and the sound of laughing and talking people soothed my soul when I arrived. I desperately needed normalcy.

I slid down a polished pew to sit next to Joyce and David. After short greetings, they asked in urgent whispers if I was all right. They had heard about the torched houses on State Street.

I reassured them that I was fine, and so was my family and home.

The pianist struck the chords of the first song.

It felt good to sing to God. He was bigger than all of my fears, and bigger than all my problems. He'd proved it last night in the church parking lot. Finally, a sliver of peace settled into my soul.

Pastor Warner took the platform. "Last night's fundraiser was a huge success," he boomed.

Applause resounded.

With a smile, Pastor Warner scanned the sanctuary. "Good news is, we raised a lot of money. It will help a lot of people." His smile faded. "I'm sorry to say I bear bad news, too. The FGA called me this morning. They're furious."

"Why, you ask?" His fingers clenched the sides of the podium. "Because I preached Jesus at the fundraiser. I told people that he died on the cross for our sins. A message of hope, right?"

A few people nodded.

"Wrong, according to the FGA. They approved the fundraiser for one reason, and one reason only; to help the community, and to improve the public's opinion of our church. Preaching Jesus was not approved. They said they've received dozens of complaints. Apparently, I've offended the entire town."

"Their voters, more likely," David muttered beside me.

"Some of you know I went to an FGA vision meeting on Thursday. It was a real eye-opener." Pastor Warner spoke slowly now, as if choosing his words with care. "They rebuked me on a number of issues, but the central sin I've committed is preaching the Bible as the truth. As the literal Word of God. The FGA insists that premise is false, and even archaic."

He thumped open his Bible. "I tell you it is not! Second Timothy three, verses sixteen through seventeen say,

"'All Scripture is God-breathed and is useful for teaching, rebuking, correcting and training in righteousness so that the man of God may be thoroughly equipped for every good work.'"

He gazed at us over his glasses. "The Bible is my witness. Our faith stands on this book." He hefted it. "I must preach God's Word.

"But here's the rub. The FGA will fire me, and expel us all from this church building if I keep preaching the Bible as the truth."

My gasp mingled with that of the congregation's.

"The FGA's 'politically correct' stance reminds me of Second Timothy chapter four, verse three. Read it. It's an indictment against the FGA." Pastor carefully lay down the Bible. "I have more bad news. The FGA also accused us of flagrantly ignoring their directives three times in a row, now."

How did they know, I wondered. Where were they getting their information?

"So they're going to put a freeze on our money. All of it. Effective Wednesday, we can only spend it on expenses *they* approve. The FGA is sending a representative this week to collect the money from the fundraiser, and they've already told Driscoll Shelter to tear up their check. The FGA wants to audit their finances."

I gasped again.

"As you know, I already gave the money to Driscoll Shelter." Pastor's voice rose in passionate anger. "I tell you now, I've advised them to keep the check. They will get the money, and I won't ask for it back! We promised it to them, and they need it, so they'll keep it.

"What's more, the FGA's suggestion that the shelter's finances are corrupt is hogwash!" His voice erupted like a volcano, making the mike squeal in protest. "Three separate churches audit the shelter's finances every year!"

"I'll be honest with you, friends. I don't know where things will go from here. We've reached an impasse with the FGA. We need to pray, or we could lose this church."

"I think the FGA wants the money for themselves!" Sophie spat after Sunday school class.

"For Oak Woodward's campaign," Anne agreed.

The FGA's ridiculous demands were the hot topic this morning.

"Money aside, I want to know the real reason why they're so upset with Pastor Warner," I said. "Didn't the FGA start twenty years ago by preaching the Bible as the truth?"

"This isn't about the Bible," David said. "It's about politics—all of it—which includes the money and the message. Christians are unpopular. The hate attacks prove it. The FGA is trying to whitewash our church's negative image. They probably think the more community events our church does, and the less said about the Bible, the more Truesdale will like and accept our church—a.k.a., the FGA."

Everything finally clicked. "It's all to help Oak Woodward become Senator." The theory was almost unbelievable. Censorship, outright persecution of Christians and the Bible, and an attempt to steal funds by First Gospel of America, our parent church. All for the sake of political power.

I felt sick to my stomach.

"Something needs to be done," Sophie said with a disgusted lip curl. She grabbed her coat. "What is this country coming to?"

Joyce frowned to herself. She had been unusually quiet this morning, and I wondered what she thought about it all. Her father's job was on the line. In fact, her whole way of life, growing up at Truesdale First Gospel, was on the line.

"Are you okay, Joy?"

"I'm fine." She abruptly grabbed her purse and stood. "I need to write up my term paper on last night's fundraiser. Talk to you later, okay?"

I nodded, remembering that the fundraiser had doubled as a project for one of her business classes. Clearly, she was busy. Did that explain why Joyce kept running off these days? Either she ran off, or she snapped at someone. It was almost as if she wanted to escape church...or us. Obviously, something was bothering her, but what?

Didn't she want to talk anymore? It hurt that she might not.

But she *was* busy. We both were, actually. A business degree took a lot of work, and she was the type to put in hundreds of extra hours. It was her focus in life. She was on the career—warpath, really—to become a business woman.

But doubt niggled. Was "busy-ness" really the problem? Or was our friendship slipping for another reason? It wasn't the first time the thought had crossed my mind. It bothered me, because we were the best of friends.

At least, we used to be.

At home, the football game blared from the den. My family jostled in the kitchen, assembling snacks.

"Hi, honey." Mom lifted a crystal pitcher of iced tea from the counter. She paused on her way out the door, silver bracelets clicking against the glass. "How was church?"

I blinked. Mom never asked about church.

"Good," I said, snagging a potato chip and popping it into my mouth. *Mmmm.* Crispy and salty. It took a second to remember the sermon. "Pastor Warner said God is the ultimate authority. We should humble ourselves and live in obedience to him."

"Oh." Mom lifted her eyebrows, but still hovered. Interest glimmered in her eyes.

Surprised but encouraged, I said, "He also said that for our own happiness, God's way is the best path for us to follow. But sometimes we don't believe that. Or we forget it."

Dad patted my shoulder as he brushed by, beer in hand. "I like your pastor. He's a real down-to-earth kind of guy."

I blinked again as the two exited.

Theresa's fingers tightened around the wooden chip dish. "Was David there?"

I fetched the pottery sombrero filled with tortillas and salsa. "Yes." Did Theresa still like him? The thought disturbed me.

"Does David like girls?"

The dish almost slipped out of my fingers. I stared at her in shock. "Yes! He does."

Theresa looked down. Confusion flickered across her face.

"But he's kind of picky," I said awkwardly.

Theresa tossed her head up. "I know he doesn't like me, Kay."

"Of course he does."

She laughed shortly, and shook her head. "I know. Like a friend. He's a real nice guy." She looked at me with suddenly bright eyes. "And I know he likes girls, too. That was a mean question to ask."

I took a surprised breath, but my sister hadn't finished. Her next question shocked me more than the first one.

"What does 'growing in the Lord' mean?"

"Um..." I gaped for a second. "It means," I said, trying to order my thoughts, "that when a Christian spends time praying, reading the Bible and obeying God's Word, she—or he—grows closer to the Lord. God changes the person's heart, and the Christian begins to show more and more of Jesus' character qualities. Like love." I paused for a breath. "Why?"

Theresa shook her head. Almost indifferently, she tossed out, "Are you growing in the Lord?"

I bobbled again. "Yes. I hope. Slowly. But I wish God would change me faster."

"Okay." Theresa brushed by me, heading for the den. Clearly, the conversation was over.

I stared after her. Where on earth had Theresa heard the phrase, "growing in the Lord?" And why did she care what it meant?

Our favorite team, the Forty-Niners, lost.

As Dad ate the last chip, we listened to Mick Murray's local news commentary on Channel 23.

"Police caught several of the rioters who vandalized State Street last night. Thanks to fast community action, only five million dollars in damage was done.

"In related news, new government statistics show that drugs, gangs and crime are on the rise again. It's a trend echoing around the world.

"But here's some good news, straight from the conflict-riddled world front. Sources say they hear a whisper of *peace* on the horizon..."

Monday

"What happened to you?" I stared in horror at Mary's puffy, black and blue right eye.

"Nothing." Mary fumbled in her backpack and slipped on sunglasses. "Nothing happened, okay? I'm fine."

But she did not look fine. She looked desperately unhappy.

"Jack hit you, didn't he?"

After a long moment, Mary whispered, "Yes." Then it all spilled out. Rushing, shaking words tumbled over one another. "He...he wouldn't believe I'd spent the day with my mom yesterday, going to church." Tears slipped down her cheeks, and escaped from beneath the sunglasses. "He thought the fundraiser was on Sunday. And that I spent the day with you and your friends." A high sob choked off. "So he hit me."

"Leave him, Mary! Come stay at my house."

"No. It's okay now." She swiped the tears from her cheeks. "Jack apologized. He said he'd never do it again."

"You don't *believe* him, do you?"

Mary looked away. It was clear she did.

"Mary! He treats you like trash. Can't you see that? For your own safety—for the *baby's* safety—leave him!"

Mary shook her head, "It's not that bad..."

"Will you stop it? Listen to yourself," I cried in outrage. "You're a special person, Mary. A valuable person! Obviously, Jack doesn't see that. You deserve far better. Don't you see that?"

Tears cascaded down her cheeks, but she jerked her head in a silent "no."

Frustrated tears formed in my own eyes. Why wouldn't she listen to reason?

"I care about you, Mary. *All* of your friends care about you. We don't want you to be treated like this. And you know what? God loves you so much you can't believe it! And he *hates* the way Jack is treating you."

Mary's head jerked toward me. But then her shoulders slumped. "I know you care about me, Kay. But God doesn't seem real to me. He's so far away. It's hard to believe he loves me."

I realized this was the crux of the problem. Mary felt unworthy. She felt unclean. Nothing she did, in her eyes, could cleanse her of her sin before God. She believed God despised her, just like Jack did. Just like her father did. And so it was impossible for her to feel good about herself.

"None of us is worthy of God's love, Mary. But that doesn't change the fact he does love us. He loves you, and he loves me. And to prove it, he sent his Son, Jesus, to die on the cross for our sins. All of our sins. Past, present, future. We can be completely forgiven if we just believe in Jesus, and what he did for us on the cross. It's that simple."

"I just can't believe it," she whispered.

I tried one last tack. "Jesus said, 'I have come that they may have life, and have it to the full.' Do you know what that means? It means a relationship with the living, loving God."

Mary rubbed her eyes, but her voice sounded dull now. "What does that mean?"

"It means that even though we're born sinners and dead spiritually—separated from God—Jesus came to bridge that gap. If we accept him as our Savior, God does a wonderful thing for us. He regenerates our spirit. He gives us new life. Jesus said it best." I flipped through my tan Bible to John 3:3,5-6.

"In verse three Jesus says, 'I tell you the truth, no one can see the kingdom of God unless he is born again.'"

"Born again?" Mary frowned in disbelief. "What does that mean?"

"'Jesus answered, "I tell you the truth, no one can enter the kingdom of God unless he is born of water and the Spirit. Flesh gives birth to flesh, but the Spirit gives birth to spirit. You should not be surprised at my saying, 'You must be born again.' The wind blows wherever it pleases. You hear its sound, but you cannot tell where it comes from or where it is going. So it is with everyone born of the Spirit.'"

"I don't understand that."

I sighed. "It means what I said already. That God, when we accept Jesus as our savior, gives us new life. We're made alive by his Spirit, who comes to live within us. We are born again. And we enter into a real relationship with God.

"I can't explain how it works exactly. All I know is that when I accepted Jesus as my Savior, God became *real* to me in a way I can't even describe. I know that he is really *there*. He is really real. I know it with every fiber of my being. And since then, he's been changing me from the inside out."

Mary looked troubled. "I don't know." She twisted her hands. "It sounds nice. But I don't think I'm ready to make a leap of faith like that."

"Just think about it," I said. "Please."

Mary said nothing, but I sensed that she would. All I could do was pray. *Lord, please turn Mary's heart to you. Please save her soul. And please, I pray she'll leave Jack before it's too late.*

I briefly spoke to Trent in journalism class. Again, Friday night's uncertain, confused emotions welled in me, so when he asked me to lunch on Wednesday, I jumped at the chance. I wanted to figure out what was going on with our relationship, once and for all.

Tim and Randy attended class today, too. I tried to ignore them, but lost that battle when something hard flicked into the side of my head. A pencil eraser bounced into the aisle.

I pretended not to notice the juvenile assault, but felt tense for the remainder of the class, waiting for the next missile. It never came, but I did feel their malevolent stares boring into my back. And I felt their hatred, like a live, pulsating thing. It frightened me.

I still felt their eyes on me when I exited the classroom at the end of the period. Creepy crawlies skittered down my back, but I tried my best to ignore them.

I pushed through the door at the end of the hall, and slipped outside with the rest of my class. I inhaled a cold lungful of fresh air. Free. Free from the suffocating class. And free from Randy and Tim...

An elbow smacked hard into my side.

"*Ow.*" I whirled.

Randy sneered down at me. "Get out of my way, girl."

Rage flashed through me. Enough was enough. I was so sick of being the victim. "You get out of *my* way!"

"Watch your mouth! It's gonna get you a pack of trouble."

"That's right." Tim flanked my other side.

I whipped around to face them both. "Get a life. Leave me alone!"

Tim's lips stretched back, baring his teeth in a snarl. His face swooped toward mine. Despite myself, I stepped backward. That made him smile.

"We enjoy putting narrow-minded bigots in their place. Makes life sweet for us, right, Randy?"

"Uhhmm." Randy glowered.

I quivered with fury. "Why do you keep attacking me?"

"Why?" Tim's jaw jutted toward me again, but this time I didn't retreat. "Why? I'll tell you *why*. Because we're sick of people like you. Always sticking your nose in where it doesn't belong. Telling people how to think!"

Randy thrust in his own words. "Mind your own business! And keep that trap of yours shut."

The full blast of their hatred made me shake. Finally, a pinch of fear took hold. Reasoning with them was like grasping for the wind. Logic did not motivate them. Tim and Randy were consumed by hatred.

"The world needs to be freed from religious fanatics." Tim's eyes slitted. "It's our job, see, to keep you in your place."

"It's a free country," I returned, probably unwisely. "Remember? No law prohibits believing in God. *Vandalism* is another story."

A satisfied grin curved Tim's lips, and he glanced at Randy.

I felt sick. They had accomplished their goal. Clearly, they had wanted to remind me of the parking lot on Saturday night. All three of us knew they had been there.

Tim turned away. "Come on, Randy. We've got better things to do."

Randy shoved by me.

Trembling with anger, I watched them go. I felt helpless. Frustrated. And scared.

I couldn't stop them. Tim and Randy would keep harassing both me and my church. Calling the police hadn't helped. Obviously, they had never been able to track down the car that had tried to run me over. And I couldn't prove they'd attacked us at church on Saturday night, either.

Lord help me. I'm scared. I don't know what to do anymore.

Legs trembling from an excess of adrenaline, I headed for my next class.

At home, the warm smell of cheese and baking broccoli, along with the rich scent of ham and potatoes au gratin wafted to my nose. My mouth watered as Mom delivered each steaming dish to the table. Each course had taken several hours to prepare. Except for the ham, perhaps.

All of these dishes were Dad's favorites.

Mom wore her fanciest gold lame pantsuit, and delicate pearls and diamonds dripped from her ears and from the necklace clasped around her throat. Dad sat silently at the head of the table. He glanced at Mom out of the corner of his eye. He looked wary.

"Looks wonderful, Helen," he finally grunted. He picked up a silver spoon and reached for the potatoes.

"Thank you, dear." Mom sailed by in a waft of expensive perfume. She sat across from Dad. Her frosty blue eyes looked watchful, and her smile tentative. "I hoped you might like it."

He slid the spoon with a soft squish through the potatoes. "Makes a man wonder what you might want."

I swallowed a soft gasp.

The cruel words hung in the air.

I speared up a slice of ham, unable to suppress a flare of anger. Why couldn't they get along? I was so sick of their petty arguments.

I banged the ham fork sharply against my plate.

"No." Mom's voice was level. She glanced down for a second, masking the hurt in her eyes. "Actually, Winston, I decided you were right. Maybe I have been spending too much money. I wanted to ask your opinion about something. Do you think we need new drapes? Or should we keep the old ones for a while longer?"

Theresa and I glanced quickly at Dad, who blinked. He tapped the heaping potato spoon against his china plate. "Well," he cleared his throat. "I think we should keep the ones we have." As he shoved the spoon back into the potatoes, his voice gathered strength. "At least until I find out if I get a Christmas bonus."

"All right. That's what we'll do." Placidly, Mom began to eat. Theresa and I glanced at her, and then at Dad, not sure what to make of this sudden change in tactics.

Dad didn't know what to make of it, either. He cleared his throat and abruptly reached for the ham. "All right, then."

The rest of the evening passed tranquilly. I didn't understand it, but was grateful for it.

Lord, thank you for the change in Mom's heart, and thank you that my parents were able to get along this evening. I ask that their relationship will improve and that they'd love each other again. Thank you for my parents. I love them so much.

And please protect Mary from Jack. Please give her wisdom about that situation, and that she'll get out of it soon. Please turn her heart to you. In Jesus' name, Amen.

WEDNESDAY — MORNING

"*HOW ARE THINGS GOING* between you and Trent?" Mary's bruised eye had a grayish yellow cast this morning, and her lids looked puffy, as if she had been crying.

Clearly, she wanted to steer the conversation away from herself. "I'm not sure," I admitted. "I'm confused, but trying to work it out in my head. Has Jack hit you again?"

"No." Mary's face closed up. Tears glittered in her brown eyes.

"Why don't you leave him?"

"I can't. Try to understand. Jack has always *been* there for me."

"Let your friends support you, too."

She closed her eyes. "Please. Can we talk about something else?"

"I'm worried about you. He hit you once. Who's to say he won't hit you again?"

"He won't." The rebuttal came fast. "But if he does, I'll move out." She lifted her head with gentle dignity. "I won't let him hurt my baby."

I hoped that was true. But her relationship was already horrible, and she hadn't moved out yet. I didn't understand why she stayed with Jack. But Mary was her own person. I could not live her life for her.

I changed the subject. "I'm having lunch with Trent today."

My own life was complicated enough.

"My treat. What do you want?" Trent smiled as I gazed at the menu printed above the cash register in the student union's snack shop.

"A turkey sandwich with Swiss on rye. And a root beer. Thank you." Trent had already refused my money.

"Okay." Trent ordered the food, and while he waited for it to be made, I scouted out a free table. I found one in the middle of the student union. The lunch crowd noise swirled around me as I sat, and my backpack slid to the floor at my feet.

The excitement this lunch would have inspired in me only a few weeks ago had not materialized. I enjoyed spending time with Trent, but the feeling that the relationship was going flat continued to plague me.

I still didn't understand why my feelings for Trent had changed so rapidly—in the wrong direction. Unless, of course, I'd only had a superficial crush on him. That was certainly possible. He was suave, handsome...almost everything I thought I'd wanted in a man.

But something was missing. I had asked God to take away my romantic feelings for Trent if they weren't his will. Maybe God was answering my half-hearted prayer.

I did like Trent, and I valued his friendship very much. But did I want to continue to date him? That was the crux of the matter.

"Here you go." Trent slid my wrapped sandwich across to me.

"Thank you." I smiled, and spread the napkin across my lap and peeled open my sandwich. I felt oddly at a loss for words. Not an affliction with which I was usually cursed.

Trent helped me out. "How'd the fundraiser go Saturday?"

I smiled again, and met his intensely interested gaze. "Good. We raised thousands of dollars for the shelter. But we almost lost it."

"How?"

"A gang ambushed us in the parking lot. Pastor Warner scared them off with his gun." Actually, God had scared them off, but I didn't know how to say that to Trent without raising his skepticism.

"A gang. Maybe the one that's been attacking your church?"

"Yes. I recognized Tim's voice."

"Wow!" He stared at me. "Will you write that article? I know the *Press* would print it."

I hadn't thought about the article since he'd mentioned it last Friday, but found myself saying, "I think I will. Someone needs to expose them. But I'll need to do a lot more research to find out who they all are, and who's behind it."

"Good luck."

"I know." It sounded like an impossible task.

A short, awkward silence followed, which Trent quickly filled. "So, is the FGA still giving you problems?"

"Yes. They're threatening to throw us out of our church building. And out of the FGA, too."

"*What?* Why?" His blue eyes sharpened. He picked up a French fry and shoved it in his mouth.

I explained that the FGA didn't want us to preach the Bible, or about Jesus, or about sin and turning to God in repentance.

"Sounds like a strange position for a church organization to take."

"I know. David thinks it's all about politics. A public relations ploy to help Oak Woodward get elected."

"Really. Seems like a lot of trouble to go through to promote a candidate."

"I know. But power is power. If Oak Woodward gets elected, the FGA will be in a position to directly influence the federal government."

"And coat their own pockets," Trent muttered.

The distasteful idea could be true. "Maybe so."

"So, does the FGA believe in Jesus anymore?"

The change in topic took me by surprise. Trent's eyes glittered, as if he'd deftly orchestrated the change of topic on purpose.

"I don't know."

He leaned toward me, and it felt like a high wattage light beamed at me when he turned on every ounce of charm he possessed. Why was he doing it? Did he sense our relationship was slipping? Did he want to fight to rescue it?

I felt flattered.

Trent said, "I've been chewing over what you said about Jesus. And how he claimed to be God."

"Really?"

"Yes. Maybe he did claim to be God. But I can't believe one thing."

"What's that?"

"The resurrection."

He threw that at me and sat back, as if throwing a bone to a dog. His gaze still looked oddly intense.

Did he really want to hear what I thought? Or was he manipulating me for some other, unknown reason?

I decided to respond with a question.

"What happened to his body, then?"

His lean fingers drummed the table. The strained charm faded, and I sensed an odd tension in him. I didn't have a clue what was going on, but I felt more drawn to him in that moment, and at the same time, more uncertain of my relationship with him, too.

"Maybe the disciples stole it."

"Would you die for a lie?"

"What?"

"Almost every apostle died a martyr's death. Peter died hanging upside down on a cross. Paul was beheaded. Would you die a horrible death for a deliberate lie?"

He frowned harder, his intellect clearly caught by the argument. "No. I guess not." He shrugged. "Maybe the Romans stole Jesus' body. Or the Jewish leaders."

"Then why didn't they produce it? The disciples infuriated the Jewish leaders with their teachings about Jesus, and how he'd risen from the dead. Don't you think the officials would have revealed Jesus' body if they'd had it? It would have stopped the Christian movement dead in its tracks."

His drumming fingers stilled. "So, what do you think happened?"

"I think he rose from the dead," I said simply. "Just like the disciples said. They saw Jesus in his resurrected body, and so did hundreds of other people.

"And look at the changes in the disciples' lives after Jesus rose to heaven. After Pentecost, Peter—who had denied the Lord three times—suddenly started preaching, unafraid, in front of huge crowds of people. And that's just one story. There are tons more. To me, it's only logical that something dramatic happened to change their lives. Something like Jesus rising from the dead."

"Interesting." His stilled fingers started drumming again, and his expression shuttered. He swallowed the last of his cola.

"Hi." David's voice startled us both.

My heart leaped, and I glanced up. David's tall, dark form blocked the rays of sunlight shining through a window. "Hi." I smiled.

Trent wrapped up the remains of his sandwich. He glanced at me. "I've got to go. Just remembered research I need to do for next class. See you on Friday?"

I nodded. A bit surprised, I watched him stride away.

David lowered himself into the vacated chair. "What's with him?"

"I don't know. The internship is keeping him pretty busy." I took a sip of root beer and sighed. "Everyone seems busy lately."

"Midterms are coming up. It's a busy time of year."

"I know."

David's gaze narrowed. "What's wrong?"

"I don't know. I guess I feel like I haven't been able to really talk to people lately. Like we're growing apart."

"Who, people? Trent?"

"No." Then I knew what was bothering me, and had been, in the back of my mind, for several weeks.

"I miss talking to Joyce. We've been friends forever, but I feel like we're drifting apart. We never talk about anything important anymore. She always seems so busy."

David fingered the salt shaker in the center of the table. "Joyce is changing. You're changing, too. Her life goals are different than yours or mine."

"What do you mean?" But I thought I knew what he meant.

His serious gaze met mine. "I like Joyce a lot, but she's on the fast track now. She's making new friends, and new plans. Her career is everything to her. Just like Trent's career is everything to him."

"What do you mean? You don't know anything about Trent."

"I do. He has a one track mind, Kay. Even I can see that. It's journalism. Just like Joyce's focus is business. Period."

Was he right? Was that why Joyce was drifting away? Did her business career mean more than her old friends?

"Do you think we still matter to her?"

"Sure, we do," David said, his voice rough.

"Then why does she keep snapping at me? And why do you both keep fighting? It seems like she keeps getting angrier and angrier. Why?"

"I don't know. But remember, the church has been attacked five times this last month. And midterms are coming up. Combined together, that's pretty stressful. Maybe she doesn't know how to deal with it all."

"You're probably right." I still felt there was more to it, though. But it was my responsibility, as much as Joyce's, to keep up our friendship. If something was troubling her, I should ask about it. I wanted to help, if I could.

And, as far as her business career was concerned, she probably needed support in her new path, just as much as I did in mine.

What *was* my new path? Besides journalism, of course. I felt like I was growing. Growing toward something I couldn't see yet.

"Hey, how's Mary?" David changed the subject. "She wasn't at the dinner Saturday night, but I thought she bought tickets— or her parents did?"

"Her mother donated money, but she didn't come." I told David how Jack had punched Mary because he thought she'd been with us on Sunday.

David's high cheekbones whitened with anger. "I can't believe that!"

"I asked her to come stay at my house, but she wouldn't. I don't know what to do. She won't leave him."

David's hands closed over mine. "We can pray."

He prayed in a low murmur, and I ended the prayer.

"Lord, please protect Mary from Jack, and please give her wisdom about her relationship. And please tell us what we can do to help her."

David released my hands, and smiled suddenly. "Mary's lucky to have a friend like you." One brow flicked up. "And so am I."

I smiled back at him. Gentle peace stole through my soul. Why did I always feel so happy when I was with him? Maybe because we'd been friends forever...

Week Six — False Prophets

*For the time will come
when men will not put up with sound doctrine.
Instead, to suit their own desires,
they will gather around them a great number of teachers
to say what their itching ears want to hear.
They will turn their ears away from the truth
and turn aside to myths.*

2 TIMOTHY 4:3-4

Wednesday — evening

"THERESA! YOU'VE BEEN CHEATING?" Furious red mottled Dad's face when I mistakenly stepped into the kitchen that evening. He shook a paper in his fist. *"That's* what the college said?" He turned to Mom.

"Yes." Mom appeared more thin and frail than usual, and her eyes looked large and pleading. She reached for the paper. "Please. I shouldn't have opened Theresa's mail. It was a mistake."

Theresa's eyes were puffy and her face blotched. "It's *my* life, Dad! So I made a little mistake. Let me deal with it."

"A *little* mistake?" Dad roared. "A little mistake? You've made a mistake all right, missy, but I'll be the one who will handle it. No more dates for the rest of the semester!"

"Dad," she wailed. "That's not fair! I only cheated once or twice..."

"*Quiet!*" he erupted. "I've always believed in you, Theresa. Always! I thought you could handle your social life and college, but clearly, you cannot. One of them has to go, but it won't be college."

"Dad!" Theresa appealed mutely to Mom.

Mom's distressed gaze darted between the two of them. "Perhaps we are being a bit harsh, Winston. Maybe we should..."

"No!" Dad rounded on her. Cringing, I stepped backward, into the doorway. "She's run amok for two months, thanks to you. Now we'll handle things my way. This young woman has to learn priorities."

I retreated into the hall and waited for Mom to explode. She always stood up for Theresa.

"All right, Winston." Mom's calm voice surprised me. "I agree that Theresa should be punished. But three months of grounding seems a little severe."

Dad flung the paper at Mom. "We'll reevaluate in two months."

Sobbing hysterically, Theresa fled from the room and lumbered upstairs. A door slammed.

The house fell deathly silent. I didn't know where to go. Certainly not the kitchen. I was sure my parents would begin fighting again, and I didn't want to hear it. And I didn't want to hear my sister cry. All I wanted was a little peace.

As I slipped into the living room, Mom called after me. "Kay? It's time to eat. Come help set the table."

Surprisingly, dinner was hushed, but civil. The table seemed empty without Theresa. I felt sorry for my sister, but Dad was right. Theresa needed to face the consequences of her actions.

Thankfully, college group met tonight. My parents were still behaving cordially when I left, but the tension in the house remained palpable.

I sprinted to my car in the cool, swiftly deepening dusk, and slammed and locked the door behind me. I still couldn't forget the gangs of people who had marched down State Street on Saturday night, brandishing torches and flames. And guns. How many had also worn the hate group's black bands?

The blackened houses looked shadowed and eerie in the soft purple dusk. After turning the corner, I headed for Truesdale First Gospel.

I met up with Sophie and Anne in the parking lot, and was glad I didn't have to walk alone to the church. The darkness scared me now.

Inside the warmly lit sanctuary, cheerful laughter swirled around us. Laura and David stood on stage, preparing for worship, and Joyce chatted in a corner with friends. I decided to sit with Sophie and Anne this evening, but was determined to speak to Joyce after church.

A few minutes later, Bobby jogged up to the microphone. "Evening, guys and gals! Glad you could make it tonight." The microphone squealed briefly.

"Just wanted to say you did a great job on Saturday. Driscoll Shelter thanks you for your hard work, and so do the Pastor and I. You guys made a real difference in people's lives."

On stage, David ran a pick through the guitar strings, and Bobby grinned. "I see David's ready. Worship will go a bit longer than usual. Let's give God a big thank you for all he has done."

Clapping in time to the music, I sang with enthusiasm. Joyce stood on stage now, singing next to Laura. Usually they asked me to join, but that didn't matter. Singing on stage or not, it felt good to worship the Lord. By the end, the joy welling up in my soul had melted away the uncomfortable feelings lingering from home. I felt close to the Lord. I knew he would take care of me. I didn't have to worry, or be afraid. If only I could always remember to trust him this much.

After the meeting, I headed over to talk to Joyce. Our friendship wouldn't die of neglect if I could help it. Although I wanted to ask what was bothering her, too, that would probably have to wait until we could sit down and have a long talk.

"Hi, Joyce."

Joyce turned, and her glad smile instantly matched my own. "Oh, hi, Kay! I was wondering where you were. We could have used a third up on stage."

"Oh, thank you—maybe next time. Has your dad heard from the FGA again?"

"Yes, he has." She frowned. "Remember that FGA man who came a few weeks ago? Mr. Crawford."

I nodded.

"Well, he came today, and demanded that Dad give him the money from the fundraiser. But of course the bank has it, and Dad refused to stop payment on the check."

"I'm glad he didn't back down."

"He wouldn't. Dad will never renege on a promise." Joyce glanced at the laughing, talking people who filed out of the church. "How's your mom?"

An odd question. "Well... Actually, she's been acting a little strange."

Joyce's eyebrows flew up, and she grabbed my arm. "Don't you *know*?" Her tone sounded incredulous.

"Know what?"

"Your mom gave her life to Christ on Saturday night. She told me at the gym on Monday."

"*What*?"

"Yes. Honestly, I'm just as surprised as you are."

My mouth finally snapped shut. "But how? Why?" I sputtered. I'd never talked much to Mom about Jesus. She'd never seemed remotely interested.

Joyce's eyes sparkled. "I don't know. The Lord has a way of working in peoples' hearts, doesn't he?"

Suddenly I had to know every detail. "Have you been talking to her about Jesus?"

"Not especially. She's asked questions about our college group, so I told her what we do here. I thought she was interested because you go."

"Anything else?" I prodded, still feeling overwhelmed and overjoyed that my mother was a Christian. She was saved! Tears of joy stung my eyes.

"I did tell her about Jesus," Joyce admitted. "A little. But I didn't get the impression she was very interested. She just seemed unhappy and lonely, that's all."

I felt unable to grasp the enormity of what had happened. Then another incident flashed to mind.

"Theresa," I breathed. "On Sunday, she asked what 'growing in the Lord' meant. Do you know why she asked? Or who she heard it from?"

"Me." Laura's hand movement caught Joyce's eye. "Last week, she said David is a hundred times nicer than the guys she dates. I told her David is really growing in the Lord. That's probably where she heard it." She edged away and offered an apologetic smile. "Talk to you later?"

I nodded. A bit of our old camaraderie had returned, and my mother was saved! Suddenly, I had to tell someone.

I spotted David heading out the door with his guitar case in hand. I sprinted after him and hugged my jacket close about me as I stepped into the chilly night.

"David!" I half-ran, half-walked after him.

"What?" His grin looked surprised, and happy.

"I have to tell someone, or I'll burst!" I gasped. "My mom's saved! Joyce just told me. She became a Christian on Saturday night."

"That's great!" A wide grin lit his face. He hesitated a moment, and rested the guitar case beside his car door.

"And Theresa might be interested in God, too! Can you believe it? The Lord is really working in my family!"

Sudden tears slid down my face. I felt so excited, so happy, and yet so humble before God. That he would do this for them. For me, too, because I loved them so much.

"I don't know why I'm crying!" I choked on a laugh.

"Come here." Smiling, David pulled me into his arms, and I wept there, with my face buried against the edge of his cotton jacket. His flannel shirt felt warm against my cheek. "I'm just so happy!" I sobbed helplessly.

"I know."

He held me, and a moment later I found that my hands had crept around him, too, and I hugged him close.

His strong arms held me tight. They felt warm and secure. I did feel happy. *Very* happy. Sweet, intense joy filled my soul. But it wasn't because of Mom, I suddenly realized. It was because David held me in his arms.

With a startled gasp, I stumbled backward. "Sorry. Didn't know I was such a basket case."

Why had I just felt like that in his arms?

His smile gleamed through the inky dusk. "Don't apologize. It's one of the things I like most about you."

"What?" I smiled weakly. "Being an emotional wreck? Bursting into tears all the time?" I wanted to flee from the confusing new feelings. Instead, I heaved a great breath and rubbed my eyes dry with my coat sleeve.

"You're honest. Even when it makes you vulnerable. It's a rare quality these days." His deep tone told me how serious he was.

"Thanks." I managed a cheeky grin. "I'll remember that. Next time I have a crying fit, you'd better run for cover."

He smiled and pulled keys from his pocket. "See you later, Kay."

"See you."

Trembling a little, I watched him slam the door. I felt scared inside. Confused.

Hugging my arms tightly against myself, I turned toward my Mustang. Why had I felt so happy in David's arms?

I had a guess. But honestly, I wasn't ready to understand it, or face it yet. I had another problem to figure out first.

I slid into my old brown Mustang. A cold weight of acknowledgment dampened my spirits. I never could have shared my happiness over Mom's salvation with Trent. He simply wouldn't have understood.

I did like Trent, but how much, beyond a basic—not to mention new—friendship? And what did we have in common, besides journalism? I was beginning to think, *not very much.*

SUNDAY

BOTH OF MY PARENTS sat at the table eating breakfast when I entered the kitchen. My ivory dress, printed with an abstract, golden leaf pattern, swirled around my ankles. Mom wore a pale blue silk dress, and Dad wore slacks, a gray shirt, and a red paisley tie.

"Where are you going?" I poured a glass of orange juice and pulled a pineapple flavored yogurt from the refrigerator.

"We'd like to go to church with you today," Mom said.

Dad said gruffly, "I like your pastor. Decided it couldn't hurt to hear him preach once."

"That's wonderful!" I beamed in surprise.

I hadn't talked to Mom yet about how she'd become a Christian, although I longed to. I hated the gulf that still separated us. I would be the one to take that first step. Today.

Both Mom and Dad seemed to enjoy the service. When we got home, Theresa was still asleep upstairs. It was her way of rebelling, I supposed. She couldn't date anymore, so she'd make up the time in sleep.

I paused in the den doorway, clad in jeans now, and an old gray sweatshirt. Mick Murray's voice rumbled from the T.V. "...Oak Woodward plans to speak tomorrow at Truesdale State University. It'll be at noon sharp, according to the latest press release. Security will be tight, since he's received several death threats..."

Grimacing, I stepped away. The FGA. Oak Woodward. I hated how they were trying to destroy my church.

Mom stood in the kitchen, preparing a pot of macaroni and cheese. Football fare for Dad. After lunch, I would study for midterms and work on my current affairs article. Dr. Williams wanted a rough draft in less than two weeks.

"Smells good." I hovered at the stove, sniffing appreciatively.

Mom's warm smile appeared a touch vulnerable. "Thanks, honey. Would you hand me that spoon? You father hates it when the noodles clump."

I handed her the spoon, and searched for something else to say. "Did you like church?"

"Yes. It was good." She ripped the packets of cheese open and dumped the orange, powdery substance into the pot, followed by milk and butter. "Your pastor seems nice."

"Joyce told me you became a Christian on Saturday night."

Mom's hand faltered, and then quickly resumed stirring. "That's right, I did."

"I'm so glad." I said awkwardly, "I don't know if I can explain..."

Mom smiled at me. Her eyes brimmed with tears. "I understand, honey. And I'm more happy than I've been in my whole life. I had no idea..."

"That Jesus is real? That he loves us more than we can understand?"

A tear slipped down her face, and she quickly brushed it away with a silver bangled wrist. "Yes. All that and more. I never understood why you love church so much. And why you love God so much. But I'm beginning to see now. A little. I know I have a long way to go."

Joy welled in me. "I have a Bible you can have. That way you can read more about Jesus."

"I'd like that."

I sprinted up to my room and returned with a paperback Bible I'd won in a Bible quiz tournament. "I've marked the Gospel of John. That's a good place to start."

"Thank you, honey." Mom scraped the pan clean.

"Have you told Dad?"

"No. I'm not sure he would understand."

"I think you should tell him. He's already seeing that you're acting differently. I think it would be good if he knew why."

"Maybe I will."

Sudden tears brimmed. "I'm sorry I don't tell you this more, Mom. But I love you...so much."

Mom's lips pressed tightly together, and her eyes brimmed, as well. She hugged me tightly. "I know you do. And I love you, too, honey."

That afternoon, I found my mind wandering as I worked on the article for Professor Williams' class. Last Saturday night's ambush at the church returned to mind. How many attacks had our church suffered lately? At least one every week.

Disquiet slipped through me. An attack every week. And each week was worse. What would happen this week?

Foreboding settled into my gut. The hate group was planning something new. Something big. Someone hated my church, and he—or she—would never be satisfied until it was destroyed.

Who was behind it all? And would it really help if I found out? I'd need proof in order to get the police involved.

I picked up a pen and quickly jotted an outline for the *Truesdale Register* article. A ton of research lay ahead of me. But I had to believe that writing this article would make a difference. I had to expose the hate group, and the people in it, before they hurt anyone else.

MONDAY

"HOW WAS YOUR WEEKEND?" I asked Mary. I felt happy today. Chipper, in fact—a word I'd never thought to apply to myself. I'd woken up this morning in one of those rare, cheerful good moods that have no explanation. A precious gift from the Lord.

Mary smiled. "Good." She touched her rounded stomach. "Jack smiled when he felt the baby kick this morning."

The glow in her eyes shadowed. Perhaps more had happened over the weekend than she wanted to mention. For once, however, I didn't jump in and tell her what she should do. Mary could make her own choices.

"Do you plan to listen to Oak Woodward at the plaza?" My latest essay crinkled as I pulled it from my backpack.

Mary's expression brightened. "Yes. Well, for a few minutes, anyway. I have to work an extra shift this afternoon. I wish I could hear more of his speech, though. It sounds interesting."

"I wonder what he'll talk about."

"Politics," Mary laughed frankly. "And he'll promise us a better future. Isn't that what they all do?"

The hazy sunshine beat down on the crowded plaza. The sticky warmth reminded me of summer, and it was a radical departure from the recent cool weather. Thank goodness I'd worn a short-sleeved blouse today. Trent had dressed for comfort, too. He walked beside me now, wearing a sky blue polo shirt and tan slacks.

Professor Williams had canceled class today. In fact, Trent and I wouldn't have seen each other at all, except we'd almost run into each other. I'd been leaving the building and he'd been heading inside. He'd invited me to eat lunch with him, and I accepted. I wanted to settle the questions in my heart about our relationship today, once and for all.

"Where do you want to sit?"

"I don't know." I glanced around, and waved to Mary, who spoke with Mitch a few steps away.

Both waved, but Trent nudged me away from them. I didn't mind. In fact... A thought occurred. If only Mary would spend more time with Mitch! Jack might lose his appeal if she got to know an awesome, nice guy. Mitch would treat her right, and how she deserved to be treated. If only Mary could see that.

Trent and I plopped down on the edge of the crowd, up on a little hill so we could see the stage, and I pulled a sack lunch from my backpack. Trent had bought a sandwich at the student union. Munching, we waited for Oak Woodward to appear.

"Any hunch what he'll say?" Trent's intense blue eyes flashed at me. His gaze conveyed sharp intelligence, and yet emotionally, he appeared withdrawn. I got the fleeting impression, as I had before, that more lay below the surface than he wanted to reveal.

I glanced at the stage, which bristled with armed security officers. News cameras flanked the platform. "He'll try to convince us to vote for him."

"Think he'll mention your church?"

I shrugged. "Why would he?"

"Just a reporter's guess. Have you researched your article for the *Register*?"

"I'll start today. I'd like to discover who's leading the hate group."

His aristocratic brows drew together. "Good goal."

"I know," I ruefully agreed. "I'm not sure how to go about it. It's not like I can look him up in the phone book."

"You'll think of something." Trent's gaze returned to the platform.

Biting off a rich, mayonnaisy mouthful of ham and cheese sandwich, I glanced at Trent again out of the corner of my eye. How did I feel about him? For both of us, I needed to figure this out today.

I felt pretty certain God didn't want me romantically involved with Trent. I had been struggling against that conviction for a while. But I also struggled with my feelings for Trent.

What were they, really? Friendship? Yes. I did like him. And I knew he liked me. He'd gone to a lot of trouble to become friends with me. That fact made me feel special. And he was very good looking.

But as I swallowed, I realized that loving someone required more than physical attraction, and even more than friendship, although both were important. Love needed time, and depth of relationship. A communion of souls. The attraction I'd felt for Trent was exciting, but it wasn't a solid foundation for a deep, meaningful relationship. Peel away the sizzle and what was left?

Well...a guy I barely knew. And with whom I had little in common. I liked him, but I wasn't in love with him. Not even a little bit.

The easy clarity of my feelings surprised me.

I wasn't in love with Trent.

He was a nice guy, and I liked him, but it wasn't enough. At least not for me. He wasn't the right guy for me.

I swallowed. I had to tell him. But how? Would he be hurt? Or had his feelings for me changed, too?

No matter what happened, I did want to stay friends. I liked him a lot.

"Here he comes." Trent's voice interrupted my muddled thoughts, and I glanced at him, feeling bad. I didn't want to hurt his feelings.

A flurry of movement drew my attention to the stage. A tall man, dressed in dark slacks and a crisp gray shirt rapidly stepped up onto the platform. His silver hair shone in the sun. A small squadron of security officers dogged his heels.

Oak Woodward, the Senate candidate from the FGA; the organization which was harassing my church.

Our school president, a balding man dressed in a charcoal gray, pinstriped suit, grabbed the microphone. Sweat gleamed on his chubby face.

"This man," his thick arm motioned toward the silver-haired gentleman, "needs no introduction, but I'll give it anyway. He's the head of the biggest church denomination in the United States. U.S. Senate candidate, Oak Woodward!"

Onlookers clapped.

Oak Woodward stepped forward, and his perfect white teeth flashed in a smile. But even from this distance I could see his eyes. They looked chillingly empty. A shiver snaked down my spine.

"Good afternoon! It's wonderful to be in Truesdale, California. What a beautiful place. It reminds me of my own home town." His fake smile twitched higher, and beamed sincerity.

"Your school president said it right. I am the head of the biggest church denomination in the United States." His body posture appeared relaxed. "But I want to shoot from the hip, and get a few things straight right now. Because I know for most of you, church is a big turn off."

He pulled the microphone from the stand, pushed up his sleeves and paced the stage.

"First off, First Gospel of America—or FGA, as we like to call ourselves—believes in universal love. Human kindness. The basic themes of the Bible.

"But we're not Bible thumpers. No. We welcome all faiths. All viewpoints. We want to work together with *you* to create a peaceful, loving society. That's something we all want."

In the middle of the crowd, a young man with a purple bandanna on his head leaped up. "You talk the good talk, Woodward," he spat. "But you're narrow-minded, just like every other Christian!"

Oak Woodward paused. To my surprise, he graciously nodded to the heckler. "Go on, I welcome your viewpoint."

The heckler's face flushed. "Your *FGA* church here in town preaches it different, Woodward. They say there's only one way to God, through Jesus Christ."

Woodward opened his mouth, but the heckler made a violent, obscene gesture. "You believe the same thing, don't you, Woodward? You won't get my vote!"

"Now hold on a minute." Woodward raised his hand. "Truesdale First Gospel is *not*, I repeat is *not* like other First Gospel churches across the country."

The heckler spat a disbelieving epithet.

Oak Woodward's face reddened. "Hear me out! Please." His fingers whitened around the mike. Sincerity oozed from him like oil.

"It's not a well known fact, but Truesdale First Gospel has been a thorn in our sides for months. We've dealt with them quietly to solve the problem. In fact, we've given them scores of warnings, but nothing works. They refuse to stop their dogmatic preaching."

"Wait a minute!" the heckler cried. "Are you saying *you* don't believe in Jesus Christ?"

I held my breath and waited.

Woodward paused. His expression smoothed, but managed to look incredibly pious at the same time.

"I believe Jesus taught wonderful principles for living. But do I believe this whole book..." he hefted up the black book lying on the table beside him, "is true? Of course not. It's a collection of fables."

I could not believe my ears. "*Heresy*," I breathed. Oak Woodward had just denied the whole Word of God! A verse came to mind. 2 Timothy 4:3:

> *For the time will come when people will not put up with sound doctrine. Instead, to suit their own desires, they will gather around them a great number of teachers to say what their itching ears want to hear...*

Those words had come true today with Oak Woodward and the FGA. And with hundreds of churches across the country. The FGA wanted to make it true of our church, as well. I felt sick to my stomach.

"What's more..." Woodward's oily voice felt like an abomination to my soul. He wanted to kill my church; and clearly all for the sake of political power. "Truesdale First Gospel has committed a sin much worse than violating FGA's preaching standards."

What could he possibly mean? I glanced at Trent, but he stared at Oak Woodward with an odd, salivary look on his face. It almost appeared as if he eagerly licked up each word that fell from the Senate candidate's lips.

Even more sickened, my attention returned to Woodward.

"Truesdale First Gospel put on a fundraiser last week. Remember? It was for the earthquake victims. In fact, one young lady advertised it right here on campus."

Me. He was talking about me.

"They raised over ten thousand dollars." Woodward's words sharpened into clipped, staccato blasts. "That money has disappeared!"

A gasp ripped through the crowd. Someone made a rude hand gesture. It was Tim. Randy and Mr. Carlisle flanked him. Suspicions about my World Religions teacher rocketed to the surface again.

"That's right." A grim smile flickered. "We sent a financial officer to Truesdale First Gospel on Wednesday to pick up the money. But Pastor Warner didn't have it."

Murmurs of outrage swirled about me. I felt disjointed and cold; an angry mass of whirling, chaotic emotions. Woodward *knew* we hadn't stolen the money. Why would he lie? Why didn't he say that we'd given the money to Driscoll Shelter?

"Luckily," Woodward's eyes narrowed, "the FGA has a faithful steward in that church. ...There he is! Come on up here, Bobby. He might know where they stashed the money."

Bobby Page climbed the steps to the stage. I stared. *Bobby?* What was he doing here, with Oak Woodward?

Woodward extended a gracious hand to him. "Bobby deserves our congratulations. Thanks to his loyalty, federal investigators are in the process of recovering the stolen money. What is more, I'd like to announce that effective immediately, Pastor Warner and his entire congregation have been evicted from our church building. They're no longer a part of First Gospel of America!"

I gasped. Cheers whistled. My heart pounded. Adrenaline pumped through me like an overdose of caffeine. We hadn't stolen that money! And Woodward knew it. How could he lie like that? And Bobby...he was a *traitor*?

It was wrong. All of it.

The injustice of it nearly choked me. What was worse, the crowd and media clearly lapped up Woodward's every word as if it were the gospel truth. It wasn't right! Someone had to set the record straight. Someone had to report the other side of the story.

But no one spoke up.

No one *would* speak up, I realized.

I leaped up and found myself darting jaggedly between people, running for the stage. I shoved past the bodyguards and snatched the mike from Woodward's hands.

"He's lying!" I shouted. My face felt hot with rage. People plucked at my arm, but I shoved them off and glared at Woodward.

"We raised that money for the homeless! You know that, Woodward. And we gave the money to Driscoll Shelter. How dare you try to steal it from them? You have no *right* to it! Tell us, why do you really want it? To beef up your campaign budget?"

Rough hands seized me, and the air blurred as I hurtled through the air and off the stage. I landed on my knees. Painfully. Tears formed in my eyes. The landing jolted me back into my right mind.

What had I done? I was lucky I hadn't been arrested. I staggered up and blindly stumbled through the milling crowd. Where was Trent? I needed to talk to someone.

"Excuse me, miss?" A reporter with sunglasses and her hair scraped into a ponytail shoved a mike in my face. "Do you have evidence to prove your allegations?"

"Yes." I allowed the reporter and cameraman to shuffle me over to a clear square of grass. Although I trembled and felt a bit numb, one thing rang clear in my mind; I had to tell the whole story. Every bit of it, if I wanted to save the reputation of my church.

Haltingly, and shivering a bit, despite the warmth of the sun, I told my story from the beginning. I escaped as soon as I could, and brushed past clutching hands who begged for my story, too. I was looking for someone. I didn't know who.

And then, on the edge of the crowd I heard a familiar voice. *Trent.* I whirled. He stood next to a tree, cell phone to his ear. His back was to me.

"Yeah, stuck to Kay. She turned me onto a great story. Yeah, that's right. She gave me the whole inside scoop on the FGA. I knew dating her would pay off."

I gasped aloud. A high, keening wail rose in my throat.

Trent whirled. "Kay."

But I ran.

"Wait! Stop."

But I felt blind, deaf and dumb. Tears streamed down my face. Gasping, I flung open the door to Kale Hall and dashed inside. It was quiet and cool in there.

My shoulder slammed against the beige "Women" door and I staggered inside, weeping helplessly. The room was empty. Stumbling around a corner, I sank onto the cold linoleum and wept harshly, wretchedly. For a long, long time.

I couldn't believe it. Trent had used me! This whole time. Just to get a story.

My face ached from the the shuddering, jaw clenching sobs, and my cheeks burned hot against my cold, trembling hands.

How could I have been so stupid? Why hadn't I suspected something was up the instant a guy with movie star looks pretended interest in me? Why was I so stupid? Why hadn't I listened to God? Why had I trusted Trent? And Bobby...

I wept until I could weep no more, and then I cried dried, hiccupping sobs. I felt drained. Wretched. And I'd made a fool of myself, running up in front of everyone to the stage. I'd been thrown off. Like a common criminal.

I began to laugh quietly, hysterically. What was *wrong* with me? As fresh tears welled in my eyes, I pressed my hand to my mouth, trying to stop the empty, hollow laughter. Had I come unhinged? It felt like it. I needed help.

And I hated Trent, for what he had done to me.

I lay my head on my knees. *Lord, please take away this pain. I know you love me. Please help me.*

After a long time, I pulled myself up and stepped on stiff legs to the sink. Splashing cold water on my face felt good. It cooled the swelling in my eyes. But not in my heart. My face looked blotchy. I'd been in the restroom for a long time.

I needed to rescue my backpack, if it was still out there. I hoped Woodward's speech was over. I hated the man with a perfect hatred. And I hated Trent.

With a paper towel blotted against my wet face, I squeezed my eyes shut. *Lord, help me. Please help me to forgive, because I know that's what you want me to do, but I just can't. Not yet. Please help me.*

A tiny sliver of peace entered my soul, and I grasped at it desperately, knowing the Lord was with me, and that he loved me. His opinion of me was the only one that mattered.

The crowd had dispersed when I finally ventured outside. Inside, I felt still. Aching. I still wanted to talk to someone. But who? Who could make it right? No one.

Thankfully, I found my backpack. I slipped on my sunglasses, wanting only to blend in and be unrecognized. Reporters still milled near the stage. I knew I should go talk to them and set as many straight as possible about the FGA and Truesdale First Gospel, but I couldn't. I felt raw inside. I just wanted to run and hide.

"Kay." Mitch's voice stopped me. I hadn't realized I'd been walking. Wandering, really. "Are you okay? I've been looking for you."

I managed a wan smile. "Did you see my grand performance?"

He offered a bracing smile. "I thought you were great. That took guts."

"Or stupidity. I wish I'd think first, instead of jumping head first into hot water."

"I think the official saying is, 'rushing in where angels fear to tread.'" But his grin looked sympathetic and understanding. Tears again filled my eyes. Mitch was on my side. He was a true friend.

"Are you okay?" he asked again.

"I'm just angry," I swallowed back the ache in my throat. I couldn't tell him about Trent. I already knew Mitch disliked him.

I noticed the sketch pad clenched loosely in his hand, and grasped for a change of subject. "What did you draw?"

He tilted it toward me. "Thought I'd do a portrait of the Senator-to-be." A grim smile edged his lips, and his gaze sharpened in intensity. I guessed it was one of his odd pictures.

The spare, black strokes captured the essence of the politician. It was a cartoon sketch. He'd captured Oak Woodward in motion, striding forward, microphone tilted toward his mouth, which was open, as if speaking great and mighty things. But the cartoon blurb above his head was empty. And around the stage, people bowed in worship to him.

A bubble of laughter caught in my throat. "It looks just like him. He's not saying anything. Only empty words that people want to hear."

With narrowed eyes, Mitch stared at the picture. Then he lifted a muscled shoulder. "Don't know what it means, really. Except politicians tend to blow a lot of hot air."

"And he's denied the Christian faith, just like Paul said would happen in the last days. First Timothy four, verse one says, 'The Spirit clearly says that in later times some will abandon the faith...' It goes on from there."

He stared quietly at the picture for a moment longer before glancing back at me. "I knew that would fit in somewhere."

I felt rebuked. "I guess you're tired of me talking about the last days all the time." For the first time, I felt self-conscious about my faith with him.

"Not at all. Actually, it intrigues me. That's not a comfortable thought, since I'm Jewish."

"Jesus was Jewish. He came to the Jews first." I tugged my backpack more securely up on my shoulder and glanced at the news teams, who wandered toward the parking lot now. "Look, I'd better go. I need to talk to a few more reporters."

"I know some of them." He flipped his sketch pad shut. "I'll introduce you."

After dinner, I watched the news with my parents. To my relief, Channel 23 gave the story fair coverage—probably not out of a desire to back the home church, or to be impartial, I thought cynically. But because they didn't know which story was juicier—a Senate candidate trying to steal over $10,000 for his campaign, or a church being stripped of its FGA membership for giving money to a shelter.

"What is your church going to do?" A heavy frown creased Dad's brow.

"I don't know." Depression settled again in my spirit as the truth finally rammed home. Our church had been kicked out of its building. What would we do now? I should talk to Joyce, but didn't feel up to it right then. I felt drained, and bitterly upset with the back stabbing FGA, and with Trent.

"Are you all right, honey?" Mom said when I lurched to my feet.

"Yes. I'm just tired. I'm going to bed."

"Goodnight." Concern echoed in my parents' voices. On the news they'd seen my embarrassing flight for the stage, and how I'd wrestled the microphone from Oak Woodward. Did they think I had jumped off the deep end? I just didn't care.

The phone rang as I passed by the kitchen.

"I'll get it," I said dully. "Hello?"

"Hi, Kay! Saw you on the news. Good job!" Joyce's voice crackled with brittle energy.

"I was mad."

"I know. So am I. So is Dad. That's why I'm calling. The FGA ordered Dad to get all our personal effects out of the church by noon tomorrow. Crawford is going to supervise. We need help clearing everything out. Can you come?"

"Of course." My own selfish pain seemed insignificant when I thought about Joyce and her family. They'd just lost everything.

"Good. See you at eight."

I slowly replaced the receiver. I felt sad and empty inside. Our church was gone. What would the Warners do now? What would we all do? It wasn't fair. None of it was fair.

My feet dragged as I climbed the stairs. What would happen now? Only God could make things right for Joyce and her family, and for the church. I would pray more when I went to bed.

After changing into my pajamas, I hovered for a moment in the open bathroom door. Theresa sat on a stool, staring at herself in the mirror. One hand held up her hair, piled high on her head. A dissatisfied look pouted her lips.

I stepped in and mashed toothpaste on my toothbrush.

Theresa pulled her fingers from her hair. It fell to her shoulders. "I saw what you did today. That took courage."

"A lot of good it did." I scrubbed my teeth.

"It'll work out." Theresa stared at herself in the mirror. "Kay?"

"What?" I took a sip of water and spat it out, rinsing it down the sink with a blast of cold water.

Theresa said nothing for a long moment. She just stared at herself. When she finally spoke, it was in a low voice, "Sometimes I wonder if this is as deep as I go."

She grabbed up a brush and attacked her hair. "Never mind. I'm being stupid."

"You're not stupid, Theresa." But I felt too drained to ask what she meant.

However, when I collapsed into bed, I prayed for her. And I prayed that I would be able to forgive Trent, because right now that seemed absolutely impossible. I felt defeated and empty.

I hadn't thought much about Bobby's betrayal of our church. Probably because Trent's betrayal hurt so much more right now. I didn't understand what Bobby had done, or why. But Trent's betrayal was personal. He had deliberately used me. He had pretended to like me, and to find me attractive, but it was all a lie. He had dated me for a story. I felt worthless, like pond scum. It hurt terribly.

Pressing my wet face into my pillow, I drifted toward sleep. A verse sang softly through my mind.

But he said to me, "My grace is sufficient for you, for my power is made perfect in weakness." (2 Corinthians 12:9a)

TUESDAY

I ARRIVED AT THE CHURCH AT EIGHT. A moving van was parked out front, and boxes rested on the sidewalk. Slowly, I parked my car and climbed out, hugging my jean jacket tightly around me against the cold October morning.

Frost etched lacy, crystalline patterns on the brown roof-tops across the street. A perfectly clear, crisp day. It looked like the world had started off on a new slate. Everything looked clean and brand new.

But I didn't feel brand new. I'd woken up depressed, and still felt awful and betrayed. I couldn't believe Trent had used me so callously. Just for a story! It hurt. Badly.

Tears formed, but I blinked them back. He wasn't worth tears. He was a jerk, completely and simply. I was better off without him.

"Kay!" Joyce wore old clothes today, and a blue bandanna pulled her hair back into a ponytail. Her voice sounded sharp, but her manner was efficient, like usual. "Would you help me box up stuff in the kitchen?"

Martha bustled about the kitchen. Mr. Crawford, the black-haired, spectacled, dark-suited man from the FGA, leaned against the table, holding a notebook. He scribbled every time Martha pulled a box or can from the cupboard.

"Doesn't that belong to the church?" he clipped out, when Martha pulled a cake plate and server from a low cupboard.

Martha slowly turned, her white head bristling indignation.

In a sweet and reasonable voice, she said, "Young man, this cake plate has lived in my family for five generations." She motioned toward the cupboard. "I left the church cake plate. Don't you worry about that."

Crawford poked his stiff head into the cupboard. His eyebrows climbed his high forehead. A rippled, plastic platter swung between his thumb and forefinger. "This is it?"

"That's right." Martha faced him squarely, hands on her ample hips. "I hope you're not calling an old woman a liar."

The dish clattered back into the cupboard. "Of course not." Stiffly, Crawford retreated.

Joyce and I bagged up boxes and tins of food, and assorted odds and ends that Martha winnowed out. It was amazing how many things the Warners had donated to the church over the years.

Joyce worked with silent, fierce intensity. That was the only indication of her anger. Her elbow jabbed up and down, picking up items and depositing them in the bags.

It felt unpleasant to work under Crawford's eagle eye, which only served to feed the poor mood festering in me. I longed to talk to someone about Trent, and what had happened to me yesterday, but I wouldn't. My problems seemed selfish and insignificant compared to the problems facing the Warners. Joyce's family's livelihood was falling down around their ears. How could I even think about myself in a time like this?

Lugging a box out through the sanctuary, I noticed David on the sound stage, dissembling some of the equipment the Warners had bought to supplement the church's sound system. His back was to me as I shuffled by.

I couldn't talk to David about Trent anyway. He'd warned me about Trent. All he'd say now was, "I told you so."

We'd cleared everything out by eleven-thirty. Crawford and two other dark-clothed FGA men watched as we carted the last of the boxes and bags up the narrow truck ramp and deposited them in the shiny, metallic interior. The truck was half full.

"I'll take that for you." David lifted the heavy box from my arms and deposited it in the back. I thanked him, and watched him easily maneuver the box into the truck.

"That's it."

The three of us watched the Pastor, Mrs. Warner and Martha warily approach Crawford.

"I don't know what we're going to do." Joyce's strangled voice broke. It was the first time she'd spoken in two hours.

"It'll be okay." I hugged her, heart breaking for her.

"*How?* What are we going to *do?*" Tears streamed down her cheeks. Joyce, the strong one, was crumpling.

"We'll take it one step at a time," David put an arm around her, too. "Like Wednesday nights. We can still meet up for that, can't we?"

"Yes. Maybe at my house." Joyce choked on a sob. She wiped her eyes with a trembling hand. "Don't mind me, guys. It's just...*everything*. What about church? Where will we hold that? Or will we?" Her shoulders shook.

"We'll work something out," I said. But I wondered how. It was too short notice to lease a building for this Sunday, even if Pastor Warner had the money, which he didn't.

David's unsmiling gaze met mine. The three of us stood there, interlocked, for a long minute; a feeble, supportive wall bucking the crumpling world around us.

If only we could hold the church service in a house, too...

The thought crept up from my subconscious.

Like pulling a trigger on a cocked gun, images exploded in my mind. Cats and dogs running to seek refuge in my house. But there wasn't enough room...

My dream? Could this be the meaning? Could we hold the service at my house? The living room was big, but it wasn't big enough, was it?

The crazy thought refused to be dislodged. It was the perfect solution, and yet seemed perfectly impossible. Was it the answer? I didn't know. I'd have to talk to my parents about it first.

"I'm okay now." Voice resolute, Joyce pulled away, and stood alone. "Thanks for helping. I'll see you Wednesday night at my house, okay?"

We nodded.

Joyce walked toward her parents, her back stiff.

I deeply felt my friend's pain, and the loss of our church was hitting me hard. Every box we'd put in the truck had made it more real.

To make matters worse, yesterday's humiliating, betraying events again flooded my mind. I wished I could block them out, but I couldn't.

"Could I get a ride to school?" David interrupted my thoughts. "My car's in the shop."

"Sure." I blinked back the tears filling my eyes, grabbed up my jacket from the truck tailgate and walked quickly to my car, leaving David to follow in my wake. What was wrong with me? How could I even think about myself at a time like this? My problems with Trent were unimportant compared to everything else going on right now.

Quickly, I unlocked the doors, and then slid into the driver's seat and slammed the door.

David sat silently as I ground the gears, and dipped into traffic. I was glad for the quiet. I could relax. I wouldn't think about anything.

My fingers gripped the steering wheel so hard they began to ache.

We slid closer to the school, and then into the parking lot. I yanked up the parking brake, snatched the key from the ignition and reached for my backpack at David's feet.

His hand stopped mine.

"Ready to talk about it?"

"Talk about what?" I pulled my hand from his warm palm.

He raised a brow. "Whatever's bothering you."

"Nothing is bothering me." I grabbed my pack, threw in my keys, and zipped it up.

But finally, I had to meet his gaze. His dark eyes caught at my soul and pulled me in, urging me to confess all to him.

"What?" But tears hovered again. I hated that. I was sick of crying like a pitiful fool.

"Tell me what's wrong."

"Nothing is wrong!" But a hated tear slipped out. I dashed it away, and stared out the windshield. "You'll just say 'I told you so,'" I muttered. "So what's the point in telling you anything?"

Of course, this made no sense at all.

"Start from the beginning," he said quietly. "Tell me what happened."

"All right. Fine." I swallowed. "Yesterday I found out that Trent's been using me to get a story on the FGA. That's the only reason he became friends with me. That's the only reason he went out with me."

I glanced at him through eyes filled with unshed tears. "So say it. I told you so."

"I won't say that." His lips tightened. "What kind of a person do you think I am?"

"I know you hate him."

"I don't hate him. I don't like him much. And I didn't think he was the right guy for you, but I never thought he'd do anything like…"

"*I* hate him!" I burst out suddenly, pressing my hands against my hot face. "I hate him!"

I hated myself. "Why didn't I listen…?"

"Stop it, Kay." His deep voice was warm in my ear, and his arms went around me, pulling me close against him. His soft cotton shirt pressed against my cheek.

"Why did this have to happen?" I sobbed.

"I don't know."

His chin rested on top of my head. I wept until the tears slowly quieted into gulps. I rested there for a moment, feeling the wet cloth of his shirt press against my cheek. His arms comforted something deep inside of me. I felt like I belonged right there.

I pulled back and dashed my hands against my eyes. "I should have guessed he was up to something."

"What do you mean?"

I looked at him, knowing my face looked blotchy, and pushed a sun streaked lock behind my ear with one trembling finger. "Look at me," I insisted. "I'm not pretty. Definitely not the type of girl Trent should be interested in."

"Trent doesn't know what he's missing." His voice sounded tight.

"Thanks." Blinking rapidly, I dug in my pack for a tissue and pressed it to my wet eyes. His comment didn't make me feel better. Trent had never liked me. I felt ugly. Rejected. Nothing David could say would make me feel better right now.

"I think you're beautiful."

The soft words hung between us.

I looked up at him. My fingers trembled a little.

His upper body had tilted a little away from me, and his dark eyes looked uncertain, and cautious, but met mine unwaveringly for a long moment. Then he offered a half smile. "However much my opinion counts."

The first real smile in two days hovered on my lips. And tears of another sort ached in me. But I couldn't let them out. I wouldn't.

Taking a deep breath, he opened his door. "Walk you to class?" he tossed over his shoulder.

"Okay." Legs feeling a bit like wobbly jello, I grabbed my backpack and stepped up by his side.

"Maybe I could bum a ride home, too?" The question was casual.

"Maybe so." A bubble of pure joy welled up in my soul when his smile met mine.

"Hi, Dad," I said cheerfully, passing him in the hall.

"Care to keep an old man company?" Dad wore his walking shoes and a frown.

"Sure." I tossed my backpack on the kitchen table and followed him outside. I felt honored that he would ask me to come with him. Dad treasured his solitary walks.

The cold, crisp wind tugged at my hair, and I pulled my jacket more tightly around me. "Is something wrong?"

"I should ask you that question," Dad said gruffly. "I've been worried about you. You seemed pretty unhappy last night. Can I help? Is it something you can tell your old man?"

"Dad." Warm love filled my heart, and I slipped my arm through his. Dad rarely asked how I was doing. The least I could do was tell him the truth, even though it hurt to face the pain again.

"It's Trent." I told him everything.

Dad frowned. "Never cared much for that young man. Seemed shallow, like he was putting on an act. But I never guessed he'd do something like this."

"David said the same thing." The dark hurt had eased a little.

"What are you going to do?" Dad sounded protective. Angry, too.

Just like I felt. I had a right to be angry. Trent had used me.

"But I say to you, love your enemies, bless those who curse you, do good to those who hate you, and pray for those who spitefully use you and persecute you..."
(NKJV Matthew 5:44)

The still, quiet voice in my heart contradicted what I wanted to do. I wanted to be angry. I wanted to hate him.

Slowly, I said, "I have to forgive him."

"*What*? Why? Has he asked for forgiveness?"

"No."

"Then you don't have to forgive him. He doesn't deserve it."

I wanted to agree with Dad. I didn't want to forgive Trent, either. His actions still hurt too badly. But I knew I had to.

"God wants me to forgive him. Otherwise, bitterness will eat me up inside."

Dad walked silently for a few minutes. When he spoke again, his voice sounded baffled. "Then you're a better person than I am, Kay. I can't forgive him for what he did to you. And I don't see how you can, either. At least not until he apologizes."

I searched long and hard for the right words to say.

"Dad. Honestly, I don't want to forgive Trent. I want to hold onto my resentment for as long as I can. But I know I need to forgive him, and God will help me, if I ask him."

"I don't think God is too keen on forgiving Trent right now, either," he said grimly.

And that was the crux of the matter, and twisted the knife of conviction deeper into my heart.

I sighed reluctantly. "Yes, he is, Dad. That's why he sent Jesus to die on the cross for our sins. He wants to forgive us. He wants to draw us back into a right relationship with him. Forgiveness brings healing. I don't want to be bitter."

"Your God sounds like a tough customer."

"He just knows the best way to live. We'd all be a lot better off if we'd trust him and do what he says."

"Like a parent with a child."

"Yes. I guess that's exactly what it's like."

We walked in silence for a few more minutes. Even though I didn't want to forgive Trent, I knew I must. Somehow.

Lord, please help me.

"Your mother says she's a Christian now." Dad's gruff voice sounded puzzled.

"I know."

"Hmmph." A long pause elapsed. "I heard you helped the Warners clear out Truesdale First Gospel. What will your church do now?"

"I don't know."

That crazy dream returned to mind. It was impossible, wasn't it? But a small voice urged me to ask Dad about it.

"I was wondering." I hesitated. "I had an idea..."

"What is it, honey?" He looked interested.

And this pulled the words from me. "Could we hold the church service at our house this Sunday? Our living room is big. With folding chairs, it could seat at least seventy people. Even so, I'm not sure that would be enough."

Dad thought about it for awhile, and then nodded. "I like the idea. Go ahead and tell Pastor Warner he can use our house if he needs it."

"Really?" I stared at him, amazed. "You think it's a good idea?"

"Sure. I know how important your church is to you. I'd be glad to help out."

"Thank you, Dad!" I flung my arms around his neck. I couldn't believe it! It was all coming true, just like my dream had said. God must have really spoken to me. I felt over-whelmed, humbled, grateful, and overjoyed.

"...on the world front, underground peace negotiations seem to be moving forward. No concrete information is available yet..."

The words teased my ears as I padded by the den, on my way to bed. Dad watched news clips from one of the all news channels.

World peace agreement? What could that be about? A cold sensation slid through me when my hand touched the chilly banister railing.

Peace was good. Wasn't it?

An urge to review the prophecies I'd already read gripped me. I felt like I was beginning to understand a little about the end times, and how they all fit together, but tonight was different. I wanted to search out some truths, and try to put them all together in my mind.

Upstairs, I switched on my bedside lamp and plopped cross-legged onto the bed. I flipped my Bible open to Matthew 24:11,15-16:

> ...and many false prophets will appear and deceive many people...

> So when you see standing in the holy place 'the abomination that causes desolation,' spoken of through the prophet Daniel—let the reader understand—then let those who are in Judea flee to the mountains.

The prophet Daniel. I flipped back to Daniel 9:27:

> He will confirm a covenant with many for one 'seven.' In the middle of the 'seven' he will put an end to sacrifice and offering. And on a wing of the temple he will set up an abomination that causes desolation, until the end that is decreed is poured out on him.

My study Bible and various prophecy books said that the "seven" (read in context with the previous verses) referred to seven actual years. The middle of the seven would be at 3 1/2 years. I found myself flipping to 2 Thessalonians 2:4,9-12, tracking the idea of the Antichrist still further.

> He will oppose and will exalt himself over everything that is called God or is worshiped, so that he sets himself up in God's temple, proclaiming himself to be God....

> The coming of the lawless one will be in accordance with the work of Satan displayed in all kinds of counterfeit miracles, signs and wonders, and in every sort of evil that deceives those who are perishing. They perish because they refused to love the truth and so be saved. For this

reason God sends them a powerful delusion so that they will believe the lie and so that all will be condemned who have not believed the truth but have delighted in wickedness.

That was pretty sobering. Following my Bible text notes, I flipped back to Daniel 12:11-12:

From the time that the daily sacrifice is abolished and the abomination that causes desolation is set up, there will be 1,290 days. Blessed is the one who waits for and reaches the end of the 1,335 days.

So, from the "middle of the seven" first mentioned in Daniel 9:27 to the end of the "seven," mentioned here, would be 1,335 days. I liked this. It was like a puzzle that made perfect sense when put together.

And now Revelation 13:5-7a:

The beast was given a mouth to utter proud words and blasphemies and to exercise his authority for forty-two months. He opened his mouth to blaspheme God, and to slander his name and his dwelling place and those who live in heaven. He was given power to make war against the saints and to conquer them.

Daniel 7:25:

"He will speak against the Most High and oppress his saints and try to change the set times and the laws. The saints will be handed over to him for a time, times and half a time." (Year, two years, and half a year, my study note explained. Three and a half years total. (42 months.))

The Antichrist was going to be a lovely character. With a shiver, I skimmed on.

Daniel 11:36:

"The king will do as he pleases. He will exalt and magnify himself above every god and will say unheard-of things

against the God of gods. He will be successful until the time of wrath is completed, for what has been determined must take place."

Last of all, Revelation 13:14-18 caught my eye. This was talking about the False Prophet, who was evil, too. He would perform great and miraculous signs.

Because of the signs he was given power to do on behalf of the first beast, he deceived the inhabitants of the earth. He ordered them to set up an image in honor of the beast who was wounded by the sword and yet lived. He was given power to give breath to the image of the first beast, so that it could speak and cause all who refused to worship the image to be killed. He also forced everyone, small and great, rich and poor, free and slave, to receive a mark on his right hand or on his forehead, so that no one could buy or sell unless he had the mark, which is the name of the beast or the number of his name.

This calls for wisdom. If anyone has insight, let him calculate the number of the beast, for it is man's number. His number is 666.

Closing my Bible, I lay back and stared at the shadowed ceiling. Was the Antichrist—the Beast—about to appear? Was I truly living in the end times?

An affirmative *yes* whispered through my soul.

I closed my eyes, feeling a strong conviction, to the soles of my feet, that Jesus' return was near. It was here. Nearer than anyone thought. I could almost hear the door about to open in heaven.

I sat up and bowed my head. An incredible urgency burdened my soul.

Oh Lord, please turn Dad's heart to you. Please save his soul quickly, before it's too late. Please save Theresa, too.

And please save Trent. Please help me to forgive him. I want to forgive him. Please help me.

FUTURE

ISOLA LAY DOWN the notebook. It was dark outside, and the only light filtered in from the street lamps.

When she closed her eyes, her mind returned to the verses Kay had quoted about the abomination of desolation. He sounded exactly like the Chairman. The Chairman had signed a peace agreement with many nations three and a half years ago. Was it the same covenant Kay had quoted in Daniel 9:27? And the Chairman had just set himself up as God in the temple in Jerusalem. The Two Witnesses of God had warned Israel to flee to the mountains when that happened. They were gone now, of course; killed, and then miraculously raised to life. Kay hadn't quoted scriptures about that happening, but Isola bet that was written about in the Bible, too.

She shook her head. This was all too weird.

She stood and stretched her aching back. Behind her, the water faintly bubbled. So, it was after six.

Outside, the moon glowed huge and red, and hung suspended above the apartment complex across the street. A shivering shadow on the street drew her attention. Two people were locked in a silent, dark death struggle.

Fear tightened like a band around her chest, and she turned away. Too many things Kay had written about had already happened.

But it was impossible! Wasn't it?

A burning conviction, deep inside, wouldn't let Isola dismiss it so easily. She'd never felt more alone in her life than she did right now. All of her excuses to focus anywhere but the truth were gone. Her friends, her family, her chance for a college degree—all gone.

She felt sick and empty. And afraid to face the truth.

Blindly, she reached for the radio, wanting only to escape. But when her fingers touched the switch she remembered that the Chairman was supposed to make an announcement tonight. Something about a change in economic policy.

An incredible stab of fear and hope slashed through her. Would he mention something about a mark? If so, that would provide one more piece of evidence that the Bible was true.

She sank to her knees and turned up the volume. A portentous voice spoke. It was the Chairman. The Beast. Funny how she'd nicknamed him that. Was he the Beast of the Bible?

As always, involuntary revulsion rippled through her as she listened to his voice.

"I support our new economic system one hundred percent. But this is the First Advisor's baby. He'll be in charge of enforcing it." A smile curled through the hated voice. "Without further ado, I'll hand the mike to him."

After a small silence, another voice spoke. It was the First Advisor to the Chairman.

"Our new policy will ensure economic prosperity, food, and other life essentials. The Chairman and I are willing to provide these things—guaranteed—to the members of our coalition. We only ask one thing in return; that you prove you're loyal to the Chairman. To do this, everyone—small and great, rich and poor, free and slave—must receive a mark on his right hand or on his forehead. No one will be able to buy or sell anything unless he has the mark, which is the name of the Chairman or the number of his name."

Isola gasped.

The newscaster's monotone voice broke in. "In an immediate response to the proclamation today by the First Advisor, Christian leaders had this to say…"

"Do not receive the mark of the Beast, or you will be damned to hell for eternity! Repent! Turn back to God! Christians, do not take the mark!"

The newsman cut in again. "Calling the statements traitorous, the Chairman warned Christians to follow the decrees of the government. It's common knowledge that Christians have become a thorn in the Chairman's side. If the Christians refuse to take the mark, the new economic plan would be a clever way to weed the Christians from the population. Starve them, perhaps, and reduce insurrection."

Isola slammed her fist against the switch, silencing the radio. She felt numb and shaken, and trembled. No. She shook her head slowly, and then almost feverishly. *No!* This was impossible. It couldn't be true!

Her gaze fell on Kay's notebook. Almost against her will, her fingers picked it up again, and her attention riveted on the screen. The glow from the street lamp outside barely illumined the black, electronic words on the faded gray background, but she could not put the notebook down now if she tried. Her mind rapidly drank in word after word after...

Week Seven — Gospel

*"And this gospel of the kingdom will be preached in the whole world
as a testimony to all nations,
and then the end will come."*

MATTHEW 24:14

WEDNESDAY

"I admire what you did on Monday. It took a lot of guts." Mary said in World Religions class. "Did it help your church at all?"

"No," I said with a quick, rueful smile. "Woodward kicked us out of our building yesterday."

"Oh no! What are you going to do?"

"We might have a temporary solution." I felt reluctant to mention my home church idea. What if the Warners didn't like it? "I don't know what we'll do in the long run, though."

"You could start a new church. Collect donations and rent a new building. Isn't that how most churches get started?"

"That's a good idea." Talking about Woodward's speech brought another subject to mind. I smiled, and hoped it looked casual, and not devious or plotting. "I saw you talking to Mitch on the plaza. He's a nice guy, isn't he?"

Her eyes sparkled briefly. Guiltily? "Yes. He is. We have a class together. Sometimes he helps me with math problems." She smiled. "It's hard to believe an artist could be so good at math."

"Mitch is a very unusual guy." That was an understatement.

"Yes, he is." She pulled her essay from her binder. "Want to switch? Maybe we can spot each other's mistakes before Mr. Carlisle goes at them with his red pen."

I gladly agreed. Each punctuation mistake meant five points off our overall score. Who knew our irreverent World Religions teacher would be such a stickler for good English?

I quickly scanned Mary's essay, but out of the corner of my eye, I watched Mr. Carlisle stride for the head of the class. I remembered yet again how he'd stood right beside Tim and Randy at Woodward's speech yesterday.

I still couldn't believe that Tim or Randy possessed the drive or brains to head up the hate group that had been targeting my church. But Mr. Carlisle was another matter. He felt contempt for all religions—he had made that abundantly clear since the first day of class. And he was not only Tim's cousin, but also good friends with both Tim and Randy.

Could my World Religions teacher possibly be the mastermind behind the hate group?

My stomach clenched in a knot as I swept into Current Affairs class.

Trent wasn't there. A rush of relieved air escaped from my lungs.

But Professor William's cold voice stopped me in my tracks. "I'd like to see you after class, Miss Jameson." His pale green eyes looked like frozen marbles.

"Of course." The knot in my stomach tightened.

I took my seat. Dr. Williams handed back our outlines—but not mine. That made my anxiety level soar.

Still no Trent. Honestly, I was glad. I wasn't ready to talk to him yet. Someday soon, however, we would need to talk.

I was just glad it wouldn't be today.

At the end of class, I slowly put my notebook into my pack. I dreaded the coming confrontation with my teacher.

"Miss Jameson," Professor Williams barked. A few people filing out the door turned to look, and my cheeks warmed.

A paper dangled between his thumb and forefinger. "Guess what? I *almost* threw this in the trash. Care to guess why?"

My heart sank to my shoes. I stepped forward and pulled the paper from his fingers. Red marks ran like blood from every heading and subheading on the page. He'd gored it to pieces.

"What's wrong with it?" Although my gaze steadily met his, my hand trembled.

"What's wrong with it?" His mouth opened in mock, silent astonishment, and then he laughed. "What's *wrong*, Ms. Jameson, is you seem to be in the wrong class. This is *Journalism*. Not English 101."

"I know that."

"Do you?" His lips thinned. "Then explain the whiny drivel in your outline. You're supposed to write an *article*. Not a personal essay."

"It's not a personal essay."

"That..." his finger jabbed at the page clenched in my hands, "is pure shmuck! I should throw you out of my class right now. How did you get so far in the journalism program, anyway?"

How dare he yell at me like this? Anger shivered through me. "My article is on the persecution of Christians in America," I snapped. "I have pages of research to prove it's a problem."

"Then keep your own sniveling, pseudo-problems out of it."

"They're not sniveling problems," I flashed back. "I've used incidents from my own life to illustrate the facts. I've been attacked multiple times in the last few weeks, just because of my beliefs, and so has my church."

"Find other facts to illustrate your points."

I gaped at him. "A huge story is going on right under your nose, Professor Williams. Are you saying it's not newsworthy? Because I beg to differ!"

His eyes gleamed. "Not unnewsworthy, Miss Jameson. Insignificant."

I gasped, but he went on before I could respond. "You want to prove the persecution of Christians is a problem all over America, right?"

"Of course."

"Then I want stories from all over America. Not just from your own doorstep."

"Fine," I bit out. I grabbed at the zipper to my backpack and tried to unzip it. But my hand trembled so badly it took several tries. I thrust the paper in, and met my professor's gaze straight on. "I'll include those, too, Professor Williams."

"Good." His lip curled. "One more point."

"What?"

"Your central theme seems to focus on hate groups in America that persecute Christians. I want you to prove they exist. I want solid facts—figures of their memberships, their mission statement—every fact you can find about them. If you can't give me that, your article is worthless to me. Pure conjecture. Do you understand?"

A horrible, sinking feeling engulfed me. "Yes."

"Then good luck." His lips curled. Clearly, he doubted that I'd find any concrete information. I doubted it, too. I hadn't found it yet, but I'd keep trying.

I turned away.

"Oh, and Miss Jameson." I turned back to meet those freezing eyes. "I'll cut you a deal. If you *do* uncover verifiable information, I just might let you keep your *personal*, tiresome stories in the article."

Anger trembled through me as I strode from the room. How dare he? Ever since classes had started he'd had an ax to grind with me. I was sick of it. Sick of the harassment. Sick of it all!

A rough hand jerked my shoulder and made me stumble.

"Well, look who we have here." Randy's florid, jeering face looked down at me. His fingers dug into my shoulder, hurting me. "Little Kay. Guess your ears are burning now, aren't they girly?"

"Leave me alone!" Furious, I jerked free.

"Oh?" He raised a taunting brow to Tim. "She's touchy. Professor didn't like her outline."

Tim jabbed a skinny finger at my nose. "That's why we're here. Like, you know?" His jaw rhythmically moved, as if chewing on a piece of gum. "To give you some friendly advice."

I refused to flinch. But it was hard to ignore Tim's finger hovering an inch from my face.

His hateful voice oozed on. "We know all about your pathetic..." he spat, and a large, pink wad of gum landed on my shoe, "...little paper. You don't have a clue what you're up against."

"I do." I tried to keep my composure, and but it was difficult to ignore the violation of my personal space, and the nasty glob of chewing gum glistening on my shoelaces.

"Oh yeah?" Tim cast a sneer at Randy. "I guess it's true, then. A little knowledge *is* a dangerous thing."

Without warning, he thrust his jaw toward me. This time, I couldn't help but jerk back.

An evil grin twisted his lips. "You'd better be scared, girl. Because when you come looking for us, you'll find us. Trouble, that is. A pack of it. And we'll be happy to dish it up to you free. In fact, it'll be a real pleasure, right, Randy?"

"Right." Randy grinned.

Horror shivered through me, but I kept my face blank. "Are you finished?" I managed to sound bored.

Randy's face convulsed. "Your mouth is gonna get you a heap of trouble, girl!"

"One last piece of advice," Tim snarled. "A warning, since we're such gentlemen. Listening?"

I glared.

"Watch your back. Especially when you're alone. That means anywhere. This isn't the end—not for you *or* your church. Not by a long shot."

Elbows out, they shoved by me, making me stagger.

Tim laughed, but when I turned around, both had disappeared through the swinging glass doors.

The hall was silent and empty. I'd been right. They were planning more attacks. Not only on me, but on my church, too, even though the FGA had destroyed it.

Cold gooseflesh prickled up on my trembling arms. I crossed them tightly, trying to warm myself.

Maybe they were psychopaths. Or maybe they were angry because we'd chased their gang from the church parking lot on Saturday night, and foiled their robbery attempt. Maybe they wanted to deliver one last, crippling blow to my church.

I drew a shuddering breath. A lot of maybes. I pulled a tissue from my backpack and pulled the gooey gum from my shoe. A few pink strings remained, which required another tissue. No matter how hard I tried, though, I couldn't get it all off. That bothered me. A lot. I threw the disgusting mess into the trash.

I had no clue how Tim and Randy's minds worked. One fact remained crystal clear, though. I couldn't let them win. I had to defeat them. But how?

If only I could discover their plan, or uncover the mastermind behind the group. Unfortunately, I didn't know where to start looking, short of shadowing Tim and Randy day and night. A dangerous, unappealing prospect.

Only one plan of action remained clear. I had to write that article for the *Register*. Readers would learn about the hate group operating in town. As a result, the police might investigate Tim and Randy. Maybe the leader would be discovered, too. Trent had said the newspaper would be interested in the story. Well then, I'd write it, and deliver it to them myself.

At noon, I accessed the school's computer system and researched Christian hate groups with single-minded determination. Professor Williams was horrid, but he was right. I did need concrete facts. Every fact I could discover about the hate group was equal to a chink in their armor. And one step closer to getting Tim, Randy, and the whole group arrested.

But I came up empty, as far as concrete facts. Anecdotal stories, however, flooded the internet.

Disappointed, I headed home. I called the police station, and every other agency who might have solid information, but again, came up dry. No one knew anything concrete, although suspicious stories abounded.

Frustrated, I flopped back on my bed and stared up at the ceiling. How could I expose Tim and Randy if I couldn't discover concrete details about their group?

And their threats weighed heavily on my mind. What would they do next?

Whatever they planned, I had to prevent it from happening. But how? I had no idea what they would do. No idea who was in their group. No idea who was behind it. Nothing.

So how could I stop their next crime? How could I get solid evidence against them?

Catch them in the act.

A giggle escaped. Right. How?

I rolled over and scribbled on my outline:

"Try to prove the hate groups exist, and how they operate, even if I can't find out who they are. Compare attacks on me and our church with other individuals and churches across the country. Let the readers draw their conclusions. Finish research on Friday."

It was the only credible plan I could form. I had to write that article. I was an eyewitness. I could finger Tim and Randy, and expose their blatant persecution at school. Maybe that would be enough. I hoped it would be enough to trigger a wider police investigation.

I wrote a few more notes.

It just might work.

"Hi." I let myself into Joyce's house. The small living room was empty except for Joyce, who perched on Pastor Warner's old green recliner, and David, who sat on the flowered couch. I pulled off my warm jacket. My nose felt cold, and so did my hands. "Where is everyone?"

Joyce jumped up to take my jacket. "Guess no one else wants to come." Her voice sounded brittle. "Stigma of being thrown out of the church, I guess."

Bobby wasn't here, either. I wondered what had happened. Had he forsaken us for good? It was a sad, uncomfortable thought. I liked Bobby, but it hurt that he'd sold us out and become a traitor for the FGA.

I offered David a smile and casually dropped onto the couch beside him; but not too close. I felt like a violin string drawn tight, anticipating the bow stroke that would play the perfect note. I couldn't describe it. Perhaps a sliver of my feelings were fueled by uncertainty—not about Trent anymore—I'd sorted that out on Monday, before he'd betrayed me. And really, the starry-eyed, fluffy crush I'd had on him had actually sputtered out a few weeks ago. I just hadn't acknowledged that truth until Monday.

But my feelings for David were different. They always had been. Our deep, complicated relationship was real. I wanted to go slowly, and to be careful.

He grinned back and crossed an ankle over his knee. "Hey, Sunshine." His easy smile looked relaxed, but his dark eyes seemed watchful, and his lean fingers looked slightly tense on his knee.

"Hey. Is your car fixed yet?"

"As good as new. The computer needed an adjustment."

Joyce flopped into an arm chair. "I guess it's just us. What do you two want to do?"

I leaned forward. Nerves skittered through me. What was wrong? These were my friends. "I have an idea. I mean, about church this coming Sunday."

"Really? What?"

If this was truly the Lord's idea, it would fly. If not, well, I would just sound foolish, putting so much weight on a dream. I plunged in.

"...and Dad said it would be okay to hold church services at our house. At least for a few weeks," I finished.

A frown creased into Joyce's brow. "I don't know. Church services in a house?"

"What a great idea!" David leaped up and paced the room. "It'll be like returning to our Christian roots."

"What do you mean?" Joyce frowned harder.

"People held church meetings in their homes during the first century. This would be the same. Retro-church."

"You're right!" Light kindled in her eyes. "I like it. I'll talk to Dad."

David and I grinned at each other as Joyce flew from the room.

Pastor Warner returned in a minute with a wide smile. "Joyce just told me about your dream, Kay. What a wonderful idea! You say it's okay with your folks?"

I nodded.

"People will need to know where the service will be held." Joyce started planning. "I'll send a shout-out through the church's social media network."

Pastor Warner's eyes twinkled behind his glasses. "And for the old fogeys, I'll ask Martha to call church members and tell them to meet at Kay's house on Sunday at eleven o'clock, instead of at ten. It'll give us more time to set up."

"And we could put up flyers—here and where Kay lives— advertising the service." Joyce rapidly wrote on a notepad.

"I'm free on Friday afternoon," David offered. "I could photocopy and help post them."

"Let's meet at Kay's. Say, at two?" Joyce looked at us both, and we nodded. "We'll put them up then."

"Hopefully it won't rain this time." I glanced at David, remembering the last time we'd put up posters.

"No, no. It's supposed to be clear." Joyce scribbled furiously. "How about this? Truesdale First Gospel has moved to fifty-seven-o-one State Street. Services will be held Sunday morning at eleven. Everyone is welcome."

"Sounds great."

"I see you kids have this under control." Pastor Warner smiled at me. "You're really blessed, Kay, to have God speak to you that way. Thanks for having the courage to speak up."

I felt embarrassed. Yes, God had given me the dream. But I'd actually felt afraid to speak up. Why had I been plagued by doubt? Why hadn't I trusted the Lord?

Pastor rumbled, "Now I'll have a chance to preach that sermon I've been itching to do on the end times."

Joyce rolled her eyes to the ceiling when he retreated to the kitchen. "That's all he can talk about anymore." Frustration tinged her tone. "I guess we're lucky he doesn't preach it every Sunday."

"I think it sounds interesting," I said mildly.

Joyce gave a dismissive shrug. "Different strokes for different folks."

I wondered, yet again, why she seemed so hostile toward the subject of the end times

"Where's Bobby?" David asked.

Joyce frowned. "Guess he didn't feel comfortable enough to come. He *did* sell out our church, you know."

"What does your dad think about Bobby?"

"I don't know. But I do know he hasn't talked to him yet."

"I can't believe he secretly worked for the FGA this whole time." Although I was upset with what Bobby had done, I mostly felt sad.

"You mean like a traitor." Joyce's flashing eyes made it plain that she was very angry.

David flopped onto the couch and flipped through his Bible.

Tapping his finger on the page, he said, "Matthew eighteen, verse fifteen. "'If your brother sins against you, go and show him his fault, just between the two of you. If he listens to you, you have won your brother over.'"

Jesus' words had a way of cutting to the heart of the matter.

Sharply, Joyce said, "Are you saying one of us should go talk to him?"

"I think we all should." David closed the book. "We need to let him know that we still care about him."

Although Joyce frowned, we both knew David was right. Bobby was a member of our family. We couldn't let him go so easily.

"I'm with David." I stood and grabbed my jacket. "What about you, Joyce? Are you coming?"

She nodded.

Joyce told her parents where we were going, and we headed out to David's car. I wondered if David and Joyce felt as nervous as I did. Back in Joyce's living room, the right thing to do seemed clear. But out here, actually doing it, was another matter. I was glad we'd go together.

Joyce slipped behind the tilted front seat, and I sat beside David. As always, I felt comfortable in his car.

I felt comfortable being with him.

I glanced at David out of the corner of my eye as he started the motor. His high cheekbones appeared angular in the light cast by the street lamps, and his shadowed eyes looked serious. Was he nervous about confronting Bobby? I couldn't tell.

We slipped away from the curb. A few headlights approached on the dark street and flashed by.

"I'm cold back here. Is the heater on?" Joyce rubbed her hands together.

He switched the fan on high, and heat blasted my face. I tilted the airflow up so Joyce could feel the warmth, too.

"That's better." She sat back, shivering.

We rode in silence for a few minutes.

"I can't get over your dream, Kay," Joyce said. "It's amazing. Did you know right away that God had spoken to you?"

"No. I mean, I wondered. But I wasn't sure."

"Was it different from a regular dream?"

"Yes." I thought back on it. "Every detail seemed crystal clear, like I was standing right there, experiencing the dogs and cats rushing by me, into the house. And God spoke to me. That's different. I usually don't dream about God."

"Neat." Joyce fell silent.

Within minutes we'd rolled up to Bobby's house.

"Ready, guys?" Joyce said.

"Ready."

"Who'll do the talking?" I slipped out of the car, and zipped up my jacket against the crisp night.

"Let's play it by ear." This was David. "Maybe we won't have to say much at all."

Shadows shrouded the concrete path to the Page's front door. But a curtained window glowed with yellow light.

"Here goes." We bunched together on the front stoop and David rapped on the door.

Each second seemed to last a small eternity. At last, the peephole blackened, and the door swung open.

"Hi, guys." Laura looked tired, but her smile welcomed us. "It's nice to see you. Come on in."

We followed her inside. The moist smell of boiled potatoes and baked oatmeal cookies filled my senses. She waved us toward the room to the right. "Bobby's in the den. I'm sure he'll be happy to see you."

I wondered if that was true.

"Who is it, hon?" Bobby bulky form darkened the doorway. His jaw stiffened when he saw us, and his lips twitched into a strained smile. "Good to see you guys. Come in. What brings you here?"

We perched on a tweed couch while Bobby sank into his arm chair. Laura hovered in the doorway.

Ever straightforward, Joyce came right to the point. "Why did you sell us out?"

Bobby winced, and pressed his shoulders against the brown chair. "I... it was all my idea." He glanced at his wife. "Laura didn't know anything about it."

Laura shook her head. Pain filled her soft gaze as she looked at her husband. She loved him. She didn't want him to suffer alone.

"What happened?" David said quietly.

Bobby's eyes fluttered closed for a second. Misery etched deep grooves along his mouth. "It started when I wrote a letter to the FGA."

When he didn't say anything else, I prompted, "What did the letter say?"

With a sigh, Bobby visibly pulled himself together. "I asked if they'd give our church more funds so I could keep my job. I was desperate." He glanced at Laura again. "I didn't know what else to do."

"Anyway," his voice rasped, "that's what started the whole mess. The FGA wanted to know why our church was losing money, so they flew Crawford down to check it out. First, he saw the graffiti. Then he heard Pastor Warner preach about Jesus, and that made him real upset. But I didn't understand why.

"Then Crawford asked me to watch our church and give him updates. He wanted to make sure Pastor Warner complied with the new FGA orders.

"I refused to consider it at first, but when we found out Laura was pregnant, I felt I had no choice. They promised my job wouldn't be cut, and they promised to send me extra money every time I called in a report."

I understood why Bobby had caved in to the pressure. He'd needed the job for his growing family. He was desperate. Jobs in his field—in any field—were scarce these days.

"Anyway." That one word sounded tight and miserable. "I sold out our church. All for a few bucks. And the FGA lied. I have no job now, because our church no longer exists, thanks to me. I didn't trust the Lord to take care of us, even though I knew Laura trusted him. I'm sorry." Tears shimmered in his dark eyes, and his voice broke, "I'm really sorry. I understand if you don't want to forgive me."

"Of course we forgive you!" Heart full, I leaped up and hurried over to hug him. "We love you. Everyone makes mistakes."

"That's right." Joyce was right behind me. Her face softened as she gave him a hug too, and then Laura rushed over, her eyes streaming.

David shook Bobby's hand and punched him on the shoulder. "We expect you to come back, man. We'll need your help at our new service."

"New service?" Bobby said with wonder. "What new service? I thought they'd kicked us out of the church."

"They did." Joyce perched on the arm of his chair. "But Kay had a great idea. A dream, really. We'll hold the service at her house."

"What a wonderful idea," Laura breathed.

"We'll need all the help we can get. Are you in?"

"We'll need chairs." I knew Bobby had connections to get truckloads of folding chairs.

Bobby glanced first at me, and then at Joyce. "I'd like to help, but I'd better talk to your dad, first. I'm not sure he'll want me back."

"Of course he will," I said. "Just talk to him. Explain. He'll understand, just like we do."

"And forgive." Bobby's face convulsed, and tears flowed down his tan cheeks. "I don't deserve such good friends."

"Of course you do!" I squeezed a supportive arm around his shoulders.

Finally, he wiped his eyes with a handkerchief. "Thank you. I'm grateful for each one of you. You are true friends. Forgiving friends. I'll talk to Pastor Warner tomorrow, and try to straighten everything out."

Of course, we stayed to munch on cookies fresh from the oven after that.

I felt good. Better than I had in days. Was this what forgiveness felt like? Healthy, healing. Bringing happiness and laughter back into the eyes of the Pages. Maybe it could heal the bitterness lingering inside of me, too. Toward Trent.

Carrying my glass to the kitchen for more soda, I glanced at my friends. Joyce, Laura, Bobby. David. My gaze lingered on his tall frame as he joked with Bobby. I had to close the old chapter before I could ever go forward.

FRIDAY

"I LIKE YOUR OUTFIT." I told Mary as I slipped into my desk in World Religions class.

"Thank you." She fingered the slippery red fabric of her flashy blouse. It was pretty. But not quite her style. "Jack gave it to me. He's trying to be nice. He knows he's been a real jerk the last couple of weeks."

"I'm glad." Privately, however, I wondered how long Jack's good behavior would last.

"How is your church?"

"Good." I smiled, remembering the latest news. Joyce said Bobby and Pastor had reconciled, and Bobby had already lined up the chairs we'd need for Sunday. "We're going to hold the service at my house."

"Your house? Do you have enough room?"

"I think so. We're holding it in the living room."

She nodded. "It *is* huge. What a great idea."

"Would you like to come?"

Mary fiddled with the cuff of her blouse. "Thank you, but no. I don't think so." She probably didn't want to ruffle the calm waters at home. Jack would be furious if she went.

Still, I said, "It's at eleven, if you change your mind. I'd love for you to come. Mom's making coffee cake for refreshments afterward. You could just come for that, if you'd like."

"We'll see." Her tone promised nothing.

Unease slid through my spirit. I wasn't sure why.

Professor Williams left me alone today. One sneer, and that was it. Tim and Randy were absent, too. Thank goodness. But I planned to finish up my research tonight so I could give my article to the *Register* on Monday. I wouldn't live in fear any longer.

Trent attended class today. It was the first time I'd seen him since Woodward's speech. He came in after me, and sat near the door.

I found it terribly hard to look at him. In my heart, I felt insignificant, like a squashed bug. I'd meant nothing to him. He'd used me and trashed me, like yesterday's newspaper.

He glanced once at me, and for a brief second our eyes met. I tried not to look hurt or angry, but didn't know how well I succeeded.

I couldn't read anything in his blue gaze, and he quickly turned to face the teacher again. Was he ashamed of his behavior? I hoped so.

I should have confronted him today, but I just couldn't.

After class, he vanished into the crowd streaming from the building. I felt empty and sad. Was I ready to forgive him yet? *Please help me, Lord.*

Cold air nipped my cheeks and made me shiver, but I elected to eat lunch on a bench bordering the plaza. The crisp day harbored a clean, smoky smell, which tantalized my nostrils. I drew a slow, deep breath, loving the scent. Somewhere, someone burned wood in their fireplace.

With icy fingers, I unwrapped my tuna fish sandwich and took a bite.

"Hi."

I turned my head and smiled. Mitch wheeled a blue bike with one hand, and wore a black backpack slung over one muscled shoulder. He slowed to a halt.

"How're you doing?"

I nodded, and swallowed. "Good. How about you?"

"Good. Got some lab work to do." He hesitated. His black gaze looked intent. "How's your church?"

Everyone kept asking the same question. "Good. We're holding the service at my house on Sunday."

"Really?" His left brow skyrocketed. "That's kind of unusual, isn't it?"

"I guess so." A thought came to mind when I noticed his sketchbook bungied crosswise to his bicycle carry rack. "Pastor Warner's going to talk about the end times."

"Really?" Interest gleamed. "Like you've been telling me about?"

"Yes. Only he knows a lot more than I do. Would you like to come?"

He hesitated for a millisecond. "Okay. I will. I've got synagogue on Saturday, but Sunday's free. What time?"

"Eleven."

"Okay." His smile edged up, and he pushed his bike on. "I'll see you then."

"How many posters did you print up?" Joyce peered around David's shoulder. I knelt on a kitchen chair and inspected a flyer for myself. The hot pink was eye-catching, to say the least. Instructions to the church service were printed in David's bold hand.

"I like them." I grinned. "Where did you get the idea for the color?"

"I asked the girl at the counter what color would catch her attention. She said pink."

"Good," Joyce said shortly. "How many did you print?"

"Fifty."

"That should be plenty."

We mapped out our strategy and then split up, after agreeing to meet back at my house in an hour. Mom was baking chocolate chip cookies. They would be our reward for our afternoon of hard work.

I tacked up flyers on State Street and High Street. The day was quiet. No one seemed to notice or care what I was doing.

I arrived home first, and was piling warm, gooey cookies onto a plate when Joyce breezed in. She snatched one and popped it in her mouth. "Thanks." She collapsed in a chair at the table. "That was quick and easy."

I sat across from her, munching on a warm, soft cookie, and nodded. Chocolate oozed onto my fingers. Mmm. Yummy. Chocolate chip cookies were my favorite.

"I still can't get over that dream you had," she said unexpectedly.

"Want a soda?" I jumped up and headed for the refrigerator.

"Diet, please. Thank you."

After handing her the soda, I settled back down and sipped my root beer.

"I mean it." Joyce said. "And I'm amazed how well it's working out." She fingered a napkin for a moment, as if wanting to say more, but finding it hard to do so. Finally, she said, "It's really opened my eyes. I've been so tunnel-minded these days, and ignoring a lot of things. Our friendship, for one."

"You've been busy. We all have. Plus all the attacks..."

Her expression momentarily stiffened. "I know. But that's no excuse. It's my fault our friendship has been slipping. I admit it. David made me realize that last week."

"What do you mean?"

"He asked what my focus was. Remember?" Joyce looked down at her fingers, which shredded the napkin now. "I realized it's business. School. It's *all* I ever think about now."

"They are important."

"Yes. But I need balance. I've been too caught up in class projects, and planning my career and my whole future. I've forgotten what is really important. You and David. And my family."

"We understand. And it's not just you, you know. We've all been distracted lately."

Blinking quickly, Joyce shook her head. "You guys are great friends."

After a moment, I said, "Mind if I ask you something?" While our communication was open, I wanted to ask a question that had been bugging me for a long time.

"What?"

"Why don't you like to talk about the end times?"

Although Joyce tensed, she replied without her usual defensiveness. "It scares me. I like my life now—I'm not ready to be with God yet."

"I guess I hadn't thought about it happening so literally. I mean, I love to watch events happening today and match them up with things Jesus prophesied two thousand years ago. It's incredible! And I do think about him returning. But I guess I haven't thought—not concretely—about how our whole lives will change."

"What do you think it'll be like?"

"What?"

"Being raptured to be with Jesus."

I laughed. "So you *do* think we'll be raptured before the Tribulation."

"I certainly hope so! I like my life, but I don't want to live through that." Despite her quick smile, Joyce still appeared troubled.

"I don't know." My mind stilled, and I stared off into space. "I think heaven will be like..." A soft feeling of golden joy streamed into my soul. It was almost as if I could see...

"I think it will be wonderful. Filled with joy. And active, fulfilling, and meaningful. I think we'll be busy. And our new life will be so much better than this one that it really won't even compare."

I focused on Joyce again, but felt like I glowed from the inside out.

"It sounds like a wonderful place," Joyce said softly. She leaped up and gave me a fierce hug. Tears clogged her voice. "Friends always, right? No matter what happens."

My own eyes filled, and I hugged her tightly. "Of course."

I noticed David over her shoulder. He had slipped in quietly. He gave me the thumbs up signal.

I asked Joyce and David to stay to dinner. We spent the afternoon laughing and talking. I enjoyed the good time of being close friends again. When Dad came home, Joyce and I helped Mom put the finishing touches on the meal, and then I went to call Dad and David to dinner.

David lounged in the doorway to the den. I heard him say, "What do you think?" as I approached.

"It would be great." Dad winked when I poked my head in. "What do you think, honey?"

"About what?"

Dad nodded at the T.V.

Mick Murray said, "...The underground peace proposal is gathering strength. Conflicts in some areas are slowing down, anticipating the soon-to-be-announced proposal. Details will be released next week."

"What kind of peace proposal?" I wondered. "And why is it so hush hush? Who's behind it?"

"I don't know." Dad said. "Must be someone pretty power-ful to pull something this big together."

I rested my elbows on the top of Dad's recliner and glanced at David. "What do you think?"

"I don't know. But I don't think it will be the cure-all every-one hopes it will be."

The television camera panned a group of serious looking men seated at a long table. An unexpected shiver chilled me, prickling up tiny goose bumps over my arms. David was right. Something was wrong with this picture.

Dad turned. "Been meaning to ask you, David. How is the store? Any damage from the earthquakes or flood?"

"No. Business is booming, in fact. Lots of people need repairs."

Remembering my mission, I pushed away from the recliner. "Dinner's ready. Come and get it while it's hot."

Theresa sat unusually quiet during dinner. She appeared to have finally moved past her crush on David, which gave me a feeling of relief.

After dessert, Joyce said, "Thank you for dinner, Mr. and Mrs. Jameson. Sorry I have to leave so soon, but I have a paper to write."

"So do I." I'd almost forgotten my article for the *Register*! I sprang to my feet. "Thank goodness the lab is still open."

Mom frowned. "It's almost seven. I hope you're not plan-ning to go back to school tonight."

"I need to. I have to hand in the article on Monday."

"Couldn't it wait until tomorrow?" Mom cast a worried glance at Dad.

David spoke up. "I'll drive her. And bring her home again, too."

"Thank you." He'd offered this before. While I felt grateful for David's offer, I really didn't want to be a bother to him. "I appreciate it, but it'll be fine. I'll work at the lab for a couple of hours, and then come straight home."

David's gaze darkened. "I thought we had an agreement."

"I'll be fine," I insisted, and headed for the hall table, where I'd left my backpack. "I don't want to be a bother."

"I'd feel better if you'd go with David." Dad's firm voice drew my steps to a halt.

After a moment, I sighed. "All right."

David's lips twisted into a lopsided grin. "Glad to know you enjoy my company so much, Kay."

"It's not that!" I felt bad. "You know I love spending time with you. It's just—I'm so sick of being afraid. And I don't want to be a burden to you."

"You're not a burden."

Somewhere, the phone rang.

"Thank you. I appreciate that. But taking precautions feels like it's saying they've won. They keep taking away my freedom, piece by piece. I can't stand it. I don't want to be afraid anymore."

Until that moment, I hadn't realized how much anger still simmered in me because of the attacks against me, and our church, too.

David's hurt look softened. He understood, and that comforted me.

"Joyce." Mom appeared with a wrinkled brow. "It's your mother."

"Oh." She tossed us a smiling glance. "She's probably wondering when I'll be home."

A second later, I heard her muffled voice. "Hi, Mom. I'm coming home... *What?*"

A long silence ensued. Everyone in the dining room fell silent.

Joyce reappeared a moment later. Her eyes looked like shocked, dark saucers in her white face. "They did it again," she whispered.

"What?"

She fled for the front door. "I have to go! I'm sorry."

Mom turned worried eyes to Dad. "What in the world could have happened?"

I quickly turned to David. "Let's find out."

"I'm with you."

"Be careful!" Mom fretted.

I snatched up my backpack and dashed after David. Fear twisted in my gut. I was afraid. For Joyce. For her family. And for me.

Would this nightmare ever end? I squeezed into David's sports car, and we sped toward Joyce's house. Clearly, the hate group had attacked the Warners. And this incident was serious. Tim had threatened an attack when I'd seen him on Wednesday. Was this it? Or was something even worse coming?

A thought flashed to mind. I choked on a bitter laugh. "He'll probably dismiss this, too."

"Who?"

"My professor." I explained how he had ridiculed my outline. And how he'd said attacks in town weren't important enough to be included in my article.

David clenched his jaw. "That guy needs a reality check."

Emergency vehicles were parked on the street in front of Joyce's house. I slammed the car door and ran toward the front walk.

"Hold on, miss. This is a crime scene." A tall, wiry man blocked my entry. A feeling of déjà vu hit me. This same scene kept happening over and over again.

"But what happened?" I craned my neck to peer around his shoulder. "Our friend lives here. Can we help?"

"Kay." David's voice distracted me. He stood under a shadowed tree near the street. Pastor Warner, Mrs. Warner, and Joyce huddled beneath it. Joyce wept.

I hurried over. "What happened?"

"This!" A black piece of cloth shook from Pastor Warner's fist. "Those hate mongers vandalized our house!"

"When?" Horrified, I imagined Pastor Warner and his wife sitting to dinner eating, when...

"We weren't there," Mrs. Warner's quavering voice spoke. "We were visiting Bobby and Laura, and when we got back, we saw..." Her voice broke. "We saw..."

"Shh, Mama," Joyce sobbed, hugging her tight. "It'll be okay. It'll be *okay*." Her words ended in a high, keening wail.

"How much damage?"

"Enough." Pastor Warner said grimly. "I just thank the Lord we weren't home. Otherwise, no telling what they would have done. They were bent on destruction, that's..."

Joyce's harsh, wailing sobs drowned out Pastor Warner's last words.

David spoke quietly in my ear. "Apparently they took an ax to the kitchen table and a few other pieces of furniture. They also knifed the cushions, smashed the TV and lamps, and poured syrup and spaghetti sauce all over everything."

"That's *awful*." But I felt more worried about Joyce right now than the vandalized house. Her sobs sounded frantic, and her shoulders shook violently. It looked like she teetered on the brink of a nervous breakdown.

Mrs. Warner hugged her daughter. "Joyce, honey, it's okay. It wasn't that bad." With a shaky laugh, she smoothed the hair back from Joyce's forehead. "You know your dad. He'll probably have it cleaned up first thing tomorrow morning."

"That's right." Pastor Warner wrapped his arms around his shaking daughter and wife. "It's not the end of the world. We'll be all right."

"No!" Joyce's head flip-flopped feverishly. "*No*. It won't be okay! It'll never be okay *again!* Why won't they leave us alone? Why does this keep happening? Why? Why can't we stop it? Everything is out of *control!*" Her sobs screeched higher and higher.

"Joyce, honey," murmured Pastor Warner. "It may seem like everything is out of control, but it's not. God is in control. Remember? We need to trust him. Remember Psalm thirty-four, verse nineteen.

"'A righteous man may have many troubles, but the Lord delivers him from them all...'

"It's all in God's hands, honey. Not yours. Not mine. We can't control everything, anymore than we can stop the tide from coming in."

"Dad!" Joyce flung herself into her father's arms. Her lips curled back in a terrible sob. "I can't stand it! I can't handle it any more! I try to make sense of my life. I try to plan and organize. To control things. But nothing turns out the way I want it to. Ever!"

"What did you plan?"

"My career. My life! I've worked so hard, doing every single thing I can to build my future business career. I've been busy every *minute* of the day. But no matter how hard I work, things keep falling apart!"

Pastor patted her back. "It'll be okay, honey."

Gulping, Joyce pulled back, and pressed her palms against her streaming eyes. She gasped out, "I didn't want to believe it, but I think you and Kay are right, Daddy. This *is* the end!"

A bewildered look crossed Pastor Warner's features. "Then why are you so upset?"

Joyce sniffled, and choked on a laugh. "Oh, Daddy, don't you know that's why I've been so mad at you? Everything keeps happening just like you said it would. I didn't want to believe it. Because that would mean that all my work, and all my plans and dreams for the future will never come true. I hated the idea. *Hated it!* I'm sorry, but that's true.

"The attacks—everything—kept coming and coming. Like they proved you were right. It made me feel...I don't know...out of control. Fearful. But mostly really, *really* angry. I know that sounds so petty and selfish, but it's true.

"I've been taking it out on you, Daddy. And Kay, too. I'm sorry, but I didn't *want* it to be the end! I didn't want my life cut short. I wanted to stay here and carry out my dreams."

"Maybe you will, honey. We don't know..."

"Dad." Blinking, Joyce quickly shook her head. "That's not the point. Whether the Rapture happens tomorrow, or two hundred years from now, doesn't matter. I've been selfish, and only focusing on what I want. I've been running from myself, and from what's real and most important. And from God. Especially God. I haven't been listening to him at all. And I can't stop him. I've been arrogant to try. I need to trust *him*. Not me. That's the point."

Pastor hugged her tightly.

"Sir?" A fireman strode up.

As the pastor turned, I said, "It really will be okay, Joyce."

"I know." She dashed the tears away, and offered David and me a shaky smile. I suspected the tears were cathartic. A way to vent all the anger and frustration I'd sensed simmering in her over the last several weeks. It was healthy. Finally, Joyce was ready to face the future. Whatever the future might be.

"You're the best, Joyce." I hugged her. "I'm sorry I never asked why you were so upset. I've been wrapped up in my own life, too."

"That's all right. It's not like I was easy to talk to!" Suddenly, Joyce was half-laughing, and half-crying. Turning, she reached out for David, too.

His arms wrapped warmly and securely around both of us.

David and I left soon after that. Joyce was calmer, and ready to help her parents make sense of the mess in their house. We'd offered to help, but they had declined. They wanted to work through this attack together. Alone.

David pulled into the parking lot near Kale Hall. "I'll walk you up."

I didn't argue. Most of the campus lay in quiet blackness. Night classes had started twenty minutes ago, and wouldn't let out until almost ten o'clock. It explained how deserted the campus was right now.

A few yellow lamps glowed high above the sidewalks. Those pale golden globes didn't cast a great deal of light onto the path beneath our feet, however.

Several people slipped by, on bikes or on foot, perhaps arriving late to the few classes held on Friday nights. It was safe, I realized. David hadn't needed to walk me to Kale Hall, but I was glad he had.

Our steps slowed outside the brightly lit building.

"I guess this is it." He glanced at his watch, and his dark eyes gleamed down at me. "I'll pick you up in, say...two hours? Nine-thirty sound okay to you?"

"Yes. Thank you." As I looked up at him, I suddenly felt reluctant to see him go.

"Okay. Well." He flashed a crooked grin. "See you later?"

"Okay."

A wave of his arm, and his shoulders twisted right. In that instant, my hand flew out. To stop him? I snatched it back. What was wrong with me?

I watched his tall figure fade into the shadows of the night. I felt alone standing there. And a bit afraid of the emotions stirring inside of me. What did I feel for him? How deep did my feelings go, and what did they mean? And what, if anything, did he feel for me?

I turned to Kale Hall. Bright lights spilled through the glass doorways. I couldn't think about David now. I had work to do.

It seemed strange to be at school so late in the evening, but I guessed I'd be safe enough. Besides the night classes in session, surely other people worked and studied on campus right now, too. Midterms were coming up.

Eight people worked at the computers when I slipped through the lab door. It seemed like a lot of people for a Friday night, but I was glad I wouldn't be alone.

I settled down to research the hate groups. Like on Wednesday, though, I couldn't discover any reports of arrest warrants. Stories abounded, though, and hate groups did seem to be scattered across the country. Was it a national group, which spawned local chapters? Or did bands of misfits form small groups for purposes of their own? I suspected the first, but couldn't find proof.

I compiled a data file of website urls which documented the number and types of hate crimes committed, and brainstormed more ideas for my *Register* article. Finally, I printed up a new, expanded outline.

At nine-fifteen, the last person left the lab. Unease slid through me as I sat in the empty room. I felt the illogical desire to leave. A silly idea, considering all the thriller movies I'd seen, in which the heroine foolishly wandered alone into the dark night.

David would return in fifteen minutes. I wouldn't be alone for much longer.

The next few minutes passed with excruciating slowness, however. Silence seemed to weigh like a heavy cloak upon me, pressing harder by the second upon my senses.

Stop it.

I tried to focus on concrete things, like the computer screen before me. As I typed, the key clicks sounded unnaturally loud in the silent room.

Fear crept into my pores.

I didn't like the building's silence. It felt oppressive. Suffocating.

A small sound, resembling a foot scuff, drew my attention.

David?

But it was only nine-twenty. Had he arrived ten minutes early?

I tucked the outline in my pack, saved the data to my flash drive, and rose to my feet. I paused before pushing my chair in, however, and listened. Nothing.

Had I heard a footstep? I slung the backpack onto my shoulder and crept to the open door.

A small, muffled sound came from the end of the hall, near the stairwell. I peeked out and looked left. Blue plaid flashed and disappeared into a doorway. I jerked back, heart pounding. That wasn't David.

Calm down. He's probably a student. Or a teacher.

I peered out again. The man in blue had disappeared into a room on my side of the hall.

Wait. Dark spikes, looking like porcupine quills, poked into view at head height, barely visible beyond the door frame. Someone stood in the doorway. Waiting. Unmoving.

I fought the desire to hyperventilate.

One minute passed. Then two. The man didn't move.

Okay, this was freaky. What was he doing there? Who was he waiting for?

I quickly glanced right. The door to the emergency stairwell was about ten feet away.

Escaping from the building appealed more by the second. Waltzing right past the guy and down the main staircase didn't seem like a good idea. However, running in the opposite direction did.

His behavior definitely seemed suspicious. Or was that just my frightened imagination talking?

Who was he waiting for? What was he *doing*?

More alarming theories took root in my mind. What if he'd already crept by the lab and seen I was alone? What if he now waited, listening to make sure we were alone on this floor? Did he plan to tiptoe back and attack me?

I wasn't sure if I was thinking rationally any longer. All I knew was I wanted to get out of Kale Hall. *Now*. The imminent, possible threat the man posed seemed much more dangerous than escaping outside and hurrying to meet David in the parking lot.

My life wasn't a thriller movie, after all, and I wasn't a heroine. I would be fine.

A soft chuckle came from the man's direction. It made the hair stand up on my arms.

Creee...py.

I darted right, for the emergency exit, and barreled down the emergency steps. My hip hit the door's release bar, and I exploded into the dark, cold night.

Gasping, I took stock of the situation. Across the quad area, distant, small figures walked to other buildings. But here, I was alone.

I hurried for the wide sidewalk that would take me to the parking lot. I ran by Kale Hall's double glass, main front doors. No one loitered outside.

I saw no one. Had I made a mountain out of a mole hill?

It didn't matter. I'd meet David in the parking lot. He should be there in five minutes.

I walked fast. Although I'd escaped from Kale Hall, the oppressive feeling from the lab lingered. But it felt heavier out here. More pressing. The blackness curled around me.

I couldn't see very well. Lamps at this end of campus were spaced too far apart, and several had burned out. Shadows flickered in my peripheral vision. People hurried down distant walkways toward the parking lot. I hurried faster, too.

Only a little further to go down this walk, and then a twist past a huge, gnarled oak tree. It was pitch black under the tree. Someone could hide...

Stop scaring yourself.

I padded on, heart pounding. After the tree lay the home stretch; straight ahead to the parking lot. No one would attack me there—not tonight, for in the distance I saw a handful of people hurrying through the parking area. The lot was bright, too. Brighter than my path now.

I approached the tree, trying to ignore the panic squeezing through me. I wanted to run, but didn't. I wouldn't.

The tree scared me. It looked so black and hulking. Like a monster lying in wait, ready to pounce on me. I imagined evil, cruel eyes watching me, waiting for me.

Stop it. You're losing it.

Ten more steps, and I would reach the turn. My eyes darted left, then right, searching for a nearby, friendly soul I could walk with—anyone else hurrying toward the parking lot. But the shadowed paths around me were empty and dark. I was alone.

Should I have waited for David in Kale Hall, after all?

Three more steps. Two... My legs scissored fast. One...

"If it isn't Kay!" The hissing sneer made me jump, and my heart jerked hard with fear.

Someone stood at my elbow. Tim. I hadn't seen him glide out from under the tree.

My shoulders lurched forward into a run, but it was too late. Hard hands plucked at my jacket and yanked me backwards. He dragged me under the tree.

"*No.*" I jerked right and left, wriggling like a wild cat. Struggling to escape. *Help me, Lord.* "Leave me alone!"

"We just want to talk. Right, guys?"

My thrashing attempts to break free intensified when I saw two dark figures standing hidden in the shadows beneath the tree. I trembled with terror.

A hulking form pushed away from the trunk, and his face became distinct. Randy. Panting, I stopped trying to wrestle free from Tim. Somehow, I knew Randy was the dangerous one. He would take pleasure in subduing me.

I managed to calm my shaky breaths. I needed my wits about me.

Randy's pale jowls moved in the dim light. "I got a text message you might be heading our way."

From the plaid man. "Your friend followed me to Kale Hall."

Randy didn't answer. "It's dangerous, wandering around campus alone. You must be stupid."

"What about you? Trashing the Warner's house wasn't exactly brilliant."

The black figure under the tree chuckled softly, and the sound made my skin crawl. Who was it? Mr. Carlisle?

Tim's sneering voice drew my attention. "You'll never prove it."

"I don't have to prove it. All I have to do is expose it."

"What is that supposed to mean?" Tim's voice lowered to a dangerous level.

What was I doing? Trying to rile them up? I needed to escape. *Now.*

I twisted again, hard, but Tim grabbed my arm. Painfully, he wrenched it up behind my back, and I gasped.

"You're not going anywhere. Explain what you said."

Tears formed in my eyes. "I didn't mean anything. Let me *go.*"

"Oh, I think you did mean something," murmured the dark figure beneath the tree. "Tell us, Kay. We are very interested."

"Nothing! I meant nothing."

The soft voice spoke again. "You plan to write an article for the *Register*. Isn't that right?"

I managed to keep my face expressionless.

Randy's thick lips contorted into a snarl of rage. "You stupid girl. You keep talking and talking. You need to shut up!"

A meaty fist drove for my face and I twisted, trying to duck. But it wasn't fast enough. Pain exploded across the back of my head.

I gasped. Bright spots exploded before my eyes, and sudden, inexplicable words flew through my mind.

...men loved darkness instead of light because their deeds were evil. Everyone who does evil hates the light, and will

not come into the light for fear that his deeds will be exposed.
(John 3:19b-20)

I gulped back a sob as pain seared my neck. They hated me because I spoke the truth. It frightened them. It exposed their true identities.

"Randy! No." The shadowed man spoke sharply. For an instant, I almost recognized his voice. "Let her go, Tim."

Tim released my arm, and I staggered forward. Tears stung my eyes as I tried to straighten it. I wouldn't cry. I wouldn't.

I fought the pain in my head, too. I had to escape. *Help me, Lord, please!* I cupped my aching arm against my stomach.

"We need to shut her *up*," Randy bellowed. "Isn't that what I've said from the beginning?"

"She can't hurt us. All she has are silly little theories. No facts. No one to back up her pathetic stories. No witnesses." The figure slipped toward me, and the cloak of shadows fell from his hard face.

I gasped. "Professor Williams!"

"Surprised?" His lips curled into a smile. "Take a good look."

"Professor!" Tim sputtered. "What are you doing?"

"She has no witnesses. It's just her word against mine. Right, Kay?" Professor Williams slithered forward. The pale light shone off of his face, making him look like an evil, ghoulish specter. "It's ironic, really. She'll know the mastermind behind our club, but she won't be able to report it—unless she wants to be slapped with a libel suit. That would stop her career dead in its tracks."

"Why?" I managed. "Why are you running a hate club? It's so...bigoted! And small minded."

"*Wrong.*" His voice cracked like a whip. "I'm protecting my country's freedom from people like you. You're a plague. Little miss high and mighty." He stepped closer, sneering. "Sure you've found your way to heaven. Looking down on the rest of us. Judging us." He threw his arms out. "Where's your God now, Kay? Why isn't he protecting you?"

I looked up at the heavens. A few stars pierced the inky night sky.

Lord, I know he's wrong. I know you're here. Please help me! Please.

Professor Williams spat on my shoe. His eyes gleamed with hatred. "You know *nothing*. You're an egotistical, narrow-minded fanatic."

"And you're not?" I muttered under my breath.

I saw now what he got from this. Power. He felt like a big man because he trampled on other people. Persecuted them. Destroyed their churches and their lives. It made him feel omnipotent.

"Tell me something," I needed to keep him talking. David would come along soon. Two against three would provide better odds than I currently faced. "Why have you been picking on me? I'm one girl. And certainly not the only Christian on campus."

The Professor sneered, but pleasure gleamed in his eyes. He liked being asked. It inflated his self-opinion even more.

"You," he laughed softly, "were chosen by chance. A toss of the dice by fate. Right, Tim and Randy?"

Randy glared at me.

"Of course, they both knew from the beginning that you were a Christian. We've compiled a list of all the active Christians on campus. But why you? Remember the day you met them in the lab, Kay? Your shirt blazed with your love for Truesdale First Gospel. Adding to that vulgarity, you refused to let them see your paper. You put on your Christian high and mighty attitude."

Tim cut in, "That's when we chose you for our pet project."

"Soon you became a thorn in my side, as well." The Professor's eyes narrowed. "Spouting your religious drivel in class was a mistake, Miss Jameson. I decided to make an example of you. It only sweetened the pot to know you attend Truesdale First Gospel."

I pounced on that. "Why have you been attacking my church?" I had to discover every fact possible now, while I still had the chance. Soon I would escape. I hoped.

Professor Williams chuckled. "Your church has been our prime target all along. Frankly, with your brains, I'm surprised you haven't figured out why. I'll spell it out for you. Your church is run by the FGA, correct?"

I nodded.

"The FGA has a candidate running for the U.S. Senate. Oak Woodward. Here's our problem. We won't let a Christian organization gain control of the United States government!"

I laughed out loud. The FGA. Christian? Ha!

Righteous fury burned in the Professor's eyes. "We knew we needed to discredit the FGA. Persecute them. Give them a bad name so no one would touch them with a ten foot pole. And so we decided to achieve our goals through your church.

"At first, we only planned a few scare tactics. But then Truesdale First Gospel became a nuisance. With your help, they spouted off their Christian drivel to the news media. Woodward gained in the polls. He became a word on everyone's lips. It was an abomination, and made us more determined than ever to crush you both." The Professor's lips curled back. "It became personal, you see."

"You haven't beaten us."

His features contorted into a snarl, and I trembled at the hatred I saw. "So you say *now*," he hissed. His face went suddenly slack, and every expression slid away.

He turned, sounding bored. "This drama has gone on long enough."

"What should we do with her? We can't let her write that article."

"Of course not."

Randy grinned at me. I think I saw saliva drip from his lips. "I'll stop her."

Fear silenced my angry words. I was sick to death of Randy and Tim. Sick of their small-minded, hateful ways. I would not be a victim any longer.

Dr. Williams snarled, "I'll ask you once, Kay. Give me your computer access code. Now."

"No."

"She carries a flash drive with her," Tim interjected.

"Take it."

Randy grabbed my arm. When I struggled, Tim ripped my backpack open while it still swung from my shoulder. "*Stop it.*" Didn't anyone see what was happening? Where was everyone?

"Here it is."

"Good. Now for the password."

I stared at the drive clenched in Tim's hand. All of my work. They planned to destroy all of my work. "No."

"Yes!" Randy's thick, heavy arm closed around my throat, choking off the air so I couldn't breathe. I flailed wildly.

"Password!" Professor Williams snapped out.

My world slowly turned gray. A dull roaring filled my ears. Finally, as if from a far distance, faint words registered. "Loosen up, Randy. She can't talk."

The pressure eased on my throat, and I gasped in cool, sweet air. Frightened tears stood in my eyes.

"JLMJ three sixteen," I choked out. I blinked rapidly, chest heaving, trying not to be weak. Trying not to cry. But it was no use. Burning tears spilled over my lids. Everyone looked blurry. Even the dark tree trunk looked blacker and thicker than before; as if someone new stood beside it now.

"Good girl," Dr. Williams smirked. "All right, boys. Now, what should we do with her?"

My horrified breaths quickened, soaring and twisting with my heart pounding, impotent terror. I had to break free.

A shadow moved to my right, from the direction of the parking lot. Hope swelled. David?

It was all the inspiration I needed. I jabbed my elbow hard into Randy's stomach, and his breath *oofed* out. Unthinkingly, my hands grabbed his elbow and shoulder, and I twisted my shoulder down in a self-defense move. Randy flipped over my shoulder and landed with a dull, gasping thud on his back.

David stepped in and slugged Tim hard in the nose. Tim staggered, and swung. He missed. David belted him once, twice in the jaw. With his nose streaming blood, Tim swung wildly.

The Professor did nothing. He silently watched. But a chilling smile touched the corners of his mouth.

His hand inched toward his jacket pocket.

"Run, David! *Run!*" I screamed. Catching his hand, we both plunged down the path. Our sprinting feet pounded the concrete, and an explosion made me jump. A bullet whined past my ear.

"Hurry," I gasped.

"Over here." David dragged me to the left, where he'd parked facing the wrong way, next to the curb. My flying feet tried to keep up with his long steps.

"Get in on my side!" he shouted.

Another shot exploded as David wrenched the door open. He shoved me in and I scrambled frantically across the seat. He tumbled in. He slammed the door, jammed the key in the ignition, and the car leaped off in an exploding, deafening roar.

Another shot rang out, and it pinged off David's car. The professor wasn't a good shot. Thank God.

Bent over double, and hands clasped in my lap, I squeezed my eyes shut and prayed. *Lord, please keep us safe, please keep us safe...* The words chanted over and over through my mind as we screeched across the parking lot.

A squealing skid, and David whipped onto the street. He hit the gas, shifted into third, and within seconds we'd left the dark campus behind.

My heart bumped so wildly I felt it might burst right out of my chest. Slowly, I sat up.

"You okay?" David glanced at me. His face was white.

"Yes. Are you? Did he hit you?"

"No. You?"

"No." I settled back, breathing hard, and stared out the window, watching the bright lights of businesses whip by.

A shudder gripped me as the magnitude of the last few minutes hit me.

"I can't believe it! He shot at us." A sob caught in my throat, and tears blurred my vision. "He tried to kill us!"

"He didn't succeed." Only the grim, white slash of his high cheekbones showed how shaken he was.

"How can I go back to his class?" The bizarre question struck me.

"You won't."

"But how will I graduate? I need that class! I can't afford an F."

"That's not important now, Kay!" He sounded angry. "We'll call the police when we get to your house."

Tears ran down my face. David was right, but all I could think about was my professor. He'd tried to kill us! I couldn't believe it.

At last, we pulled up in front of my house.

I dashed the tears away with a trembling hand and climbed out. My legs felt wobbly. I leaned against the car after I'd closed the door.

"You okay?" David's angry, clenching jaw relaxed a bit.

"Yes." I swept a quivering hand under my eyes.

"I'm sorry I yelled at you." His eyes flashed. "I want to punch that guy's lights out."

"I wish that would solve everything."

"Me, too." He looked at me. "You ready to go in?"

"Yes." I pushed away from the car, and was grateful when he put his arm around me. My trembling, jelly legs felt like they might collapse without warning.

Mom looked up from the couch as we stepped inside. When she saw my face, her hand flew to her mouth.

"Oh my heavens, what happened?" she screamed.

Dad and Theresa ran into the room.

"Someone shot at us." David said bluntly. "Kay needs to sit down, and I need to call the police."

"My word! Oh, my goodness!"

"I'll call the police." Dad's footsteps thundered back down the hall.

David sat beside me on the couch and my family hovered, peppering us with questions. Long minutes after we'd finished telling the story, a policeman finally arrived. Then we had to tell it all over again. I felt calmer by then.

"Any injuries?" The sergeant flicked a glance over us.

"Randy choked me." I pointed to my throat, which hurt. Was it red? Did it show Randy's finger marks?

He shot it a disinterested glance. "Property damage?"

"A bullet hit my car."

He scribbled.

"And they stole my flash drive."

"*Mmmhm*. You say shots were fired?"

"Three."

"Description of gunman? Or name?"

David turned to me. "I don't know. I didn't get a good look at him."

I rattled off the Professor's name and description, and Tim and Randy's for good measure, too.

The police officer looked at his list. "Stolen flash drive. Minimal property damage. Shots fired. That's it?"

He sounded bored!

I stared at him, aghast. "Yes. Isn't that enough?"

He shook his head. "Sorry, miss, but this is minor. You have no serious injuries, and a cheap flash drive was stolen."

"But he tried to kill us!" I gasped.

"But he didn't. Look, miss. We'll look into assault charges. But he," he pointed to David, "may not be able to I.D. the guy who shot the gun. Without that nailed down, it's a slim case. Your word against Williams.' We'll talk to the professor. Scare him a little. But don't expect too much."

I gasped again when he slapped his notebook shut.

The officer flashed me an apologetic glance. "It's a crazy time, miss. Once, these would have been serious charges. But nowadays we're plain overworked and understaffed. If someone's not killed, or a house burned down, we can't afford to put much manpower on it."

He stood. "Sorry. I'll investigate and do what I can."

"Thank you, Officer," Mom hovered behind him as he headed toward the door. "Please, let us know what you find out."

He tipped his hat to her. "Good evening, ma'am." He raised an eyebrow at me. "Don't wander alone on campus, miss."

I leaped up when the door closed. "Surely we can do something!"

A thunderous scowl knotted Dad's brows. "Apparently it's up to us to protect our own families!" He stomped for the back of the house.

Looking a little shell-shocked, Mom said, "Can I get either of you something to drink? You've been through such an ordeal. Hot chocolate?"

"I'd like some," Theresa said.

"Me, too," I agreed.

"I have to go." David levered himself up. "I need to work at the shop."

"This late?"

"Dad has an order he needs ready by tomorrow." The look he gave me said it wasn't something he wanted to do right now, either.

"Well, if you're sure." Mom hurried from the room. As Theresa slowly followed, she watched David and me over her shoulder.

"We have to do *something*." I said again. "We can't let them get away with this."

"You could write an article."

"Yes." Finally, I understood why this was the only course of action that would work. They hated me because I spoke out. I spoke the truth. That's why they had stolen my flash drive. Professor Williams was afraid.

He knew if I told the clear, unvarnished truth, it could destroy his hate group. After all, I had an inside exclusive—as far as I knew, the only one in the country.

My article would expose their evil deeds to the light. It was the only possible way to defeat them right now. What was the old saying? "The pen is mightier than the sword."

My cheeks flushed with excitement. "That is *exactly* what I will do!"

"You sure you're okay, Chickadee?"

"Yes." As I looked up into his concerned brown eyes, thoughts of my article fled. Other images; warm, sharp and clear rushed to fill my mind. David. How he'd insisted on driving me to school. And insisted on picking me up.

"Thank you for rescuing me."

"My pleasure."

Our eyes locked for an inexplicably long moment, and my heart beat faster. I couldn't look away. I didn't want to.

I swallowed hard.

Stop it. What was wrong with me?

Out of the corner of my eye, David slowly reached up and tucked a lock of hair behind my ear. The breath caught in my throat as I stared up at him. I felt vividly aware of his warm fingers, lingering behind my ear. Softly, he stroked the strands of hair that lay against my jaw. I could barely breathe.

"Things have turned awfully serious awful fast," he murmured.

Was he talking about the attack? The hate group? Or us?

My mouth felt dry. "Maybe...maybe we're finally seeing things clearly."

He considered this, and slowly, his hand dropped. I gulped in a breath. My heart felt like it was squeezing out of rhythm. Why had he touched me like that?

He picked up his jacket from the couch. "Guess I should get going." His voice sounded funny.

I slid a surreptitious glance at him as we walked to the door. My nerves jumped like Fourth of July sparklers. *Stop it,* I told myself. What was wrong with me? Nothing had happened. Had it?

Shrugging on his navy jacket, David put a hand on the door knob. He sounded suddenly awkward. "By the way, have you talked to Trent yet?"

"No. I wanted to, but I couldn't. At least, not yet. Maybe on Monday."

"Are you okay...with that?"

"Yes. Definitely better than on Tuesday." I tentatively reminded him of our conversation in my car. What had he meant then? What did he feel for me now? Suddenly, I desperately needed to know.

He flashed me a sudden, warm smile. "I'm glad." He hesitated, as if wanting to say more, but a glance over my head at the clock on the wall made him turn the knob.

His dark eyes touched my face once more, and lingered. "Could we talk, do you think? On Sunday?"

My heart leaped, but I suddenly felt shy. I tried not to let it show. "I'd like that."

"Good." His familiar grin gentled. "I'll look forward to it."

"Bye." I watched his dark form merge with the shadows.

David. A warm glow filled me. After closing the door, I leaned against it and shut my eyes. I felt afraid to touch the shimmering promise—afraid it might disintegrate into fairy dust beneath my fingertips.

"Looks like you've found your Prince Charming." Theresa spoke from across the room.

"What?"

But Theresa only smiled and said nothing.

SATURDAY

The phone rang constantly all morning, and neighbors pounded on our door, furious that we would hold church services in our house tomorrow. The louder ones insisted that the neighborhood wasn't zoned for churches.

Finally, Dad slammed the door in the face of a particularly insistent lady. Then he yanked it open again.

"Is there a zone for free speech?" he shouted. The whole house shuddered when he slammed the door again.

"I'm sorry, Dad."

"It's all right, honey. I didn't know we lived near such bigots. And against the church!" Shaking his head, Dad stomped into the kitchen. "Don't open the door again."

He took the phone off the hook. After that, the afternoon passed quietly.

At two o'clock, I girded up my courage and drove to school. I made myself walk past the gnarled oak tree.

It looked serene and peaceful in the cloudy afternoon sunlight, with the dark green leaves shimmering in the cool breeze. I saw no sign of my terrifying struggle.

I scanned the grass for spent bullet cartridges, but found none. Maybe the police had already picked them up. Right. Like maybe they'd arrested Professor Williams, too.

Luckily, I found a free computer in Kale Hall. The lab hummed with activity. Papers rustled, and people murmured in low voices. The noises comforted me. I never wanted to be alone in that lab again.

Professor Williams had erased all of my files, but I didn't care. I didn't need them, because I wouldn't be attending his class any longer. I had decided that this morning.

My *Register* article needed a quick half hour of research, which I'd do on the school's article databases. I'd decided to sketch out the background of hate crimes across America, and then focus on Truesdale and specific incidents which had occurred here. *Register* readers liked to read about local problems, so most of the piece would consist of eyewitness accounts.

I quickly outlined my article. It was chilling. But would it inspire law enforcement to intervene? I must get their attention. It was the only way to stop the Professor.

At home, I typed up the article on my computer, and for once in my life, the words flowed effortlessly. It might be the best piece I've ever written.

I thought about David a lot, too, later that afternoon as I stared out the window. Dark clouds bunched overhead, shrouding the world in soft, pearly gray light.

Was I imagining that things were changing between us? A dance. A few glances. A few words that could easily mean anything at all.

I touched "save" for the final draft of my article, and rested my chin in my palm. How did I feel about him? Was I in love with him?

But hadn't I just imagined myself in love with Trent? Well, in "crush," maybe.

A bit of melancholy lingered when I thought about Trent. Finally, however, I was ready to forgive and forget.

But setting things right regarding Trent didn't clear up my feelings for David. What were they, exactly? Friendship, of course, but what else?

I'd made a mistake with Trent. I didn't want to make another one with David. He was my best friend, and I wanted to be very, very careful.

Were my feelings for David new? Or had they been there all along?

I remembered how upset I'd felt when Theresa kept insisting she had a "date" with David. And later, when David drove Theresa home several hours after bowling had finished, I'd wondered where they had been, and if David felt something for her. The idea had bothered me. A lot. Trent's kiss had left me empty that night. And I'd snapped at Theresa.

Yes. I *had* been jealous.

That was when I'd begun to emotionally retreat from Trent, too. Finally, I'd begun to see beyond my superficial attraction to Trent. It had been exciting and sizzling at first, but quickly burned up, because nothing existed to sustain the relationship. It had been a fantasy. Nothing more.

Pictures of my church college group slid across my computer's screensaver. My gaze lingered on David. I cared deeply for him. I always had. He was my best friend...and maybe more.

My heart filled with the unexpected rush of pure joy I'd felt ever since he'd told me I was beautiful—ever since the possibility of *us* had opened up in my mind. And just being with him now...something was different.

It felt so natural. So right. As if is my heart had been waiting, nurtured and protected in a safe cocoon for David all along. And now the beautiful butterfly was breaking free. I could barely touch the wonder of it, and at last I knew the truth.

I loved David. I always had.

Did he love me, too?

"Kay! Listen to this," Dad bellowed from the den.

"What?" I slipped inside the room, licking ice cream off my spoon.

"Woodward's just offered a full apology to your church."

"Really?" The television screen focused on Oak Woodward, who stood behind a podium, mouthing silent words. Mick Murray's voice gave the commentary.

"After giving a full apology to Truesdale First Gospel, Woodward announced that the federal investigation against TFG has been dropped. However, he still insists that TFG is banned from the FGA organization, and they are still evicted from their church building here in town. Apparently TFG refuses to adhere to the FGA's new vision statement..." He switched to another story.

I perched on the arm of the couch. "Why did he apologize?"

Satisfaction gleamed from Dad's smile. "Media pressure. They've been ferreting around for the real truth—hoping, of course, to throw dirt on Woodward. Guess Woodward thought apologizing was the best way to cut his losses."

"At least we have our good name back."

But we were still a church adrift, without money or a church building. Woodward had accomplished his goal.

Dad stretched, and clicked off the T.V. "That made my day. Any more ice cream?"

I nodded toward the door. "I think Mom's still dishing it up."

"Winston?" Mom appeared in the doorway. Her pale face blended into her cap of silver hair. "I think someone is at the door. Would you see who it is?"

With a frown, Dad heaved himself up. I followed him, but Mom hung back.

Dad peered through the peephole. He shook his head. "No one's there."

Splat! A soft, cracking sound squished against the door.

Mom pressed trembling fingers together. "That's the same sound I've heard for the last few minutes."

Dad frowned, but as he put a hand on the door knob, a sharp *crack!* ricocheted off the living room window.

"What the..."

"Winston, be careful!" Mom cried out.

Dad hesitated, hand still resting on the knob. Then a flurry of rocks peppered the window and door, and I heard more soft *splats*.

Dad pressed his eye to the peephole again. His face turned ruddy, then purple.

"Bunch of punks!" Spinning on his heel, he darted down the hall.

"Kay! No!"

But I ignored Mom's frantic cry and peered through the peephole myself, ice cream bowl cold in my hands. A group of toughs stood on our lawn, throwing rocks, and—a white object sailed toward the door—eggs.

The motley group of toughs wore a mishmash of jeans, designer shirts, and cutoffs. Then I froze, and my heart gave a sick lurch. A quarter of the punks wore black arm bands.

Was this a warning? A protest against the church service tomorrow?

"Move, Kay." Shotgun in hand, Dad jerked open the door.

"Winston," Mom screamed.

Dad fired once into the air. The blast made me jump.

"*Get.* Scram! I see you, McCaffrey. Your parents will hear about this. Get out! Go on!" He fired again and again.

"There." Grim with satisfaction, he stepped back inside and slammed the egg yolk smeared door behind him. "Can't believe those hoodlums."

"What happened, Dad?" Theresa stood close behind Mom, her eyes round.

"Just punks acting out their parents' bigoted biases." Dad stomped down the hall and returned the gun to its lock box.

"Will they come back?"

Dad reappeared. "Not if they're smart."

We'd just been attacked, and by our neighbors, no less. Mixed in with them were a group of black-banded toughs. Luckily they weren't carrying guns, and didn't try to torch our house.

"Don't worry about it." Dad settled down in the living room, looking remarkably calm. "I have everything under control."

But I was upset.

I'd just put my family in danger. For I knew the black banded toughs had only come because of my church; and indirectly, because of me. I had to get that article to the *Register* as quickly as possible. Maybe tomorrow morning.

"Was that *egg* on the door?" Theresa's lips twisted in disgust. "Yes."

Mom turned to Dad. "Winston, that will be *impossible* to scrub off tomorrow," she wailed. "And we're holding a church service!"

Dad stood. "I'll clean it up."

Mom seemed to gather her wits, and turned toward the kitchen. "I'll help."

"No." Dad's tone brooked no argument. He did, however, allow her to assemble the necessary cleaning supplies for him.

Fingers pressed to her lips, Mom watched Dad lug a pail of soapy water and sponges outside. She clutched my arm when I moved to join him. "No. You can't go out. It's too dangerous."

"But we could clean it twice as fast."

"No." The door clicked closed.

We waited silently, not speaking our fears. The soft swish, swish, of suds washed down the door. Mom wouldn't let us go near the pitted window. She was afraid the hoodlums would come back...with guns. So was I.

Lord, please protect us.

After a small eternity, Dad returned inside. His feet were wet, and his forearms dripped suds. "That'll do it," he said grimly. "I'll replace the window next week."

Silently, we gathered in the kitchen. Dad washed up, and Mom pulled a pack of playing cards from a drawer. We played Hearts. But our ears strained for any sound coming from the living room. We wondered when, and if, the hoodlums would return.

SUNDAY

"*ARE YOU COMING TO THE SERVICE?*" Running lightly down the stairs, I glanced at Theresa over my shoulder. She wore jeans, a frothy pink blouse and flats today. I wore flats too, and a soft, rose colored dress. Both were nice, but casual.

She arched a brow. "I guess so. It *is* in my own house."

We entered the living room.

Bright sunshine streamed through the picture window. It was a brand new day, sparkling with hope and promise. Even the pits in the window barely seemed noticeable this morning.

Last night's events seemed like a dark, distant memory, from another time and place. The hoodlums hadn't come back, and I thanked God for that. He had protected us. Again.

"Watch out," Dad ordered. He and Pastor Warner shuffled by, lugging a couch to the den. The Warners had arrived at seven o'clock this morning to help us set up for the church service. Mom had been baking coffee cakes since eight. It was nine-thirty now.

The doorbell rang.

"I'll get it." I hurried for the door.

"Hi!" Bobby and Laura greeted me with bright smiles. Bobby motioned toward a white truck parked out front. "We got the chairs. Want me to start carrying them in?"

"Uh," I glanced over my shoulder. "They're still clearing out the furniture."

"Great. I'll help." They both came inside.

"Hi, Joyce!" Laura waved to Joyce, who had just emerged from the kitchen.

The doorbell rang. "I'll get it." I twisted it open again.

Flashing dark eyes smiled down at me, and my heart skipped a beat. "Hey, Funsize," David grinned. "Need bulletins? Got them hot off the presses."

"At least they're not pink," I returned with a twinkle in my eyes. The folded papers stacked in his hand were printed on beige paper.

His grin widened. "Pink is just for special occasions."

"David," Pastor Warner bellowed. "Is that you? We need an extra pair of hands in here."

"Duty calls." David brushed by, but his gaze briefly scanned my dress. "You look nice. Is that new?"

"No." I smiled, and warmth stained my cheeks. "But thank you."

His eyes lingered on me for another second, and then, with a small smile, he turned to help the other men in the living room.

Almost everyone had dressed casually, I noticed, darting into the kitchen. All of the men wore jeans. David wore a dark brown shirt with clean, crisp lines. It matched his eyes.

Shaking myself mentally, I entered the kitchen. It was a mad house, with too many cooks in the kitchen. I helped Laura set up the serving counter while Mom, Joyce and Mrs. Warner dashed about. Joyce made iced tea, Mrs. Warner primed a huge coffee urn, and Mom pulled cake pans from the oven. The rich, full smell of cinnamon and sweet bread permeated the air.

As the clock ticked closer to ten o'clock, I headed out to the living room and set up the folding chairs the guys brought in. Theresa and Joyce helped. At the far end of the room, David assembled the sound equipment Pastor Warner had trucked over.

When we finished, Theresa and I hovered in the foyer for a minute. "Joyce told me you dreamed about having church here." Her voice was hesitant. "Is that true?"

"Yes."

"Neat." Theresa fell silent.

Before I knew it, it was ten minutes until eleven, and people streamed in the door. I recognized a few familiar faces, but most were new people, whom I'd never seen before. The noise of chatting people rose steadily in volume.

"Hi! Glad you could make it." I grinned at Mitch and ushered him in.

He glanced around with a smile. "Pretty crowded," he boomed.

"I hope there'll be enough room for everyone." In my wildest dreams, I'd never expected so many people. Especially after yesterday's unpleasant hassle with our neighbors.

"I'm sure there will be." He sauntered off, pushed by a stream of people sweeping through the front door.

Bobby and David served as ushers. The seats filled up rapidly. I wondered if I'd be able to find a place to sit later.

At five after eleven the influx slowed to a trickle, and people rustled, taking the remaining seats. Pastor Warner stood at the microphone, and I glanced around, wondering where to sit.

"Kay." David motioned from the far left aisle. I saw a free chair beside him. He sat in the aisle seat.

I stepped over. Happiness bubbled up in me. "Thanks."

"No problem."

While Pastor Warner read the announcements, I scanned the crowd and saw Mom, Dad, and Theresa. And Mitch. Happiness grew, and I shot a smiling glance toward the rafters.

Thank you, Lord. And thank you for giving me that dream. Thank you that there really is enough room for everyone!

David slipped forward to play guitar, and Laura led the singing. Then he ducked back to sit beside me as Pastor took the podium.

""As it was in the days of Noah, so it will be at the coming of the Son of Man. For in the days before the flood, people were eating, drinking, marrying and giving in marriage, up to the day Noah entered the ark; and they knew nothing about what would happen until the flood came and took them all away. That is how it will be at the coming of the Son of Man."" (Matthew 24:37-39)

Pastor looked at us. "That is how it will be at the coming of the Son of Man. That's my topic this morning. Jesus' second coming. When will it be? Will it be soon? Will we have any warning?

"I answer 'yes' to the last question. Jesus gave us signs to look for which would signal his second coming. Turn to Matthew twenty-four, verses seven through eight. Let me paraphrase.

"There will be wars and rumors of wars, nation will rise against nation and kingdom against kingdom. There will be famines and earthquakes. And Luke twenty-one includes pestilences, which are fatal epidemic diseases, in the list. All of these are the beginning of birth pains."

He looked up. "We all know what birth pains are like. Some of us know better than others." He smiled when a few women tittered, and then he turned serious again.

"When a woman begins labor, her pains are few and far apart, but as the hour of her delivery nears, her pains increase in intensity and frequency, don't they? Jesus said that's what it will be like at the time of his second coming."

He touched his Bible. "All the signs—national unrest and war, famines, earthquakes, pestilences—they're all happening now, aren't they? And no one can deny that over the last few decades they've all become dramatically worse. We can barely turn on the television without hearing of wars going on some-where in the world—or disasters—one after another, striking our planet. We know this personally, too." He looked around.

"We've experienced disasters of our own recently. Earthquakes, floods and diseases. I could go on and on."

He stepped away from the podium. "Perhaps some of you say, there's hope on the horizon. At least on the world front.

"Peace. That's what we hear whispering through the news, isn't it? Will this secret peace plan finally bring an answer to all of our world's problems?"

We waited. I probably could have heard a pin drop. "I tell you..." He flipped through his Bible.

"'...for you know very well that the day of the Lord will come like a thief in the night. While people are saying, "Peace and safety," destruction will come on them suddenly, as labor pains on a pregnant woman, and they will not escape. But you, brothers, are not in darkness so that this day should surprise you like a thief.'" (1 Thessalonians 5:2-4)

"Peace? Maybe for a while. But things will continue to get worse up to, and through the Great Tribulation. And yes, I'm convinced the Tribulation isn't far off. Things will continue to get worse—much worse—until Jesus returns at the end of the Tribulation."

A sudden, electric sort of tension hummed in the room. People listened intently, as if hungrily devouring his words. As if they nourished their very souls.

Pastor Warner's eyes looked grave. "Some of you may ask, 'What is this Great Tribulation you're talking about, Pastor?' That's simple. It will be a horrible time when God pours out His judgment on mankind. And it will be a time when man will be terribly wicked and depraved, and totally reject God; at least, most people will.

"I don't want to live through a time that horrible. Do you?"

I shook my head, as did those around me.

"Good. Because Christians have a hope of escaping it. Turn to Luke twenty-one, verse thirty-six.

"'"Be always on the watch, and pray that you may be able to escape all that is about to happen, and that you may be able to stand before the Son of Man."'

"What does this mean? When I match it with other scriptures, I believe it means that Jesus will rapture up every Christian on Earth just before the Tribulation starts.

"Paul talks in First Corinthians fifteen about the day when those of us who aren't asleep—who aren't dead—will be changed. And the dead will be raised. We'll be translated out of our mortal bodies into immortal bodies in an instant. In the twinkling of an eye, Paul says. That's a blessed hope, isn't it friends? Would you like to escape the Tribulation and be instantly translated to be with God?"

I nodded, but noticed that most people just stared at Pastor Warner, as if hearing these words for the first time. I didn't know most of them. Were they Christians, or not? The unexpected question filled me with a curious excitement. Had God called unbelievers to hear his Word on this unusual Sunday?

"...I believe that God has been warning us in recent years. Earthquakes, and many other disasters, large and small, have occurred. I believe there's a purpose to these disasters. I believe we should view them as a warning to repent, for the time is short. God is merciful and long suffering, but there is only so long he will wait."

With a sigh, Pastor put down his Bible, and stared into the audience, meeting us eye for eye. "I feel deep in my spirit, folks, that the Tribulation is about to begin. Where do you want to spend the next seven years? Where do you want to spend eternity?

"Here's the message for today: God is loving! Won't you turn to him today? He is standing at the door to your heart and knocking right this minute."

He paged through his Bible.

""For God so loved the world that he gave his one and only Son, that whoever believes in him shall not perish but have eternal life. For God did not send his Son into the world to condemn the world, but to save the world through him. Whoever believes in him is not condemned, but whoever does not believe stands condemned already because he has not believed in the name of God's one and only Son.

""This is the verdict: Light has come into the world, but men loved darkness instead of light because their deeds were evil. Everyone who does evil hates the light, and will not come into the light for fear that his deeds will be exposed. But whoever lives by the truth comes into the light, so that it may be seen plainly that what he has done has been done through God."'" (John 3:16-21)

"Jesus said, "'I tell you the truth, whoever hears my word and believes him who sent me has eternal life and will not be condemned; he has crossed over from death to life.'" (John 5:24)

""""Here I am! I stand at the door and knock. If anyone hears my voice and opens the door, I will come in and eat with him, and he with me."'"" (Revelation 3:20)

Pastor stared at us, his face ruddy and earnest. "I say, turn away from your sin! Believe that Jesus died for your sins. Ask forgiveness for your sins. Ask him to come into your heart and be Lord of your life. And those of you who are Christians already, but have fallen away from the Lord... Repent! Return to Jesus, who is your first love.

"Jesus is Lord! And I believe in my spirit that he is coming very soon."

"Even so come, Lord Jesus," I whispered.

Pastor Warner said, "Those of you who don't know Jesus, please come forward now. I'd like to pray for you. God wants to give you eternal life. He wants to raise you up at the last day."

A few people shuffled to their feet and slowly moved forward.

Tears glistened in Pastor Warner's eyes. "Thank you, Lord Jesus. Thank you. And those of you who recently gave your life to Christ, or who want to rededicate your life to him, please come forward, too. We have plenty of room. Please come forward."

More people moved forward. Mom joined them, and then Dad, too. Tears filled my eyes and overflowed. *Thank you, Lord! Thank you.* I sniffed. David's arm went around my shoulders and he held me close, comforting me.

I wiped my wet face with my palms.

"Here." David handed me his handkerchief.

I blotted my face dry with it, and stared over the edge at my parents, and scores more who knelt at the front of the room. *Thank you, Lord!* Fresh tears sprang to my eyes, but I pressed the cloth to my eyelids, soaking them up.

As Pastor prayed over them, a thought rang in my mind, as clear as a bell. How lucky they were. They could still hear the word of truth. It was so clear now. During the Tribulation people would be confused by all of the lying signs and wonders the Beast and False Prophet would do.

But even then God would send witnesses.

After Pastor Warner finished praying, I quietly flipped my Bible open to Revelation 11:3-6. I didn't know why, but these words were burning in me. I had to read them again.

"And I will give power to my two witnesses, and they will prophesy for 1,260 days, clothed in sackcloth." These are the two olive trees and the two lampstands that stand before the Lord of the earth. If anyone tries to harm them, fire comes from their mouths and devours their enemies. This is how anyone who wants to harm them must die. These men have power to shut up the sky so that it will not rain during the time they are prophesying; and they have power to turn the waters into blood and to strike the earth with every kind of plague as often as they want.

The two witnesses would warn Israel and the world to repent. Would they be the ones to warn Christians and others not to take the mark of the beast, too? The Bible said an angel would warn them. Somehow, Christians would be warned.

Revelation 14:9-13:

...A third angel followed them and said in a loud voice: "If anyone worships the beast and his image and receives his mark on the forehead or on the hand, he, too, will drink of the wine of God's fury, which has been poured full strength into the cup of his wrath. He will be tormented with burning sulfur in the presence of the holy angels and of the Lamb. And the smoke of their torment rises for ever and ever. There is no rest day or night for those who worship the beast and his image, or for anyone who receives the mark of his name." This calls for patient endurance on the part of the saints who obey God's commandments and remain faithful to Jesus.

Then I heard a voice from heaven say, "Write: Blessed are the dead who die in the Lord from now on."

"Look." David jogged my arm. I closed my Bible and looked up. People streamed back to their seats. And then I saw Trent.

I went still. What was he doing here? Had he just accepted Jesus into his heart? His dark blue gaze met mine, and then he sat down a few rows in front of us. I didn't know what to think.

Pastor spoke, his voice vibrant. "May the Lord bless you! Thank you for coming. Please stick around for refreshments and coffee. I'll stay up here if anyone wants to talk. You're dismissed."

When Trent stood again and slipped into the aisle, I rose and scooted out to meet him. I felt compelled to confront him. I needed to tell him that I forgave him.

"Hi." His gaze met mine. He spoke before I could. "I'm sorry, Kay." He moved toward the wall, out of the flow of exiting people, and I followed him. I opened my mouth.

"Don't say anything." He took a deep breath. "I had this all memorized, just how I wanted to say it. I'm really sorry I hurt you, Kay. I'm sorry I used you." One neatly clad shoulder moved. "I do like you. A lot. I have from the beginning. But maybe not in the way I was pretending."

His aristocratic nose pinched white, and he swallowed. "I've felt rotten ever since Monday. Remember how I kept insisting I was an okay guy? That I wasn't sinful, like you kept trying to tell me? Well, I realized on Monday that I'm the scum of the earth. I need to be forgiven. By God. And by you. Will you ever...?"

"Oh, Trent." Tears filled my eyes, and I hugged him. Hesitantly, his arms went around me, then he hugged me tight, too. I felt like a great weight suddenly lifted from my shoulders. "I've already forgiven you."

When I pulled away, I smiled up at him. "Actually, God worked things out for the best. Maybe we both needed a jolt so we would see the truth."

"You mean so I would find God." His eyes twinkled down at me. His smile faded. "Thank you, Kay. I can honestly say the day I met you in the journalism lab was the day that changed my life."

Laughing, I said, "Maybe that's a stretch."

He smiled, and gave my hand a brief squeeze. "I heard what happened on Friday with Professor Williams."

My happiness dimmed a little. "I wrote that article for the *Register*. I plan to give it to them today."

"Really? I'm going over now. I could bring it for you. Do you have it on a flash drive?"

"Yes." I smiled. Trent would make sure the article was published right away. Maybe even tomorrow. Could this be the beginning of the end for my professor's hate group—and would it mean safety for my family and church? "Can you wait a second? I'll get it."

I dashed off and quickly returned, pushing my way back through the crowd, and handed him the flash drive. "Thank you. I sure appreciate it."

"It's the least I can do." He grinned down at me, and then, with a brief squeeze of my shoulder, headed for the door. Smiling, I watched him disappear. Happiness glowed in my heart. *Thank you, Lord!*

"Kay?" Mitch's voice made me whirl. He glanced at Trent's retreating back. "I see you guys made up."

"We're friends again."

"Good." He handed me a rolled up paper. His black eyes looked intense and bright. "I wanted to give you this. You can keep it, if you want. It's another one of those pictures. I want to know what you think about it."

I made a movement to unroll it.

"No." He shook his head. "I have a job to go to now. Could we get together on Monday?"

"How about lunch in the union?"

"Sounds great." He made a movement to brush by me, but hesitated. "I liked your pastor's sermon. Very thought provoking." Then he was gone.

I felt overwhelmed. The Lord was working in mighty ways today. All of my closest friends had come. Except for Mary. I scanned the dissipating crowd, and a weight settled on my heart. I didn't see her.

Week Eight — Rapture

I declare to you, brothers,
that flesh and blood cannot inherit the kingdom of God,
nor does the perishable inherit the imperishable.
Listen, I tell you a mystery:
We will not all sleep, but we will all be changed—
in a flash, in the twinkling of an eye, at the last trumpet.
For the trumpet will sound, the dead will be raised imperishable,
and we will be changed.

1 CORINTHIANS 15:50-52

FUTURE

ISOLA'S HEART pounded so hard she felt it might burst from her chest. Her mind could only focus on one thing. Christians had been warned not to take the mark of the Beast! She'd just heard that on the radio. And Kay's diary had just mentioned the same thing. She'd quoted a scripture from Revelation.

Trembling, Isola's fingers flipped to the end of the Bible. *Revelation* was written in dark, bold letters on the last chapter. She would read that book. But first, she had to finish Kay's diary. Only a few pages remained in the file.

Sunday — still

Today has been a fresh new beginning. It only seemed right to make it the first day of my journal's new week, instead of Wednesday, which I've used lately.

After everyone had gone home from the church service, we cleaned up. We carted chairs out to Bobby's truck, moved the living room furniture back, and cleaned up the paper plates and crumbs left behind.

I'd changed into jeans and a new, soft gray sweatshirt with "Truesdale State" written across it in dark blue lettering. I'd also stashed the picture Mitch gave me in my room. I would look at it later. Right now, controlled chaos reigned downstairs.

Finally, the last trash bag was lugged outside, and the large coffee urn wedged into the Warners' family sedan.

Mrs. Warner stood on the stoop, wiping straggling red hair from her bright blue eyes. "We'd like you all to come over for lunch. I have stew simmering in a crock pot, and lots of French bread."

The Warners had already cleaned up their vandalized house. Joyce reported that they didn't have much furniture left, but they wanted to continue living as they had before. And that meant opening up their home to others.

"That sounds wonderful." Mom looked wistful.

With a smile, Mrs. Warner touched her arm. "It's only fair. You opened up your home to us. Please come."

"Well. All right." Mom smiled, and went in search of Dad.

I perched on the back of a living room couch, watching as Bobby, Laura and Pastor headed outside.

Mrs. Warner poked her head back in. "David? You know you're welcome, too."

David looked up from the far corner of the living room, where he clicked the locks shut on his guitar case. "Okay. Thanks. Maybe I will for a while. Dad wants me at the shop in an hour."

Mrs. Warner smiled. "You're welcome to eat and run." She looked up as Mom, Dad and Theresa approached, trailed by Joyce. "You all coming?"

At Mom's quick nod, she smiled again. "Good."

"Coming, Kay?" Joyce asked. She was the last one to file out the door, and I realized I was about to be left behind. I glanced at David, who stood now, guitar case in hand.

"Yes," I said, and locked the door behind us.

As I followed the group down the walk, David tossed over his shoulder, "Want to catch a ride with me, Kay?"

"Okay. Thanks." I couldn't contain my happy smile.

David unlocked his sports car, and I slipped inside and buckled up. The car interior felt toasty warm in the bright, sunshiny clear day. The old, familiar smells settled lightly around me, like a comfortable cocoon.

A cool blast of air entered the car when David opened his door and pushed the seat forward to place his guitar in the back seat. Flipping it back again, he angled his tall body in beside me, and started the engine while buckling up at the same time.

Somehow, even though we'd done this scores of times before, it seemed oddly intimate, with just the two of us sitting together in the warm car. We were alone.

A few nerves licked through me as David placed his arm on the back of my seat and looked over his shoulder so he could see to back up and pull out of the parking space. Bobby's white truck blocked us in ahead.

We eased free and slid into the sparse traffic on State. Light tension tickled between us. And an odd closeness. I wanted to talk. There was so much to say.

I glanced at his dear, familiar profile, and drank in his dark, rumpled hair, black slash of brows, dark brown eyes, high cheekbones, and straight, usually smiling mouth. My gaze returned to his eyes. Very expressive eyes. Communicating laughter, seriousness...tenderness.

Sensing my gaze, he glanced at me. He looked serious for a second, and then smiled. "That was a tremendous service, wasn't it?"

"Yes. It was." I settled back. "I still can't believe how many people gave their lives to Jesus. Dad. Trent..."

"Did you guys work everything out?"

"Yes."

He did not look at me, but drove intently, with fierce concentration. His next question sounded offhand. "Do you plan to date him again? Now that he's a Christian."

"No."

I looked at him and said again, "No. He's not who I'm looking for. He never was."

"Oh?" He glanced at me, and turned onto the street where Joyce lived. The block in front of her house was already parked up, so we slid into a space down the street. He turned off the engine. We sat in silence for long moments.

It felt as though a thick, unspoken current of words flowed between us. Each of us was afraid to speak first; afraid to upset the delicate balance of our friendship.

Was it worth it, I wondered suddenly. What if something went wrong? I couldn't bear to lose David as my friend.

He gave an abrupt laugh and rubbed his palms on his jeans. "Guess I have something to tell you."

"What?" I turned to him. I couldn't look away. My heart beat hard.

"I..." he took a deep breath and met my gaze. "Well, I kind of have...feelings for you, Kay. More than friendship, I mean."

I drew a quick breath. My eyes suddenly misted.

His shoulders straightened, as if self-conscious. And nervous. "Maybe you've already figured that out, by the way I acted so jealous around Trent."

I shook my head.

"Anyway," his dark eyes would not let me go. "I wanted you to know." He drew a harsh, fortifying breath. "I care about you, Kay. A lot. Much more than as a friend. And I have for a long time."

Joy rushed through my heart.

Before I could speak, he continued, "I wanted to tell you this a long time ago, but never found the right time. Then you started dating Trent."

He swallowed. "I tried to kid myself that I didn't care. But that was a lie. It bothered me a lot. Way too much. I couldn't ignore it. And then," pain twisted in his voice, "I saw him kiss you. That night I drove Theresa home."

I saw the torment in his eyes before he glanced down. He rubbed his palms across his jeans again. "I couldn't deny it anymore. My feelings for you go a lot deeper than just friendship."

His gaze met mine again, very dark with emotion. "Anyway, the plain and simple fact is, I love you, Kay. With my whole heart."

My heart felt so full of joy that I could barely speak. "David."

He cleared his throat. "I feel like something's changed between us recently. Has it? Are you ready...do you want...I know you've had feelings for Trent. You must be pretty confused right now." The hope in his eyes turned bleak.

"No." I took his hand. "I'm not confused at all. In fact, finally I'm able to see clearly for the first time. I had a crush on Trent. It wasn't anything more. Except for maybe a new friendship."

"We're friends, too."

"Yes." My heart pounded painfully hard. Fear mixed with the joy soaring through my soul. Now it was my turn to tell him how I felt. I'd never run away from a challenge before, and wasn't about to now, either. This was so terribly, vitally important to me that I felt overcome by the wonder of it.

"Yes, we're friends." I took an unsteady breath, and gripped his hand tighter. "First and foremost."

I paused awkwardly, trying to gather the strength to lay my soul bare. "This week, I finally realized how blind I've been. My feelings for you are so much bigger than... I can't even explain. I care about you so much. With my whole heart. More than as a friend, even though you're a great friend! Goofy sometimes..." I smiled shakily. "You mean so much to me. I love every minute we spend together." I took a deep breath. "I love you, too, David."

His eyes flashed, and his hand squeezed mine tight. "I wish I'd had the guts to tell you sooner. Before Trent." His voice sounded rough.

"Maybe we weren't ready," I said softly.

"Maybe not."

His dark gaze caught mine, pulling me closer. I did love him. Deeply and completely. And I had for a long time. Why hadn't I seen it?

My mind could barely touch the wonder of it. David. My best friend. And more.

Tears welled in my eyes.

"Don't cry." Tenderly, David pulled out his hanky. "Do you need this?"

"No." Laughing, I shook my head and blinked rapidly. "I'm just happy."

"Me, too." His hands tightened on mine, and his voice deepened. "Can I kiss you? I've wanted to for about a million years."

"That's a long time!" I wouldn't let the tears wobble over my lids. I wouldn't.

His gaze was suddenly serious now, and intense. And infinitely tender. My eyes closed, and a tear rolled down my cheek, but I paid no attention to it as I leaned into his kiss.

His lips were gentle and tender, and his kiss drew a response from deep within me. Wild, sweet joy slipped through me. My heart pounded so hard I felt it might burst right out of my chest. Why hadn't I realized this before? Why had I wasted so much time with Trent? Why hadn't I listened to God? How much time had we lost?

After another kiss he pulled away, his breaths uneven, and dark eyes flashing in a startled, bemused smile. "Wow."

My lips trembled into a smile, and I sat back in my seat. Joy bubbled in my soul. I felt so intensely, incredibly happy. I didn't want this close connection between us to ever end.

But then I had only to look at his special smile, just for me, and I knew it would never end. The bond between us went deeper than either of us would ever know. I knew that the Lord had drawn us together, and I could only believe that that would always remain true.

I squeezed his hand. Returning the pressure, he reluctantly touched the door latch.

"Guess we should go in. Before they send out a search party."

"Good idea." With a laugh, I reluctantly made an attempt to pull my hand from his. His grip tightened for a fleeting moment, making me look up.

"Could I see you later? I get off at seven." He looked oddly vulnerable, and hopeful.

"Yes." I smiled. "I would like that. A lot."

"Good." He hesitated, and gently let my hand go. "A little after seven, then?"

My lips trembled up in affirmation.

His dark eyes flashed with sudden, intense tenderness, and he leaned forward. His lips touched mine again, gently, briefly.

"I'll be looking forward to it, Kay."

I sat at my desk, still smiling. I hadn't stopped smiling all day. I felt overwhelmed by everything the Lord had done. Dad had given his life to Christ. Trent had, too. Mom was a Christian. Why had so many people come to the Lord today? I didn't know, but more tears of joy filled my eyes.

And David...tears slipped down my cheeks. *I don't deserve this, Lord. Why have you given me so much?* I was grateful. Humbly grateful, and as I lifted the eyes of my spirit to the Lord, I felt his love wash gently over me. He loved me. Always. *Thank you, Lord.*

My mind returned to Pastor Warner's sermon. The Tribulation. The Rapture. If there ever was a time I was ready for the Rapture to happen, it would be now. All of my family had been saved—except for Theresa. That nail poked a hole in my spirit. Would she ever believe?

I thought about the bright hope of the Rapture. It could happen any day now. I was ready to be whisked to Jesus' side. That would be the most wonderful thing in the world. My family would be there. My friends. And David, too. My eyes stung. I'd like more time with him here on this Earth. But the Lord knew best.

My mind returned to Pastor Warner's sermon again. His words had struck a deep chord in my heart today. The Tribulation would start very soon. I felt sure of that, too. What about the Rapture? Would it really happen before the Tribulation? I fervently wanted to believe this, because, like Joyce, I didn't want to live through the Tribulation. But I had never researched the idea for myself.

I reached for a prophecy book and my thin, tan Bible.

1 Thessalonians 4:16-17:

For the Lord himself will come down from heaven, with a loud command, with the voice of the archangel and with the trumpet call of God, and the dead in Christ will rise first. After that, we who are still alive and are left will be caught up together with them in the clouds to meet the Lord in the air. And so we will be with the Lord forever.

1 Corinthians 15:50-53:

I declare to you, brothers, that flesh and blood cannot inherit the kingdom of God, nor does the perishable inherit the imperishable. Listen, I tell you a mystery: We will not all sleep, but we will all be changed—in a flash, in the twinkling of an eye, at the last trumpet. For the trumpet will sound, the dead will be raised imperishable, and we will be changed. For the perishable must clothe itself with the imperishable, and the mortal with immortality.

But why should I believe that the translation of our bodies will take place before the Tribulation?

Here's one reason the prophecy book gave:

The Tribulation is when God will pour out his wrath on the earth. John says in the book of Revelation (concerning the Tribulation) that the "great day of their wrath is come" ("their" refers to the one who sits on the throne and the Lamb) (Rev. 6:17); "the wrath of God" (Rev. 15:7); "God's wrath on the earth" (Rev. 16:1), etc.

The Tribulation will be a time of God's wrath.

I turned in my Bible again.

1 Thessalonians 5:9-10:

For God did not appoint us to suffer wrath but to receive salvation through our Lord Jesus Christ. He died for us so that, whether we are awake or asleep, we may live together with him.

Luke 21:36:

Be always on the watch, and pray that you may be able to escape all that is about to happen, and that you may be able to stand before the Son of Man.

1 Thessalonians 1:10:

...and to wait for his Son from heaven, whom he raised from the dead—Jesus, who rescues us from the coming wrath.

Revelation 3:10 (To the church of Philadelphia):

"Since you have kept my command to endure patiently, I will also keep you from the hour of trial that is going to come upon the whole world to test those who live on the earth."

Those were just a few markers pointing to the Rapture of the church happening before the Tribulation begins. There would be Christians during the Tribulation too, I knew. Many, if not most—or all—would be martyred. But I wanted to believe those Christians would come to believe after the Rapture, and during the Tribulation.

I clung to the hope of escaping the Tribulation. I wondered what it would be like to be Raptured—to have my whole body changed, in the twinkling of an eye, to an immortal body. To never taste death. What an incredible privilege that would be.

My spirit quickened, just thinking about it. What could be more wonderful than being whisked up to my Lord's side, and being with him for all eternity?

"Kay?"

A knock at my door returned me to earth. The Rapture hadn't happened yet. I still lived on solid planet Earth.

"Come in."

"Hi." Hesitantly, Theresa stepped in. "Could I talk to you for a minute?"

"Of course." I twirled my chair around and Theresa perched on my bed.

"I just wanted to say I'm glad we're getting along better now. I hated it. Before."

"Me, too. I'm sorry, Theresa. It was my fault."

"No, it wasn't!"

"Yes, it was. I didn't try hard enough to be your friend. And I looked down on you for being interested in 'frivolous' things. Like clothes. I was wrong. I'm sorry."

"I'm the one who's sorry!" Theresa gasped out a laugh. "It's not your fault, Kay. I was the one putting *you* down. I was a complete snot! You know that."

"We both were pigs," I conceded. "But honestly, I still think I acted worse than you did. And I don't have any excuse, either. Except...maybe sometimes I felt like you were looking down your nose at me for my faith, and for being so involved with church, and everything."

"I was." Theresa said. "I resented you. You seemed like you had something. Even when you were down, you seemed confident. No matter how hard I tried, I couldn't find that kind of...peace, I guess. I thought finding the perfect guy would make me happy, or maybe parties would, or the right clothes, but nothing worked. Lately, I've been feeling more and more lonely—like I have a great big empty place in my heart. I resented you because you didn't feel that way, too." She sighed. "Can we be friends again?"

"I'd like that." I jumped up and hugged her tight. Then my mind flew back to this morning, when so many things had changed in my life. "How did you like the service?" I plopped back into my swivel chair.

"I liked it."

"What did you think about Pastor Warner's sermon?"

Theresa looked away. "I liked it. A lot. But I didn't want to be a part of that big cattle drive rushing to the front."

I realized what Theresa had just said. Very carefully, I said, "Do you believe that Jesus died for your sins?"

Theresa nodded her perfectly styled head, her light blue eyes sincere. "Yes. I do."

I couldn't believe what I was hearing! I pulled my Bible closer. "Can I read you something?"

At Theresa's nod, I opened to 2 Corinthians 6:2b.

"'...I tell you, now is the time of God's favor, now is the day of salvation.'" I looked up, not sure how she'd respond to my next words. "Don't let fear stop you from accepting God's free gift of salvation."

She shrugged an uncertain shoulder. "What do I have to do?"

"Do you want to accept Jesus as your Lord and Savior?"

"Yes."

Overwhelming joy welled up in my soul. "Then just pray with me, okay? Repeat these words in your heart to God. And you have to pray in faith, believing."

Theresa nodded. "Okay."

We both closed our eyes. "Lord," I said. "I am a sinner. I know no matter how hard I try I can never earn your forgiveness. But I know Jesus died on the cross for my sins. He took every one of my sins upon himself, and he paid the full penalty for all of them. Thank you, Lord, for doing that for me. Please come into my heart and be the Lord of my life. Please change me from the inside out. I want to live a life that is pleasing to you. In Jesus' name. Amen."

"Amen," Theresa murmured. When she looked up, her eyes sparkled. "What do I do now?"

"Trust that God heard you and that he has saved you. You can rest in that assurance forever.

"Also, when you become a Christian, he does something wonderful. He comes to live in your heart by his Spirit. You're a new creature in Christ. The old has passed away, and the new has come. Now you need to read his Word, pray, go to church, and follow him every day. But you won't be alone. He'll be with you, and he'll sustain you. And the body of Christ—your Christian friends—will help and support you, too."

Theresa's smile looked tremulous. "Thank you, Kay. Do you have an extra Bible I could read?"

I rummaged through my bookshelf and pulled out a thin blue paperback. "Here's a New Testament." I opened it up to the gospel of John. "This would be a good place to start. It'll tell you about Jesus, and what he did when he was on this earth."

"Thank you." Theresa clutched the book to herself, and with a final smile, stood and slipped out of the room.

I could not believe what had just happened. Theresa had given her life to Christ! And she'd chosen me to help her do it.

Thank you, Lord, I whispered. Theresa, Mom, and Dad were all saved. It was almost too wonderful to believe. God was working in a mighty way today. Even Trent had come to the Lord. What about Mitch?

Reminded of the picture he had given to me, I unrolled it and looked at it again. I didn't understand it. At least, not yet.

I folded it in half and stuck it in my Bible. I'd pray about it tonight. If there was a message in it, maybe God would tell me then.

I thought about my friends again. Everyone had come to the service today. Except for Mary.

That peculiar unease stabbed me again. Only now it was deeper, and overwhelmed me with a sense of urgency. I needed to talk to her. Now. Right away. But why?

The still, small voice inside of me spoke more insistently. Commandingly. I could not ignore it.

I would call her. I dialed the number for Mary's apartment. A busy signal. I tried again. Still a busy signal.

Go to her apartment. Talk to her face to face. The words whispered into my soul.

Talk to her now. Before it is too late.

Too late for what, I wondered, but glanced at the clock. Only five o'clock. I could go over and be back in time for dinner at six, and then David would be over at seven.

I grabbed my coat, and then found myself quickly peeking at Mitch's picture again. What did it mean?

I'm going over to Mary's now, for the Spirit is telling me time is running short.

It's so strange. Although I feel a strong urgency that I must speak to her Now, a wonderful, inexplicable peace is rushing through me, filling my heart with... Joy. Indescribable joy.

I've never felt anything like this before, and wonder, could it mean...?

FUTURE

HANDS TREMBLING, Mary Isola Campinella plucked the folded white sheet from its resting place in Kay's Bible. Almost reverently, she opened it, and pressed it flat against her knees. The last picture Mitch had drawn for Kay.

Broad, strong strokes captured the essence of a dark, rainy day. It was Kay's old neighborhood. Mitch had sketched houses, cars. A park. And a church. All looked vacant. Desolate rain slipped down their empty windows. Her gaze fell to the street dividing the foreground. Empty, except for a snake writhing down the muddy road.

Recoiling, Mary flung the drawing from her. The picture fell. Flat, open. She could not tear her eyes from it. Kay did not understand the picture, but Mary did.

It was a picture of the Rapture, when Kay, the Jameson family, Mary's mother, and all the other Christians who had declared Jesus as their Savior and Lord had been whisked away—translated to be with God—leaving Mary's world empty and desolate. And when they'd gone, the snake had come. It symbolized the evil ravaging the world now. And the Beast.

The dark clouds and pouring rain symbolized God's judgment on men living on the Earth.

Tears slipped down Mary's cheeks. A few memories slid into her mind. Kay had come over that fateful night, just as she'd written in her diary. Then, a few hours later, Kay and all the other Christians on the planet had vanished into thin air. Raptured. Just like Kay had said would happen.

Mary stumbled to her feet and stared out the open window at the silent, shadowed street below. A chill breeze made her shiver. A shadow passing over her soul?

She grabbed her heavy woolen blanket and hugged it up around her thin shoulders. But she still felt cold. Empty. And afraid.

But now she was finally ready to face the past. And the truth.

The old memories rushed in like a flood, overwhelming her mind. The first images made her gasp with pain, for she'd shut them out for so long.

But it was good.

She had to do this. She must fully face the past so she could clearly see her present, and face the future.

Jack had been furious when Kay had come over. Mary remembered standing in the living room and listening when he answered the door.

"Is Mary here? I'd like to speak to her, please."

Jack's face flushed a dull red. "Why don't you mind your own business, —— ? All you do is cause trouble!"

Rage blistered in Mary. How dare he speak to her friend like that? Wasn't it degrading and horrible enough that he treated her like a piece of trash? She would not allow him to treat Kay that way, too.

In her first flash of defiance in months, Mary hurtled her body at the door and furiously shoved it wide with her shoulder. Taken by surprise, Jack staggered backward.

"I'll talk to my friends any time I want, Jack!" Mary's face felt hot, and her lips twisted into a snarl.

Jack stared at her, and then his own lips slowly curled up. His eyes hardened into black stones. "Fine," he said in a low, sinister hiss. "You won't mind if I listen, will you?"

Her courage rapidly evaporated. "Fine," she said shortly, and slipped into the hall to join Kay. She sensed when Jack entered the hall behind her. She felt his looming, dangerous presence. But she wouldn't betray her fear. Not with Kay there.

She attempted a smile for her friend. "So? What brings you here this afternoon?"

Kay glanced at Jack. Her clear green eyes looked angry. She glanced back at Mary, and apparently decided to ignore the glowering hulk standing in the doorway.

"I don't know quite how to explain this. But have you ever felt gripped by a feeling that you *had* to do something? It's the right thing to do, but you're not sure why you should do it right this minute? But you know if you don't, someone could really get hurt. You're not even sure how, or why, but..."

"I understand," Mary interrupted. With curiosity, she said, "Is that why you're here?"

"Yes." Kay took a deep breath. "We had a great church service today about the end times, the Rapture, the Tribulation, and Jesus' second coming. Basically, God will judge the earth during the Tribulation. But people who are Christians before the Tribulation happens will be Raptured—taken away—so they won't have to go through it. I'm not sure if this is making any sense to you."

Mary didn't reply. She knew some of it, but right now, she wanted Kay to keep talking. She didn't want to be alone in the apartment with Jack.

Kay bit her lip. "Anyway, I have this strong feeling that the time is here—it's at the gates. I don't know why I feel this way, but I came over to...to make sure you understand the gospel. Who Jesus is. And how you need him to be your Savior so you can escape the wrath of God."

"Oh, ——" This disgusted snarl came from Jack. "Don't listen to this garbage, Mary. Get back inside."

"No." She glared at him, and turned back at Kay. "I think I understand, but go ahead. Explain it again." She really didn't want to listen, but Jack's order only served to peak a small amount of interest. "Go ahead. I'm listening."

"Okay." Kay heaved a great breath and repeated the gospel message to Mary. When she finished, a desperate, pleading look filled her eyes. "Does that make sense to you?"

Mary nodded. Kay had told her about salvation before. She hadn't needed to tell her again. But strangely, Mary felt a tug in her soul in that moment, urging her to make a decision for Jesus.

But she couldn't. Or wouldn't. "I understand, Kay. But honestly, I can't decide what to do." Apologetically, Mary added, "I'm sorry."

Kay shook her head. "Don't apologize to me. I'm not the one you're rejecting."

"What a bunch of ——" Jack snarled. "I can't believe you'd listen to this! Your friend's a religious fanatic, Mary. I can't believe you've been sucked in by this ——"

Kay glared at him. "The alternative is hell."

Jack cursed, and slammed the door.

Immediately, Kay frowned with remorse. "I'm sorry, Mary. He makes me so angry."

"Don't worry about it." She twisted her fingers together. "I wish I could believe, Kay. Let me think about it. I know I need to."

Kay smiled, but her gazed dimmed. It looked soul-weary and filled with grief. She hugged Mary. "Great. You take care of yourself. I'll see you in school tomorrow?"

Mary returned the pressure, and released her friend. Inside, her baby fluttered. A warning? "Of course. Mr. Carlisle would be mad if I skipped again."

"Great." Kay smiled, but something suspiciously like tears glimmered in her eyes. With a wave, she turned and was gone.

Then... Mary cringed as the horrible, knife sharp memories cut through her again.

A few hours after Kay left, Jack had flown into an uncontrollable rage. He'd been drinking, but even that could not explain why he'd beat Mary while she lay in bed, sleeping.

She'd awoken, terrified, trying to defend herself and her baby... Then his fist hit her jaw and she fell into deep, empty oblivion. It was merciful, really.

On Monday, the ringing phone pulled her from an unconscious stupor. Mary realized she lay on the cold floor, in a fetal position. Her nightgown was torn and bloody. And she hurt. Oh, she hurt so bad.

The phone rang again, insistently, on the stand above her. Her mouth felt bruised. Her stomach...horrible pain radiated through her abdomen, and she moaned. The baby. Was her baby hurt?

Ring!

The annoying noise jarred through her fogged brain. If only it would shut up!

But she needed help.

Vaguely, this logical thought penetrated her mind. Maybe someone on the other end could help her.

This spark of hope compelled her to lift one aching arm and swipe it through the air. Luckily, her finger caught the power cord. She curled her fingers around it and pulled feebly.

Crash! The phone fell to the floor. The receiver landed inches from her head. Mouth dry, she swallowed, tasting blood.

Please let the person still be on the line. Please.

Weakly, she clawed at the phone, spinning the receiver down to her mouth. "Hello?" she whispered.

"Mary? Is that you?" Mitch's voice crackled clearly through the receiver.

"Yes," she croaked.

"Are you okay? I called to ask if you've seen Kay. We were supposed to meet for lunch today, but she never showed up. I'm afraid she's gone, too."

Mary had no idea what Mitch was talking about. And she didn't care. All she could think about were the horrible waves of pain seizing her body. And her baby...she couldn't feel him moving.

Tears trickled down her sore cheeks. "Help me, Mitch," she whispered. "Help me. Please." This ended on a choke.

"What's wrong?" Alarm rumbled in his voice. "Are you okay?"

"No. Come get me. Please. Hurry." She wept helplessly, incapable of speaking any longer. The severe pain made it difficult to think.

"Hang on! I'll be right there."

Mary closed her eyes, longing for sleep. She must have blacked out, because the next thing she knew, Mitch knelt over her, his black brows drawn together in fierce concern. He spoke to her. She saw his lips moving.

"Mary, are you all right? Answer me!"

She felt his hand on her bruised shoulder.

"Ow," she groaned, and closed her eyes.

"Sorry." Instantly, the pressure eased. His deep voice murmured unintelligible, soothing things.

His tone sharpened. "Going to get you to the hospital. Do you feel this?" Mary felt her foot move.

"Yes."

"Good..."

"Hey!" It was Jack's voice. Rough, surly. "What are you doing in my house, man?" The slurred words rose in volume.

Trembling with fear, Mary heard the approaching clump of his heavy boots. "No," she whimpered. Tears trickled from her eyes. Feebly, she pulled her arms protectively around her head. Jeans rustled as Mitch stood to meet Jack.

"Leave. Now." Mitch's words sounded hard.

"Get out of my way, man!"

Mary cringed, knowing Jack's fist would follow that outraged bleat. Instead, all she heard was a stagger, and then a wild roar.

"I'll get you!" Another lunging step.

The pain flooded over her in black, tormenting waves, and she drifted in and out of consciousness. Feet scuffled. Hard fists hit flesh. Someone moaned, and a thump indicated he'd fallen to the floor.

Who was it? Mitch? Was Jack coming for her now? Fear seized her, and she curled up tighter. *No.*

A gentle hand brushed the hair from her brow, and then strong arms lifted her from the floor.

Mitch. It had to be.

"What happened...Jack?" she mumbled.

"I punched him. He's out cold." Mitch sounded grimly satisfied. "Now relax. I'll drive you to the hospital."

The next thing she knew, it was nighttime. Mary lay on a crisp white hospital bed. An I.V. dripped into her arm. She felt woozy, but felt no pain, thanks to the drugs.

"Glad to see you're awake." Mitch's deep voice spoke from nearby. Weakly, she twisted her neck. He put down a magazine and placed a large warm hand over one of her bandaged ones. His funny, quirking eyebrow tilted up. "Glad to see you're okay."

The memories flooded back. Tears slipped from her eyes. "My baby?"

The pressure on her hand tightened, but not before she saw the deep sorrow, tinged with anger, in his black eyes. "I'm sorry," he said gently. "He didn't have a chance."

Tears streamed helplessly toward her hair.

"You're lucky, though. No broken bones. Mostly bruises. Your spleen was partially split, but they fixed that up, as good as new." His warm voice tried to encourage her.

"Where's Jack?"

"In jail. And he'll stay there for a long time, if you press charges."

"I will." She closed her eyes. Bleakness filled her soul. "I will."

Mitch visited her every day in the hospital, and stayed for as long as he could. He helped her through the worst of her emotional trauma. Gradually, she learned about the Rapture. Her mother had been taken. And her father remained here. He'd been notified of her injuries, but had not come to visit her. At least, not as far as she knew, for the first day and a half were mostly lost to her.

Mitch brought the newspaper, and pointed out Kay's front page article. The article was powerful. Moving. And it had shocked her. She'd had no idea how much persecution her friend had been suffering. Evidently, the article had shocked the community, too. The police department immediately launched a full-scale investigation into Professor William's activities.

Surprisingly, Mr. Carlisle had stepped forward, and reported that he'd been a witness to the attack on campus. Mary's thoughts flitted back to the thick tree shadow Kay had seen just before David had rescued her from the Professor. Had that been Mr. Carlisle, hiding behind the tree? If so, it meant he'd come upon the scene toward the end of the brutal attack. Knowing Mr. Carlisle was Tim's cousin made her all the more surprised that her former, atheistic teacher had stepped forward. It just went to prove that the complex human soul was past figuring out.

A week after Kay's article was published, Mary learned that bullet cartridges found at the school matched the Professor's personal gun, which confirmed Kay and Mr. Carlisle's testimonies. He was arrested. The university fired him. And he fingered Tim and Randy, and they were arrested, too. Their hate group was disbanded. A victory for Kay.

Unfortunately, more—many more—hate groups sprang up later. Some, Mary was certain, were sponsored by the government. Persecution grew worse. Just like the Bible had said would happen. And chaos... National and world governments were still in turmoil as a result of all the people who had disappeared. A huge hole gaped in the social fabric of the nations—and in Mary's own personal life.

When she was released from the hospital, Mitch took Mary into his own apartment. He was concerned for her safety. Jack was already out on bail, despite the charges she had pressed. His first offense, and all. Bitterness made her soul hurt.

That black emotion rooted deep into her heart, and stayed.

A few weeks after she moved into Mitch's guest room, he sat down to talk to her at the kitchen table. His dark eyes looked serious and sad, but excitement also lurked in them.

"Mary," he hesitated. "I feel torn. I don't want to leave you here alone. But I've decided that now is the time for me to go to Israel. I've dedicated my life to Christ. And ever since I've done that, I've felt an incredible urgency to go to Israel, like I've planned for so long. I think God wants to use me there. Do you understand?"

She stared at him. Terrible grief and loneliness overwhelmed her. Mitch, the only friend she had left, planned to leave her.

"I'm sorry," he said quietly, and touched her hand. "If I thought you were interested, I'd ask you to come with me."

"No." Mary choked on a laugh, and quickly brushed the tears from her eyes. She knew one thing: Mitch was supposed to go to Israel. And she was supposed to stay here. At least, she thought so. She felt so lost.

"I understand. Really." Blinking, she withdrew her hand.

"I'll leave in one week." His voice sounded gentle. "After that, this apartment is yours. I don't think Jack will look for you here. But if he does, the security gate will keep him out."

"I'll be okay." Mary offered a watery smile. She didn't deserve such a good friend as Mitch. He truly was a wonderful guy. "I know you're doing the right thing. I'm glad you'll finally get to go."

"Thanks." He smiled and leaped to his feet. His strong hands pushed in the chair. "How about an omelet? Don't know about you, but I'm starved."

The last week spent with Mitch had been bittersweet. She'd wondered why she hadn't seen earlier what a wonderful guy he was. Jack couldn't even compare. She'd been blind...about so many things.

At the airport she could not help but cry, and she could tell he was sad, too. But she knew that deep in his heart, joy consumed him because he could finally fly to the promised land. He gave her a brief, hard hug, and a kiss on the forehead.

"Take care of yourself, kid. I'll miss you. I'll write. Write me back. I mean it. I don't want to lose touch."

Mary closed her eyes, and briefly touched her cheek to his shoulder before letting him go. She forced a smile. "I'll miss you, too. Vaya con Dios."

He smiled. "You too, Mary."

Then he headed toward the security check, and was gone.

Loneliness stripped all hope from Mary after that. The deep hurt gradually turned into anger, and deepened into bitterness. Her friends and mother were all gone. Her father wanted nothing to do with her. He'd died during the Interrogations, probably still hating her. Jack had tried to track her down, but a gang member killed him in a street fight.

Mitch wrote to her, as he'd promised. He'd written often, at first, but then his emails dwindled. The last one she'd received had been five months ago. In it, he'd repeated his invitation for her to join him. Five long months ago. It was her own fault, of course, that he'd stopped writing. He probably thought she was dead. She'd only written him once—over two years ago, and that was to give him her new email address.

She'd lived on bitterness and depression ever since Mitch had left, and it had swallowed her whole.

Now, with unseeing eyes, Mary stared into the pitch black night. A lone street lamp flickered. So many horrible things had happened to her, and she had been so angry at God. Oh, so terribly angry about everything. But the anger had brought her nothing but aching, bitter unhappiness.

It was time to stop. She'd gone to Kay's house today because she was finally ready to hear the truth. To discover if God was real. If he really loved her. And if hope still existed for her life, even now.

Her mind returned to the Rapture. Pastor Warner had been right. The Chairman—the Beast—had been revealed shortly after the Rapture, with a great peace plan that many had signed. But it wasn't long before the real troubles began.

Denial flashed. It couldn't be true. It was crazy! Wasn't it? And yet everything Kay had said would happen, had happened. The Rapture. The Beast setting himself up as God; the mark of the Beast; the two witnesses; the persecution of Christians; the terrible catastrophes that had fallen upon the earth, causing earthquakes, famines, and so many other horrible things. It was the judgment of God, like Kay had said. It was the only logical answer. It fit all the facts.

The burning conviction in her heart flamed. Everything Kay had tried to tell her was true. She was living through the Great Tribulation of the whole Earth!

Numbly, she slipped down to the floor, and lifted her eyes toward heaven. "I believe," she whispered incredulously.

And then she wept, stormily, as the flood gates holding all of the hurt in her heart burst open. She lay her soul bare before God. "I believe!" she gasped.

Her jaw ached from clenching it, and her eyes felt hot and aching when the storm finally eased. But it wasn't over yet. She still needed to get right before God. Remembering the prayer Kay had prayed with Theresa, Mary prayed earnestly, her eyes toward heaven, and she knew Jesus was watching her, and listening. And she knew that he was smiling.

Her voice sounded loud and halting in the small, empty room, but she knew she wasn't talking to herself. She was not alone. "I believe you died for my sins, Jesus. Please forgive me for my sins, and come into my life. Please be the Lord of my life. Please tell me what to do now. I believe!"

She closed her eyes, and new tears ran down her face. And as she sat there, emotionally drained and empty, quiet joy poured into her soul. She smiled; her first radiant smile in years. Then she burst into tears. God loved her! He was real!

As she wept, joy continued to flood through her. Waves of peace and strength watered, healed, and gave life to her parched soul. How could she have been so blind? God *was* real. She had just never sought him out with her whole heart before.

Mary felt as if a great new light had turned on in her mind. She could clearly see and understand so many things that she had not before. The words in the Bible were truth. The Word was alive, and real, and nourishing her soul.

Several verses she had learned during childhood sprang to mind. The Gospel of John. Eyes straining through the darkness, she hesitantly flipped through Kay's Bible. Here it was. John. Chapter one.

> *In the beginning was the Word, and the Word was with God, and the Word was God. He was with God in the beginning. Through him all things were made; without him nothing was made that has been made. In him was life, and that life was the light of men. The light shines in the darkness, but the darkness has not understood it.*

She skimmed on. It talked next about John the Baptist, who came to testify of that light. Here, in verse 10 it went back to talk about the light, and the Word.

> *He was in the world, and though the world was made through him, the world did not recognize him. He came to that which was his own, but his own did not receive him. Yet to all who received him, to those who believed in his name, he gave the right to become children of God— children born not of natural descent, nor of human decision or a husband's will, but born of God.*

> *The Word became flesh and made his dwelling among us. We have seen his glory, the glory of the One and Only, who came from the Father, full of grace and truth.*

The Word was Jesus.

She paged back in Kay's electronic notebook to the Pastor's sermon. Here it was; a verse from Matthew chapter 24.

"...he who stands firm to the end will be saved. And this gospel of the kingdom will be preached in the whole world as a testimony to all nations, and then the end will come."

The end was here. And she was saved. This she knew for certainty. And she would stay true to the end. For she knew the truth now, and the truth had set her free. Gloriously free.

She hugged the Bible to her chest as peace and joy engulfed her, filling her soul to overflowing. Tomorrow she would read more about Jesus. And she would read Revelation. Certainly she needed to learn many more things about the three plus years remaining in the Tribulation. What else would happen? What would be the end of it all? And what would happen to the Chairman?

And finally, she would write to Mitch and apologize for her neglect and poor friendship. She'd explain everything, and she knew he would understand. And most of all, she would tell him about her decision for Christ.

And if Mitch asked her again to come to Israel, maybe she would consider it. She'd saved a modest amount of money in the bank by automatically saving a little every week from her check. And if the mark of the Beast would be implemented soon, she may not be able to buy tickets in the near future without the mark. If she was ready to make a life change, now would be the time.

Now was the time to set aside all of the fear and hurt of her past.

Now she was ready to face the future. No matter what came. For Jesus was with her.

"I will never leave you nor forsake you."
"...lo, I am with you always, even to the end of the age."

HEBREWS 13:5B
MATTHEW 28:20B (NKJV)

Acknowledgements

I DEEPLY APPRECIATE the many people who have helped make this book possible. First, as always, I'd like to thank my editor, Lori, for pointing out issues I never would have noticed on my own. (I'm unable to see the forest for the trees after reading this book for the millionth time—slight exaggeration, but it feels that way!)

Believe it or not, this story has been twenty years in the making. I wrote the first draft in the mid 1990s. At that time, my writing friends Cindy, Diane and Bev read it and provided the first round of constructive feedback. A shout out to all three of you—you are the most amazing friends. Although this book has been polished considerably from that first draft, the main details of the story remain unchanged.

Also, I am so grateful to my current beta readers for taking the time to read and provide valuable feedback on this final version. Claire, Charlotte, Melissa, Colleen, Marilyn, Betty, Kristy, Briana and Debbie, thank you so, so much! Each of you is a true blessing, and each of you brought fresh insights that I had never considered before. This book is so much better as a result of your help.

And, as always, thank you to my wonderful husband, Dale, and my three terrific kids. I love you so much.

One final note: As a small press author, getting books before readers can be a challenge. You can help! If you liked this book, please consider writing a review on Amazon, or on the retailer's website where you purchased the book. Each review encourages Amazon to promote the book to more readers. Each and every review counts, and means so much! Thank you!!!

About the Author

Jennette Green has always had a passion for writing. She wrote her first story over thirty years ago, and her first romance novel, *The Commander's Desire*, was published in 2008. It was awarded "Readers' Favorite Hero for 2009," and has received "Top Pick" and "5 Star" accolades from a number of review sites. Other books by Jennette include *Her Reluctant Bodyguard*, a Christian romantic suspense novel, and *Ice Baron*, a science fiction romance, packed with action and romance. These books have received awards such as "Top Pick," "Recommended Read," and "Reviewer's Choice Award" from popular review sites, and Ice Baron placed third in the science fiction category in an international ebook competition.

Jennette loves to travel with her husband and children, and particularly likes long walks along the ocean, dreaming up new stories.

She loves to hear from her readers.

Drop her a note, or join her "Street Team":
jennettegreen@jennettegreen.com.
Visit her website to discover new and upcoming books!
www.jennettegreen.com